TWISTED
ROOTS

The Dollanganger Family Series
Flowers in the Attic
Petals on the Wind
If There Be Thorns
Seeds of Yesterday
Garden of Shadows

The Casteel Family Series
Heaven
Dark Angel
Fallen Hearts
Gates of Paradise
Web of Dreams

The Cutler Family Series
Dawn
Secrets of the Morning
Twilight's Child
Midnight Whispers
Darkest Hour

The Landry Family Series
Ruby
Pearl in the Mist
All That Glitters
Hidden Jewel
Tarnished Gold

The Logan Family Series
Melody
Heart Song
Unfinished Symphony
Music in the Night
Olivia

The Orphans Miniseries
Butterfly
Crystal
Brooke
Raven
Runaways (full-length novel)

The Wildflowers Miniseries
Misty
Star
Jade
Cat
Into the Garden (full-length novel)

The Hudson Family Series
Rain
Lightning Strikes
Eye of the Storm
The End of the Rainbow

The Shooting Stars Series
Cinnamon
Ice
Rose
Honey
Falling Stars

The De Beers Family Series
Willow
Wicked Forest
Twisted Roots

My Sweet Audrina
(does not belong to a series)

VIRGINIA ANDREWS®

TWISTED ROOTS

BCA

This edition published 2004
by BCA
by arrangement with Simon & Schuster Inc.
A Viacom company

CN 127269

Printed and bound in Germany by
GGP Media, Pößneck

TWISTED ROOTS

Prologue

Hannah's Story

I have always felt like someone with a pimple on the tip of her nose because my last name is different from my mother's. First you try to cover it up, and then, when you can no longer do that, you pretend it's nothing and act as if it certainly doesn't bother you.

I have my father's last name, Eaton, and my mother, Willow, who remarried a year after I was born, has my stepfather's last name, Fuentes. My father, who is an important and successful Palm Beach attorney, has always refused to permit my stepfather to legally adopt me and thus take on his name, even though my daddy, too, remarried a year after I was born and has twin boys, now fifteen years old, Adrian and Cade.

The irony about all this is my Eaton paternal grandparents have never had anything to do with me. Neither has my aunt Whitney, my father's sister, or her children, my cousins Quentin and Laurel, both of whom have their own families. I have seen my Eaton grandparents, my aunt, and her husband Hans, only from a distance, and I know they have seen me from time to time, but they have never acknowledged me. Once I saw Quentin, but I've never seen his family, and I've never seen Laurel or any of her family. Even when I was very young, it didn't take me long to realize the Eatons built a wall around themselves, so they were the castle-keeps, especially in regard to me.

Whenever I've been with my father, I've also been with Adrian and Cade, but I'm not very fond of my half brothers, who suffer from 100 percent snob-quotient. I won't deny that they are very good-looking and very good students, but they love reminding people of that, especially me. Even though I'm just as good a student as either of them, they often try to make me feel inferior by bragging about how much more they have or how many more friends they have. They have what they call their "Invite Board" in their game room, and they pin up their party invitations on it. They love showing it to me, especially when almost every available space is taken.

My father's second wife, Danielle, is polite and nice enough to me, but I've always thought she was afraid to be much more. She gives only about a 70 percent smile and stops short whenever she is about to invite me to do something or give me something that might somehow seem to be extra and above what is absolutely necessary. Perhaps she thinks my brothers would be jealous. I'm sure they would be.

Danielle is pretty with doll-like features. My father

met her on one of his trips to France. She was working for a travel agency. All I know is they had a whirlwind romance, and she became pregnant almost the day they were married. She always seems quite overwhelmed by her twin boys. I've caught her looking at them with an expression of astonishment on her face after something they said or did, making me think she was wondering how two such conflicting and explosive personalities were ever a part of her. I've even heard her jokingly say that they kicked so hard in her womb, she was afraid they would induce labor.

Mommy calls Danielle my father's "trinket wife." She says he has a charm bracelet with pictures of all his past trinkets, with Mommy excluded, of course. I know that's not true, and I know that Mommy doesn't really believe it, but she likes to say things like that about him. There is what I would best describe as a shaky truce between my mother and father, and I walk the tightrope between them afraid to say one nice thing about either to either for fear their anger and disappointment will shake the ground I'm on, causing me to fall off and then lose them both.

The only family I really have is what I call my "stepfamily," the Fuentes. They have never made me feel like anything less than a member of their family, making sure to always include me in their celebrations and events. I expect there is really a word in the dictionary like *stepfamily*, but the word is in my own private dictionary along with *snob-quotient* and *nongrandma* and *nongrandpa*, which is what my father's parents Bunny and Asher Eaton are to me. I suppose I could call the Eatons my *nonfamily*.

I do have some family on my mother's side: an uncle, my mother's half brother, Linden. He lives in a residency in the Boca Raton area, in what my mother terms an "intermediary home." He's spent years and years in a very controlled environment, a mental health clinic, and he's not quite ready to be on his own in the outside world. She never says it, but she doesn't have to say it. She knows I know she doesn't believe he will *ever* be quite ready. So it's not really an "intermediate place" for Linden; it's a dead end. No matter how deeply set his problems are, however, my uncle Linden loves me very much and I love him.

My father is always warning me about Uncle Linden and telling me things like "Insanity runs like an underground sewer through that family bloodline," which makes me wonder if he doesn't think I have the mental pollution in me as well. His parents, his sister, and even his children certainly treat me as if I do. Sometimes I get the impression that Adrian and Cade think I'm going to break out in mad babbling or stick my finger in an electric socket. (They would love that.) I know they deliberately do things, tease and shock me with their words and behavior, in the hope that they will bring on a seizure of madness. There is always that slight pause, that hesitation of anticipation, waiting for my reactions. I try to ignore them, but sometimes it's like pretending a mosquito hasn't landed on your arm.

My stepfather, Miguel, who is a psychology professor and was even once my mother's teacher, told me that it's my father's family that has the mental problems. I told him that doesn't help me because in either case, I might be inheriting it.

"Not this kind of mental illness, Hannah," he replied. "This kind is home grown in Palm Beach. You can't inherit it. You have to wander into those gardens to contact that sort of poison ivy, and thankfully, your mother keeps you out of those gardens."

We both laughed at that, me not so much because Mother was keeping me out of that world, but because that world wasn't inviting me to enter. Whenever I walked down Worth Avenue with Mommy, I felt we were both invisible. People who knew who we were seemed too terrified to look at us for more than a split second. Maybe they thought they would be turned into pillars of salt, or if they smiled at us, no one would ever again smile at them. This was especially true about snobby salespeople in the better Palm Beach stores, who often made us wait or even ignored us for as long as they could or until Mommy put herself aggressively in their faces.

"When I tell you these things about Palm Beach, it's not a case of the fox and the grapes, Hannah," my stepfather insisted. "Believe me. You don't want to be part of that social scene. It's cannibalistic. They eat each other for breakfast.

"Pass me that child from Coconut Row, or can I have a piece of that young man from Esplanade Way, please?" he added, pretending to be seated at some Palm Beach fancy restaurant. We both roared with laughter.

I really love my stepfather as much as anyone would love a natural father, maybe even more than I love mine. I know my father thinks I do. Whenever he sees me wearing something new, especially a ring or a bracelet, he always says, "I see your mother's Cuban lover is trying to buy your love again with some cheap imitation jewelry."

I always want to say, "He's not her Cuban lover. He's her husband, and this isn't cheap imitation jewelry," but if I defend Miguel too vigorously, it only convinces Daddy he's right, so I usually pretend I don't hear him. More often than not, when I am with either my mother or my father, I feel like I am floundering in the world of jealous adult quicksand. A critical glance, a sarcastic word, even an innocent question can pull me down into their swampy underworld full of green-eyed monsters.

It's better for me to say nothing, to look bored and disinterested. Both take it as a sign of agreement, and I think that's all right. Let them believe what they need to believe. Little silences are like antimissiles I use to keep all the missiles of unhappiness from striking my heart.

I might not be able to do that today, however. Today is one of the strangest, if not *the* strangest, day in my life: My mother is a psychologist who specializes in the problems of young people. She said she likes to get to someone before his or her emotional and psychological difficulties are not too comfortably seated. She has been in practice for more than ten years, and she is very well known and respected. All during that time she and my stepfather put off having a child of their own, and then they decided right after my sixteenth birthday to have one. Just a little more than two months later at dinner, Mother announced she was pregnant. It was the most surprising thing I had heard my whole life. My mother, pregnant? It was so strange to realize she was actually going to give birth. There were girls my age giving birth!

"Your brother or sister might even be born on your birthday," she declared. "Wouldn't that be wonderful? We could have one big birthday party every year!"

I know Mommy was just trying to be excited for me because she never had a brother or sister in her home when she was growing up. But no, I thought. It *wouldn't* be wonderful. Who wants to share your one special day with someone else? I used to feel sorry for Adrian and Cade because they had to do that, being twins. Adrian's solace is his gleeful bragging about being born a good two minutes before Cade. Cade counters by saying that was because he kicked Adrian out of their mother's womb first.

"I couldn't stand the smell," he bellows and laughs.

"That was exactly why I came out first. I couldn't stand your smell," Adrian throws back at him.

It's hard to believe they are brothers, even though they are mirror images of each other. They so enjoy belittling each other or defeating each other. It's as though they were put on some mysterious starting line and their births came after the report of a starting gun. Cade will always be in pursuit of Adrian, who had that two-minute advantage. However, at least when they are making fun of each other, they are not making fun of me. If I try to stop them from hurting each other, I know they will only turn on me.

Anyway, this morning I was woken by a great deal

of commotion, shouting, doors slamming, footsteps on the stairs and in the hallway. My heart skipped a beat when I heard Miguel yell, "We're going to the hospital!"

When I went to the door, Miguel turned to me and cried, "Your mother's water has broken!"

I knew it was almost a month too soon, so I understood why she and Miguel were in a panic about it. Mommy had always been nervous about being pregnant this late in life, so she had been very intense about her prenatal care, her vitamins, doctor's visits, diet, and exercise. Now, despite all that, she was being rushed to the hospital to give birth to what I already knew would be my baby brother, Claude, named for my maternal grandfather. Even before little Claude, as he would come to be known, opened his eyes and cried for the first time, I was already jealous of him, more jealous than Cade was of Adrian and Adrian was of Cade.

After all, my brother Claude would have my mother's last name. He would be a Fuentes, and he would belong in this family more than I did. He would never have a nongrandma or nongrandpa.

Certainly, he would never feel like a stranger in his daddy's home. He had dozens of real relatives to call his family, not his stepfamily. He wouldn't need little silences to keep him from being too unhappy, nor would he have to worry about saying the wrong things to his father or his mother. He would never think he was on an island, cut off from the sea of society around him.

In short, he would never wonder who he really was.

Lying there and listening to the shouting and the footsteps dying out in the hallway as they left the house, I had one deep regret on this the most confusing of all days for me. Anyone who heard my regret might think it was probably the strangest thing of all, in fact.

Why was I born first? Why couldn't I be the one who was to be born today?

1

An Early Baby

I was too young to remember her before she died, but my mother had a nanny, who, according to the way Mommy talks about her, was more of a mother to her than certainly her stepmother was. Sometimes I think how weird it is that Grandmother Grace, Mommy, and I have each had at least one stepparent in our lives. Are some people meant to be brought up that way? I asked Mommy about that, and she said so many marriages end in divorces these days that it is not at all uncommon for a child to have stepparents.

"People marry and remarry the way teenagers used to go steady and break up to go steady with someone else years ago," she says. She's very bitter about it, although she would be the last one to admit to that. Psychologists, both she and Miguel remind me, are not supposed to be judgmental.

"We help our clients make those decisions on their own. We don't impose our values on them," she said.

However, I have heard her angrily remark many times that the marriage vows should be updated. "They should be rewritten to say, 'Do you take this woman to have and to hold—for a while or until you get bored?' "

Sometimes she is so down on male-female relationships that I have to wonder if I will ever find anyone with whom I might be happy and spend the rest of my life. According to what he has told me and how he acts, my stepfather, Miguel, has no doubts about it. He seems to be very happy and very determined to spend the rest of his life with Mommy. I have never said anything to her about it, but I think he loves her more than she loves him. I know he makes her happy. He makes her laugh a lot, and I can see she enjoys her conversations with him, especially when they are discussing social and psychological topics. But sometimes, more often than ever, I think, she can be very distant. Her eyes take on a glazed look, and she stares at the sea or suddenly goes off to walk alone.

She steals away when Miguel or I least expect it, walking through the house on "pussy willow feet." I have watched her without her knowing, observed her on our beach, and have seen her moving slowly, as slowly as sand sifting through your fingers, idly watching time go by, her face sometimes taking on that dreamy far-off expression, her beautiful lips in a soft smile. It makes me think she hears voices no one else can hear, remembers a whisper, a touch, or even a kiss she has lost. Something wonderful slipped through her fingers years and years ago, perhaps, and now all she can do is resurrect the memory.

"All our memories are like bubbles, Hannah," she once told me. "They drift by and burst, and all you can do is wait for another chance to blow them through your thoughts so they can drift by again. Reach out to touch them, and they will pop and be gone. Sometimes I envy people who have suffered loss of memory and who are never tormented with their pasts. I even envy Linden, lost in some world of his own."

I hate it when she talks like that. It makes me think she would like to return to a time before I was born, as short as that happier period in her life might have been, and if she could, she would sell her soul to do so.

How can she be unhappy here? How could anyone? We live on an estate called Joya del Mar. We have an enormous main house with halls so long and rooms so large, you could bounce your echo along the walls. The property is vast, too. On it we have a beach house, our own private beach front, a magnificent pool, beautiful patios and walkways with enough flowers and bushes to fill a small public park. She doesn't have to do any household chores. We have a cook, Mrs. Haber, and a maid named Lila who has been with us nearly ten years. Twice a week a small army of grounds people manicure our property.

Professionally, Mommy is very successful. She has a psychotherapy practice with an office in West Palm Beach, not far from the magnet school I attend. Magnet schools provide a more specialized curriculum. Mine emphasizes the arts, and since I like to sing, Mother arranged for me to attend the A. W. Drefoos School of Arts in West Palm Beach. We get up and go together most of the time, or my stepfather takes me.

This was the year they were supposed to buy me my own car so I could drive myself places, but they have yet to do it. They have this idea that I should first find some sort of part-time job to at least pay for my own gas and insurance.

"When you accumulate enough to pay for at least one year's insurance, we'll get you the car," she has promised.

She also promised to help me by looking for a job that could fit into my schedule. I moaned and groaned, wondering aloud in front of them if my taking on a job wouldn't hurt my schoolwork. Miguel laughed.

"Oh, having a vehicle and driving all over the place won't cut in on your study time?"

I hate having parents who are so realistic. The parents of other girls my age accept at least a fantasy or two. However, it is very important to Mommy and Miguel that I develop a sense of value, the one sense they both insist is absent in Palm Beach.

"Here, people would think it justifiable to go to war over a jar of caviar," Mommy once quipped.

I do understand why she doesn't like the Palm Beach social world. My maternal grandmother Grace wasn't treated well here, and Mommy blames many of her own difficulties on that. At times Palm Beach doesn't seem real to me, either. It's too perfect. It glitters and feels like a movie set. When we cross the Flagler Bridge into West Palm Beach, Mother claims she is leaving the world of illusion and entering reality.

"Rich people here are richer than rich people most everywhere else," she told me. "Some of the wealthy people here are in fact wealthier than many small or third-world countries, Hannah. They keep reality outside their gold-plated walls. There are no cemeteries or hospitals in Palm Beach. Death and sickness have to stand outside the door. While the rest of us get stuck in traffic jams of all sorts in life, the wealthy residents of Palm Beach fly over them."

"What's wrong with that?" I asked her. "I'd like that."

"They haven't the tolerance for the slightest inconveniences anymore. Sometimes it's good to have a challenge, to be frustrated, to have to rise to an occasion, to find strength in yourself. You need some calluscs on your soul, Hannah. You need to be stronger."

"But if you never run out of money and you can always buy away the frustrations, why would it matter?" I countered.

She looked at me very sternly.

"That's your father talking," she replied. Whenever she says that or says something like that, I feel as if she has just slapped me across the face.

"You'll see," she added. "Someday you'll see and you'll understand. I hope."

Should I hope the same thing? Why do we have to know about the ugly truths awaiting us? I wondered that aloud when I was with my stepfather once, and he said, "Because you appreciate the beauty more. I think what your mother is trying to get you to understand is that not only do these people she speaks of have a lower threshold of tolerance for the unpleasant things in life, but they have or develop a lower threshold of appreciation for the truly beautiful things as well. The Taj Mahal becomes, well, just another item on the list of places to visit and brag that you have seen, if you know what I mean."

I did, but for some reason, I didn't want to be so quick to say I did. Whenever Mommy or Miguel were critical of the Palm Beach social world, I understood they were being critical of my father and his family as well, and even though they weren't treating me like a member of that family, I couldn't help but think of them as part of me or me, part of them. I'm full of so many emotional contradictions, twisted and tangled like a telephone wire with all sorts of cross-communication. It's hard to explain to anyone who doesn't live a similar life so I keep it all bottled up inside me. I never tell anyone in my classes at school or any of my friends about these family conflicts and feelings.

Feelings, in fact, are often kept in little safes in our house. There is the sense that if we let too many of them out at the same time, we might explode. Everything is under control here. We're never too happy; we're never too sad. Whenever we approach either, there are techniques employed. After all, both Miguel and Mommy are experts in psychology.

Daddy is always urging me to be different from them, warning me that if I'm not, I'll be unhappy.

"Don't be like your mother," he says. "Don't analyze every pin drop. Forget about the *whys* and *wherefors* and enjoy. She's like a cook who can't go out to eat and take pleasure in something wonderful without first asking the waiter for a list of every ingredient and then questioning how it was prepared, always concluding with 'Oh, if he or she had done this or that, it would be even better.' Don't become like that, Hannah," he advises.

Maybe he's right.

But maybe, maybe I can't help it. After all, I am my mother's daughter, too, aren't I?

Or is my mother going to forget that I am her daughter? Is she hoping for that little loss of memory she often wishes she had?

I have another fear, a deep, dark suspicion that I remind her so much of my father that she can't tolerate it anymore and that was and is the real reason why she finally wanted another child, a child with Miguel.

Perhaps it is my imagination overworking or misinterpreting, but all throughout these last months of her pregnancy, I felt her growing more and more distant from me. She had less time to talk to me about my problems and concerns. Helping me find a suitable part-time job and getting me my own car seemed to have slipped out of both her and Miguel's minds. She had more concern for her practice, finding ways to continue to treat or have her clients treated while she was recuperating from giving birth than she had for me. She wanted to stop going to work the last month, and she was always very busy trying to make arrangements. I could see that even our morning ride together had changed. How many times did I say something or ask something and she didn't hear me because her ears were filled with her own worries and thoughts?

"What was that?" she would ask, or she would simply not respond and I would give up, close up like a clam, and stare out the window wishing I had woken with a cold and stayed home bundled up and forgotten.

However, my school, my teachers and some of the friends I had filled my life with more joy now. Staying home would have been punishing myself for no reason, or at least, no reason for which I could be blamed. In fact, some of my girlfriends actually felt sorry for me. They thought it would be weird if their mothers became pregnant like mine at this point in their family lives.

"I can tell you right now what's going to happen," Massy Hewlett declared with the authority of a Supreme Court judge. "You're going to end up being the family baby-sitter, and just when you should have more freedom to enjoy your social life."

"No," I told her. "They have already decided to hire a nanny. My mother had one when she was little. She didn't need one when I was born because she wasn't working yet, but she has to get back to her clients, so it's different now."

"It's not the same thing," Massy insisted. "You'll see. Older mothers are more neurotic. They have less tolerance, and they tend to exaggerate every little thing the baby does. A sneeze will become pneumonia."

"Don't you think Hannah's mother would be aware of all that?" Stacy Kreskin piped up. "She just happens to be a psychologist, Massy. It's not going to be the same for Hannah."

"We'll see," Massy said, refusing to be challenged or

corrected. To Massy, being right was more important than being a good friend. It never even occurred to her that she was making me unhappy. I don't think she would have cared anyway.

Reluctant to be defeated, she simply shifted to another level of criticism.

"Even if she doesn't find herself baby-sitting or being asked to hang around the house, she'll feel like she doesn't exist anymore. There's a new king or queen. It happened to me!" she cried, shaking her head at the looks of either skepticism or disapproval. "My baby sister is nearly eight years younger, so I should know, shouldn't I? I'm just trying to give her a heads-up about it."

Our little clump grew silent and then broke away like blocks that had lost their glue and exploded, sailing off in a variety of directions. I was left alone to ponder the way my world would change, feeling as if I was floundering on the border between childhood needs and adult responsibilities. Should I be whining about the way our lives were changing or should I accept and adjust?

Maybe I shouldn't care. Maybe I should be happy. I'll be more on my own. I won't be on everyone's emotional radar screen. It's good to be ignored, isn't it? Or will I feel more unloved and unwanted than ever?

The conflict in me kept me so distracted, I felt like I was lost and drifting most of the time. Sometimes I felt I had stepped into the quagmire of emotions. I had to face it and find a way out. Now, with Mommy's water breaking and little Claude on the threshold of our home and family, there was no more putting it off for later.

Whether I liked it or not, whether I was ready or not, the whole situation was in my face. It was all happening and it couldn't be ignored.

There was going to be another child in this house, a little prince.

The princess would have to step aside.

On those rare occasions when either Mommy or Miguel were unable to drive me to school, our head grounds keeper, Ricardo, drove me in his pickup truck. Unfortunately for me, these occasions were so rare, I couldn't use them as an excuse or reason for them to get me my own car before I had a suitable job or earned the year's worth of insurance.

"What good is my driver's license?" I whined more than ever lately. "I don't get much of an opportunity to use it. It's not safe for someone to drive as little as I do."

"Now, there's a good one," Miguel teased. "In order to make the highways safer, we should increase the number of teenagers with their own cars."

"I'm sure we'll make it all happen soon," Mommy promised. "As soon as I get free of these other issues, I'll help you find suitable employment, and Miguel will look into what car we should get for you. Soon," she repeated.

Soon: That was an easy word to hate. Adults, especially parents, used it as a shield to ward off requests and complaints. It was full of promise, but vague enough to keep them from having to make a real commitment.

Even rarer were times when Mommy's car was there for me to use. Right up to the last week of her pregnancy, she wanted her car at the house. It made her nervous not to have it available for an emergency. Ricardo could drive her anywhere if Miguel wasn't home, or even I could.

The morning Mommy's water broke, Miguel asked me if I would rather go with them to the hospital and wait for my baby brother to be born, but I told him I couldn't. I had an important English exam to take. I didn't, but I didn't want to be at the hospital. From simply listening to conversations Mommy and Miguel had about different clients of Mommy's, I knew enough to describe myself as being in denial. I resented little Claude so much I refused to admit to his coming and being. I actually imagined Mommy returning from the hospital without him and Miguel explaining it had all been an incorrect diagnosis. It had turned out to be a digestive problem easily corrected. There was no little Claude after all. Our lives, mine in particular, would not change. My world would no longer be topsy-turvy.

"Well, all right," Miguel said with disappointment flooding his face. "I'll tell you what," he said. "Let Ricardo drive you this morning, and I'll come to the school to get you if your mother gives birth before the day is over. I think that just might happen even though it's nearly a month too soon," he added with some trepidation in his voice.

"You could call the school and let them know to tell me, and I'll drive to the hospital," I said. "Just in case she doesn't give birth that quickly."

Once again his eyes darkened with disappointment.

"Your mother is nervous, Hannah. I don't want her worrying about you at this time," added.

"Why should she worry? I'm a good driver."

He stared without replying. It was his way of pleading for understanding.

"All right," I said petulantly. Little Claude hadn't made his first cry and already he was causing me unhappiness. I had to swallow it down.

"Thank you," Miguel said.

After they had left and I had my breakfast, I got into Ricardo's pickup truck.

"Today you become a sister," he declared with a joyful smile. "I bet you are excited, eh?"

"Yes," I lied. I didn't like airing my inner feelings, especially ones that had me feeling guilty and ashamed. I hated myself for that, but I hated what had made me that way even more.

Ricardo started to talk about his younger brothers and sisters. He was the oldest in a family of seven, but all of them had been born relatively close to each other. They all had much more in common than I would have with little Claude. By the time he was old enough to talk to me and understand anything significant, I would be in college. How could I ever think of him as a brother or ever care?

Ricardo's voice droned on. Even with its musical cadence and his happy tones, it became a monotonous stream of noise behind me, behind my dark and dreary thoughts.

"You can go a little faster, Ricardo," I interrupted. "I don't want to be late for school."

"*Si, si,*" he said.

As we rode on, I glanced occasionally at pedestrians and the scenery, but I really saw no one or nothing, and when I arrived at school, I was surprised. Somehow, I didn't even realize the trip. I had been in too much of a daze. I hopped out quickly and barely uttered a thank-you and goodbye.

Not one of my friends seemed to notice how unhappy I was. It caused me to wonder if to them I always appeared this sad and depressed. Everyone seemed to be used to my silence, my dark eyes, my downward gaze and lack of energy. They rambled on with their usual excitement, swirling around me, show-ing off new clothing, new makeup, different hairdos, and passing on stories and rumors about this boy and that. I almost felt as if I had woven a cocoon about myself and none of them could see, hear, or touch me.

There was finally a reaction to and an awareness of my existence when Mrs. Margolis, the principal's assis-tant and secretary, appeared at my classroom door and announced I was to be excused.

"For a happy occasion," she added, unable to contain the news.

All my friends knew what that meant, and all turned to me, Massy's face a scowl of pity. I quickly gathered my books and hurried out, head down, my heart feeling more like it was growling than beating.

"Your stepfather is waiting for you in the lobby," Mrs. Margolis said as we walked down the hallway. "Congratulations," she added, and I muttered a thank-you and hurried along.

Miguel stood smiling proudly near the front entrance.

"I told you it would happen quickly. Little Claude has arrived," he announced.

"How's Mommy?" I asked.

"She's doing fine, but . . ." he added letting the *but* hang for a while as we walked out and to his car.

"But what?"

"Your little brother is smaller than we had expected him to be because he's technically a premature baby even though he weighs enough. He's doing fine, but to be on the safe side, the doctor would like to keep him there a little longer than they usually keep newborns."

"Oh," I said, caught in a rainstorm of different feelings and thoughts. A part of me hoped he stayed there forever, but a larger part of me felt very sad for Mommy and for Miguel.

"Naturally, your mother is concerned, so I thought it would be very good for you to visit, see little Claude, and tell her how beautiful he is," Miguel said. "I'm sure you understand," he added.

I nodded, but I also always believed Mommy could tell if I was not sincere about something. Even my father believed she had a second set of eyes that slipped in front of her regular eyes and pierced through any mask of deception.

"She ought to work for the CIA," he quipped on more than one occasion.

When we arrived at the hospital, we did as Miguel wanted and went to see little Claude first. He was in a bassinet that looked like it was built for a baby ten times his size. I couldn't believe how small he was and that this tiny creature in that miniature form was a full human being related to me. His head looked no bigger than an apple, and his hands and feet were so doll-like, I couldn't help doubting he was real. He was crying with such intensity, his face was actually the hue of a ripe apple. Despite his being only hours old, his skin around his tiny wrists and even under his eyes and his neck resembled skin wrinkled with age. I saw nothing beautiful about him and was actually happy about that. How could they make such a fuss over something like him?

"Isn't he remarkable?" Miguel asked, standing beside me and looking through the window.

"Yes," I said. "But you're right . . . he's so tiny."

"But he'll grow fast. In a few weeks you won't believe you're looking at the same child," he assured me. "He has my hair, although not much of it yet, huh?"

"Dipped in ink," I said, and Miguel laughed. When I was little, it was something he used to tell me about his hair and his beard.

"Right, right. Well, let's go see your mother," he said, and I followed him to her room.

Maybe I had a second set of eyes, too, because it only took one glimpse of her to know she was wading about in a pool of worry.

"Did you see him?" she asked almost before I stepped through the door.

"Yes. He's so tiny, but he has Miguel's hair," I said quickly. Miguel laughed, but Mommy held her expression of deep concern.

"I did everything I was supposed to do. I ate right. I don't smoke, and I didn't even have a glass of wine for nearly nine months. Those vitamins," she told Miguel, "we should have them analyzed. Vitamins and health foods are not inspected and analyzed by the government. Maybe they weren't what they were advertised to be."

"It's not the vitamins," Miguel said softly, closing and opening his eyes. "It makes no sense to flail about searching for some demon, Willow. You gave birth and that's it. He'll be fine. The doctor assures us."

She raised her eyebrows and looked at him with the face I knew my real father hated, the face that made a liar, a dreamer, a procrastinator swallow back his or her words. Miguel called her "lie-proof."

"Fibs and exaggerations bounce off and come back at the people who send them in her direction," Miguel told me often, leading me to think he was trying to warn me never to attempt to deceive her.

He raised his arms. "What?" he cried.

"They don't keep a baby as long as he wants to keep Claude under observation, Miguel. Too early is too early. Please. You're not talking to an idiot."

"All right, all right. Still, it will be fine. You will see."

"I hope so," she said and turned to me and finally smiled. "He is beautiful, though, isn't he, Hannah?"

"Uh-huh," I said even though my idea of a beautiful baby were the babies I saw in television commercials.

"You finally have a little brother. When I was growing up, I longed so for a sister or a brother. Most of my friends had one or the other, and even though they were always teasing or arguing with each other, I knew they at least had someone, had family. I'm sorry we waited so long to give you a sibling, honey. But you will be older and wiser and almost a second mother to him."

"When he's my age, I'll be thirty-four," I said. "I'll probably have my own children by then."

"Yes," she said. "But he will love having nieces and nephews, too. You'll see. If I've learned anything from marrying Miguel, it's how important and wonderful family can be. You'll see," she promised.

"I was thinking I would run back to the college and attend that faculty union meeting. It's important," Miguel said. "I should only be an hour or so."

"It's fine, Miguel. Hannah can stay a while with me."

"You're not tired?"

"I'll doze on and off, I imagine, but I wouldn't mind the company, if you wouldn't mind staying a while, Hannah."

"No, I want to stay," I said quickly.

"Fine, then," Miguel said. He walked to the door, turned, and raised his shoulders and puffed out his proud father's chest. "I'll be back," he added, pretending to be Arnold Schwarzenegger.

Both Mother and I laughed at his poor imitation, and then he left.

"Are you going to have Miguel bring Uncle Linden here to see him?" I asked her.

"No. I think it would be better if we just waited until we bring Claude home. Then we'll either have Linden over or take the baby there."

"Why? He can come out and go places," I said sharply. "We take him to restaurants, don't we? Why can't we bring him to a maternity ward?"

She scrunched her nose like she had just sipped some sour milk.

"I don't think it's a good idea to bring him to hospitals of any kind, Hannah. He doesn't feel good about that. Too many unhappy and unpleasant memories from his time in clinics and such. Why do that to him?" she asked.

"We leave him out of too many things," I complained.

She smiled. "He's not being left out."

"Yes, he is," I insisted.

"No one stands up for Linden like you do, Hannah. That's very nice."

"He doesn't have anyone but us," I said. "He's not related to Miguel and you're very busy. He's always saying you don't visit him as much as you used to visit him."

She shook her head. "He doesn't remember when I do."

"Yes, he does," I insisted.

"All right, honey, all right. Don't get yourself so upset about it. We won't leave Uncle Linden out of anything. I promise."

"I don't know why he's still in that place. He paints beautiful things. People buy them! He doesn't bother anyone. Why don't we just have him come home and live with us? Our house is certainly big enough, even with a new baby. We have rooms that have been shut up for as long as I can remember."

"He does well where he is, Hannah. Everything is organized for him, and he doesn't have to be reminded of bad memories, memories that made him sick."

"You have said that often before, Mommy, but I still don't understand what that means. What bad memories? What's in our house that would remind him of them anyway?"

She closed her eyes and let her head sink back on the pillow. The nurse came in to check her blood pressure and see how she was doing. Mommy introduced me to her, and I could see by the expression on her face that she was surprised my mother had a child as old as I was. Anyone looking at the two of us could see that I was really her daughter, too. She hadn't married Miguel and inherited me. We had the same nose and mouth. My eyes were my father's blue, but my hair was Mommy's light brunette shade. I had a slightly darker complexion. I was about an inch or so taller than she was, and I had a fuller figure. Some of my girlfriends were jealous of that, but I always wished I was more diminutive even though they thought I would be more attractive to most boys.

I've had boyfriends on and off since the ninth grade, but no one I would drool over or suffer heartbreak over when we went our separate ways, no one until this year. His name was Heyden Reynolds, and he was a new student in our school and very much a loner. Massy said he was weird and blamed it on his having a mother whose family came from Haiti and a father who was white and from New Orleans. His father was a musician with a jazz band and traveled a great deal. He had a fourteen-year-old sister, Elisha, who attended a regular public school, but being he was a talented songwriter and guitar player, Heyden came to our magnet school when he moved to West Palm Beach. He came every day on an old moped that other students teased him about, but he didn't seem to care.

I had spoken to him only a few times, but I sang with him once in vocal class, and the way he looked at me afterward made me tingle inside. I thought he was handsome with his caramel complexion and his dark, curly hair, strong mouth, and black pearl eyes. He was lean and tall like Miguel. I didn't find him weird because of his standoffish manner. I found him mysterious and a lot more interesting than the other boys in the school.

As soon as the nurse left Mommy's room, Mommy turned back to me. I didn't think she was going to say anything more about Uncle Linden. She never liked to talk about him all that much, especially with me, but she surprised me.

"Your uncle Linden has a hate-love relationship with Joya del Mar, Hannah. When you were little, we brought him around often, but he literally trembled as we drove through the gates each and every time."

"Why?" I asked, intrigued. She had never told me anything like this.

"You know he and my mother used to live in the beach house after my mother's stepfather practically bankrupted my grandmother Jackie Lee. It was difficult and sad for Linden to be forced to move out of his home and live in an apartment under the help's quarters. It made him bitter and he resented the Eatons."

"But you brought them back to the main house and paid off the debts. You fixed everything," I said.

She started to smile and stopped.

"Fixed," she said as if it pained her tongue. "Hardly

that, Hannah. It was true that thanks to my father, I had inherited enough money and property to bail out my mother and Linden from their debts and make it possible for all of us to return to the main house, but I was also a foolish, impressionable young girl who allowed your father to charm and beguile me with his elegance and his promises. Even with your uncle Linden's mental turmoil and difficulties, he was wiser about your father than I was. I should have listened to him."

"If he was so wise and you were becoming a psychologist, why did he end up in a mental clinic?"

She took a deep breath. Was I being selfish by making her talk when she was tired and weak from giving birth? I couldn't help it. It was as if she were finally opening a door to a secret room, a room I had wanted to peer inside all my life.

"You know that his father, Kirby Scott, seduced and performed what amounted to rape of mine and Linden's mother. Linden had a very difficult and confused upbringing. For a while he was given to believe my grandmother was actually his mother. It was an attempt to sweep the disgrace under a rug. When he learned the truth about himself, it triggered his manic-depressive condition. He lived on the darkest edges of the world he envisioned. Right from the beginning Mother and he were not treated nicely by the people here. They made him feel freakish, and because of that, he became even more introverted.

"It became very serious after our mother died. He wanted to shut us both up and shut out the world outside our gates. He had something of a nervous breakdown over it, in fact. So you can see why our home is not the happiest of places for him to be, Hannah."

She smiled.

"You can see it in his art. The work he is doing at the residency is brighter, happier than the work he did here. Right?"

I nodded. "I wish, then, that we could sell Joya del Mar and find another place, one where he would be happier."

"I don't know if that would solve all his problems, honey," she said.

I sensed that there was more to see and know in this dark shut-up room, but she didn't look like she was going to tell it all to me.

"When I get married and move away, I'll make sure I have a home big enough for him, too," I vowed.

"Maybe you will," Mommy said smiling. She closed her eyes again. "Claude is beautiful," she muttered, "isn't he, Hannah? I hope and pray he'll be all right. You pray, too, sweetheart, pray for your little brother."

I watched her drift off right in front of my eyes. Her breathing became soft and regular. For a few moments I sat there, pouting, and then I rose and went back to the nursery to look through the window at my new brother, at the little being who could bring so much joy to my mother and Miguel simply by appearing.

Looking at Claude caused me to wonder about Uncle Linden, born secretly in that beach house, barely knowing his mother before she was sent to my grandfather's clinic. Do babies sense the separation, long for their mothers without even realizing what it is that makes them feel so lost? Was Uncle Linden terrified at night when he cried and was comforted not by his mother, but by his grandmother?

Something made little Claude shudder, and then a moment later he waved his arms and small fists wildly, screaming. No one seemed to notice. I looked about frantically until finally I saw a nurse go to him. She held him for a moment, but that didn't stop his crying. His face looked even redder, and I thought, *Do something before he chokes to death on his own tears.*

I was about to pound on the glass and shout it, but the nurse smiled as if there was absolutely nothing wrong, then she said something to another nurse and took him out. I worried about where she had taken him until I saw she was bringing him to Mommy's room.

"What's wrong with him?" I asked.

"Nothing. He's just hungry," the nurse replied and went in to wake Mommy so she could breast-feed him. She had decided she would do that.

Nothing brought home little Claude's favored place and status in our family more than watching him suckle at Mommy's breast and seeing the angelic joy in her face. Mommy never told me whether or not she had breast-fed me, and suddenly it became very important to know.

"He's so hungry," Mommy said. "That's good."

"Was I breast-fed, too?" I asked abruptly.

Mommy looked up at me, holding her smile.

"No, actually, you weren't. I was so crazed back then. Your father and I had separated. I was feeling so abused. Despite what everyone was telling me, I couldn't help believing I had permitted him to ruin my life."

"Then you didn't want me to be born?"

"Yes, of course I did. I was just feeling terribly sorry for myself. My mother had died; Linden was not doing very well, as I explained to you, and here I was, pregnant with a husband who considered adultery less important than a parking ticket.

"But the moment you appeared on the scene, it all changed. It was as if the sun had finally come out on a rainy day."

"Then why didn't you breast-feed me, too?"

She hesitated, glanced at Claude, and then looked at me and forced a smile. Mommy's forced smiles always looked like she could go either way: cry or laugh.

"I just told you, Hannah. I was in somewhat of a state of turmoil. I had no one but Miguel really. I needed to get back on my feet as quickly as I could. I tried to stay home with you as long as I could, but eventually, I had to get out in the world and occupy myself. You had a wonderful nanny in Donna Castilla, and Mrs. Davis, bless her soul, watched over you as though you were her very own grandchild. In the beginning I had my hands full arbitrating the arguments between the two of them concerning what was best for you and what was not. Do you remember any of that?"

"A little," I said.

"Yes, well, I'm glad I didn't keep a nanny as long as my stepmother did, even though Amou was more my mother. You, thank goodness, had me and had a stepfather who has always loved you like his own."

"Now he has two children to love," I said.

She gazed down at Claude. I wondered if she could hear my fears in my voice. I really meant he'll love him more. It's only natural, I thought. Claude is his real child and Claude is his son.

"Does that hurt?" I asked.

"Breast-feeding? Just the opposite. However, you won't find many Palm Beach mothers doing it. They're terrified of losing their figures."

"Aren't you?"

"No," she said firmly. "Besides, I want to do what's best for him," she added.

Then why didn't you do what was best for me? I wanted to ask, but I didn't. I watched for a while, and then, after the nurse returned and took Claude back to the nursery, I went to get Mommy some magazines at the hospital gift shop. When I returned to the room, Miguel was there. He was ranting on and on about his faculty meeting, and Mommy was lying back on the pillow, a smile of amusement painted across her face.

"I mean, they will, they won't. Talk, talk, talk, but no action!" he exclaimed.

"They're afraid, Miguel. They have to talk themselves into it first. It takes time."

"Time is not something they have in abundance here, Willow. Oh, what's the use!" he cried and collapsed in the chair, his arms dangling. The he looked up at me and shook his head.

"Don't marry a schoolteacher unless he's independently wealthy," he told me.

"I'm not getting married," I retorted.

"What? Why not?"

"I want to have a career."

"Your mother has a career and she's married," he said, nodding at Mommy.

"She's different," I said. "She can be a psychologist and stay in one place. I will have to travel, do tours, be in shows. I won't have time for a husband and especially not for a child."

"Sure you will," Miguel said.

"No, I won't. I especially won't be able to breast-feed," I practically screamed.

The smile lifted off his face. He looked at Mommy.

"It's all right, Hannah. You're too young to have to worry about those things anyway," she said. "What did you get me?" she asked, and I brought her the magazines. "Good," she said, looking them over. "You guys better go home," she told Miguel.

"Sure," he said, standing. "I'll be back after dinner."

He leaned over and kissed her softly on the mouth.

"Thank you for my son," he whispered loud enough for me to hear.

She beamed.

I turned toward the door.

"Hannah?" she called, holding up her arms.

I went to her and let her embrace and kiss me on the cheek, but my own lips were still stuck in a firm pout.

"Take care of Miguel," she said. "Make sure he eats a real dinner and doesn't stop at some taco stand and call that a meal," she added, eyeing him with pretended fury.

He laughed. "She reads my mind, that woman. No wonder she is such a successful psychotherapist."

If she could only read mine, I thought, she would know how deep the hurt I felt was and how it seemed to travel through my body, even affecting the way I walked. Miguel insisted on stopping by the nursery on our way out.

"One more look to be sure it's all real," he said.

Little Claude was contentedly asleep, his tummy full of Mommy's milk. There was no umbilical cord between them, but he was still dependent on her.

He wasn't a day old, and he was already more a part of this family than I had ever been, I thought.

Maybe more than I would ever be.

2

Brothers and Sisters

Suddenly I was the center of attention for all my friends at school. They practically attacked me with their questions when I returned the following day. With Mommy in the hospital, I had use of her car. It was one of those rare heavily overcast days with a marine layer that grew thicker and thicker with every passing hour, the clouds rolling over each other and growing darker, looking more scuffed and bruised, until the skies exploded in thunder and seared the underbelly of the stormy ceiling with lightning. Finally a downpour brought some cool air, but the clouds still seemed embedded in my thoughts, and the lightning still sizzled in my eyes.

My girlfriends surrounded me as soon as I entered the building. They fired their questions in shotgun fashion.

"How much did your little brother weigh?"

"Who does he look more like?"

"Does he look at all like you?"

"What's his name?

"Why did they call him Claude?"

"Did your mother hire the nanny yet?" Massy asked pointedly, pushing her way to the forefront.

Mommy hadn't hired anyone even though she had conducted interviews and had a dozen or so résumés. She had decided only during the final few weeks not to do so immediately.

"I think it's important for me to be home and continue the breast-feeding," she announced at dinner one night. I looked at her and thought Massy was right after all. Despite Mommy's knowledge of psychology, she would be the neurotic mother Massy had predicted.

"Not yet," I was forced to admit.

Massy practically illuminated, her eyes filling with candle flames.

"Not yet?" She laughed. "I told you," she declared with such an expression of self-satisfaction, I felt my stomach churn. "I told you your mother would be too nervous to put her trust into anyone but family."

"Yes, you told me. You're so brilliant and the rest of us are all stupid," I retorted, shaking my head in front of her and burning my eyes into hers.

"Don't get mad at me for being right," she fired back.

Everyone looked at me. My face was flushed. I was already in a mood that serial killers would envy, and here was Massy putting her fat, self-satisfied face in mine.

I smiled coldly at her. "I'm not mad at you for being right, Massy. I'm mad at you for enjoying it so much and for taking your frustrations out on me."

"Huh?" she moaned, stepping back, her cheeks swelling so much, her eyes seemed to disappear. "What frustrations?"

"Not being able to get Raymond Humphrey to give you the time of day," I replied in a voice loud enough for the boys behind us to hear, Raymond being one of them.

Massy's face turned more blue than red. She looked at the other girls, and then, with her eyes filling with tears to drown out those candle flames, she lifted her heavy shoulders, squeezed her books against her ample bosom, and spun around to march away. The boys laughed aloud behind us.

"That was mean, Hannah," Brigitte Sklar said. The others nodded in agreement. "You know she told us that in confidence. We were all trusting each other with our heartfelt, deepest secrets."

"It's her own fault, making me feel bad first," I said. I hated sounding like I was whining, but that was exactly what I was doing.

"What did she say that was so terrible? She was just trying to give you heads-up about your mother and what things might be like for you at home," Tina Olsen said.

"You should know better," Brigitte insisted. "That wasn't fair."

"Fair has nothing to do with anything!" I snapped back at her. "It's childish to think it does."

She didn't reply. She looked at the others and then

the bell rang and we headed for our classes. At lunch I felt like being by myself. It wouldn't have mattered if I hadn't because all my friends were comforting poor Massy, who was milking their sympathy and throwing glances full of darts my way. I had sulked all through my last two classes, not answering questions I could have easily answered. Everyone kept her distance between classes, too. They could see in my face that I was full of anger and self-pity and not fit company. I found an empty corner at a table and attacked a cheese-and-tomato sandwich as would a ravenous dog.

"Are you that hungry?" I heard and turned to look up at Heyden Reynolds.

"No," I said. "I don't even know what I'm eating," I replied.

He smiled and looked toward my friends.

"Trouble in paradise?" he asked me.

"Some paradise," I muttered. His smile widened to reveal how pleased he was about that. Was this a case of misery loves company? I wondered.

"I heard you singing in Mac's class the other day," he said, sliding himself onto the chair across from me. "You have a nice voice. It has timbre."

"Timbre?"

"Yeah. When you want to, you can bellow it out. Your voice has a thickness, a resonance. It's deep and rich," he continued like a professional music critic. "I like the way you hit the low notes and then lift the melody when you have to and get into the high ones. You've got the range someone needs to make it out there," he added.

I simply stared at him. He raised his eyebrows at my silence and at the way I glared. Then he tucked in the corners of his mouth and began to rise.

"Sorry," he said. "I didn't mean to poke my nose in your life."

"No!" I cried when he turned to walk off.

"No?"

"I mean, you're not poking your nose into my life. I mean, you are, but that's okay. I appreciate it. Thank you. Poke all you want."

His annoyed expression flew off and a smile of amusement settled in to replace it. He glanced back at my girlfriends, who were all looking our way with interest, and then he slipped back into the chair across from me.

"So, what's up? Why are you ostracized from the henhouse today?"

"I'm not ostracized. I'm just . . . just not in the mood for their silly talk."

"Who ever is?" he said. "What happened to put you out of the mood—or is that me sticking too much nose into your life?"

"It's complicated," I said.

"What isn't?" he retorted.

I glanced up at him. When he spoke, he had an accent that suggested his Haitian mother's influence. There was a unique sort of cadence and melody. He had an intelligence in his eyes, a look that reflected something more mature than most of the boys I knew, and all that was reflected in the confident way he held himself, walked, and talked to people.

"My mother gave birth yesterday," I said. "I have a

new brother. His name is Claude. He's named after my mother's father."

"Any other brothers or sisters?"

"I have twin half brothers, my father's sons, but they would deny they're related to me in any way if you asked them."

He sat back. "Is your mother your real mother?"

"Yes. I know what you're thinking, and that's part of what makes everything so complicated."

"What am I thinking?"

"Why did my mother wait so long to have another child?"

"Did your mother just get remarried or something?"

"No. She's been remarried about sixteen years."

"Okay, I'll bite. Why did she wait so long?"

"She didn't want to interrupt her career, I guess."

"And now she does?"

"I don't know," I said with more annoyance than I had intended, but I did hate answering the questions. "Like I said, it's complicated."

"So, make it simple," he said, standing again.

"How?"

"Do what I did," he replied, picking up his books. "Start thinking more about yourself. Stop worrying about everyone else, and especially," he added, glancing at the girls again, "what they think."

He walked away. My eyes followed him until he was gone, and then I looked at my girlfriends. They were all chattering at once.

It made me laugh.

They did look like hens in a henhouse.

I saw Heyden a few more times in the afternoon

between classes. He smiled, but he didn't stop to talk to me. I couldn't help being disappointed, and that just added weight to the burden of heavy emotions I was lugging about all day. When the school day ended, I was looking forward to going to see my uncle Linden. His home, his world never seemed more appropriate. I felt like moving in with him.

Neither Mommy nor Miguel really knew how often I visited my uncle Linden. Whenever I was able to get Mommy's car, it was the first place I thought I would visit. It was an easy ride, only a mile and a half off I-95. Nothing about the house Uncle Linden was in suggested it was a supervised residency. It was a big, front-gabled house with a two-tiered porch. The flat jigsaw-cut upper balustrade and the gable trim were all in a fresh-looking linen white. The rest of the building, except for the shutters, was in a dark chocolate wood cladding.

Stuart and Elizabeth Robinson, who owned and operated the residency, were a very pleasant couple in their fifties. There were only four clients, as they were known, presently living in the house. They had supervised as many as six since I had been visiting Uncle Linden, but two were now gone, one to live with her family, and the other, an elderly man, had become very ill and passed away in the hospital.

Uncle Linden was barely two years older than Mommy, but he looked more like twenty years older. I once asked Mommy about that, and she said it was probably a result of years of medication and depression.

"The mind has more influence on the body than

most people think, Hannah," she told me. "Stress, emotional turmoil, worry, and depression all take a great toll."

To be sure, Uncle Linden was still a rather good-looking man. Although he had some premature graying in his temples, his hair was thick and an interesting shade of blond, more like a light olive-brown. He had dark brown eyes that he directed with such apparent intensity at whoever spoke to him or he spoke to that the person always thought Uncle Linden was concentrating hard on what he or she was saying. Actually, he often turned his brain inside out but left his eyes fixed like that, just the way someone might direct a flashlight on something and walk off. It took me a while to realize it when I was younger, but he could and often did drift away on the shoulders of some thought or some memory. It was my way of knowing my visit had come to an end. My kiss goodbye on his cheek would flutter his eyelids and bring the trace of a smile to his lips, but not much more.

Lately, though, I found him doing this less and less, especially with me, and either Stuart or Elizabeth had told me on more than one occasion how much my uncle looked forward to my visits.

"When he's not absorbed by his painting, he often sits on the porch and watches the highway, hoping, I'm sure, to see you drive up, Hannah," Stuart told me. Then he added in practically a whisper, "He has this fear in his face that he missed you or that somehow you were there and he hadn't paid enough attention to you. I know. He's said as much," Stuart said. He patted my hand and added, "He needs reassurance, lots of reassurance. I'm not a psychiatrist and I don't have a degree, but experience has taught me that people who are in his state of mind are constantly afraid of abandonment."

"I'll never abandon him," I said, sounding furious at the very suggestion. "If anything, as soon as I am able to, I'll take him out of here to live with me."

"That's very nice," Stuart said. "He's lucky to have a loving niece like you."

I knew that smile was a smile meant to humor a young girl who fantasized, but he didn't know me. He didn't know how determined I could be and how loyal I was, especially now. Uncle Linden was all the family I had, real family, other than Mommy. Daddy was in a class by himself along with his children. I stopped trying to figure out where I would fit in his view of things.

As lean as he was in the pictures we had of him when he was much younger, Uncle Linden still wore his hair long and dressed casually, favoring a windbreaker I had bought him for his birthday two years ago. Most of the time he wore jeans and a pair of sandals. One of the things I did do with him occasionally was go for a walk along the street, passing the gates of home developments with their security guards peering out of glass booths at us with what looked like paranoid eyes, expecting us to rush the entranceway and crash into their precious housing development. People knew that the residency was just down the street, and that drew up terrifying scenarios and nightmares for them, I was sure. The Robinsons told me that there had been a number of challenges to their existence over the years, attempts to use zoning ordinances to stop them from housing what was politely referred to as the mentally disabled. It was another in a growing list of reasons why I wanted us to bring Uncle Linden home. He and the other residents had problems, but that didn't mean they couldn't sense being persona non grata.

When I drove up to the home this time, I was pleased to see Uncle Linden sitting on the front porch. He recognized Mommy's vehicle and stopped rocking. As soon as I stepped out of the car, he rose and came to the railing to call out, only he called out, "Willow," instead of Hannah.

"It's me, Uncle Linden," I replied.

He stood there strangely gazing past me as if he was really a blind man trying to hear or somehow sense what he was supposed to see.

"It's Hannah," I said, hurrying to the steps.

"Oh, Hannah. Hannah," he said, nodding. He smiled and I rushed up to embrace him.

"How are you today?"

"Good," he said, nodding and looking thoughtful about it. "Good," he concluded. "Where's your mother?"

"She's still in the hospital. She might be coming home tomorrow morning. It all depends on Claude."

"Hospital?" He sat in the rocker, his face turning ashen with concern. "What's wrong with her?"

It simply hadn't occurred to me that neither Mother nor Miguel had called the residency to tell Uncle Linden about little Claude's birth. I knew from previous visits and one visit, nearly seven months ago with Mommy, that Uncle Linden knew she was pregnant. She didn't spend very much time talking about it, and I remember he seemed unimpressed, even though she had gone so long without becoming pregnant.

Maybe they were planning on telling him today. They didn't know I was coming to see him, but Mommy hadn't told me to wait for her to tell him or anything like that. However, she always made it seem like I should tiptoe around Uncle Linden and never volunteer any more information about our family life than he actually asked about.

"I know it's hard, maybe even impossible for you to realize how ill he was and still is," she instructed, "so please especially try to avoid talking about the past. If he brings anything up from our past, just say you don't know anything and you're not comfortable talking about it. He'll understand and stop.

"I'm not saying you can make him sicker or anything like that, Hannah," she added when she saw the expression on my face. "I just don't want you to feel any sort of pressure."

"I never do," I said.

"No, I'm sure you don't, and I am happy about that. I do know he enjoys seeing you very much, so spend your time talking about yourself, your school, your music lessons, things like that. He has no other way of learning about that sort of thing, you know. Okay? You understand?" she asked, and I nodded even though I didn't understand. Why was our family past filled with so many minefields? I knew so little detail about everything anyway. What was she afraid I would say? It did make me nervous.

And so whenever Uncle Linden did begin to drift off, to talk about life before me, I interrupted and mentioned something that had just happened. Sometimes he would bite and ask me about it, and sometimes he would simply clam up and take on that far-off look, and I knew he was hearing another voice, seeing another face. That was my clue to end my visit.

In the beginning when I started to visit Uncle Linden by myself, Mommy questioned me in detail about each occasion, wanting to know what was said, what sort of things Uncle Linden wanted to talk about, and how he reacted to the things I told him. I assumed she had a purely professional interest in it, but the time before last, when Uncle Linden mentioned his desire to do a painting of me, she became very agitated and concerned, so much so, that I was frightened.

"No!" she cried almost before I was able to get the news through my lips. "Absolutely out of the question. Don't you even think of it."

"But why not? What harm could that do to him?" I asked, disappointed. I was actually looking forward to posing and having the picture. I couldn't help but be curious as to what he would see in me and how he would portray me. He had done one other portrait while he was at the residency, as far as I knew, and that was of another resident, a woman who was at least twenty years older than he was, and yet she looked twenty years younger, and I thought there were resemblances to Mommy.

"He's always talking about how much you and I look alike," I told Mommy. "I guess he just wants to paint that."

"I forbid you to do it, Hannah. If you don't listen to me, I'll have to tell the Robinsons not to permit you to visit Uncle Linden without my being present, too," she threatened.

I felt hot tears come up under my eyelids.

"I don't see what's so terrible," I muttered.

"It's complicated psychological business," she explained. "His doing a portrait of you or me or anyone so close to him is a catalyst bringing on deeper emotional issues. You won't understand if I go into great detail. You will have to trust my judgment, Hannah. I don't mean to say or do anything that is painful or unpleasant. You have to believe me that what I am telling you is best for Uncle Linden, okay? Will you promise? Will you?"

"Okay," I replied in a small voice of disappointment. "I promise."

I didn't bring it up again, but it left me feeling so tentative and uncertain whenever I visited him now. I hated lying to him and when he asked me again to pose for him, I had to tell him I couldn't spend that much time there. I had this or that to do for school or something at home. I could see he was so disappointed it made him sulk, and I hated myself for doing that to him, but what else could I do?

"You remember that Mommy was pregnant, Uncle Linden," I told him. "She gave birth to a boy and she named him after her father, Claude. He was born underweight, actually premature, and so they are keeping him under observation for a week, but the doctors believe he will be fine. I'm sorry no one has called to tell you everything, but I'm sure Mommy and Miguel just didn't want you to worry. They have been very occupied, too."

He looked at me and nodded.

"I told her what to do," he said. "I told her what to take and what to eat and I told her not to depend so much on doctors. You can become just another number, a statistic. I explained all that to her. I gave her things to read, too."

Read? What things did he give her to read? I never saw anything. And where would he get such material?

"But she didn't listen, did she?" he continued, more vehemently. "Now, as I feared, there is a problem. Thatcher," he said, practically spitting out my father's name. "Thatcher Eaton."

"What does he have to do with it, Uncle Linden?"

He looked at me and twisted the corner of his mouth up into his cheek for a moment and then shook his head.

"Nothing," he said. "He has absolutely nothing to do with it."

He sat back in the rocker and gazed up at the clouds that spiraled in the wind toward the horizon. The breeze had picked up, and the American flag the Robinsons had on their front lawn snapped briskly, sounding like the striking of a wooden match. The sound seemed mesmerizing for Uncle Linden.

"I'm working on a new song for the next school variety show, Uncle Linden," I said, deciding to quickly change the topic. I could see I was already losing him, and I had just arrived. I had never seen him this bad. It frightened me and turned my heart into a tin drum. It put some panic in my voice. "You told me once that it was your mother's favorite, and I'm singing it in French. *La Vie en Rose*. You'll come to the show, won't you? You said you would."

He rocked slowly, nodding at his own thoughts now, his lips firmly pressing against each other, his eyelids blinking rapidly. He was no longer hearing me

"Uncle Linden?"

The front screen door opened, and Elizabeth Robinson stepped out, smiling as soon as she saw me.

"Hannah, how nice to see you. I was just coming out to see how Linden was doing. How are you? How's your mother?"

"She gave birth two days ago, nearly a month too early."

"Oh, is she all right?"

"Yes."

"And the baby?"

"Yes, although he's small."

"Well, I'm sure everything will be fine. As I recall, you all already knew it was to be a boy, right?"

"Yes. They named him Claude, after her father."

I spoke quickly, so quickly someone would think the words and the facts were fermenting poison in my brain.

"Good. Well, please, give your mother our congratulations. And your stepfather, too. Did you hear all about that, Linden?" she said, turning to him. "You're an uncle again. You have a little nephew."

He continued to rock and stare.

"Oh," Elizabeth said, realizing he was in one of his deep trances. "How long have you been here, honey?" she asked me.

"I just got here. I just told him about Mommy and little Claude."

"Um," she said. She stared at him a moment. "Well,

don't let this upset you. He's doing real well, you know. He's been working regularly and eating well, too."

She put her hand on his shoulder. "Linden, aren't you happy to hear the good news? You have a new little nephew," she repeated, hoping to get a response and bring him back from whatever thought or memory had seized his brain.

He continued to stare blankly.

"He gets quiet like this sometimes. It's not usually good to force him to listen. He'll come around when he's ready. I'm sure you'll have a better visit next time," she told me and turned back to him. "Hannah's leaving now, Linden."

"I wasn't going to leave," I said.

She smiled and squinted. "I'll get him to go in and rest a while before dinner. That always works best," she said. "Linden, would you like to come inside and rest up for a while?"

He lowered his head slowly and then nodded.

"Yes, I'm tired," he said. "I'm very tired."

"Sure you are," Elizabeth told him. "He was working all morning on a new painting. He was at it intensely. Weren't you, Linden?"

"Yes," he said.

With her urging, he stood.

"Tell Hannah you'll see her another time, Linden," Elizabeth suggested.

He looked at me as if he had completely forgotten I was there. It put a cold chill in my heart.

"Tell Willow to come with you next time," he said. "I haven't seen her for a long time. We have things to talk about. She's not taking proper care of herself for a pregnant woman," he said and turned with Elizabeth toward the door.

She looked back at me and mouthed, "Don't worry. He'll be fine."

I watched them go in. I felt like I had swallowed a rock. Was this why Mommy was always warning me not to talk to him about the past? This wasn't the past, but something triggered his withdrawal so quickly and got him confused, I thought.

Frustrated and disappointed, I stepped off the porch and walked to the car. I wanted to tell Mommy about this, but then I was afraid she would be angry I had been the one to tell Uncle Linden the news. She might tell me he wasn't prepared properly or something, and she might forbid me to come back without her.

I felt so alone. I thought about calling Daddy. I sat in the car and dug into my bag to find my cell phone, a birthday present from Miguel.

"I know kids your age have too many electronic toys and such, but this makes sense. It's good to have it in an emergency," he said, more for Mommy's ears than mine. She was always warning him about spoiling me or trying to buy my affection, something she knew Daddy loved to accuse him of doing. She hated giving my father the opportunity to pounce on anything, which only made it harder for me when I was alone with either of them, part of that tightrope I walked.

"Why did you tell him that?" she would ask, annoyed after he threw something I had said back into her face. "Why is it any of his business?"

What should I tell him then? I wondered. What was his business? It wasn't my fault there was a No Man's

Land between them. I didn't create it; they did. I never said any of this to either of them. Maybe I should have, I thought. Maybe I should have asked her for a list of permissible subjects.

Daddy's secretary, Mrs. Gouter, answered on the first ring.

"Eaton, Cooperman, and Robatille," she said.

"It's Hannah," I said. Usually that was enough.

"Just one moment, please," she replied. All these years I called his office, Mrs. Gouter never was anything but correct and businesslike with me.

"Hannah, I'm right in the middle of something. Anything wrong?" Daddy asked quickly.

"No. I just wanted to tell you Mommy gave birth."

"Yes, I heard," he said.

"Oh."

I don't know why it surprised me, even though I was sure neither Mommy nor Miguel would have told him. Gossip was the lifeblood of this community, I thought.

"Some family planning," he muttered. "You'll probably be married with kids of your own before he's out of diapers."

"I will not, Daddy. That's silly."

"Yes, well, silly is as silly does," he said. "I'll call you tomorrow. I might be home for dinner Friday, and you can come over and have a normal evening," he said. "No one will analyze the salad dressing."

"Daddy . . ." I began.

"Sorry, Hannah, I have to get back to work. I'm in the middle of winning a half million dollars for a client whose poodle was accidentally on purpose dropped down a laundry shaft in one of our better hotels."

"Really?"

"Gotta go," he said, and the phone went dead.

My feelings seemed to do the same thing: just come to a stop and drop away, leaving me numb and silent inside. There was nothing to do but go home.

That must mean something terrible, I thought, to think of home as the absolutely last place you wanted to be.

There was a message waiting for me. Miguel had gone to the hospital, and I should either follow or have dinner at home by myself. Reluctantly I was going to go to the hospital, but a surprise phone call stopped me from doing that.

It was Heyden Reynolds.

"I decided to keep poking my nose in your life," he began. "Before you ask, Selma Warden gave me your phone number. She was guarding it as hard as she's been guarding her virginity," he added, and I laughed.

"Then how did you get her to give it up to you?"

"Can't tell you. If I did, I would have to kill you immediately."

It felt good to smile. He was like some antidote for depression, a dosage of fun.

"I know it's a precious school night and all, but I was wondering if you would like to go for some fast food. I can afford as much as a royal, deluxe supreme burger or chicken delight supreme, if you don't order any extra French fries.

"I know," he added before I could respond, "someone has already prepared dinner for you."

"For your information, Mr. Know-it-all, no one has,

and I was on my way out to eat some hospital cafeteria food."

"Oh. Well, if you would rather do that, I can meet you in the emergency room or even the OR."

I laughed again.

"I'll meet you at your favorite fast-food restaurant. Just give me directions," I said and he did.

When I hung up, I felt a surge of new energy and excitement. The heavy cape of dark depression slipped away, and I hurried to fix my hair, put on some fresh lipstick, and change into a one of my prettier blouses and a pair of designer jeans. Then I thought I was over-doing it for a fast-food restaurant and felt a sense of new panic. Would he think I was silly? Was I being too anxious? Confusion added to delay, which intensified my panic. Stop acting stupid, I finally ordered myself and shot out of my room, down the stairs, and out the front door. I heard the phone ringing behind me, but I didn't wait to see who it was.

Minutes later I was heading for the Flagler bridge to drive into West Palm Beach. Both Mommy and Miguel didn't like me going into new places without them or without them being aware of it, but I wasn't feeling like paying much attention to their rules at the moment. The particular area of West Palm Beach into which I was driving was not an area featured in any tourist maga-zines. The housing was the least expensive and the least attractive. It was home mostly to the people who served as menial laborers and service employees in the fancier resorts. The storefronts were dull and weathered, the streets not as clean looking. Coming directly here from Palm Beach's Worth Avenue was one of the best ways to appreciate the vast gap between the rich and the poor in America.

Sometimes I think rich people are threatened by the mere sight of poor people, of poor communities. They prefer to ride through them quickly or pull down the shades on their luxurious limousines following the premise that what you don't see, what you don't know can't hurt you. Who wants to be reminded just how disgustingly wealthy he or she is? As Mommy often says, "Rich people here put a gag on the mouth of their conscience."

Heyden was standing outside the front entrance of the fast-food restaurant when I drove into the parking lot. Mommy's Mercedes C-class looked out of place. Heyden wore a smile of amusement as he started toward me.

"Feel like you're slumming?" he asked.

I looked around. "Actually, I'm here every other day."

"Sure, and there really is a Santa Claus," he said, laughing. "C'mon. I've decided to splurge and buy you extra large fries, too."

It seemed like everyone was looking at us when we entered, but I blamed that on my own nervousness. We got right in line, and he read off the choices printed on the wall. I really wasn't hungry, but I let him order me the deluxe hamburger and the fries. I chose a bottle of water as an offering to the god of diet and nutrition, and then we sat at an outside table.

We were right at the center of a busy intersection. There was a constant stream of traffic going by the fast-food restaurant and a continuous flow of traffic and people coming to it and leaving it. This was certainly not the most romantic or private place to meet someone for the first time, but for some reason, that was what gave it its charm.

"I have this philosophy as far as being creative is concerned," he began, noticing how I was looking at everyone and everything. "I think you have to be in it, to feel the rhythms of real life. You can't hide out behind those high walls and hedges all your life and do anything good.

"In other words," he said, "I'd be here even if I didn't have to be. At least, once in a while," he added with a smile.

"The hamburger is as delicious as I've had in fancy places," I said and he laughed.

"How's life at the palace?"

"My mother is still in the hospital. I haven't been there yet today."

"Oh." He thought a moment. "I didn't mean to interfere. I guess I could have met you there. I just assumed you had come back from visiting and—"

"No. I was visiting my uncle instead," I said.

"Your uncle is in the hospital too?"

"He's in an adult residency near Boca."

"Oh? Is he that old?"

"It's not that kind of residency. It's for people who can't live on their own."

"Really? What's wrong with him?"

"He suffers from manic depression. He was in a clinic for years and years and then improved and was placed in the residency. Some day I'm going to get him out of there," I declared.

"Is he your mother's or your father's brother?"

"Mother's."

"Your house is as big as a small hotel, isn't it? Why wouldn't she want him to live with you if he could?"

"She doesn't think he can," I said bitterly, "but she's wrong."

"Well, isn't your mother a psychologist? Shouldn't she know better than you?"

"No. It's—"

"—complicated," he finished for me. "I know, I know."

"No, you don't know," I flared.

"Why is it all the other students at our school, especially the girls, believe they have a monopoly on emotional and psychological problems? I call it the 'No one has it as bad as I do' syndrome.

"Poor Massy Hewlett can't control her weight. She never met a bonbon she didn't like. Poor Brigitte Sklar hasn't found a decent hairdresser, and Tina Olsen? If Tina doesn't get her mother to let her go to Aspen the next spring break, she'll run away from home. Not to mention Natalie Alexander's crisis over zits."

I laughed and then, looking critical, said, "So you listen in on our conversations? Everyone thinks you're bored to death most of the time and couldn't care less about anything anyone says."

"That's true, I am bored to death, but I'm not deaf, and to tell you the truth, it gives me some moments of amusement."

"I'm glad you think that's all we are, moments of amusement. My mother is always telling me that rich or poor, emotional and psychological baggage is still a serious problem. If someone makes a mountain out of a molehill, it's still a mountain to him or to her."

"Very charitable."

"If you can't be compassionate, compassionate with everyone, you can't be a good doctor or a good psychologist or anything that has to do with helping people, Heyden. Don't be so smug just because you have a normal life," I snapped.

"Normal?" He laughed the hardest he had.

"Well, I don't know much about you, except what I've heard on the rumor network."

"And what have you heard exactly? Go on, tell me," he urged, seeing my hesitation. "It's okay. I'm a big boy and I have the skin of an alligator."

"I know your mother's Haitian."

"And practices voodoo," he said.

"Really?"

He laughed at how quickly I believed what he said.

"No, but I enjoy fanning the flames of stupid prejudice. My father is a jazz musician. He's away from home twenty or so days a month. I have a sister who is studying to be a terrorist, I think. She's fourteen and goes to public school here. She already has a record some of your hardened urban criminals would envy. Last night I found ecstasy pills in her room. I flushed them down the toilet and didn't tell my mother, not that it would do much good if I did tell her."

"Why not?"

He looked away a moment and was so quiet, I thought he wasn't going to explain. But then he turned back to me, his eyes smaller, darker.

"You ever wonder if animals get reincarnated as people? You know, you look at someone and say he or she reminds you of a bird or a hog or something?"

"Yes," I said smiling.

"My mother is definitely a reincarnated ostrich. Her head is buried so far down . . ."

"Oh."

"I'm sure there is a psychological term your mother could apply."

I nodded and said, "I'm sorry."

"I'm tired of being my father, know what I mean?"

"I think so," I offered, but I really didn't. I had few if any adult responsibilities and was fighting to be given some.

He smirked and then turned it quickly into a smile. "Anyway, why talk about depressing things? All that does is depress you."

I was happy to agree to that and ate another French fry. We just stared at each other for a long moment. I could almost hear the wheels turning in his head. Why was I here? How interested in him was I really?

"What?" I finally asked.

"I don't know if you have the time, but I'd like you to hear a song I wrote for my guitar. I thought of everyone in that school, you'd be someone who might appreciate it. Not that I'm saying I'm that great or anything."

"I don't think I'm any authority on the subject, but I would like to hear it very much," I said.

"Okay. I'm not far. Actually, just a block down and to the left. I walked here rather than take my moped."

I glanced at my watch. By now Miguel and my mother were surely wondering where I was. It was unlike me not to let them know where I was going, especially when I had Mommy's car. I thought about calling on my cell phone, but I knew they would be upset and would want me to come to the hospital immediately or go home immediately. Better I call them after I hear Heyden's song, I thought.

"I'm ready," I announced, taking my last bite of my hamburger.

"Great."

We got into Mommy's car and I pulled out of the parking lot.

"First time I've ever been in a Mercedes," he said.

"It's the only car I've ever driven. It's my mother's car. My parents want me to get a job before they'll get me my own car."

"The nerve of them," he quipped.

"Actually," I said, "it's not that important to me."

"As long as you get to use this when you want, huh?"

"I don't, but for some reason, I've lost interest."

"That's just temporary. You're going through something. You'll snap out of it."

"Yes, Dr. Reynolds," I said, and he laughed.

"Sorry," he said. "I'm no one to give anyone advice. That's for sure."

"Now who sounds like he's cornered the market on suffering," I said.

He raised his eyebrows. "Wow. You're tougher than I imagined."

I smiled to myself, thinking, finally a compliment I really appreciate.

"Here it is," he said, nodding at a duplex. "Joya del street."

"Very funny," I said. Actually, I was flattered he

knew so much about me already. Obviously, I had been in his line of sight for some time. Was I simply oblivious or was he that good at hiding his intentions?

Before we reached the front door, it flew open and Heyden's sister came charging out. She was almost as tall and lean as he was, but with a darker complexion, short licorice black hair, and what were at the moment blazing coal black eyes.

"You were in my room again!" she screamed at Heyden, stepping right up to him and putting her face into his. "You went through my things again and you took it. You're not my father! You have no right to do that!"

"You shouldn't be playing with that stuff!" Heyden yelled back. "And you certainly shouldn't be bringing it into the house."

"I hate you!" she cried, barely taking note of my presence. "I wish you weren't my brother."

"That makes two of us," he said.

"You'll be sorry soon," she threatened, and then she smiled so coldly, it even put a chill in my body. "You'll see," she added and charged past us.

"Elisha!" he screamed after her. She just kept going, her head down, her arms tightly crossed under her small breasts, crossing the street and gone before he could call out to her again.

"Damn," Heyden muttered. He looked at the front entrance. "Better go inside," he said. "I have a bad feeling."

It was a small apartment, the living room being the biggest room, the kitchen not much bigger than our pantry closet. The furniture looked ten years past its retirement, and the rug was worn thin enough to see the wood floor beneath it in the living room. Some dirty dishes were piled next to the sink, and a partially filled coffee cup with what looked to be morning coffee was on the small yellowish table.

"Elisha didn't do her chores again. My mother is still at work," he said. "She takes as much overtime as she can get."

"What does she do?"

"She's a chambermaid at the Breakers, so we have a lot of hotel soap," he added bitterly.

He walked slowly through the kitchen to the hallway and paused at an open door. I saw him bring his hand to his forehead and then lean against the doorjamb.

"Damn her to hell," he said.

"What?"

"Look for yourself."

Slowly I stepped up beside him. There, smashed to pieces on the floor of his bedroom, was his guitar.

3

Parental Concern

With his guitar broken, Heyden was unable to play and sing his song. I offered to listen to it anyway or at least read the lyrics, but he was too despondent.

"It won't be the same. Another time," he said, picking up the pieces.

"I'm sorry," I said.

"Me, too." He paused and looked at me as if he were first realizing I was there in his room with him. "You're lucky your only brother is so much younger than you. You won't have to go through stupid stuff like this. You'll be out of the house by then. Me, I'm trapped. I'd leave tomorrow, if I could, and I won't hesitate the moment I can," he vowed.

"Wouldn't your mother be upset?" I asked.

"She'd just pretend I was in school or something. I told you. My mother would do anything to avoid crying or being sad. People don't mind lying to themselves if it will make their lives easier."

He gazed down at the broken guitar.

"But isn't that what you would be doing by running away?" I asked.

He looked up so quickly, I thought he was going to be angry at me, but instead, he smiled.

"Now you sound like a psychologist's daughter. How come you can be like that with other people but not yourself?"

"Why do you say I'm not?'

"Because you fume and pout and rage just like the rest of us. At least, that's what you were doing in the cafeteria when I spoke to you."

I laughed and nodded. "You're right," I said. "But remember what Miss Foggleman always tells us in music appreciation class: Do as I teach, not as I do."

"As far as I'm concerned, that's the oath of a hypocrite," he replied.

He threw the pieces of his guitar into a corner roughly, kicking the splinters into a small pile.

"What are you going to do about this?" I asked.

"Strangle her with one of the guitar strings."

"No, seriously?"

He shrugged and sat on his bed. "I've got some money saved," he said after a moment. "I had my eye on a JB Player that's in the window of this pawn shop. You know anything about guitars?"

"No."

"This one is mint with the exception of a small surface crack at the heel of the neck. It has a flame photo top, a maple neck, rosewood fingerboard in a cherry finish. It's in the window for three hundred. I was planning on buying it anyway. I'm using money I've earned as a part time waiter. I'm supposed to be saving for college, but I'd rather have the guitar. College can come later, if at all," he said. "You don't have to go to college to do what I want to do."

"What's that?"

"Write and perform my own songs."

"My mother says a good liberal education gives you the background to do most anything. You have to draw on something when you create."

"I draw on real life," he said with a fierce look of pride in his eyes. "My stuff rings with truth. It's all out there on the street," he said, gesturing at his window. "It's authentic. That's what I was trying to tell you before. You've just got to be willing to listen, to not be so uppity and snobby that you miss it."

"I'm not snobby. My half brothers have cornered the market on all that as far as my family goes," I said.

He nodded. "No, you're not or you wouldn't have met me for a hamburger and you certainly wouldn't be here in this house with me. Can you imagine Stacy Kreskin or Natalie Alexander coming to my house? Well?" he demanded when I hesitated.

"No," I admitted.

"So why did you come?" he followed with a little more aggression than I anticipated. "It wasn't just to see how the other side lives, was it?"

I stared back at him, shooting my own fiery darts at him.

"I came because you invited me, Heyden Reynolds, and I don't consider myself the other side. If anyone is taking sides here, it's you!"

He stared a little longer and then he laughed. "That's good," he said. "You do that real well."

"It's not an act. Maybe you are so used to phony girls that you can't recognize sincerity when you see it. I feel sorry for you," I said and started out.

"Hey, wait."

"What?"

"I'm sorry. I didn't mean to offend you. I was just . . ."

"Just what, Heyden? Amusing yourself with me, seeing how far I would go or how far you could take me before I would get disgusted?"

I stepped toward him.

"I'm sorry your sister is a big brat and your mother won't face up to her responsibilities and your father is away from it all too much, but I think hating the world is only going to hurt you in the end.

"And that," I added, "is from the psychologist's daughter."

I pivoted like a military guard and strutted out, my heart thumping so hard, it felt like it was pounding a hole through my back. He came after me and stopped me on the front steps.

"Wait. Holy psychosis. You have a worse temper than I do," he said.

"So?"

"So, I meant what I said. I'm sorry if I insulted you in any way, shape, or form. I didn't mean it. I apologize!" he cried, his arms lifted.

I relaxed.

"It's all right. I'm not leaving because of what you said. I've got to be going anyway. My mother and my stepfather are probably on the phone with the FBI by now."

He laughed. "Well, when can I see you again?"

"I'm in school tomorrow."

"You know what I mean," he said.

"No, I don't. Say what you mean," I ordered.

"Okay. How about coming with me to check out the guitar after school tomorrow and then, since it's Friday night, we'll go have something to eat in a slow food restaurant and maybe see a movie or something?"

"So you're asking me on a real date?"

"Yes," he said, laughing. "A real date, only I can only take you on my moped. No car."

"Don't worry about the car. Okay?" I said and continued to walk to my car.

"Okay?"

"Yes, okay. We'll discuss the details tomorrow," I added and opened the car door. He hurried to my side.

"Don't you have to check it out with your parents or something?"

"They are very busy at the moment. Stop worrying about it, and thanks for the fast-food dinner."

I got into the car. He stood there holding the door open and looking in at me.

"What?" I said.

"You're about the prettiest girl in that school. You know that?"

"No."

"Well, you are. I'm just surprised you're not with one of the rich Palm Beach boys that hover like arrogant roosters over the hens."

"I'm not."

"Why not?"

"Some day I'll tell you," I said.

"Tell me tomorrow. Maybe I can turn it into a song," he said, and now I laughed.

"I bet you could," I said, inserting the key in the ignition.

He leaned in before closing the door and kissed me quickly on the cheek.

"Bye," he said and closed the door. Then he turned without seeing my look of surprise and walked back to his house, his shoulders slumping as soon as he reached the first step. I waited. He paused, turned back, flashed a smile, held up his hand, and hurried inside.

As I pulled away, I saw his sister walking slowly up the street, her head down. She glanced my way when I reached her, and in that face I saw more pain and fear than the rage she had been wearing before. I felt sorry for her even though she had done a very bad thing to Heyden. I knew he would be upset with me for feeling that way, but I couldn't help it.

I was my mother's daughter after all.

And I couldn't help that, either.

Mommy and Miguel had been very concerned about my whereabouts and let me know as soon as I arrived at the hospital.

"You don't call to let us know where you are and you don't show up for dinner? Why?" she asked. "Where have you been, Hannah?"

Miguel stood to the side, his arms folded, staring at me and waiting.

"I met someone for a quick bite, a hamburger, that's all."

"You met someone? Who?" she followed.

She was sitting up. When I had stepped out of the elevator, I saw the nurse carrying little Claude back to his nursery, so I knew she had just breast-fed him.

"A boy I met at school."

She looked at Miguel and he shrugged.

"Well, why didn't you tell Miguel anything about that?"

"It all happened so quickly."

"It all happened so quickly?" she parroted.

"Besides, Miguel was gone long before I returned from school."

"That's true," he told my mother, but then he turned to me. "Why did it take so long for you to come home? I waited for you so you could go to the hospital with me."

"I went to see Uncle Linden."

They were both silent.

"I would appreciate knowing when you go there, Hannah," Mommy said.

"Nobody told him about Claude. You said we weren't going to leave him out of anything, but no one bothered to call and let him know what was going on. He didn't even know you were in the hospital!" I fired back at her.

"I told you we were going to tell him. I thought I explained how complicated it can be, Hannah. What did you tell him exactly?"

"I told him Claude was born and that he had to remain in the hospital longer because he was too small."

"What happened then?" she asked.

I saw Miguel move closer to the bed in anticipation of my response. I had no idea why, but it put a trickle of ice down my spine.

"He . . . he got confused. He said things that made no sense, and then he got the way he can be sometimes."

"How?"

"You know, staring at nothing, not listening."

She looked at Miguel, who shook his head slowly.

"What things did he say that made no sense?" she asked.

"I don't know, things. He claimed he gave you books or information on giving birth and that you weren't taking good care of yourself. He mentioned Daddy's name, and when I asked him what he had to do with any of this, Uncle Linden said 'Nothing.' It was just confusing."

"What did you do?"

"Mrs. Robinson came out and talked him into going in for a rest and I left."

"Good," she said. She looked like she relaxed, and Miguel's posture softened as well. "So where did you meet this boy? Who is he? Where did you go to eat?"

"I met him at school, Mommy. Where else would I meet someone?"

"There's no reason to be irritable, Hannah," Miguel said. "Your mother is asking you a simple question, taking interest in what you do and whom you get to know. There's nothing wrong with her doing that, is there?"

"No," I muttered, even though to me it sounded more like a police interrogation.

"So?" she followed, her arms folded under her breasts. "Tell us."

"His name is Heyden Reynolds and he plays guitar and writes his own songs. We went to a fast-food restaurant near his home."

"Where was that?" Miguel asked.

I told them. Neither spoke for a moment.

"You have to be careful in that neighborhood at night," Miguel said.

"I am careful. I'm not an idiot," I shot back.

"You don't have to be an idiot to find yourself in a difficult situation," Miguel said softly.

"No one wants to attach a ball and chain to you, Hannah," Mommy said. "We're just concerned for your welfare. That's all. Especially now," she added.

"Why especially now?" I asked, looking up at them quickly.

"Well, for one thing," Miguel said, smiling, "you've become a rather beautiful young woman. Your mother and I have discussed this many times. We've been anticipating lots of male interest in you, and we want you to have a wonderful social life without any of the problems that can ensue."

I smirked. Sometimes Miguel's calmness was irritating, I thought. Sometimes you need a show of emotion. I hated the feeling that I was being handled. Miguel didn't often resort to what I and my friends called *Teacher Talk,* words that seemed to come directly out of a textbook, but I couldn't help feeling he was doing it now.

"And for another thing I am going to be quite a bit busier and more occupied because of little Claude," Mommy added. "I don't want to neglect you and miss something important, honey."

"Right," I said and looked away, tears simmering beneath my lids. You've already missed something important, I thought. I've grown up, and you still think I'm eight years old or something.

"You know, you marched in here without asking how your little brother is doing," Miguel said softly.

"No one gave me a chance to ask," I shot back at him.

He nodded. "Maybe so," he said generously. "Well, the doctor was here a little while ago and told us he was doing better than they had expected and he might not have to be here as long as they had anticipated."

"Good," I said.

"Oh honey!" Mommy cried, holding up her arms. "Let's not have any arguments or unpleasantness now, not now when we've all got so much to be thankful for and happy about, okay?"

I nodded and went to her. She embraced me, kissed my cheek, and stroked my hair.

"What sort of a young man is this Heyden Reynolds?"

"Mommy, I just met him for a hamburger. We didn't get engaged!"

She laughed. "I know, I know. I was simply curious, that's all. It reminds me of when I started seeing boys as not just the other species," she said, and Miguel laughed.

I felt the walls come down, my defensive attitude slip away.

"His mother is Haitian and his father is a jazz musician who is hardly home. He has a fourteen-year-old sister, but she doesn't go to our school. She gets in trouble a lot, and he bears the brunt of it."

"Oh. Sounds like he has to carry a great deal of emotional and social baggage," she said.

"He does, and he doesn't have many friends at school. He transferred in for his senior year. Because of his father's traveling, they have had to move about a great deal."

"Well, be careful about how much you get involved with his problems, Hannah."

"You get involved with other people's problems," I reminded her.

"Yes, but your mother is a professional, trained and schooled in how to do that without it seriously impacting on her own life," Miguel said.

"I thought you wanted me to be a compassionate person," I told Mommy. "You're always telling me to empathize, to feel the other person's pain so I can understand him or her."

"I just don't want you getting into anything too deeply, Hannah. Sometimes, we get ourselves into trouble even though we have every good intention, and we find ourselves trapped by our own decency and charity. It's all right to feel sorry for someone, but it's not all right to let that burden your own life. It's like someone who can't swim well trying to save someone who can't swim at all . . . the result is usually both drowning. What good is that?"

"I can swim."

"Your mother means emotionally. It takes wisdom, years, maturing to involve yourself deeply in other people's problems, Hannah."

Everything they were saying sounded so right, of course, but at the same time, it did feel like they were wrapping tight, nylon cords around me, binding me so tightly, I couldn't breathe. It made me furious inside. My nerve endings felt like Heyden's guitar strings, twanged.

"Both Miguel and I want you to enjoy yourself, have fun, have a social life," Mommy said. "Don't misinterpret our concern for you. Okay?"

I nodded.

Then I blurted, "We're going to the movies tomorrow night. After we look at a possible new guitar he might buy and then have something to eat," I added.

"Tomorrow, but I'm coming home tomorrow. I thought we'd have a relaxing dinner and talk about little Claude and things we could all do together," Mommy said.

"How can you come home tomorrow? Aren't you breast-feeding him anymore?"

She smiled.

"Yes, of course, but I'll pump milk for him that will be kept refrigerated and come back twice a day until he is released."

"Pump? Ugh," I said.

Miguel laughed.

"It's not as unpleasant as it might sound," Mommy said. "In time I'll begin to alternate formula and slowly wean him off. There is a great deal of evidence that babies are healthier when they are breast-fed," she insisted.

"I already promised to meet him and go to the movies," I said in a snappy voice. I didn't want to hear how wonderfully she was going to treat little Claude compared to how I was treated when I was born in the midst of a shattered marriage.

"Well, of course, if you have already made plans."

"Where will you go to eat dinner?" Miguel asked.

"I don't know yet."

"Why don't you take him to Havana Malena. I'll call my brother and have them set you up, if you like," he offered. "My treat," he added.

I gazed at him with some suspicion. It was nice of him to make the offer, but in the back of my mind, I thought he was doing it just so he and Mommy could find out more about Heyden. On the other hand, the food was wonderful at Miguel's family's restaurant, and Heyden might not be as embarrassed as he would be if I paid for our dinner or even shared the cost. This way we were both being treated.

"Can I have the car again? He doesn't have a car," I said, "Only a moped."

"I don't like you driving into that neighborhood," Mommy said.

"It's not *that* bad, is it, Miguel?"

He looked caught in the middle. "Well, as long as you remain in well lit areas and just drive in and drive out, I suppose it's fine," he relented. "I would rather she was in a car and not on his moped anyway, Willow," he added.

She didn't look happy about it, but she reluctantly agreed.

"I'll ask Heyden about going to your family's restaurant and call you from school tomorrow, if that's all right," I said.

"Sure."

Mommy sighed. "I guess I just have to let you grow up," she said.

"Your father and stepmother let you," I replied.

She raised her eyes. "Oh, my stepmother would have let me out of the house to play in traffic when I was only five, if she could."

Miguel laughed and then she did, too.

"Time turns turmoil into comedy," she said, and he nodded. Then she looked at me. "You can go look at little Claude, if you like."

"I'm sure he's sleeping contentedly," Miguel said. The way he smiled at Mommy told me he was implying he would be sleeping contentedly if he had been little Claude and had just breast-fed. Mommy actually blushed and glanced at me to see if I had been perceptive enough to catch the small but clearly sexual suggestion.

Except for the time Selma Warden told us about her walking in on her parents making love when she was only seven, none of us ever referred to our own parents when we talked about love and romance and sex. Miguel and Mommy could be very affectionate toward each other, but I couldn't recall them ever kissing each other passionately in my presence. It seemed to be true for all my friends—parents kept their sexual relationships well locked behind closed doors. It was somehow different to hold hands as a husband and a wife, different from holding them as lovers.

Even Mommy's getting pregnant seemed to be something that happened immaculately. All of our mothers were Mother Marys, and to some of us, our fathers were like gods, worshiped and idealized. In my house and in my life that wasn't true, of course. My father was this Hollywood-handsome, sophisticated

lawyer whose kisses were birdlike pecks on my cheeks
and whose love for me often felt more like something
grown out of the soil of vengeance and spite. Nothing
underscored that more than his refusal to permit Miguel
to adopt me and change my name. However, it didn't
appear to come from an overriding love for me as much
as it did from an overriding indignation that someone,
anyone, would dare even think to cast off the Eaton
name.

Miguel was certainly a good-looking man, and no
man was or could be sweeter to me than he was, but it
was still easier for me to imagine Mommy in a loving,
passionate embrace with Daddy than it was to imagine
her with Miguel. I suppose I was never convinced of
Mommy's distaste and dislike of Daddy because of
that. Despite her self-deprecating talk, her continuous
expressions of amazement at herself for ever being
taken in by someone like Daddy, I had an easier time
believing she would fall in love with him than I did
believing she would find it one of the most stupid and
foolish things she could have ever done.

Of course, I believed that was because I was still too
young and still not smart enough to see. I had to accept
on faith that she was right—one should never fall in
love with a man like my father. A girl had to be careful,
smarter, more aware, and know when her own body
was lusting and blinding her.

But how do you ever trust your heart? I wondered.
When do you know it's right? When do you know that
it's not just lust? If someone as brilliant as my mother
could have been fooled, what hope did I have?

Maybe that was why she and Miguel were so con-

cerned about my seeing someone. Suddenly, and maybe
for the first time ever, I realized how hard it was to be a
parent. It was like holding on to the string of a kite that
was caught up in the wind. If you pulled too hard and
too fast, it would snap and be gone forever, and if you
let out more string and gave it more room, the wind
might still have its way with it so that when it returned
to earth, it was not what it had been.

I started out to see Claude, and Mommy seized my
arm. She smiled.

"Don't blame me for wanting you to be my little girl
forever, Hannah. I know it's wrong and it can't be, but
don't hate me for it."

"I can't hate you, Mommy," I said.

She let go of my hand.

I felt like the kite in the wind and continued on.

It was like pulling a curtain of fury away from my
eyes, a sheer curtain of red. The more I gazed through
the window at little Claude, the more the curtain moved
to the sideline. Today he looked more like a little person, his mouth and chin showing resemblances to
Miguel. His tiny body twitched. Do infants dream yet?
I wondered. How could they? Maybe he was hearing
the cries of the other infants and he hated it. Now I
wanted him to come home and come home immediately. He needed protection. He should have his own
place. I could see myself hurrying home to be with him,
to give him his bottle when he was finally on formula,
to change his diaper, and to hold him and keep him
from crying and being afraid. He made me recall my
best childhood dolls. Here he was, a living, breathing

toy. Wouldn't it be fun to see him recognize me, to see him looking forward to me?

"Amazing how much he has grown in twenty-four hours, isn't it?" Miguel said, coming up beside me after I had been there a while.

"Yes."

"I think he's going to look more like your mother, despite my inky hair."

"I don't."

"Check these out," he said, drawing some pictures from the inside pocket of his jacket.

They were pictures taken in Mommy's room, pictures of her holding little Claude, of Miguel holding him, and then the two of them standing side by side with little Claude in Mommy's arms.

"Do we look like doting parents already?"

"Yes," I said, and he laughed.

"I'll get a picture of you holding him before we take him home, too," he promised. "Ready to go home?"

"Yes."

"I told your mother I'd follow you. You know her—Nervous Nellie. Despite her brilliance, she still harbors this silly superstition about family curses and such. It's probably why she comes off sounding a little too protective," he added.

"Why is that, Miguel? What family curse?"

In our home it was always a forbidden topic, but somehow, I felt the lid had been opened on our personal Pandora's box, and like it or not, the past with all its dark days and troubled moments was let loose.

"Well, you know how difficult it was for her to be brought up in a home with a stepmother who despised her and a father who felt he had to restrain his love.

"And then, after they were gone and she learned the truth about her birth, she confronted your grandmother Grace and met your uncle Linden for the first time. He was already quite an emotionally wounded young man. To add insult to injury, he tried to commit suicide, and your mother blamed herself."

"I knew all that, but I never understood why Mommy blamed herself."

"She kept their relationship secret when she first arrived. She was afraid of the truth. To her it was like a big, blinding light in everyone's eyes. It had to be done slowly, carefully, and Linden wasn't strong enough emotionally for all that.

"Then there was the trouble with your father and the Eatons and everything just piled up on her fragile shoulders. When your uncle Linden got hurt, your grandmother Grace was convinced there was some sort of perennial dark cloud over their heads and nothing could sweep it completely away."

"Do you think it could be true?"

"Of course not," he replied quickly. "And your mother doesn't really believe it in her heart, either, but it's like anything else that haunts a family's past. It takes time to see just how untrue and foolish it is.

"You are your own person. You will make the choices that determine your fate, and not some skeleton in some closet," Miguel assured me.

I glanced at little Claude.

I hoped Miguel was right, of course, now for little Claude as well as me.

After we returned home, I went to my room and

found a message on my answering machine. It was from Heyden.

"Just want you to know I haven't murdered my sister. I have her shut up in a trunk and I'm burying it in the backyard, but other than that, things are fine. Thanks for being here with me. I know I wouldn't be as calm and collected if you hadn't been. I'm looking forward to our official date," he concluded. I could almost hear the laughter behind his voice as he pronounced the word *official*.

There was a second message. It was from Daddy. I had completely forgotten what he had said when I called him with my cell phone after I had visited Uncle Linden. Our conversation had been so short and he had been so flippant, I hadn't paid much attention to it.

"Hannah, I will be home for Friday night dinner. I'll pick you up at six-thirty."

Oh, no, I thought. It was not that often that Daddy invited me to dinner at his home. Most of the time, he picked me up with Adrian and Cade in the car and we all went to a restaurant, sometimes with Danielle coming along as well, but not always.

Daddy's home wasn't as big as Aunt Whitney and Uncle Hans's estate, an estate I had seen only in pictures and had passed by and gazed at from our car, but Daddy's home was one of the prime North Lake Way estate properties.

Adrian and Cade never stopped reminding me that they lived in a more desirable location and an even bigger house than I did. It had a very wide and long entry hall with Italian marble flooring, a dining room about one and a half times larger than ours, also with marble floors. Daddy's house had a more elaborate library, too, with black granite floors and a floor-to-ceiling bay window that provided a magnificent view of his wonderful gardens and tennis court. The pool had been recently redone with an expansive travertine terrace, and he had renovated his cabana, creating a living room with a travertine flooring and sliding doors that opened to the pool. There was a new steam sauna installed as well. The cabana had a guest bedroom. Adrian and Cade had practically taken to living there, considering it their private club. I knew they had friends over frequently, and from what they told me, their parties weren't the sort Mommy would like to see me attending.

Daddy was always into boating and now had his own yacht at his own dock. Adrian and Cade had been given Jet Skis for their birthdays last year. They bragged to me how popular they had become at their school, claiming an invitation to their house on the weekend was a "prize."

I felt terribly pulled in two directions. Should I call Heyden and tell him I had to go to my father's for dinner and try to get him to consider the following night? On top of what I had seen happen at his house, he might not believe me. I hadn't known him very long, but I hated the idea of disappointing him or giving him the impression that I was trying to find an excuse to get out of the date. Actually, I would rather be with Heyden, I thought.

On the other hand, it was so rare that Daddy wanted me at his home. I knew that it was usually when he was sure his parents weren't going to be there, or his sister. I didn't see him all that much these days.

I really didn't know what I was going to do when I called. To my surprise his butler didn't answer. Adrian did. It was difficult to decide who enjoyed tormenting me more, Adrian or Cade.

"The Eaton residence," he said, parodying their butler, whom I knew they tormented as well. Adrian was somewhat more nasal than Cade, so I could tell who it was immediately.

"Adrian, it's Hannah," I said.

"Hannah? Hannah who, please?" he replied. He loved to tease me about my last name.

"You know who I am, Adrian. Stop it."

"Is this a prank call? Are you going to whisper obscenities into the phone? If you are, please begin. I have my tape recorder ready."

"Adrian, I have to speak to Daddy."

"Daddy? There is no one here by that name. We have a caddy, but he is at the golf course."

"Stop it!" I shouted.

"Stop what?"

"All right, Adrian. You've had your fun. Please let me speak to my father."

"Your father? Isn't he that Cuban person?"

I didn't answer.

"Hello? Is there anyone there?"

"I'm waiting," I said.

"One moment, please," he said. He put me on hold and I know deliberately took his time. It was nearly two full minutes before Daddy picked up. I was ready to give up and call again.

"Hannah?"

"Oh, Daddy, Adrian is so mean."

"What did he do now?"

"He teased me and teased me and then left me holding the phone for so long."

"I'll speak to him," he said. "What's happening?"

In the second or two it took for me to reply, I envisioned Heyden's dark eyes seizing on mine, and I saw the look of interest and wonder in his face.

"I can't come to dinner tomorrow night."

"Oh? Why not?"

"Well, you didn't sound absolutely definite about it, and I forgot and agreed to go on a date with a boy at my school. We're going to dinner and a movie."

"Really? Well, I don't blame you for choosing that over dinner with your old man," he said. "We'll get together next week some time, maybe."

"Really?"

"Sure. No problem," he said.

I was waiting for him to ask me about Heyden, but he didn't ask a thing.

How different he was from Mommy when it came to me and my life, I thought. Did I like this better? I hated the way Mommy had begun to ask her questions, and yet I resented Daddy not taking an iota of interest or concern. For all he knew, I was going out with a serial killer.

"I'm sorry about it," I repeated.

"Nothing to be sorry about, Hannah. I'll call you. Have a good time," he added.

"Thank you," I said.

He hung up and the line went dead. I held the receiver as if it hadn't and imagined another conversation.

"Who's the boy? What's he like? Does your mother

approve? Don't stay out too late. Be careful, Hannah. Don't give your heart away easily or cheaply. Let me tell you about men. I know. I'm an expert when it comes to being a cad. Matter of fact, I'd like to see you tomorrow before you go out. We should talk. I'll take you for coffee and we'll sit on the patio. I'm sorry I haven't done this before. You've grown up so fast and right before my eyes. How beautiful you have become. I have a responsibility to fulfill. After all, I am your father."

Where were these words? Were they lying dormant in his mind? Had he ever thought of saying them to me?

I hung up my phone and for a while just stood by my window, staring out at the sea and wondering if my grandmother Grace's fears weren't well founded.

Maybe there *was* a curse, a dark cloud just waiting to rain its misery down upon me, too.

Maybe it already had and I just didn't know it yet.

4

A Kiss of Love
and Hope

I was disappointed Heyden didn't seek me out first thing in the morning at school the next day. We didn't share a class until third period, but I had hoped—even expected—that he would be there to greet me. I looked for him in the usual places, but I didn't see him anywhere, and I was so distracted because of it, I didn't hear my English teacher, Mr. Mullens, call my name to answer a question about the play we were reading. I wasn't even aware that the whole class had turned to look at me.

"Well," Mr. Mullens said, moving down the row to my desk, "I've hypnotized another student, it seems."

The class laughter brought me back to earth.

"Are you all right, Miss Eaton?"

"What? Yes," I said. "Why?"

"Oh, nothing. I was just wondering since I asked

you a question twenty minutes ago and you continued to stare out the window as if neither I nor the rest of these students existed. In love, are you?" he continued.

"No!" I said sharply, tears piling under my lids. I blinked them back.

"Pity. I was hoping that was it rather than me or the material," he added, scowled at me, and turned away.

Massy Hewlett was practically bursting apart with glee.

"Now that you are back with the living, can you tell us why you think Iago is doing what he is doing to Othello?" Mr. Mullens asked me.

I threw my own eyeballs of fire at Massy and then reread my homework.

"I know there are a few possible reasons," I began. "He says Othello might have slept with his wife, but I don't think he really believes that. It's just an excuse."

"An excuse? For what?"

"For liking what he's doing. I think Shakespeare is telling us some people are just driven by pure evil and enjoy hurting other people. They don't need a whole lot of reason. They take pleasure in someone else's pain," I continued and then glanced at Massy again.

"Interesting," Mr. Mullens said. "Maybe you should continue daydreaming," he added.

There was some more tittering, but somehow I had deflected the brunt of his reprimand and escaped any more embarrassment. Afterward, I apologized to him.

"It's all right. I know you've had a great deal of new excitement in your life. Just hang in there," he advised and smiled at me. I was running an A in his class and I did enjoy it.

When period three began, I took my seat and watched the classroom door with anticipation. I thought Heyden might have just come late to school this morning. The students filed in, a few rushing to beat the bell, but Heyden did not enter, and his seat remained empty when the class began. Trying not to appear too interested, I asked Michael Scranton, the only boy I had seen speak with Heyden much, if he had seen him today. I tried to be as casual as I could.

"He didn't come to school," he said. "Probably just didn't feel like it," he added with a smirk. "Why? He owe you money or something?"

"No," I said.

"You're lucky," he replied and turned away as the teacher began.

Where was Heyden? Why didn't he come to school? He hadn't mentioned any other problem when we had spoken the night before. It troubled me all day. My girl-friends, urged on by Massy Hewlett, I'm sure, caught up with me at lunch and started to ask questions about him.

"I don't know any more about Heyden Reynolds than any of you do," I told Tina Olsen. "Why are you all asking me these questions?"

"You looked very cozy with him yesterday at lunch," Brigitte said.

"So?"

"So we were just wondering, that's all. Why are you so defensive?" she asked.

"I'm not. I just . . . just don't know anything that would interest you."

"Bet you'd like to know more about him," Massy said, looking for a way to satisfy her thirst for revenge.

I shrugged. "Maybe. Now that you're making me think about him, maybe I would," I said.

"You're kidding," Natalie Alexander said. "You know where he lives and what he is."

"Where he lives isn't important, and last I looked, he was a human being."

"Yeah, right," she said. "Miss Liberal America," she added, and they all laughed.

I wondered if they could see the smoke flowing out of my ears. I was that hot and angry, but I smiled back at them.

"Be careful, girls. Your snob-quotient is rising. You'll all start looking like you have flies in your noses," I said. It was an expression our old housekeeper Betty Davis used to use.

"If you hang out with Heyden, you'll be the one swatting flies," Massy quipped.

They all laughed. I decided not to talk about Heyden anymore, and they quickly went on to other topics. After school, still concerned about him, I made an impulsive decision to drive to his house instead of returning to Joya del Mar. I knew Mommy would be home from the hospital by now, but I thought another half hour or so wouldn't matter that much. When I pulled up in front of his home, I hesitated, wondering if I should have tried to call him first. I sat there, my heart thumping. Was I being too forward?

Finally I told myself I had come this far. It would be stupid to just drive off and go home without speaking to him and seeing if he was all right. I stepped out and walked to the front door. There was a buzzer button, but after I pressed it, I heard nothing and thought it might not work. I knocked and waited. A few moments later the door was pulled open so abruptly, the suction nearly pulled me inside. Elisha stood there glaring out at me.

"What do *you* want?" she demanded. She had her hair down and wore a thin, V-neck brown blouse and a short brown skirt. I also noticed she had a small nose ring, something I had not seen. She was barefoot and looked like she had been crying.

"I would like to see Heyden," I said.

"He locked himself in his room," she replied. "He hasn't even come out to eat. Maybe he's dead in there," she added.

"Why did he do that?"

"I don't know. He does lots of stupid things," she said.

"Where's your mother?"

"At work. Where's yours?" she fired back at me.

"Didn't you go to school today, either?" I asked her, ignoring her sarcasm.

"What do you care?"

"I work for the truancy department," I said, marching in and past her.

"Huh?"

"If you're not in school on Monday, we'll send a padded wagon for you," I told her.

She pulled in the corners of her lips.

"Very funny. You're as crazy as he is," she said, nodding toward Heyden's room. "You belong together."

She walked away and I went to Heyden's closed door and knocked gently.

"Heyden? It's Hannah. I missed you at school and came by to see how you were," I added.

I heard nothing and the door remained closed. Suddenly his sister's angry and silly quip concerned me. Why had he locked himself up all day? Mommy once told me that suicidal people don't always appear suicidal, especially teenagers whose self-inflicted deaths surprise their own parents. Depression was a deeply seated and insidious disease that wormed its way into every remaining bright place, putting out the lights and leaving gloom and doom behind as it made its way toward your very heart. Could this be true for Heyden?

I knocked harder.

"Heyden? Are you in there? Please answer me. Tell me to go away or something, but answer me," I pleaded.

Elisha stepped up behind me. She had a lit cigarette in her hand, and she was smiling.

"Maybe you should have the padded wagon come for him instead of for me," she said. Then she went to her own room, closed the door, and started to play her rap music loudly.

"Heyden?" I knocked again. I was about to give up and go home when I heard the door being unlocked.

He stood there shirtless and barefoot in a pair of jeans.

"Are you sick?" I asked after a few moments of having him simply stand there and stare out at me.

"Yes, sick of life," he muttered and turned away. He returned to his bed and flopped back to stare up at the ceiling. He put his hands behind his head. I remained in the doorway a moment and then entered, closing the door behind me softly.

"Did your sister do something else terrible?" I asked.

He continued staring at the ceiling and not replying.

"I was worried about you when you didn't come to school, Heyden. You didn't say anything about any other problems when you and I spoke last night."

"I didn't know then what I would soon find out after we spoke," he said and sat up.

"What?" I asked. He remained quiet. "I'm not just trying to be nosy, Heyden. I am sincerely concerned."

He took a deep breath and turned to me.

"When my mother returned home from work, I told her what Elisha had done and what I had found. I knew nothing would come of that so I insisted she call my father to tell him. I wanted her to impress him with how out of control Elisha has become and how he should devote some time to her when he comes home. My mother kept ignoring me and when I started to shout at her, she finally turned to me and told me my father wasn't coming home this time, maybe never."

"Never?" I held my breath. "Why?"

"Apparently, he has gone off with someone from his quintet and told my mother he didn't want to remain in their marriage."

"Oh. I'm sorry."

"That's a funny way to put it, isn't it?" he asked. "Remain in their marriage? It makes it sound like a room, a place, rather than a relationship.

"Anyway, according to what I managed to pull out of

her, my mother revealed that this had happened a little more than two weeks ago. Can you imagine keeping that a secret or, as in her case, ignoring it for more than two weeks? Maybe she thought that the next time he called, if he bothered calling again, he would not mention ending their marriage, or maybe she thought he would just show up and none of that conversation would matter. Who knows how she thinks!" he screamed and pounded his own legs.

The sight of someone inflicting such obvious pain on himself made me wince.

He laughed rather than show it had hurt.

"Imagine how stupid I must have looked insisting she talk to my father about my sister. Heyden who? Elisha who? he would probably say."

"I'm sorry, Heyden."

"Yeah, me, too. Actually," he continued, "I'm not sorry anymore. I'm out of sorry. I'm on to what's the difference?"

He sighed deeply and shook his head.

"She started to cry, of course, and moan about our troubles. I felt so bad I gave her the money I was going to use to buy the guitar today. With my father deserting us like this, we're not even going to be able to afford this rathole if I don't get more work. She doesn't make enough. My father's checks were important. I guess I'll have to drop out of school," he added.

"Oh, Heyden, no."

"Not no, yes. So anyway, you can see why I didn't bother to go to school today. Why pretend the inevitable isn't going to happen? Why be like my mother?"

"Maybe you can get some sort of student aid," I said.

He raised his eyebrows. "Yeah. What I can do is get a cheaper guitar and play on the corner for small change. I'll put a sign on the can that reads *Student Aid.*"

"I know I have no right to encourage you, Heyden, but you can't give up."

"Who's giving up? Who even had a start?" He studied me a moment and nodded. "I knew when I first entered the magnet school that I shouldn't, I shouldn't go where so many well-to-do students were going. I never expected to feel comfortable there. I let some do-gooder guidance counselor give me advice, pump me up with myself.

"But there I was among all of you in your expensive clothes, many driving your own cars, most taking private music lessons. I might as well have tried to go to school on the moon."

"That's not true, Heyden. There's no one there better than you."

"Not better, no; but better *off,*" he said. "Hey, thanks for coming to find out why I didn't show up. I appreciate it, but now you can see why you're better off turning around and forgetting you ever met me, okay?" he said and lay back again.

"No," I said approaching him. "It's not okay."

I sat beside him on his bed. He kept his face turned away from me, but I leaned over and kissed him on the lips.

"What are you doing?" he asked.

"You promised to take me on an official date and show me a good time. I'm collecting on that promise."

"Didn't you hear anything I just said?"

"Sorta. It went in one ear and out the other," I told him, beaming my smile down at him like a ray of sunshine.

"I'm not going to go look at that guitar, Hannah. It would be like torturing myself."

"No, it won't. If it's good, we'll get it. I'll loan you the money."

"I wouldn't take money from you," he snapped indignantly.

"You won't be. I'm not giving you the money. I said I would lend it to you. Say at 7 percent interest annually. You'll pay me back from your first royalties."

He shook his head. "This isn't some cheap toy we're talking about, Hannah. It's three hundred dollars."

"It wouldn't be worth it to lend you much less," I said. "How am I going to make any money otherwise?"

"You have that kind of money on you?"

I dug into my pocketbook and produced my charge card.

"My father gave it to me last year for my birthday. I have a five thousand-dollar limit. I haven't used it very much, I'll admit, but I have it to use when I need to or want to buy something special.

"My mother calls it his conscience money. Actually, because of her, I haven't used it very much, although recently she told me I should do it just for spite."

"I don't know," Heyden said, but there was the breakdown of some resistence in his tone of voice.

"I have another selfish reason, too," I said.

He raised his eyebrows. "You mean, besides making all that money on the loan?" he asked skeptically.

"Yes."

"What?"

"I thought if you play guitar so well and write a decent song or two, maybe I could sing it. Maybe you could play other songs as well, songs we could both sing."

"And be an act?"

"Maybe."

He sat up again, his sad, heavy eyes suddenly brightening.

"You would do that?"

"I was more afraid you wouldn't want to," I said.

"Oh, yeah, right. I wouldn't want the prettiest girl in the school with the best singing voice to do a duet with me, especially singing some of my own songs."

"I'm not the prettiest girl in the school, Heyden, and I'm not saying I have the best voice."

"I said it," he insisted.

"Well . . . I'm not going to argue with you anymore," I said, and he laughed.

"I'm adding on 'best personality,' too," he said.

I held my smile and he held his. It was magical. Some guardian angel had waved a wand over us, and the dark clouds, the heavy and morbid sounds in our ears, were gone.

"Hannah, you are terrific," he whispered and leaned forward to kiss me. It was a long kiss that grew more demanding every passing second. I could feel him trying to draw hope from me like some strange new vampire who fed not on blood, but on hope and love.

He pulled back and brought his fingers to my chin to gently lift my face, forcing me to look into his eyes so he could search mine for truth and sincerity.

"Are you sure about this, Hannah?" he asked.

"Yes," I whispered.

There would be times when I would question whether or not I had come to him out of just as much desperation as he had when he had come to me. In a sense I still felt deserted, too, felt alone, drifting. My mother and Miguel had a whole new world to live in and develop, and I didn't feel as much a part of it as they would expect. Most of my life I had been caught in that vacuum that existed between my mother and my father. Now, with the little attention he had given me my whole life diminishing, and with Mommy having a new top priority in her thinking and taking up her time, I could sense the vacuum growing bigger, wider, deeper.

"Yes," I whispered again. It brought our lips back together. His moved off mine and to my neck. He took me back with him on his pillow, and he stroked my hair and gazed into my eyes.

"I think you could make me forget the end of the world," he said.

He kissed me again and then his hands slipped under my blouse and to my breasts. When I moaned, he lifted himself over me and flooded my face with more kisses. He unbuttoned my blouse and kissed me just above my bra. Then he reached behind and unfastened it. When he pushed it up and over my nipples and brought his lips to one and then the other, I began to question myself.

What are you doing, Hannah Eaton? Aren't you throwing yourself at someone too quickly?

I didn't even care to answer my conscience. I felt so good, so warm, so detached from all the unhappiness and pain in the world.

His kisses grew more demanding, his fingers playing me, drawing the music out of me. I soon saw myself rolling down a hill of passion, speeding so fast, there was no possibility of putting on the brakes. He had his hands under my skirt. When his fingers went over the elastic band in my panties, I thought I had stopped breathing. Even my heart waited like some hammer held back.

He paused, too, and his hesitation was so long, I opened my eyes and looked up at him.

I felt him retreat.

He looked down at me with suspicion clouding his eyes.

"What?" I managed.

"How many boys have you been with, Hannah?"

"None," I said. "Not like this."

His lips twisted with doubt.

"I'm telling the truth."

"Then why are you letting this happen so fast?" he asked.

I pushed him away and sat up.

"Now you're making me feel guilty," I said and reached back to fasten my bra. I started to button my blouse.

"I don't mean to do that."

"Well, you are," I threw back at him and stood.

"I've been with other girls," he said, "and the ones who were fast the first time were always the ones who didn't matter to me after a short while or the ones I never mattered to very much at all. I just don't want that to be how it will be between us."

Now it was my turn to look skeptical.

"I mean it. Maybe I'm fantasizing, but I was hoping you and I were on the way to being very special," he said. He looked so conflicted, I couldn't help but believe him.

"You're not fantasizing."

"I'm just tired of disappointments and betrayals," he said with a sigh.

I stopped buttoning my blouse.

"I'm not going to betray you, Heyden, and when I do or say something, I mean it. I know you have trouble accepting what I tell you, but please try to stop thinking of me the way you think about the other girls at our school. I have a lot more than bubbles and straw in my head."

He laughed. "I know you do," he said. "And you're right. I'm being guilty of the very thing I accuse people of doing to me: stereotyping. Sorry," he said, holding up his hands.

"It's all right. Actually, I'm glad you hesitated and put on the brakes. We could have gotten into trouble, or at least, I could have. I'm dangerously close to that zone of ovulation. Imagine me making my mother a grandmother just when she has become a new mother," I said.

He nodded. "My fault, too. I'm usually not this carefree, forgetting to take precautions. Everything has just got me nuts. I feel like I'm sinking into some cesspool of oblivion."

"Well, let's get you up and out of that immediately,"

I said, standing. "Take me to your new guitar," I ordered.

He laughed and reached for a shirt he had draped over the back of a chair. Then he hurried to get on his sneakers.

"If you're really sure you want to do this," he said. "If you're really sure . . ."

"I'm sure, Heyden. Stop talking about it already and let's just do it."

"Right," he said. "Right."

We started out of his room. He stopped in the hallway. Elisha's music was still loud. He looked at her closed door and then shook his head.

"C'mon," he urged. "Let's get out of here. This is the only chance I'll ever have to get out of here."

I followed slowly, wondering what would become of Elisha. At least Heyden had his song writing and his guitar. He was using music to lift himself up and out of the din. She was using it like a blanket to cover her misery.

Maybe Mommy would give me some suggestions as to how to help her, I thought.

But then again, maybe she wouldn't. Maybe she would be angry at me for trying to involve her and myself in Heyden's family problems. She had warned me about it already.

There wasn't time to really think about it, but I was glad of that. I wanted to keep rushing, to keep charging forward with Heyden. Together, we would make the music that could drown out both our voices of sadness and disappointment.

Couldn't it?

*   *   *

Heyden cradled the guitar in his hands with as much pleasure in his face as Mommy had holding little Claude, I thought. It was so rare that anything I was given gave me such pleasure. I was actually jealous of the instrument and not jealous of Heyden. It put him into such a pure ecstatic state, he practically glowed. Would he love anyone with as much passion as he loved his music? I wondered. Maybe he was more like his father than he cared to admit.

In one of her more revealing moments with me, Mommy told me she loved Miguel because it was so clear to her that there was nothing more important to him than her. She made it sound almost as if she was therefore obligated to love him, and I wondered if anyone could truly love someone out of obligation. It seemed to me it had to come from a different place, sprout from a garden different from the garden of responsibility and expectation. It had to have more of a spontaneity. It was richer and far more exciting when it surprised you, when you looked again at someone and realized a force greater than anything you had experienced before was drawing you to him.

Was that too romantic, too fantastic to come from the mind of Dr. Willow Fuentes's daughter?

Watching the careful and loving way Heyden handled his guitar made me think of the careless way Adrian and Cade treated all their possessions. There was always a nonchalance and often an indifference. Neither of them was ever surprised at receiving anything, truly believing that for some reason, it was all coming to him. They deserved it all simply because they existed.

Heyden smiled his pleasure at me and then tuned the strings while the store clerk watched us with a half-annoyed, half-suspicious expression on his face. He couldn't decide if we were just toying with him and the guitar or if we had the wherewithal to actually purchase the instrument.

Heyden tried a cord and nodded. "It's in cherry condition," he said. "It's a find."

"Well, then, let's get it," I said.

The clerk's eyebrows were nearly hoisted off his head. "Is this the best price?" Heyden asked him.

His smirk returned. "Absolutely," he said. "As you just said, it's cherry," he tagged on with a gleeful smile.

"Right." Heyden turned to me and I produced my credit card.

The clerk looked at it carefully.

"Do you have a driver's license or any other form of identification?"

"Yes," I said and showed him my license. Still skeptical, he processed the card, looking as if he expected it would be kicked back. When it wasn't, he became more pleasant.

After we had left the store with the guitar in our possession, Heyden couldn't contain himself. All the way back to his house, he played.

"This is the song I wanted you to hear," he said and began. It was a beautiful song about someone who was afraid of falling in love and yet very much wanted to fall in love. He warned his lover that when he was touched, he would be too weak to keep from falling in love.

This is for forever, he sang, *so don't touch me with your eyes, your lips, or your fingers unless you mean for us to be true.*

Before he finished, I joined in with him on the final chorus. I pulled up in front of his house and he played the song again, this time with me singing as much as I could remember. After a third time I knew most of the song and we were both laughing.

"Just come in a little faster and don't be afraid to reach for that high note. I'll be there like a net to catch you if you fall," he said.

We were at it again. While we were singing and he was playing, I saw the front door of his house open and his sister come out. She stood there watching us and listening to us and then she walked toward the car. Heyden stopped and looked out at her.

"You comin' in for dinner?" she asked.

"Why? You making it?" Heyden retorted.

"No. Mama's home."

"She's home?"

"Yes, she's home and she's just workin' in the kitchen and cryin' at the same time," Elisha said.

Heyden looked at me.

"Go on," I said. "I'd better get home anyway."

"Where'd you get that guitar? You take it from your precious school?" Elisha asked.

"Where I got it is none of your business, Elisha, but you touch it, even look at it too long, and I'll—"

"Kill me? Get in the back of the line," she muttered and then glared at me, but with more of a plea for help, a look of desperation than empty anger.

She turned and walked back into the house.

"Don't be too hard on her, Heyden. I'm sure she's very frightened."

"As frightened as a shark," he said. "Don't worry, Dr. Hannah. I'll be a good big brother."

I laughed.

"Call me later if you can," I told him.

"Okay," he said, leaned over to kiss me on the lips, and then smiled and stepped out of the car. "Drive carefully . . . partner," he said.

I smiled back at him and started away. In my rearview mirror I saw him holding on to his guitar tightly, embracing it lovingly and protectively before walking into his home the way someone would embrace and protect a little loved one in a hurricane.

Back at my home, Miguel came bouncing down the stairs the moment I opened the front door and stepped inside. He paused near the bottom step.

"Where have you been, young lady?" he demanded. It wasn't often that Miguel was angry at me, but I knew whenever he referred to me as young lady, he was about to reprimand me for something.

"I had to help my friend Heyden get his new guitar," I told him.

"Do you realize your mother has been home for hours and has been lying there thinking all sorts of terrible things? Don't you ever turn that cell phone on, Hannah? Why did I buy it for you if you're going to let the battery die down or forget to turn it on? How can you be so self-centered at a time like this? Don't you realize how traumatic it is for a woman to give birth and then have to leave her newborn infant back in the hospital? I had a lot more respect for your intelligence until today, Hannah."

"I told you!" I cried back at him, the tears streaking down my cheeks, "I had to help Heyden. It was very important. He needed me."

"Your mother needed you, too, and I would think she would have some priority over someone you just met, Hannah."

"She doesn't need me. She has you; she has little Claude," I shot back.

"What kind of a dumb thing to say is that?"

"Maybe I'm just stupid!" I screamed and shot past him, pounding my way up the stairs and to my room. I slammed the door shut behind me and threw myself on the bed.

Moments later Mommy, dressed in her robe, came to my door, knocked softly, and entered.

"What's going on, Hannah?" she asked.

I turned and looked up at her. She looked drawn, tired, even a bit pale. I had a terrific surge of guilt rush through me and just started to cry, bawl like a girl half my age.

"Oh, Hannah, what's wrong?" she asked coming to me.

"I'm sorry, Mommy. I just lost track of the time."

"That's all right," she said, sitting on my bed, "but tell me what you're doing? Why did you lose track of time?"

"Heyden didn't come to school today," I began.

"Heyden? Oh, yes, your new friend. And?"

"So I went to see what was wrong and learned his father has deserted his mother, sister, and him. He ran off with someone from his band, and it had happened weeks ago, but Heyden's mother never said anything until last night."

Mommy nodded. She didn't look impressed with my story, and I imagined that over the years she had heard many similar tales of woe.

"What does his mother do?"

"She's a chambermaid at the Breakers."

"I see," she said. "How old is Heyden's sister?"

"Fourteen, I think."

"And Heyden?"

"Seventeen, I think."

"Well, his mother should have his father pursued for child support at minimum," she said.

"She can do that?"

"Of course she can."

"Will you tell me how so I can tell Heyden and he can tell his mother? They don't have much money," I added quickly, "and Heyden thinks he has to drop out of school to get more work."

Mommy sighed. "It's like an epidemic," she muttered to herself. "I'll tell you, Hannah, but you're getting yourself in too deeply with someone else's problems. These are not simple problems. They don't get solved over a weekend and then everyone forgets them. I'm sure Heyden's mother has her hands full with his sister, too. Was she close to her father? Is she heartbroken about the breakup?"

"I think she is, but she likes to appear tough and unaffected."

"Classic," Mommy said. "Oh, sweetheart, you're too young to get yourself so involved in these sorts of matters. Can't you take a few steps back?"

"*You* wouldn't," I said with accusatory eyes.

"Yes, I would," she replied firmly. "Especially after

knowing what I know now, living what I lived through. What good is all that if I don't pass on my experience to you and you don't take heed, Hannah?

"You're too young yet, too vulnerable yourself," she insisted.

"I am not. Stop telling me I'm too young for everything. I'm nearly seventeen years old."

"I just don't want you to be hurt, Hannah. Please. I'll give you information to pass on to your friend, but promise me you won't get too involved."

I was silent.

"I'm going to need you now, especially with little Claude coming home soon. He's very fragile. We're going to have to pass through a difficult time. I'm going to depend on your support," she said.

I looked at her. For almost all of my life, my mother was a rod of steel in my home. She had learned from her troubled past, and she had become an impressive guide, leading other people through the dark corridors of their own fears and troubles successfully. That took strength and self-confidence. I depended on that, on her far more than I depended on anyone else. Maybe this was the reason I was so ambivalent about my new brother. I was afraid she would give him everything and there would be little or nothing left for me.

For the first time I heard a note of fear in her voice, saw a wobble in that rod of steel. Would she really need me as much as she was claiming?

"I made promises and I like Heyden. I can't just turn my back on him, Mommy."

"You don't have to do that, Hannah, but you do have

to be careful and use good judgment. Most important, you have to realize you are limited and can do only so much. People get themselves in trouble when they take on more than they can handle. Don't make the mistake of thinking you can rescue him, his mother, and his sister completely? Okay?" she asked.

I nodded.

But why did I feel even this concession was my abandoning Heyden just when I had filled his heart with so much promise and hope?

"Good," she said and leaned over to kiss me. "Are you still going out for dinner?"

"No."

"Then see to it Miguel eats, will you? He's been hovering about me like a worrywart ever since I came home from the hospital."

"Okay," I promised.

She smiled again and stroked my hair. "Your birthday is a month and a half away," she said. "We'll have to do something very special. Seventeen. It all seems to have gone by so quickly. Don't be in a mad rush to grow up," she advised. "After you do, you spend lots of time wondering why you were in such a hurry."

She rose slowly, acting as though it took some effort to stand and shuffle her way out of my room.

"Are you all right, Mommy?"

"Yes," she said, smiling. "Just tired. It's to be expected. I'll be fine. We'll all be fine," she said.

But it didn't come out like one of her firm pronouncements that carried such muscle you couldn't help but believe. It came out more like a small prayer.

I whispered it myself when she closed the door

behind her and left me in my childhood sanctuary, surrounded by my dolls, my beautiful pink world of dreams and fantasies where people were always forgiven for their little failures and where tomorrow always began with a breakfast full of new promises.

5

A Sudden Syndrome

Mommy had already eaten her dinner in her room, so Miguel and I had dinner together. I could see he was sorry for yelling at me earlier. He confessed to being more high strung and nervous than he had ever been, and he admitted it was all because of his concern for little Claude.

"I thought you said he was doing fine and would be coming home sooner than you thought."

"We're not really out of the woods yet, Hannah," he revealed. "Your mother won't let me pretend we are. I just don't want her blaming herself for waiting too long before deciding to have another child. I was part of that decision, too."

"Why *did* you wait so long then, Miguel?" I asked. I never believed Mommy's career was a good enough excuse for putting off another child. She would manage it now, wouldn't she? Why couldn't she manage it ten years ago?

"As you know, she took longer to complete her education. She never liked leaving you even with your nanny for such long periods. Afterward, I wanted your mother to get her sea legs, so to speak, to develop her career and feel strongly enough about herself. It's really impossible for you and for me to truly appreciate how difficult her early life was living as a stepchild in a home where she really had only the nanny to think of as family, and then to come into all these problems here. When you consider all that, you realize how remarkable a woman she is, what a remarkable woman she has become," he said.

Of course, I had no doubt about that, nor did I ever doubt that I had a wonderful mother. I think what made me distrust and wonder about my father the most, in fact, was that he could ever have done anything that would result in his losing her. Danielle was sweet, but she was like a bump in the road compared to a mountain when it came to putting her up against my mother.

"Some men don't want women who challenge them or compete with them," Mommy once explained when she was talking about my father and Danielle. "They don't want a woman who can see their flaws and failures. That puts too much weight on their egos. I'm sure your father is very happy with Danielle. I was tight shoes. Danielle is comfy soft slippers."

"Then why did he want to marry you in the first place?" I asked.

"Probably that same ego at work. He thought he might be able to turn me into another trinket." She squinted and smiled. "I was more like a pin poking his balloon of hot, selfish air.

"But," she added, "he's capable of giving you as much love as he is capable of giving anyone, so don't let me tout you off him. You develop your own relationship with him and trust your own instincts, Hannah," she advised, putting on her psychologist's face.

Does anyone live in a world that is uncomplicated and simple? I wondered. Psychologists and counselors were as much a necessity in this world as medical doctors. No wonder Mommy was always busy.

After Miguel and I had dinner, I went up to see her, but she was dozing off already so I went to my room and completed my homework. I was about to go to sleep when my phone rang. It was Heyden.

"I just had a conversation with my father," he began.

"Really? Where?"

"He called me to explain himself. I don't know why he waited so long. He said he was traveling and wanted to get settled in somewhere first. He and his quintet have a gig that will last six months in New Orleans."

"What did he say?"

"He tried to explain himself, of course. He moaned and groaned about my mother, how hard it has been for him to live with her because she is so oblivious. He knows he has neglected Elisha and me, and he made promises that he would try to get to see us more. Promises like checks written on water. Anyway, he swore that he was sending money. He said he was particularly concerned that I would drop out of school. He thinks I have talent."

"He's right about that."

"In the end I couldn't get myself to hate him. I was angry, but I just couldn't tell him to go to hell, if you know what I mean. In fact, I'm calling you because I figured you were someone who would know exactly what I mean. You still get along with your father, don't you?"

"In a vague sort of way, yes. I'm not in love with my half brothers, and my father's family has nothing whatsoever to do with me."

"Still, you manage to hold on to something. I'll see if that will be true for me as well. We'll see," he added. "Anyway, I'll be in school tomorrow."

"Good."

"Thanks for what you did today, Hannah. I won't let you down. We'll make beautiful music together."

"Okay," I said.

"Good night," he said in a soft, small voice.

"Good night."

When I lowered my head to my pillow, I couldn't help but think about Mommy's warnings and concerns. But Heyden's face, his eyes, his kisses and touch rode like a wave over the memory of her voice and her warnings.

She just doesn't understand, I thought. *She doesn't know Heyden, or she wouldn't be as worried as she is. In time she will see, especially the first time she hears us singing together.* Those thoughts were so soothing and wonderful, I had no trouble falling asleep.

I couldn't wait to get up and ready for school the next morning. Mommy let me take her car again. Miguel was going to drive her to and from the hospital for the next day or so. I knew he wanted to be with her every possible second, and especially when she was with little Claude. He had rearranged his schedule to make it all possible.

When I arrived at school, Heyden was there to greet me. He was very excited.

"I was up late thinking of songs we could do together. Not all mine, of course, but there are a number of great tunes that I'm sure we would sound great doing, Hannah. Here's a partial list," he said, offering it to me. "Can you find time after school today? There's no problem practicing at my house. My mother is at work, and Elisha hangs out with her girlfriends most afternoons."

"For a while, I guess," I said. "As soon as things settle down with my new brother, I'll have you over to Joya del Mar," I told him.

He smiled, but his eyes were full of doubt.

"Yeah, right," he said.

If my girlfriends were talking about me before, they were absolute chatterboxes after they saw how intimately Heyden and I were in the school corridor. He kissed me before hurrying off to his first class. Like a fuse lit with gossip, the subject of my relationship with Heyden singed its way down the halls, through the classrooms, and finally exploded in the cafeteria. The chattering sounded more like tiny firecrackers. We ignored the eyes that followed us to our table and continued to talk about our singing together.

That afternoon and the following three, Heyden and I worked on our music together at his home. Most of the time I stayed for two hours. Occasionally I would sense his eyes on me and not the music and words of our songs, and when I turned to him, the look in his face stole my breath away.

"What?" I asked, stopping.

He put the guitar down slowly and closed his eyes, seemingly holding his breath for a moment.

"Every once in a while," he said, "I have to reassure myself that this is really happening, that it's not some fantasy of mine.

"I confess I felt that way before I got up the nerve to approach you," he continued, "I had been watching and dreaming about you, Hannah."

His words and his expression made me blush.

"Well, if we're into confessions, I have to say I stole a glance or two at you as well, Heyden Reynolds."

"Did you? Must have been when I felt the warmest in that place. Okay, here's a second confession," he announced.

"I feel like a Catholic priest," I said, and he laughed. Then he grew serious again.

"When I first proposed we sing together, I did it more out of a desire to be with you, to have you next to me, than out of my love of music."

"Why, Heyden Reynolds," I declared with my hands on my hips in mock indignation, "I thought you said I had the best voice in the school."

"You do, but . . ."

I laughed at him and he pushed me playfully onto his bed. I braced myself back on my hands and looked up at him.

"Hannah," he said, as if he could express all he felt just by saying my name.

He approached me and leaned over to kiss me. After

he did, he started to undo the buttons of my bodice. I continued to lean back on my hands, looking down at his fingers as they undid my dress and gently brought it out to my shoulders. He slipped his hands in and around my back and kissed me again. I didn't move, and he unfastened my bra and kissed my stiffened nipples and nudged my breasts gently with his face, moaning softly with pleasure.

Feeling a wonderful weakness take over my body, I let myself fall back on the bed. I didn't open my eyes until he had taken off my clothes and then his own. My heart pounded harder and faster at the sounds of his shirt and pants being tossed to the side. I heard him rip the envelop of his protection, and then I opened my eyes and looked into his.

"Just tell me to stop, Hannah, and I will," he said.

I closed my eyes.

Mommy had told me to go with my instincts, and there were no sounds of warning, no cries of regret coming from that place in my heart. *There is no more intimate act, no closer or stronger way to make yourself part of someone else,* I thought, and that was what I wanted. Whatever mystical and magical energy had brought us together now wrapped itself around us, tying us to each other. Few things you do, few things that happen to you, or things you see remain with you as does the first time you make love. That memory is there until you take your final breath and can be resurrected with little effort. I had seen that in Mommy's face, in Mommy's quiet moments full of special remembrances.

This day will live forever in me, I told myself. *It will never die.*

I felt him there, gently prodding, coming to me in small sweet increments of love, holding me as he would a delicate piece of china, waiting for my anxiety to pass, my pain to dissolve into passion. I held on to him like someone afraid of drowning or disappearing might, and together we redefined who we were forever and ever.

Once you have done it, does your face really change? Do you walk and talk differently, have a look in your eyes that tells people you have crossed into a more sophisticated, mature, and knowing place? I wondered. Would Mommy take one glance at me and immediately know?

Afterward, the next day in fact, small intimacies grew between Heyden and me. In school Heyden and I seemed always to find each other's hand when we were walking together. We brushed against each other whenever we talked and brought our faces closer. I grew accustomed to his breath caressing my neck, his lips grazing my ear. My girlfriends suspected we were intimate immediately anyway, so I couldn't judge how I appeared to others on the basis of how I appeared to them, but I imagine most thought we were truly lovers. Their smiles and giggles bounced around me like silly bubbles I could swipe away with a reprimanding glance.

Now when Mr. Mullens caught me daydreaming in his class, he smiled knowingly, for he, like most of our teachers, took some interest in the way the students socialized and co-mingled at our school. They saw us walking hand in hand in the halls. I'm sure they gossiped, too. I could see it in all their faces and felt like I had blushed so much in two days, my face must appear sunburned.

Mommy said nothing different to me, and surprisingly asked me little about Heyden except for an occasional "How's your friend doing?"

"Fine" was enough of an answer to get her off the topic. I hadn't told her about our rehearsals. I was afraid of her forbidding me to continue, and also I hoped to surprise her and Miguel one day by having Heyden over and the two of us singing for them.

Mommy and Miguel were spending more and more time at the hospital anyway, and often weren't home before I returned from Heyden's. The doctors had given an approximate date on which they hoped to release little Claude. Mommy was absorbed by all of it and had now turned her attention to perfecting the nursery, even though she made it clear little Claude would sleep at her bedside for the first few months at least. I told Miguel I pitied the students in his early-morning classes. He laughed but nodded in agreement.

"I might soon be yawning as much as they do," he joked.

At the start of the following week, I finally met Heyden's mother. Before this she was never home when I was there. She looked much younger than I had anticipated. Only about five feet two and maybe one hundred and five pounds or so, she immediately appeared overwhelmed by the problems in their lives. *A stiff wind could lift her and carry her away,* I thought. Heyden had obviously inherited her beautiful ebony eyes, which now were downcast and troubled.

She appeared embarrassed when Heyden introduced us. I couldn't imagine how so shy a woman could perform any work outside of her home. Being a chambermaid obviously gave her a minimum of contact with people, however. She did invite me to stay for dinner one night, but I explained how important it was for me to be home for my mother.

Rehearsals, schoolwork, attending to Mommy, all took up so much of my free time that I let nearly two full weeks go by without visiting my uncle Linden. I felt so bad about it that I told Heyden I had to skip our rehearsal. When he heard my reason, he was not only understanding, he wondered if he could go along.

"Really, you would do that?"

"Even from the little you've told me about him, especially about his painting, he sounds interesting. Unless you think I might disturb him, of course."

"No," I said quickly. "He would want to meet you. I'm sure."

Of course, I really wasn't sure, but if Uncle Linden was ever to be released into the outside world, as I liked to call it, he had to be able to meet new people and get along. I thought it was nice of Heyden to care.

We drove down right after school that day. I was disappointed he wasn't sitting outside when we pulled up. During the past two weeks, I had asked Mommy about him, and she had said she had spoken to him on the phone and he was doing fine, so I had no reason to assume otherwise.

"Maybe he's working," I told Heyden after I parked. My voice was heavy with concern.

Mrs. Robinson greeted us at the door. "Oh, Hannah.

I'm glad you've come. He has been asking for your mother and you quite a bit this past week. In fact, he's been a bit depressed, and he hasn't done any work."

"Did you tell my mother?"

"Yes."

"Didn't she speak to him on the phone?"

"He doesn't do well on the phone, Hannah. In fact, he always complains about it." She smiled. "He says he's an artist. He has to look at the people he speaks to." She shrugged. "It makes sense to me," she said, smiling at Heyden.

"Me, too," he replied, and I introduced them.

"Where's my uncle now?"

"Just sitting in his room. I tried to get him to sit outside today, but he wouldn't budge from his rocking chair. Maybe you will be able to get him out for some fresh air. Take him for a walk."

"Yes," I said.

She stepped aside, and I led Heyden down the hall to Uncle Linden's room. I knocked and waited, but he didn't respond.

"Uncle Linden? It's Hannah," I said.

"Hannah? Come in, come in," we heard, and I opened the door.

He was sitting in the rocker. His hair looked more disheveled than usual, and he was wearing a thin short-sleeved shirt and a pair of dungarees with his usual sandals. He looked as if he hadn't shaven for nearly a week. It took that long for his blond beard to show itself. He sat forward.

"Close the door," he leaned toward us to whisper as soon as we had entered.

I did so and glanced at Heyden, who looked more concerned than curious. Before I could introduce Heyden, Uncle Linden sat back and said, "Okay. Now that you are here, tell me exactly what happened."

"Happened? You mean with Mommy?"

"Of course. I spoke with her on the phone, and when I asked her about Thatcher, she said she didn't want to talk about him anymore. So?" he said.

"She doesn't like to talk about him, Uncle Linden. She says it's over and done with and that's that. It's been years and years anyway, so why bother?"

I smiled and stepped aside.

"I want you to meet a friend of mine, Uncle Linden. This is Heyden."

He glanced at Heyden and nodded quickly, barely acknowledging him.

"Why is it over and done with, Hannah? What happened?"

"When, Uncle Linden?"

"I don't know when." He thought for a moment. "It could have happened anytime, I suppose. I warned her about that."

"Uncle Linden, you're just confused. I just told you. Mommy and Daddy have been apart for years and years. They rarely see each other and rarely speak to each other anymore. Everything they want to say to each other, they say through me. I'm the messenger and I hate it. In any case, nothing new has happened."

He smirked. "Sure. That's just Eaton propaganda you're hearing. Nothing new. It's not new, but it's not nothing, either," he said. He leaned back. "I knew when she wasn't coming around that something had happened. She's too trusting, too vulnerable. I tried to show her that in a picture I painted once, but she just didn't understand."

"Speaking of your pictures," I said, jumping on the opportunity to change the subject, "Heyden would love to see what you're working on now, Uncle Linden. I told him all about you, how many of your pictures have been in galleries and sold. Can we see your latest work? Mrs. Robinson told me you were at hard work on something new."

"I sold it," he replied quickly.

"Sold it?" I smiled at Heyden.

"Yes, yes, yes, sold it. Mrs. Valby's mother bought it. Mrs. Robinson put the check in the bank for me the other day," he said. He leaned over, opened a dresser drawer, and produced a deposit slip. I took it and read it and nodded.

"Five hundred dollars," I told Heyden. "That's wonderful, Uncle Linden."

"It's not the first I've sold while I've been living here," he said proudly.

"How many have you sold all told?" Heyden asked. "Here and in the galleries?"

"I don't know. Quite a few, I suppose." His looked up at me quickly, his eyes narrowed. "He's not telling you that it's because of him again, is he? It's not, you know. He never did me any favors."

"Who?"

"Thatcher Eaton. Bragging to Willow about how he got my pictures into galleries. *I* got my pictures into galleries. People wanted them because of the pictures, not because of what Thatcher Eaton told them."

"I'm sure that's true, Uncle Linden."

"Yes," he said. He put the deposit slip back in the drawer, closed it, and looked at Heyden. "Who are you again?"

"Heyden Reynolds," Heyden said, smiling. "I go to school with Hannah."

"He writes songs and plays the guitar, Uncle Linden. We're singing together."

"Writes songs. That's good," Uncle Linden said.

"Do you want to go outside, take a walk with us? It's a cool enough afternoon. Nice breeze."

"Yes," he said and stood up without hesitation.

Heyden smiled at me. "I was hoping to see some of your work, Mr. Montgomery," Heyden said. He looked about the stark room, but there was nothing.

"I have a few in the room next door," Uncle Linden said. "We can see them on the way out." He paused and looked at me. "I want you to pose for me. Did I ask you?"

"Yes, Uncle Linden. As soon as school is finished, I'll have more time," I said and winked at Heyden.

"Right. Where's Willow? Why didn't she come with you?" he demanded.

"I told you, Uncle Linden. Mommy gave birth recently. She'll be here soon and with the new baby."

"Yes," he said, smiling. "The baby." He laughed. "Won't that set their tongues wagging on Worth Avenue?"

"What?" Heyden asked.

Uncle Linden didn't answer.

"We're going for a walk," he said instead and headed for the door.

Heyden looked at me and I shook my head.

"He's all right," he said. "Just a little confused. I like him," he added, and we walked out after Uncle Linden, who was already down the hallway, marching to his rambling thoughts. He didn't stop at any room to show Heyden his paintings, and I didn't think I should mention it. We were getting him outside and that was good.

We took a nice walk. The fresh air, being outside the residency, had a good effect on Uncle Linden and reinforced my belief that he should be living with us by now. Almost as soon as we started away from the house, he asked Heyden questions about his songwriting and wanted to hear something.

"Well, I usually sing to a guitar," Heyden said.

"I can sing one," I offered and sang the song we had been working on the past two days. Heyden had obviously written it about us. It was a modern day Romeo and Juliet story with a refrain that went *Nothing anyone can do will ever take my love away from you. It's bigger than the bright blue sea. It keeps the life inside of me.*

Uncle Linden stopped walking and looked at us.

"I like that. I like that a lot," he said. "In fact," he said, walking on, "it gives me an idea for a new painting."

Heyden smiled at me. Uncle Linden's walk became more energized. He couldn't wait to get back to the house and to work.

"It's good being around creative people," he told us. "Creative people feed each other's imaginations."

Heyden looked proud, his chest swelling.

"Thanks for coming with me," I told him afterward. "You made the visit very beneficial."

"I'm glad I did. I don't know anything about psychology really, but I agree with you. I don't see why he has to be kept in any residency. So he gets a little confused once in a while. Who doesn't? Especially someone who is so isolated from the people he loves."

"That's it," I said excitedly. "That's what I have been trying to tell my mother for some time."

"I wish we had mountains of money and we could just run off together and set up a home with a studio for him," Heyden fantasized.

"Sounds good to me," I said.

"I'm not kidding, Hannah," he said, his face screwed tightly in a serious expression.

"I'm not kidding, either," I told him, kissed him goodbye, and headed back to Joya del Mar.

The moment I opened the front door, I sensed a major change. Our maid Lila was hurrying up the stairs, carrying a tray of food. She didn't even pause to look my way. Miguel came charging down the hallway toward the stairs, too.

"He's home!" he cried. "Claude is here!" he announced. I could almost hear the fanfare. However, his excitement was infecting.

"That's wonderful!" I cried.

"Come on," he urged. "Before he falls asleep. You won't believe how alert he is for an infant so small. There's no doubt he knows your mother's voice and touch. You can see the pleasure in his face."

I followed him up to their bedroom. Mommy was sitting up in bed, and little Claude was in his bassinet beside her. Her face was lit with such happiness, it could have illuminated the room, I thought.

"Hannah, where have you been? The doctors just decided it would be all right to take him home. You can't imagine how surprised and overjoyed we were to hear it. I'm so happy I had everything prepared in anticipation."

"For months, she means," Miguel kidded.

I approached the bassinet and gazed down at my little brother. He waved his arms vigorously and then paused for a moment when my shadow moved over him.

"You can hold him if you like," Mommy said. "Just be sure you give his head good support."

"I'm afraid to," I admitted. "He's so tiny. He looks even smaller than he did behind the window."

"He's not. He's two pounds heavier," Miguel said with a boasting that made it seem he had done it all himself.

"Pick him up, Miguel, and let her hold him," Mommy insisted.

Miguel did with expert care.

"Hold out your arms, put your hand here," he instructed, then gave me little Claude.

I felt his squirming and the warmth in his body; however, he sensed my tension, too, and that made him uneasy. Almost immediately he started to cry. I looked up with panic.

"He doesn't like me holding him," I said.

"It's all right," Mommy said. "He just has to get used to you and you to him. Once you relax, he will, too," she assured me.

I held him a little longer, and then Miguel mercifully took him from me. In a moment little Claude stopped crying and looked relaxed again.

Miguel's face blossomed with just as much happiness as Mommy's. The two of them never looked as radiant nor as blissful. I couldn't think of a time when they were as contented with me or with something I had done. All little Claude had to do was wiggle his nose and they would break into ecstatic delight.

"He's already developed your thoughtful expression," Miguel told Mommy.

"That's not thoughtful, that's plotting," she replied. "I can see you in those eyes."

"Look at these fingers." Miguel continued gently holding little Claude's tiny hand between his thumb and forefinger. "He'll be a pianist or a brain surgeon, for sure."

"Maybe he'll be an artist like Uncle Linden," I inserted, and they both looked at me as though they had forgotten I was in the room, too.

"Yes," Miguel said, but without any sense of conviction.

"Uh-oh," Mommy said, "I know that twist of his lips. He's getting hungry."

She put her tray to the side and held up her arms. Miguel placed little Claude gently in them and stepped back as Mommy lowered her nightgown to begin breast-feeding. I turned to leave.

"You don't have to go, Hannah," she called.

"I've got a lot of homework and two tests tomorrow," I told her. It wasn't so, but I felt a need to leave.

"Okay. Come see me after dinner," she said. "You can hold little Claude again then."

I nodded, forced a smile, and left. I had no idea why, but my stomach felt full of bees buzzing angrily like bees who had been misinformed as to where the nectar would be found. Soon they would head for the hive in my heart and chastise the worker who had made the error.

After dinner I returned to Mommy's bedroom and, at her insistence, held little Claude again. This time I was more relaxed, and he closed his eyes and fell asleep.

"See how easy it is?" Mommy said.

Miguel came in and stood by watching. It intrigued me as to just how fascinated he and my mother were with little Claude. It was truly as though every new move he made, every sound he uttered, was a remarkable, earthshattering new achievement.

"Look at those lips twitching when he sleeps," Miguel said. "He must be having a real Freudian dream, Willow."

Mommy laughed.

"Right," she said. "He was promised better lodging outside the womb, and it isn't exactly as comfortable out here."

"Can't blame him for complaining," Miguel said. "Can you, Hannah?"

"I don't think he's complaining," I said. "He's just nervous."

They both laughed.

"Well, he is," I insisted. I returned him to Mommy's arms. "Babies don't dream anyway, do they? They can't have nightmares."

"Maybe not with as much sophistication as they will after they learn language," Mommy said, "but there is most certainly a flood of images under the thin layer of sleep he experiences," she said gazing down at him.

"Who knows how often he relives the trauma of birth?" Miguel added. "Some psychiatrists and psychologists think we never forget it, right, Dr. Fuentes?" he asked Mommy.

"I don't want to think of anything unpleasant in relation to him, Miguel. His life is not going to have anything like the turmoil mine had," she vowed.

Did she make the same vow when I was born? I wondered. She never told me she had.

It's because of my father, I thought. *It will always be because of him.*

I left when I heard my phone ringing. It was Heyden calling to sing me the first stanza of his new song.

"I got the idea from visiting your uncle," he said. "It's about a painter who falls in love with his own painting."

"Pygmalion," I said.

"What?

"The Greek myth, remember? The sculptor prayed to Aphrodite to find him a wife like his statue, and she brought it to life."

"Yes," he said excited. "I remember. I'll use that. Thanks. I knew we'd make a great team, Hannah."

He was so up and excited, he boosted my morale.

"I may be late for school tomorrow," he said. "I'm going to work on this until I pass out."

"Don't get in trouble with your attendance, Heyden," I advised.

"I don't care about that. This is what I care about: my music and you," he said with conviction. In fact, I envied him for his determination and his strong sense of purpose. I felt like a ribbon in the wind, tossed from one place to another, but he didn't hear any longing, any sadness, any emptiness in my voice. He was flying too high. And he had so much more weighing him down and bringing him back to earth.

"Oh," I said before we ended our conversation and finding it remarkable that I had forgotten.

"What?"

"They brought my baby brother home from the hospital."

"Hey, great," he said. "Lot of excitement there, huh?"

"Yes," I said.

"I'll be in school by third period," he promised and said good night.

I fell asleep faster than I expected I would. I was anticipating a night of tossing and turning, my bed becoming a small rowboat on a wild sea of dark dreams. When I heard the commotion in the hallway, I thought I was trapped in some nightmare. It took me a few moments to realize I wasn't asleep and that it was all really happening.

I got up quickly and went to my door. Miguel, in his pajamas pants but with his jacket and shoes on, was charging down the corridor toward the stairway.

"What's going on?" I called.

"Oh, Hannah," he said. "Your mother is in a panic. She woke up and looked at little Claude and is convinced that he wasn't breathing. It's all the fault of that damn intern who put SIDS in her head."

"SIDS? What's that?" I asked.

"Sudden infant death syndrome," he muttered. "I'm getting the car ready. We're taking the baby over to the hospital to have the doctor check him out. Your mother won't sleep a wink if we don't."

"But what is . . ."

He continued down the stairs. I walked down to Mommy's bedroom. She had her coat on over her nightgown, and she was holding little Claude.

"What happened, Mommy?" I asked.

She was staring down at him and gently rocking him. I couldn't believe she hadn't heard me.

"Mommy?"

She looked up quickly. "What? Not now, Hannah!" she cried before I could utter another sound. "Just go to sleep. I have to take the baby to the hospital."

"But—"

"Where's Miguel? What's taking him so long?"

"What's SIDS?" I asked her.

Her eyes went wide with terror.

"Why did you say that?"

"I just spoke—"

"It's not that! It can't be. Can it?" she asked, looking down at little Claude as if she expected he would begin to speak intelligent sentences and reply to her question and concern. She continued to rock him gently.

I had never seen her so unhinged. Was this the same woman who coolly and intelligently evaluated other people's hysteria and emotional crises, the woman who was always there for me before, helping me cope with the disappointments I had with my father's family and with my half brothers?

When she looked toward the doorway where I was standing, she didn't appear to see me at all. Her face was contorted, her lips twisted, her eyes still very wide and wild.

"Okay," I heard Miguel say behind me, and I stepped

back. He came charging into the bedroom and guided Mommy out. She didn't even glance at me as she passed me in the hallway. I followed behind them slowly and watched as they descended. Miguel lunged to open the front door, and a moment later they were gone.

My heart stopped pounding, but I knew I wasn't going to fall asleep again, not for a long time. Instead, I went to my computer and pulled up my encyclopedia to read about SIDS. According to what was written, I learned that it was a medical disorder that claimed the lives of nearly 3,000 babies one week to one year of age in the U.S. each year. It had also been called crib death and occurred during sleep, striking without any real warning, even though the babies appeared to be healthy. The cause, according to the article, remained vague.

I read on about the recommendations concerning prevention, but nothing seemed to be a 100 percent guarantee. How horrible, I thought. A mother like Mommy could live within the confines of this terrible nightmare for well into a year before the fear was reduced.

Surely, this would reinforce her belief that a curse hung over this family. Maybe it did, I thought. Maybe it wasn't so foolish to think so after all.

I dozed off and on for hours. Just before the light of day I heard them return and come up the stairs. They both looked exhausted.

"What happened?" I asked. Miguel helped Mommy down the hallway. She didn't turn to me. He looked back.

"We left him there for observation. Just a day," he said.

I heard Mommy groan.

"It's just a day," he repeated for her benefit and continued to guide her down to their bedroom. I waited until their door closed, and then I went back to bed and overslept.

None of my friends missed the fact that both Heyden and I were late for school. I could see their little minds going a thousand words a minute. I felt like a bull, eager to charge into their red faces of glee and knock those smirks and coy, twisted smiles off them.

Heyden was surprised I was late, too. We were both sent to the office for special passes. Then I explained why and he understood.

"I'm sorry. It must have been a hairy situation. Everything will be all right, I'm sure," Heyden said quickly. "At least I finished the song. I can't wait for you to hear it and then sing it."

"Not today, Heyden," I said. "I've go to get home. My mother will need me," I said. He looked more disappointed than I had expected.

"What can you do?" he asked.

"I can't do much maybe, but my being there is important. She would want me there."

It annoyed me that I had to explain, but I would soon discover that was very optimistic.

It would make me think Heyden was right after all, and it would leave me feeling like I was the one who should have suffered SIDS.

6

A Pair of Earrings

Lila, our maid, told me little Claude was already home again by the time I returned from school. Surprisingly, however, Mommy's bedroom door was closed. I knocked on it gently, and when it opened, Miguel stepped out and closed the door softly behind him. The moment he turned to me, he pressed his right forefinger against his lips.

"She's asleep," he said. "She wouldn't go to sleep unless I promised to be at her and little Claude's side while they both slept."

"What about your afternoon classes?"

"My intern is administering an exam for me in both classes."

"Can I see the baby?" I asked.

"Not right now, Hannah. For the moment let's just keep things quiet."

"What happened at the hospital?"

"Nothing remarkable. Your mother might just have overreacted," he said, whispering.

"But isn't this something that could happen at any time during the first year and without any warning and something you can't tell by examining a baby?"

Miguel raised his eyebrows.

"Done some research, have you?"

"Yes."

"Maybe it's better we don't talk about it," he said. "Let's not keep it on the front burner, always on her mind, if you know what I mean."

"I just thought she would appreciate my knowing all about it," I said, not hiding my disappointment. When would I do something right in relation to my new brother and my mother?

"Oh, she would. She will," Miguel said. "But not right now." He gazed back at the door. "I better go back inside," he said. "If she wakes and doesn't find me there . . ."

"I could sit with her, if you like."

"Maybe later. Right now she's just a stick of dynamite. Oh," he said, just as he reached back for the doorknob, "your father wants you to call him when you get a chance."

"Daddy? Why?"

"He didn't say. Actually, it was his secretary who called for him."

"Thanks," I said and watched him go back into the bedroom, closing the door softly and closing me out.

Even if my mother was a stick of dynamite, I thought, why would my presence set her off?

I went to my room and called my father's law offices.

"It's Hannah," I said as soon as Mrs. Gouter answered.

"One moment and I'll patch you through to his cell phone," she said. A few seconds later I heard him say hello and knew from the background noises that he was in his car.

"Hannah, how are you? How's life in the maternity ward?" he asked with laughter in his voice.

"Not easy," I replied.

"I'll bet. Anyway, I would like you to come to dinner tomorrow night. Special occasion. It will just be the five of us," he added.

"What special occasion?"

"Don't tell me you forgot your brothers' birthday," he said. "Don't worry," he continued before I could admit that I had, "I asked Mrs. Gouter to get something that will be coming from you. I'll tell you what it is when I pick you up about six-thirty, okay? You can sign their birthday cards then, too."

"I can drive myself, Daddy. I can use Mommy's car."

"No, no," he insisted. "I'll come by to get you. I have a baby gift I'm bringing, too. Does he look Cuban?" he asked.

"He looks like a little baby, Daddy. He's cute and he has Miguel's dark hair."

"I thought he would. Better warn everyone I'm showing up on the grounds. I don't want them to sick any dogs on me."

"We don't have any dogs, Daddy," I said.

"I know, Hannah, but if you did, they would be

trained to get Thatcher Eaton," he said and laughed. "Wouldn't be the first time," he added. "Okay, gotta go. I'm anxious to see you," he concluded, and then the line went dead.

At least you are, I thought to myself and hung up.

Just before dinner Mommy awoke and I was permitted entry to the bedroom, which to me now had the religious, sanctified atmosphere of a church. For some reason both Miguel and Mommy kept their voices to a volume barely above a whisper, even though little Claude was also awake and stirring. I thought Mommy looked drawn and pale, still quite exhausted from last night's ordeal and crisis.

"What did your father want?" she asked. Miguel had obviously told her he had called.

"Tomorrow night is the dinner celebrating the twins' birthday," I told her. "He's coming by about six-thirty for me, and he said he's bringing a baby gift as well."

"Something his secretary bought, no doubt."

"I forgot to buy the twins any gifts," I confessed. "He remembered for me."

"He doesn't remember those sort of things, Hannah. Mrs. Gouter has a detailed calendar she keeps for him. I once saw it. It had my birthday, your grandmother's birthday, even our wedding date written in it so she could remind him to get gifts."

"He even forgets his own birthday," I said, defending him. "But when he remembers, he always takes me out then, too."

"That's just a ruse, Hannah. The Eatons don't forget their own birthdays, believe me. Asher Eaton once hired a plane to drag a birthday greeting for Bunny

Eaton around and around Palm Beach for nearly two hours, and that was followed by a party that rivaled a coronation."

"If you hate them so much, why did you get involved with them at all?" I asked with a petulance that raised Miguel's eyebrows. Mommy just shook her head.

"Might as well ask Eve why she ate the apple," she muttered. "Oh, I don't want to think about them. I have far more serious and important things to think about than the Eatons," she added and leaned over to gaze into the bassinet. Little Claude was swinging his arms and kicking his feet under the blanket.

Mommy's face brightened. "He's so precious," she said. "A marvel."

"When are we bringing Uncle Linden here to see him?" I asked.

She looked up quickly.

"Oh, not yet, Hannah. Not until we're sure everything is all right."

"Why? What would Uncle Linden do?"

"I just can't deal with him and this situation at the same time," she whined. I couldn't remember hearing that sort of note in her voice. I stared at her just like someone wondering if it was really her mother. Giving birth seemed to have changed her whole personality. Gone was the assurance, the strength that practically radiated from her and gave other people some self-confidence.

"But you promised," I moaned.

"Hannah, can you suspend this obsession you have with your uncle for a while?" she snapped at me.

It felt as if she had slapped me.

"I don't have an obsession, Mommy. What kind of thing is that to say?"

Miguel stepped in between us.

"Your mother just means for you to cool it for a little while, Hannah," he said in a soft, reasonable tone. "She wants Linden to see the baby just as much as you do, but we're going to try to keep things very quiet around Claude for a few days. The doctors think that's best, too," he said, closing and opening his eyes. "Best for Claude and best for your mother," he added, lifting his eyes toward the ceiling as a way of urging me to let it go.

I still didn't understand how having Uncle Linden over would jeopardize anything, but I pressed my lips together and looked down.

"Miguel," Mommy said with a voice full of panic and concern. She leaned over the bed and hovered above little Claude. "Hurry!" she cried.

Miguel moved quickly to the bassinet and touched the baby's hand.

"He's just dozing, Willow," Miguel said in a soft, calm voice. "It's all right. He's doing fine. Look at the color in his cheeks."

She nodded, released a deep breath, and sank back against her big, fluffy pillow. Her eyes drifted by me to the wall. Once I felt she and I were invisible to people in Palm Beach. Now I felt I was invisible to her.

"Maybe we should all go down to dinner tonight, Willow," Miguel suggested. "It's been a while since we all sat and had dinner together. We'll bring the baby, of course," he added quickly.

"No, no," she said. "That's not important. There's no

need to go through all that just for a dinner. You and Hannah can have dinner together. Send Lila up with my food. I'm fine," she said. "I *am,*" she emphasized sharply when he didn't immediately agree.

Miguel smiled. "Well then, maybe we'll all eat dinner up here. How's that?"

"I'm not that hungry," I said. "I'm just having a sandwich and getting to my homework since I won't have time to do stuff tomorrow night."

"Why not?" Mommy asked.

"I just told you, Mommy. Daddy's coming to get me for the birthday dinner."

Hadn't she heard a word I had said?

"Oh, yes, right," she said, but I could see the information pass right through her head as she sat up again and leaned over to look at little Claude. "He should be hungry soon," she said. "I can almost feel his body churning with the need for nourishment. It's truly amazing. It's as if he's still inside me, still connected," she said, her voice full of awe and wonder. "I'm sure it's because of the breast-feeding."

Rubber bands stretched and snapped inside my chest.

"Then you shouldn't worry about him not breathing, Mommy," I told her. I could feel my eyes narrowing. She looked up, surprised. I shrugged. "If he stops, you'll feel it, too," I said.

I glanced at Miguel. He looked very displeased with me.

"There is nothing funny or frivolous about this, Hannah," Mommy said. "He could be susceptible to SIDS. It's a serious condition that—"

"I know what SIDS is," I interrupted. "Sudden infant death syndrome."

She glared at me. "Then," she said in measured tones, "you should know better."

The tears felt like drops of boiling water beneath my eyelids. I kept them back.

"Sorry," I muttered, turned and headed out. "Sorry I was ever born," I added under my breath and hurried down the hallway to my room, but instead of going in, I paused at my door and then continued slowly until I was standing at the door of the infamous bedroom, the forbidden room, shut up and ignored like some unwanted child.

I knew bits and pieces of the story that haunted our family, a story that climaxed in this room. Mommy had doled out the details to me in measured doses, adding more information as I grew older, just recently explaining why Uncle Linden was bitter about Joya del Mar. I knew in my heart that there was much yet to be learned and even more to be understood.

What I did know was that after my great-grandmother's husband, a naval officer, was killed in a helicopter accident, she and my grandmother, who was about twelve at the time, moved to West Palm Beach, where my great-grandmother, Jackie Lee Houston, worked as a waitress to support herself and her daughter. One day she met Winston Montgomery, a very wealthy widower twenty-five years her senior. He fell in love with my great-grandmother, who I could tell from pictures was a very beautiful woman. He married her, bringing her to Joya del Mar. After Winston died, my great-grandmother foolishly fell in love with and married a Palm Beach playboy named Kirby Scott.

I knew that it was in this room that he had seduced his wife's daughter, my grandmother, who then became pregnant with Uncle Linden. Mommy had explained how my grandmother's attempt to keep her pregnancy a secret resulted in a great deal of confusion and bitterness for Uncle Linden.

I thought about this room from time to time, and from time to time, I took glimpses of it, but the onus of sin and the understanding that all of our family troubles originated with a single lustful act within the room kept it forbidden and even a little terrifying for me. If there was such a thing as a curse on our family, it lived and breathed within the walls of this scene of a sex crime, and if I spent too much time within it, or even touched anything inside the room, that curse might leap into me and live under my heart, waiting for a chance to do its wicked work.

But at the moment I was so twisted and turned inside, I felt the need to be reckless, to challenge Fate itself. I glanced back at Mommy's bedroom. The door was still closed. Miguel was still with her. I knew Mommy didn't want me wandering around in this room. It made her nervous, but defying her at the moment seemed not only satisfying, but delicious. She talked about the forbidden fruit, compared herself to Eve in Paradise. Here it was for me to taste, and taste I would.

I opened the door and stepped into the bedroom. Although it was never used for guests or otherwise, Lila, as Mrs. Davis before her, kept it neat and clean, althought not dusted and vacuumed as often as the other rooms in the house. However, there were no cobwebs permitted here, no dust or grime. The linen was not changed, but with the curtains drawn, the lights off, nothing looked faded.

The dark pine four-poster bed had cream silk drapes down each post that puddled at the floor. The headboard was embossed with the figures of two terns facing each other but soaring, their heads and eyes lifted toward some heavenly destination, the tips of their wings touching each other. I once overheard Miguel tell Mommy that the artist who designed and constructed the headboard was suggesting that the inhabitants would find ecstasy within its sheets.

"They hardly found *that,*" Mommy told him in a tone of chastisement. I remember wondering why she was so mad at him for saying something that sounded so innocent.

Whether by design or accident, all the artifacts in the room were sexually suggestive. There were small bronze statues of naked men and women on the dresser and nightstands, one with a man and a woman kissing passionately. There was a large statue of the goddess Diana, the huntress with her bow drawn against her naked bosom. It was set on a pedestal in the far right corner, but she was aiming at the bed.

The bed had three large pillows and two small ones set atop a crimson spread. When I was very little and had only quick glances of the room, I imagined the bed was soaked in blood. Now, standing and gazing at it in the light of the afternoon sun filtering through the curtains, it looked as if it had the folds of two bodies imprinted, two people who had just recently lain side by side on the bed. When I drew closer, I saw that wasn't so. It was just an illusion of shadows and light.

I had never opened the closet door, but turned to do so now. Surprisingly, I found a sheer nightgown still hanging on the inside of the door. The closet had some garments, a few skirts and blouses, and on the shelf above, some shoe boxes. I sifted through the clothing and looked at some, measuring the skirts against me. They were all about my size. I imagined they once belonged to my grandmother, Grace Montgomery. I wondered why no one had ever taken them away or given them away.

In fact, as I studied the room, I realized the hairbrush was still on the vanity table as well as hairpin holders and hairpins, some pearl hair combs, makeup brushes, and even tubes of lipstick. When I opened the drawer I saw some costume jewelry, earrings and bracelets. In another drawer I found two pearl necklaces and a half dozen boxes of pearl earrings to match.

I remembered Mommy telling me that Uncle Linden once stayed in this room. How could he want to sleep in here? What did it do for him? Was he trying to kill the demons or face them down? Surely, they had moved all of this out when he was living here. When he left, everything had been returned, but why? It was eerie how everything had been restored. It was almost as if my grandmother was expected back, that she wasn't dead, only away. Maybe it was something Uncle Linden had insisted on doing, I thought, and made a mental note to ask Mommy about it someday. Of course, she would wonder why I was exploring in this room in the first place. Maybe I was better off asking Uncle Linden himself. If it upset him, however, Mommy would be very angry at me.

There were just too many secrets, too many unanswered questions, too many forbidden topics in our family, I thought, and all because of what had happened in this room.

I returned to the side of the bed and put my hand on the red comforter. Closing my eyes, I tried to envision my grandmother, not too much older than I was, trusting this handsome man who portrayed himself as her loving guardian, assuring her that he wasn't going to hurt her, but instead would only help her step into maturity and sophistication, confusing and blinding her with his soft words, his gentle, loving touch until he was at her, consuming her in his own lust and passion and then leaving her innocence smashed and crushed on this very bed, leaving her like some wilted flower that had lost all hope of sunshine. She would draw the curtains on her shame and choke back her tears. All the crying she would do would be inside herself.

What was it like for her to realize she was pregnant with Uncle Linden? Her shame was so great, making her keep it secret too long. She was embarrassed and felt guilty and at fault. How do you tell your mother you have slept with her husband? I'm sure she felt that it was somehow her fault, that she had done something she shouldn't have done.

The same was true for poor Uncle Linden living under the cloud of despair, believing his very existence was destroying his own mother. No wonder he had tried suicide, I thought. No wonder he was so confused and lost. He was as innocent as my little brother down the hall. He didn't deserve the self-inflicted punishment, and he certainly didn't deserve to be treated like an unperson, a pariah in this snobby, rich community.

And he certainly didn't deserve to be kept out of this house at such a supposedly happy time!

I gazed about this room with fury. I hated this room. Why was it kept so sacrosanct? Why wasn't it stripped to the bone and left to be what it was? Why were its walls protected so the sin that happened in it could remain? *Defy any curse!* I cried inside. *There isn't any curse. There is just stupidity and fear.*

In a burst of anger I pulled off the bloodred comforter and tossed it to the floor. Then I threw off the pillows as well and tore away the sheets until there was nothing but a naked mattress. Not satisfied, I ripped away the silk drapery from the posts and heaved them beside the bedding. When I stopped and stepped back, the bed looked reduced to merely what it was: wood, cloth, and springs. It was indistinguishable from any other old furniture. It was no longer a stage or a scene of anything. It was merely a bed.

Contented, I left it like that and closed the door behind me. The house was silent, so silent, I could hear the pounding of my own heart. It took the remainder of the afternoon for me to calm down.

In the end Miguel did not have dinner with me. He told me he thought it would be better if he ate with Mommy in her room.

"She says she doesn't want company, but she really does. I'm sure you understand," he said.

I didn't, but I didn't tell him so. Sitting alone at our long dining room table, I not only felt silly, I felt like a stranger. Above me, Mommy, Miguel, and little Claude were together. I had little appetite and didn't eat much. When I went upstairs, I heard laughter behind Mommy's bedroom door. For a moment I debated going there, but decided to delve into my homework instead. I shut my own bedroom door and put on some music. It was hard to concentrate. Every once in a while I would stop to think about them.

As the evening continued, I anticipated the discovery of what I had done to the forbidden bedroom, but no one came to my door. I didn't know Lila's schedule. It could very well be a day or two before she or anyone would go into that bedroom, which was fine with me. I had no idea what I would say or how I would defend what I had done.

I called Heyden, but his sister said he had gone out. She said she would tell him I had called, but I knew she wouldn't.

As I expected, the next day at school he told me she had never given him the message.

"Which doesn't surprise me," he said. "The drugs she uses and the music she blasts through her head have blown out half her brain."

He paused and squinted a little as he ran his eyes over my face.

"Something wrong?" he asked. "You look down."

I told him what had happened with little Claude and the way Mommy had behaved.

"It's been so long since she was a mother. I guess she's just very nervous," he said. I thought it was ironic that he was the one finding ways to defend her. If he only knew how much she wanted me to stop investing my time and emotions in him and his family problems, he might not be so charitable, I thought.

"I know what SIDS means. I'm nervous, too, but no one seems to notice," I moaned.

Heyden nodded, but I could see he didn't fully appreciate how I felt. Not being noticed in his own home was not as unusual for him as it was for me. At the moment I wondered who was really better off. When you don't have many expectations, even in relation to the people you love and who are supposed to love you, you don't suffer disappointment or sadness as often. I envied him his independence.

I told him why I couldn't be at his house for another rehearsal: my half brothers' birthday.

"They never treat me like a sister, but my father tries to keep our relationship alive," I explained.

"Your life is so complicated," he said, his voice dripping with disappointment. "Maybe we're just fooling ourselves about the music and performing."

"My life is not so complicated, Heyden. We'll rehearse tomorrow night. I promise," I said.

I hadn't seen his skeptical look for some time now, but it was there again, seemingly emerging from the darkest places in his heart.

"We'll see," he said, sounding as uncommitted as he could.

It bothered me all day. My twin half brothers would certainly not appreciate my being at the dinner as much as Heyden would appreciate my being with him, but I couldn't help wanting to be with Daddy. Little Claude's arrival, as wonderful as it really was, left me feeling like a small boat left out at sea, searching desperately for a lifeline. I was bobbing about on wave after wave of conflicting emotions. They twisted and turned like a tornado in my heart. Who could blame me for searching for blue skies?

I wasn't finding them in my mind or outside. The sky became more and more overcast as I returned from school. By the time I arrived at Joya del Mar, there were sprinkles turning into a steady downpour. I put my briefcase over my head and charged for the front door.

I could see that nothing had changed very much at home. The downstairs was deserted, few lights on. Although Mommy was out of bed, she was still locked up in her bedroom, hovering about little Claude, monitoring his every breath and movement. She looked up quickly when I came pounding up the stairway and rushed to her door.

"Easy, easy," she ordered. "You'll frighten the baby and bring in a cold draft."

"I was just anxious to see how he was doing," I said.

She shook her head. "He's doing all right, but he has to be watched carefully."

"You'll make yourself sick jumping at every movement he makes," I said.

She turned to me with a face I couldn't recall ever seeing. From the way she had described her to me, I imagined it was just the sort of face she had often seen turned on her by her stepmother. The anger around her eyes made them dark, and her lips thinned and whitened in the corners.

"An infant is completely helpless, Hannah. He doesn't understand what's happening to him. Of course I have to study every movement he makes. I'm surprised at you for saying something like that."

"I just . . . I was just worried about you," I said.

"Worry about little Claude, not me," she snapped, and then she turned back to the baby. I was about to leave when she spun around and cried, "Hannah!"

"What?"

"I don't understand you."

"What? I told you I was just worried about you and—"

"I don't mean this. I just remembered what Lila came to tell me a few hours ago. Did you go into that bedroom and make a mess of it?" she shrilled.

I simply stood there gaping back at her. For a moment or two I went numb inside. This morning when I had awakened, what I had done had seemed more like a dream.

"How could you do something like that and especially now? What's going on in your head? Well?"

The tears were streaming down my face.

"Well!" she demanded so sharply, I winced.

"I went in there and I kept thinking about Uncle Linden and all the terrible things that have happened to him because of what had happened in that room. You told me about it yourself."

"So you took it out on a bedroom, on blankets and sheets and pillows? What sort of behavior is that for a girl who is nearly seventeen years old, Hannah?"

"I was angry."

"I don't understand you, Hannah. When this situation eases up, I'm going to have a serious talk with you. You are obviously spending too much time with Linden, and it's causing you to have some very serious confusion."

"Right. Just consider me one of your clients," I snapped back at her.

Before she could respond, I pivoted sharply and left her to march quickly to my bedroom. I heard her call after me when I closed my door. For a few moments I just stood there, shaking all over. The sound of a thunderclap made me jump. Seconds later the rain began pounding so hard against my windows, I thought the drops would shatter the glass. The storm seemed very appropriate. It was as if Mother Nature was tuned in to me. The gloom that fell over the house fit my mood.

But the downpour didn't last very long, and by the time Daddy arrived to pick me up, the clouds had begun to drift apart and permit the remaining sunlight to leak through and make the wet leaves, flowers, and grass dazzling. Talk about schizophrenics, I thought; Mother Nature was the biggest one of all.

I hadn't forgotten about the party for my half brothers. I showered, fixed my hair, and then put on one of my prettiest dresses: a mock two-piece with a metallic ribbed tube top and a metallic chiffon A-line skirt.

Dinners at Daddy's were most often formal. The twins were usually in matching sports jackets and slacks. Daddy wore a suit and Danielle wore an elegant dress as well. Guests, who were most often clients of Daddy's, came just as dressed up. There were always two maids serving, even when there were only the five of us.

I heard the front door open below and Daddy ask for me and then for Mommy. Miguel, who was downstairs, greeted him. They were speaking in the hallway at the foot of the stairs when I emerged from my room and began to descend. Both my fathers looked up at me.

"Well, well," Daddy said. "Here comes the heartbreaker. She's going to leave a string of lovesick corpses behind, eh, Miguel?"

"Absolutely," he said. I knew that Mommy had told him everything I had done. I could see it in the restraint in his face. He had the gift Daddy had brought in his hands and turned back to Daddy. "Thanks for this. I'm sorry Willow is unable to greet you, Thatcher."

"Oh, that's all right. I understand. I have a few new mothers as clients for one reason or another. They are a separate species, if you ask me," Daddy replied. "Ready, Miss America?"

"Yes, Daddy." I looked at Miguel. "Tell Mommy I'll stop by before I go to bed," I said.

He just nodded.

"Have a good time," he said when Daddy opened the door. "And give our best wishes to your boys."

"Will do," Daddy said. I knew he wouldn't, and even if he did, neither Adrian nor Cade would care or even acknowledge it, especially if they hadn't been given anything to add to their mountain of possessions.

"It's like a morgue in there," Daddy muttered as we headed for his car. "I thought the birth of a new baby would add festivity and sunshine to Joya del Mar. The place reminds me of what it was like when Linden lived there. Gloom and doom," he muttered and opened the door for me.

"Wasn't Uncle Linden ever happy, Daddy?" I asked when he got in behind the steering wheel.

"Oh, he had his moments, I suppose. But then he realized it and quickly shifted back to a creature of the night," he said, smiling.

We pulled away. I gazed back at the house and thought about Mommy and how angry she was with me. I didn't want this to happen. Everything just seemed to be going in the wrong direction. No matter what I did, I felt like a fly caught in a web of confusing emotions. It wrapped itself around me so my life could be drained of any pleasure.

"Hey," Daddy said, poking me playfully. "Stop looking like you're on your way to the death chamber. This is supposed to be a party. Join me in celebrating another year closer to setting the two of them loose on the world and on their own," he said, smiling.

I smiled back.

Maybe Mommy was right. Maybe Daddy was a selfish person, but I rarely, if ever, saw him unhappy or depressed. His loose approach to everything, always seeing something funny in the events that happened around him, was never more refreshing to me than it was at this moment.

"Here are your birthday cards for them," Daddy said, tapping a small paper bag.

I took them out. They were humorous ones and both the same. Was it always like this for twins: everything simply duplicated? I was glad I had no twin. It seemed difficult to get people to treat you as an individual, to see you a separate being with your own likes and dislikes.

"Here," Daddy said, offering me his pen.

"I feel funny doing this, Daddy."

"What?"

"Pretending I bought the cards and the gifts. What are the gifts?"

"Hand-held PCs. They can use them for addresses, notes, calculating—they can even get on the Web with them. They're the best out there."

"But I didn't really buy them."

"What's the difference who buys them? They still come from you to them and that's all that matters," he assured me.

I signed the cards, but I didn't feel attached to anything or any real emotional involvement. We shared a father, but to me Adrian and Cade were almost alien creatures. Unless Daddy brought me there, they never spoke to me, called me on the phone, or ever thought to visit me. One of my girlfriends at school, Natalie Alexander, knew them because her father was friends with Daddy. She just loved being the first to tell me news about them, underscoring how little contact I had with my own brothers.

"Oh, didn't you *know* that?" she would sing, stinging me with her sweetness.

Daddy's butler greeted us at the door and took the gifts he and I had supposedly bought and brought them into one of the three sitting rooms. The moment she had heard us arrive, Danielle came down the stairs quickly to greet me. She looked so young, far too young to be the mother of the twins, I thought. I knew she liked to read, but I always wondered how she occupied her time. Daddy's house had far more servants than ours. Mommy wanted only Lila and Mrs. Haber, who did most of our cooking. Lila did it on Mrs. Haber's day off.

Daddy had three full-time maids, a cook, and a butler. Danielle had no house duties whatsoever. She had no career as such, unless you considered being Daddy's wife and the twins' mother a career. Mommy categorized it as being more like a prison sentence. A good deal of her time was taken up with what Mommy sarcastically called her beautification. When I once made the mistake of saying Danielle was very pretty, Mommy turned on me with fiery green eyes of jealousy.

"Thatcher wouldn't tolerate it any other way. She has to look young and beautiful all day and all night," she said.

Truthfully, I never saw Danielle caught by surprise, looking untidy. Her hair was always perfect, as was her makeup, and she was always well put together, everything from her earrings down to her shoes well coordinated, just as they were tonight. I was sure all that did take a lot of time and effort. Maybe Danielle believed she was constantly on a stage, but surely it was the life she wanted, I thought.

"Hannah," she called as she descended. "*Bon soir, cherie.*"

"Hi, Danielle."

"Isn't she looking like a femme fatale, Danielle?" Daddy asked.

"*Mais oui.* Every time you come, you are more beautiful than you were the time before," she said.

She said it with such sincerity, she brought a blush to my face. Then she kissed me on both cheeks, French style, and took my hand.

"Come and see how we have decorated the room for the twins' birthday dinner," she said.

"Go on," Daddy said. "I'll be right along."

He headed for his home office, and I followed Danielle, who chatted with such happy energy, I couldn't help but leave my doldrums at the door. Her bright, melodic, and youthful voice was truly a welcome relief. Maybe being Daddy's wife wasn't as miserable a situation as Mommy made it out to be.

We stopped in the doorway of the dining room, and I looked at the crepe paper decorations, the balloon displays, and gold and silver cutouts. It was obvious they had hired a professional party decorator.

"Wait until you see the cake. It's three feet high with two dolls made by an artist who duplicated their faces."

All this just for a family dinner, I thought. *What will they do for a big party?*

"There's just the five of us?"

"*Mais oui*. Tomorrow, they will have their friends over for a barbeque. Thatcher wanted so much to have a quiet, private dinner first. *Naturellement*, your brothers complained. They hate getting dressed up in their tuxedos. Your father, he is battling with them every day not to look like homeless people," she said, laughing. "Boys. We should have had two girls, eh? Then you would see what spoiled is."

"Why don't you try to have a little girl?" I asked.

She laughed. "Thatcher says he would drive himself into the ocean if he had to bring another child into this mad, crazy world." She sighed. "But I wish he would want it."

She took my hands and stepped back to look at me closer.

"But I will borrow you to be my daughter, yes? I love your dress," she said. "I have a pair of earrings you will adore. They are perfect for this. Come. We have time to indulge ourselves," she added, pulling me back to the stairway.

We went up to her and Daddy's bedroom, which was nearly twice the size of Mommy and Miguel's. It had an entirely separate living room area and a large, long vanity table and mirror for Danielle. Her closet was as big as my bedroom. It had a wall mirror, a dressing table, and a television set so she could watch her soap operas or whatever while she considered what she would wear.

Her jewelry chest had more than a dozen drawers. She rifled through the third drawer until she found the earrings she wanted me to wear. I couldn't imagine how she remembered what she did and didn't have. There was so much.

"So," she said and gave them to me.

I put them on, and then she turned me to the mirror.

"*Voilà!* I was right, no?"

"They're very pretty, Danielle."

"Good. They are yours," she said.

"But—"

"No *but*. They look wonderful on you. I insist," she said, smiling. "Do you know in some places, when it's your birthday, you give your guests gifts. The best gift is one that fits you, and these beautiful earrings fit you perfectly. They belong on you, Hannah," she insisted, turning me so I would look at myself again.

It felt so good to have someone focus fully on me and see me for a change. Maybe I should move in with Daddy until little Claude was a year or so old, I thought. The idea actually didn't seem so outrageous.

"So," Danielle said as we headed back to the dining room. "Tell me news. You have a beau, maybe?"

"Maybe," I said, smiling, and she laughed conspiratorially, as if she were my friend and not my stepmother.

Daddy was already in the dining room waiting.

"Where were you two?" he asked.

"I had to give Hannah these earrings," Danielle explained.

Daddy nodded and looked at his watch.

"Where are those idiots? They can't even be on time for their own birthday dinner."

He started to rise when we heard a door slam and laughter in the hallway, but it was coming from the rear of the house and not the stairway. Daddy's eyebrows lifted with curiosity, and we all turned to the doorway.

Adrian and Cade appeared. They were both in bathing suits, towels around their necks, both their sleek, muscular bodies gleaming. Why did the two of them have to be so perfect? I moaned to myself.

"What the hell . . . why aren't you guys dressed?" Daddy demanded.

"We just saw what time it was," Cade said nonchalantly. I always though he had a shrewder, more conniving glint in his blue eyes. Usually, his gaze lingered on someone a bit longer than Adrian's. I could almost feel him plotting some prank or mean thing.

"This is the way you treat your birthday dinner!" Daddy shouted. Adrian glanced at me and looked down, at least pretending some shame. Cade, on the other hand, held his defiant gaze.

"We'll be ready in a few minutes, Dad. Don't worry," he said confidently.

"You're supposed to be here now!" Daddy shot back. "You have a guest."

"It's only Hannah!" Cade cried.

Daddy took a threatening step toward them.

"All right. We'll be right down," Cade assured him and nudged Adrian.

They started away. As Daddy turned back to the table, his face red with fury, we heard Cade's laugh and then a challenge to beat Adrian up the stairs.

Danielle looked at Daddy.

"Sometimes," he muttered, "I think God punishes us through our children."

He collapsed in his chair and stared down the long table, glittering with beautiful dinnerware and crystal glasses.

"Not Hannah," Danielle said, smiling and trying to resurrect the happy moments we had just shared.

Daddy raised his eyes toward me and shook his head.

"No," he said, "not Hannah."

I know that should have made me feel very good about myself, but it didn't. Instead, it sent a small flutter of panic through my body. He had given me the compliment with such definiteness, such assuredness, it seemed as if he had just nudged the lid on another secret, buried and shut away, patiently waiting to be reborn.

From Joya del Mar to here, the darkness followed me, slithered like a snake, and coiled up in the shadows, listening with gleaming eager eyes for its opportunity to strike.

7

A Not-So-Happy Birthday

"**Y**ou see how much easier men have it than women when it comes to preparing for an evening," Danielle said to me when Adrian and Cade returned in less than fifteen minutes, each with his light brown hair brushed neatly and each in his tuxedo. As mannequins modeling the newest in black-tie styles, they were flawless, both already close to his mature height at five feet eleven inches tall. Their competitiveness had them bodybuilding when they were only twelve, and I couldn't remember a visit when one of the twins wasn't demonstrating how much bigger his biceps were than the other's.

Daddy grunted, reluctantly complimenting them on how good they looked and how fast they had dressed.

Adrian and Cade both looked pleased with themselves and took their seats like perfect little gentlemen, flipping their napkins and placing them in their laps before they assumed proper posture. My daddy's mother, Bunny, had paid for them to have private charm school lessons when they were barely five years old. To me they were the perfect example of why proper etiquette had nothing to do with the quality of a person. The moment the adults turned their backs to them, one or the other did something disgusting.

"Well, it couldn't have taken Hannah very long to dress," Cade said after a moment. "Look what she's wearing, a metallic sock."

"What a terrible thing to say, Cade. She is wearing a lovely dress, and I'm sure it took her much longer to fix her hair than it took both of you to fix yours," Daddy said, defending me.

"Is hers fixed? It looks like it's still broken to me," Adrian teased, and they both laughed.

"A year older and a year less mature," Daddy said, shaking his head.

"And happy birthday to you both," I told them dryly.

"Thank you, Hannah Banana," Cade said.

Adrian laughed and added a thank-you.

The maids began to serve our dinner. About halfway through the meal, Cade, who had been teasing his brother about a girl he claimed Adrian liked, paused and turned to me to say, "I hear you have quite a boyfriend, Hannah."

Daddy paused in cutting his London broil and looked up with interest.

"Oh?" he said. "Hannah has a boyfriend?"

"Yeah, he's a guitar player and a songwriter, right?" Cade pursued.

"Yes," I said, a little surprised at how much he knew.

"Is this who you went out with the other night?" Daddy asked, smiling.

"Yes," I admitted.

"Well, that's okay. Someday these two might find girls who can stand being with them," Daddy joked.

"We can find them, Dad. We're just very particular about whom we date, a lot more particular than Hannah apparently."

"What's that supposed to mean?" Daddy asked sharply.

"Her boyfriend's half black, right, Hannah?" Cade asked, smiling.

Daddy turned to me. "What?"

"His mother happens to be Haitian," I said.

"Black is black," Cade insisted.

"Haitian?" Daddy asked. "A Haitian boy is going to your magnet school?"

"Yes, Daddy. He's a talented musician. He plays guitar and he writes songs. His father is a jazz musician who is presently working in New Orleans," I said. One thing I didn't want to do was describe his broken family situation.

"We heard he goes to school on some rusty old moped. What a sight that must be," Cade said.

"He wasn't born with a silver spoon in his mouth like some people," I snapped. "It's all he can afford."

"What's you mother have to say about all this?" Daddy asked as he patted his lips with his napkin.

"She hasn't said much about anything that concerns me these days," I replied, almost under my breath.

Cade's smile spread from ear to ear. It suddenly

came to me where he had gone to drink at the pool of gossip.

"If you're hearing things from Natalie Alexander, Cade, you can be sure they are full of exaggerations and lies and whatever," I said with fire in my eyes. "She's jealous of everyone because she is such a loser."

He shrugged and looked at Daddy. "You're always saying where there's smoke, there's fire, Dad, right?"

Daddy looked at him and then at me.

"How long have you been seeing this person, Hannah?" he asked.

"Not long at all. We're rehearsing an act," I added.

"An act? That's a new name for it," Cade said, and Adrian laughed hard.

"Cade," Danielle snapped. "That is rude, and especially in front of your mother."

"I'm not the one in rehearsal," he said, without a sign of remorse. I couldn't recall when I had ever seen either of them intimidated or even respectful of Danielle.

"What I meant is we're singing together," I told Daddy and Danielle.

"I bet," Cade said.

I threw him the most furious look I could, but he only widened his smile.

"You want to be careful about your friends and other people with whom you associate, Hannah," Daddy warned. "Unfortunately, too often we get labeled by the company we keep."

I looked down. "Heyden Reynolds is a very nice young man, Daddy. I am not ashamed of being with him and"—I continued shooting darts of rage at my twin brothers—"he has never done anything at our school for which he had to be reprimanded. His father didn't have to plead with the principal to keep his son from being expelled. Unlike some people at this table," I added. Both of my half brothers had been suspended twice from their private school, and one time Daddy had to donate money toward the new gymnasium to keep them in attendance.

"Yes. Well, that's fine," Daddy said. "I think you are a sensible and responsible young lady, and I have full confidence in you doing the right things. Unfortunately, I can't say that yet for our guests of honor," he added, looking hard at Cade and Adrian.

They both took on the look of the wounded. Then Cade raised his eyes to me, his face full of bloodred anger because he and his brother were getting the reprimand and not me. Adrian was a mirror image. It did amaze me how they not only shared looks and physical characteristics, but very often feelings and emotions as well.

"So tell us about the new baby," Danielle said, breaking the heavy silence that followed.

"He's very small, so he has to be watched carefully. They are afraid of SIDS," I added.

"Who's Sid?" Cade quipped.

"It happens to be a very serious, often fatal illness that affects babies," I told him.

"What happens to them?" Adrian asked.

"They stop breathing and die."

"So they commit suicide," Cade said.

"They hardly know what's happening to them, Cade."

"How can you not know you've stopped breathing?" Adrian asked.

"Something happens to their nervous systems," Daddy said. "If you were better students, you wouldn't say so many stupid things." He turned to me with concern. "Miguel didn't mention it to me when I met him earlier. Is that why Willow is shut up in her room like that?"

"Yes."

"How sad," Danielle said.

"Very hard, very hard," Daddy said.

"Is it because his father is Cuban?" Cade asked, unintimidated by Daddy's reprimand.

"No," I said sharply and quickly. "SIDS affects people of all races, religions, and even income levels. It occurs during sleep and strikes without warning. And you can't tell from looking at the baby, either. Seemingly healthy children can suffer from it."

"Still sounds like suicide to me," he muttered.

The maids began to clear off our dishes.

"I knew someone in France whose baby suffered SIDS. It's hard on everyone in the home," Danielle said. "Always tension in the air. Everyone nervous, worried." She thought a moment and turned to me. "Why don't you say here for the weekend?"

"Stay over?"

"You can be here for the barbeque. Your mother won't have to worry about you while she is worrying about the new baby."

"Oh, no, I don't think—"

"She wants to 'rehearse' tomorrow, I bet," Cade said. "Right, Hannah Banana?"

"Stop calling me that, Cade." I blushed because I knew why they were always calling me that. He had once done a very nasty thing with a banana in front of me and from that day on, tagged on the nickname. Daddy was under the misapprehension it was a term of brotherly endearment. I wasn't about to explain why that wasn't so.

"Rehearsal," he muttered.

"As a matter of fact we do have a session planned for tomorrow."

Cade broke into laughter.

"A session?"

Adrian smiled at me.

"You're more than welcome to stay, Hannah," Daddy said. "I'm sure the boys would like it, too," he added, sounding more like he was threatening them.

"Sure. Maybe she could sing for us, too," Cade said.

"I can't stay, but thank you, Daddy, Danielle."

"All right," Daddy said, folding his napkin. "Let's adjourn to the den where we'll have some birthday cake and watch these two juvenile delinquents unwrap some undeserved gifts."

"Did Grandmother Eaton send us something yet?"

"Of course," Daddy told them.

I had never so much as received a card, much less an actual gift from our grandmother.

"She usually spends a bundle. Last year they bought us the water jets," Adrian told me, even though he knew I knew. They so enjoyed rubbing in my grandparents' rejection of my very existence.

We rose and walked down the long hallway to the sitting room Daddy referred to as a den. It had more informal furnishings, a long circular leather sofa with recliner chairs on both ends which faced an in-the-wall wide-screen television set. There was a long, rectangular glass table in front of the sofa and piled on it at the moment were the twin's gifts.

"These are all from the family," Daddy explained. "My parents happen to be in Cap Ferrat on the French Riviera at the moment. Your aunt Whitney and uncle Hans are in Switzerland," he told the twins, but neither seemed very interested. They were eyeing the impressive pile like ravenous wolves. "Your cousins have all sent you gifts, boys. I want you to be sure to send out thank-you cards this year, hear me?"

"Just have Mrs. Gouter do it, Dad. She does it better than we can," Adrian said.

"That's not the point. It should come from you."

"It will. We'll sign a dozen and have them available ahead of time like you do, Dad," Cade followed.

Daddy blanched, but his lips whitened. He looked at Danielle, who quickly dropped her eyes.

"They're impossible," he told me.

"Should we start?" Adrian asked.

"Start," Daddy said and turned to one of the maids hovering at the door. "You can bring in their cake, Claire," he told her.

The boys lunged at their gifts, tearing away the wrapping and the cards without even taking care to see who gave them what. Danielle had to check each card for them. Their gifts included very expensive imported silk shirts, Rolex watches, digital cameras, the hand-held PCs Daddy bought in my name, binoculars, and what they considered their pièce de résistance: the keys to their own speedboat. It was going to be delivered tomorrow. There was a picture of it along with the keys.

"She got it for us! She got it!" Cade cried. "I told Bunny what we dreamed of having, and she got it."

"Mon Dieu, Thatcher. Should they have such a gift?" Danielle asked.

"No," Daddy said. They both looked up at him with disappointment on the verge of rage. "But it doesn't surprise me that my mother would do such a thing. She loves providing dreams for people. You're not to take the boat out without first having me give you a full course of instruction," Daddy warned them.

"Sure," Cade said.

"I mean it, Cade. If I hear that you have, I'll have it towed off and sold, understand?"

"We understand, we understand. Don't we, Adrian?"

Adrian looked at him and then turned to Daddy and nodded, but I had no doubt in my mind that they would disobey him first chance they had.

Just then the maid brought in the cake, moving slowly so the candles would stay lit.

"Oh, my, my!" Danielle cried, clapping her hands.

It was an impressive cake, and the two dolls did resemble my half brothers, both with a small arrogant smirk on their lips, I thought.

The maid placed the cake on the cleared table, and the twins leaned over and started to blow out the candles, racing with each other to see who would blow out the most. When they were finished, the other servants gathered obediently at the door, and we sang happy birthday to Cade and Adrian. They both stood back, glowing as if they were finally getting what was always rightfully theirs. Two more ungrateful, spoiled people did not exist anywhere, I thought.

"Happy birthday," I told Cade and kissed him on the cheek. I did the same for Adrian.

As Claire began cutting the cake and putting the pieces on plates for us, Daddy's butler stepped in to tell him he had a phone call. He left and the four of us sat eating cake and reviewing their presents.

"I've got to run out," Daddy announced when he returned. "Something has come up."

"Now?" Danielle asked, "but—"

"I'll be back in an hour. I promise," he said. "You two behave yourselves," he warned the twins.

Danielle rose. "I can't imagine what it could be," she said sadly, and then she followed him to the front door.

"So," Cade said turning to Adrian, "not a bad haul this year, huh, brother of mine?"

"Not bad," Adrian agreed, turning his new Rolex watch over and over.

"Too bad your mother dumped dear old dad for Fidel Castro," Cade said to me. "Or you would be enjoying birthdays like this with piles of expensive gifts."

"There are a lot more important things in life than accumulating more possessions, Cade."

"Like what? Making music?" he said with ridicule.

"Yes, I think so." He started to laugh again. "At least I am doing something that pleases other people, too, and feeling good about myself. I don't have to have something new every week to keep me from being bored to death, either."

"Really," he replied, lowering the corners of his lips.

"Yes, Cade, really. The two of you think you have loads of friends when all you have is a bunch of people who use you and wouldn't care about you if you didn't have all this to offer. They don't like either of you for who or what you are, only for what you can give them, and that to me is not having friends at all."

Both of my half brothers stared at me, my words seeping in to their reluctant brains.

"I bet you think you're better off with your Cuban stepfather," Cade finally retorted.

"He has never been nasty to me or not cared about my feelings, and his family have always welcomed me with open arms."

"Of course they would. They're honored you give them the time of day," Adrian said. "You have the Eaton name."

"That's not true. It's just the opposite. I wouldn't trade them for a pile of gifts five times as high as this," I said, pointing to their small mountain of gift wrap and boxes.

"Sure."

"Yes, sure," I said.

They both glared at me.

"Having fun?" Danielle said, returning.

"Loads," Cade said dryly.

"Your father has a client who was just arrested for drunken driving. He had to go down to the police station. He'll be back very soon," she explained. "I'll be right back," she added. "I have to see about some things I have scheduled for tomorrow."

I was sorry to see her go, too. I always felt uncomfortable when I was alone with my half brothers too long. It wasn't getting any better as they grew older, either.

"Our father and his clients," Adrian said, shaking his head.

"His clients are very important to him, and they should be to you," I said. "How do you think he provides all this for you?"

"If he died tomorrow, we wouldn't be a penny poorer, Hannah," Cade said. "Our grandparents have created a trust fund for us. We'll be millionaires for the rest of our lives. We're millionaires now!"

"Good for you."

"If you were really part of this family, you would have had a trust created for you as well. Bunny and Asher are very, very wealthy people."

"Whether they like it or not, they are my grandparents, too. It's not my fault I'm not recognized as part of this family," I said and folded my arms under my breasts.

Some birthday party celebration this was turning out to be, I thought. I should have had the courage to refuse to come and spend the time with Heyden, as we had planned.

"No, it's not your fault; it's your mother's," Cade shot back.

"Look, I told you—"

"You don't know the real story," he said before I could finish. "We might be younger than you are, but we know more than you do about yourself, right, Adrian?"

He looked up from his watch and then looked at me. There was something in his face that frightened me. He looked afraid himself, I realized. He started to shake his head.

"Stop pretending. You and I agreed that we would tell her the truth one day, didn't we? Well? What better day is there than our birthday?"

Adrian just stared at Cade.

"It's time we did, Adrian. She's no longer a baby. She's rehearsing with a Haitian."

"Stop it!" I stared at them. "What truth?" I asked, smirking. "I don't think you would recognize the truth if it had the word *truth* tattooed all over it."

"Really? Well, try this tattoo on for size, Hannah Banana. Our father is not really your father. We're not related at all," he said.

I started to laugh at him, but Adrian's expression stopped me. He looked even more terrified than he had just a moment ago.

"It would probably be my best birthday gift to know I wasn't related to you, Cade."

"Well, it's true. You're not. So happy birthday, Hannah Banana Montgomery."

"My name is Hanna Eaton."

"No, it's Hannah Montgomery. Tell her, Adrian."

Adrian shook his head. "We're not supposed to. We agreed. Daddy would find out what we did."

"What did you do, Adrian?"

He turned sharply to me and shook his head. "Nothing." He looked back at Cade. "Shut up, Cade. I'm warning you."

"Don't tell me to shut up, stupid. She's sitting there like she's better than us, isn't she? You heard her. We have no real friends. We are selfish bastards. She's better off with her Cuban family. She's the one who said the Eaton name isn't all that important, didn't she?"

"I didn't say that."

"Yes, you did. Didn't she, Adrian?"

"Yes," he said, looking at me. "She did."

Cade turned back to me, full of satisfaction. "Adrian's afraid to tell you what we know because he doesn't want our father to know we listened in on a conversation he had with our mother one night when he had too much to drink. They talked about you," he said, pointing his forefinger like a pistol in my face.

"I don't believe you."

"So don't believe me," he said with a shrug. "Whether you do or not isn't going to change anything."

"Cade," Adrian warned.

"Shut up, I said. She's going to hear it. She's going to have that arrogant smile wiped off her face." He turned back to me. "My father told my mother that your idiot uncle made your mother pregnant and not him."

"That's a disgusting and terrible thing to say!" I shouted and practically leaped at him.

"It was a disgusting thing to *do*," Cade replied casually. "My father said he was away when your mother got pregnant, and he always knew you weren't his child. That's why he arranged to have the marriage ended."

"He did not arrange anything!" I looked at Adrian, who gazed at me with pity on his face. "Why would he refuse to permit my name to be changed, then?"

"It was part of a deal they made. He did it for you. He thought it was terrible enough for you to be left behind in that asylum. Look at us," he insisted. "We don't really look much like you, do we? Did you ever look good at your crazy uncle? I'm sure you'll find the resemblances if you do."

"Dad's going to be real mad at you, Cade," Adrian said.

"Hannah Banana isn't going to tell. Are you, Hannah Banana? You're just going to keep your mouth shut and do what we tell you to do or we will tell everyone the truth about you."

"Shut up," I said.

"How about if we call up your black boyfriend and tell him your mother and her half brother are your real parents? Think he'll still want to make music with you? Even *he* might be disgusted."

I stared at him with so much fury, I thought I was burning up inside, but he remained cool and collected.

"What if we tell Natalie Alexander, Adrian? Think she can keep a secret?"

"You are a rotten, spoiled—"

"Why don't we give her a call tonight, Adrian?" Cade said, staring into my face.

I stood up. "I won't listen to any of this!" I cried and charged out of the room, down the hallway to the stairs. I wanted to find Danielle and ask her to arrange to get me home.

"Hey, where are you going?" Cade called after me. "We're having so much fun on our birthday, Hannah Banana."

"Shut up," I threw back at him and hurried up the stairway, searching for Danielle. I wanted her to take me home. I could hear both Cade and Adrian laughing and following me with that stupid chanting: Hannah Banana, Hannah Banana.

It was a long corridor, and it wrapped around to the right. I headed for the bedroom Danielle shared with my father, but when I got there and called for her, I didn't hear her. This house was so big, she could have been downstairs in another wing, I thought. I went into the living room area of their suite and sat dejectedly on a sofa. When I heard the bedroom door close, I looked up.

My twin half brothers stood there, looking down at me.

"Leave me alone!" I cried, tears streaming down my cheeks now. "You're both mean and horrible, and you can't stop being that way, even on your birthday!"

"No, we're not. We've actually been very considerate of you, Hannah. We've known the truth all this time, but we've never told anyone, have we, Adrian?"

Adrian shook his head.

"Never, and we could have many times."

"And we're willing to keep it a secret now, too, right, Adrian?"

Adrian nodded.

Cade stepped closer.

"If you're cooperative, that is," he said. "If you give us a nice birthday present, not that phony one our father probably had purchased for you anyway," he said.

I looked up at them suspiciously. There was a note in their voices that I hadn't heard before, but it was dark enough to scare me.

"What are you talking about now? What do you want?"

Cade's smile was thinner and sharper than ever. His eyes brightened as he drew closer.

"Take off your clothes for us," he demanded.

I thought my heart had turned into a tight fist and closed on my lungs. For a moment I couldn't breathe.

"What?"

"Go on. Show us what you have. You do it for your Haitian songwriter boyfriend, don't you? And he hasn't got anywhere near as much to offer. Take off your clothes, and we'll keep our mouths shut."

"You're both more disgusting than I could have imagined," I said.

"Don't make me angry," Cade threatened, "or we'll withdraw our offer."

"I don't care what you do."

"Oh, you don't? Do all your friends know about your crazy uncle? They don't, do they? From what Natalie was telling us, you're not Miss Popularity right now anyway. This would really do you in, don't you think? Tell her, Adrian," he commanded, gesturing for Adrian to step forward. "Tell her we're serious about this."

"We're serious," Adrian said. "And you know we can do what we say."

"Get away from me," I warned them.

"How is this information going to sit with your mother at the moment, huh? Her and her SIDS baby. What is she going to tell people when they call to tell her what they have heard?"

I shook my head slowly.

"You know she'll hear about it, too, don't you? You know how everyone spreads stories in this town. You won't be Miss Goody Two-shoes anymore, and your mother . . . do you think people will want to go to her for mental and emotional help after they hear what a sinner she was?"

"You bastard, Cade."

"Just take off your clothes. Give us a real birthday

present and show us your birthday suit," he said, smiling. "It's as simple as that. You do it every day, undress. So do it here. Go on. Do it!" he ordered.

Adrian drew closer, his eyes full of interest, wondering if I would do as Cade ordered.

"I'm going to tell Daddy," I said.

"You do that and we'll really get the story out." He smiled. "Maybe we and our older friends will go out to see your uncle and ask him to confess. We'll tell him he should do it for you."

"You wouldn't dare do such a thing."

"Why not? It's not a crime or anything to visit him, is it? We're just trying to help our sister, right, Adrian?"

"Right. We're just trying to be good brothers."

"I hate you both," I said.

"I'll tell you what," Cade said, stepping only a few feet from me now. "You can keep your eyes closed. I'll take off your clothes for you, and then we'll leave and you can open your eyes and it will be as if nothing happened. How's that?"

"You should do it, Hannah Banana," Adrian said. "It's a good deal."

"Is this the sort of sick games you play with your so-called friends?" I asked them.

Cade smiled. "You'd be surprised at what some girls will do to get invited here, right, Adrian?

"C'mon," Cade said, closing in and reaching toward my dress. "Just close your eyes. Go on. It's easy and then it's all over. We swear we won't say a thing about your uncle and your mother. Just think of it as a birthday present from us before your birthday. C'mon," he urged.

His fingers were on the zipper of my top.

"Stop," I said but not as firmly as I wanted. Everything they had threatened really frightened me, especially the part about Mommy. My mind was reeling. I couldn't think. He took it as encouragement.

"Close your eyes. In a few minutes we'll be gone. C'mon. What's the big deal?"

I felt the zipper being lowered and I started to pull back.

"Hannah, be cooperative. I'm warning you. Our patience is running out."

"Stop," I said, tears emerging.

"It doesn't hurt and it gets you off the hook," Adrian said, stepping to my left. He put his hand on the strap and edged it over my shoulder as Cade continued to lower the zipper.

"Close your eyes," Cade whispered. "It'll be over before you know it."

He lowered the other strap, and then they both seized the bodice and pulled it off my breasts. Just as they did, the bedroom door opened and Danielle appeared. Her eyes nearly bulged out of her head.

I clutched at my dress to cover myself.

"What are you doing?" she cried.

"She wanted us to!" Cade immediately shouted. Lies were always stored at the tips of their tongues and on alert for instant use.

"She brought us up here and said she would give us a real birthday present," Adrian added.

"No," I said, shaking my head. "They made me. They said terrible things. They—"

"Why would we bring her to your bedroom,

Mother?" Cade asked, his arms out. "We'd bring her to our own bedrooms. She led us up here. We had no idea what she meant by a real birthday present."

"Hannah, this is not so?" Danielle asked.

"No, it's not." I backed away from them. "They're lying."

"She's into this stuff now, Mother," Adrian said. "She was telling us about her and this Haitian kid, how they rehearse in the nude."

I shook my head. "That's not true. They're lying," I said, my chest full of hot air, I couldn't breathe. Danielle looked like she was believing them. "They're lying, Danielle. Honest!" I cried.

"But why are you in this room?" she asked.

Cade's face filled with glee. "She's the one who wanted to come here, Mother. You know we never come into this room. Why would we have done it now?"

Danielle turned and looked at me. I shook my head so hard, I thought my eyes would fall out, and then I charged past her, out of the room, rushing down the stairs.

"Hannah!" Danielle called behind me.

I didn't turn back. The twins were too good at lying and getting people to believe anything they said. What good would it do for me to stay there and deny and deny? I thought.

Claire froze in the entry hall when she saw me clinging to the top of my dress and rushing toward the door. The look on her face put even more panic into my feet. In seconds I was out the door and down the portico steps, running over the driveway toward the entrance of the property. Only when I reached the gate did I pause and fix my dress. Then, as calmly as I could, I pushed the button that opened the gate and stepped out on the highway.

Moments later I was heading back toward Joya del Mar, the traffic whizzing by, my own tears flying off my cheeks, the sea breeze catching my hair and flailing it about my face. I was sure I looked like a madwoman, but I didn't stop walking, even when my legs and feet began to ache.

I must have walked and run nearly two miles before I finally stopped to catch my breath. My skin was clammy with sweat, my heart pounding so fiercely, I thought it would soon shatter like a piece of fine china. Traffic continued to whiz by. If anyone saw me standing there, he or she did not think to stop to see what was wrong.

I had left my purse behind at Daddy's house. My cell phone was in it as well as my wallet and my credit card. What would I do? I walked on slowly until I came to the gate of another estate and pushed the button on the call box. After a very long pause, a deep male voice said, "Yes?"

"My name is Hannah Eaton," I said. "I've broken down in my automobile, and I don't have my cell phone with me. Could I come in and make a call, please."

"No," the voice replied. "However, if you will give me the number you wish to call and whom you wish to speak with and tell of your plight, I will do so for you. Well?" he demanded instantly.

I couldn't think. Should I call Miguel? Would this upset Mommy and get everyone angry at me? I made a quick decision and gave him Heyden's phone number.

"Please ask for Heyden and tell him I need him to come to this address to get me," I asked.

"Very well. Remain at the gate," he said.

It was so strange: a deep, unemotional, unsympathetic-sounding voice coming from this metal box embedded on a stone pillar by the tall, black cast-iron gate. It was as if I had called into hell itself.

"Please let me know if he's coming," I pleaded, but there was no response.

More frightened than tired and angry now, I crunched up under the lights from the entrance and tried to calm myself. It seemed like hours had gone by and no one stopped. Where was Daddy? Hadn't he returned when he said he would and didn't he know I had run out of his house onto the highway? Why wasn't he looking for me?

Despite a clear night of dazzling stars, the sky felt so close and oppressive to me. Every shadow along the highway, every sound other than an automobile that I heard was a threatening sound. It wouldn't surprise me to discover my twin half brothers lurking in the dark, making noises to see how terrified they could make me.

Oh, why did I run away? Why didn't I remain there and do battle with them and prove to Danielle that they were vicious liars? I knew she wouldn't want to believe that, but it would still have been better for me to stand my ground, I thought. Now, I probably looked guilty to her, and Daddy might believe it as well. He would have only their side of the story to hear and Danielle's shock at seeing me in her bedroom, bared to the waist.

I couldn't stop crying. My shoulders heaved and fell, and my chest and stomach ached. Did the man inside this impregnable estate really call Heyden? Had Elisha answered and deliberately pretended he wasn't home and not tell him about me? She was certainly capable of doing that. And what if he did reach Heyden? I realized. He had no automobile. What good would it have done? Would he come get me on his moped? Why didn't I ask the man to call Miguel?

I thought about getting up and walking on until I came to someplace where I would find a phone, but when I stood up, my legs were shaky. Instead, I returned to the call box and pressed it again. Again, it took an exceptionally long time for any response. Finally the same voice full of obvious annoyance said, "Yes?"

"It's me again. I was wondering if you had made the call for me."

"I did and the individual you requested said he would find a way."

"You could have told me," I said.

"This is *not* a public phone or any sort of rescue service. Do *not* use the call box again," he ordered and went silent.

"I won't!" I shouted into the box microphone. "And you can go to hell if you're not already there."

My voice echoed away and died.

I took a deep breath and gazed down the highway. After another half dozen or so cars went by, I saw one pair of headlights closing in, the vehicle slowing down. It was a taxicab and it pulled up to the gate. Heyden was in the backseat looking out the window for me. The moment the cab stopped, he jumped out.

"Hannah, what's going on?"

I rushed into his arms and just cried. He guided me back to the taxicab, and we both got inside.

"Where to now?" the driver asked.

I couldn't see his face, but he sounded amused.

"Hannah?" Heyden asked. "You want to go home?"

"No," I said. "Take me back to your house, Heyden," I said.

He gave the driver the same address at which he had been picked up, and the driver turned around and started back.

"I don't have any money," I whispered, "or my credit card. I left it at my father's house."

"Why? What are you doing out here?"

I just shook my head. I didn't want to tell him the story. I was afraid the driver would hear everything, and I was still very embarrassed.

"Don't worry," Heyden said. "I have enough."

"I'll pay you back tomorrow," I promised.

"With interest?" he asked, smiling.

I started to cry again, but more softly, with my cheek pressed to his chest and his arm around me, holding me snugly and safely.

After we arrived at his home and he paid the driver, we went inside. It was so quiet, I asked where his sister was.

"She's at a friend's house, probably doing some drugs or drinking and who knows what else? My mother let her go even though I told her what Elisha has been into these days. It's just easier for her to say yes. I warned her I wasn't taking care of Elisha or going anywhere to rescue her if she gets into trouble," he said.

"Like you just did for me?"

"There's no comparison," he said.

I went to the bathroom, and after washing my face with cold water, I joined him in his room. He was sitting on the bed, tinkering with some chords on his guitar. He looked up.

"Well?" he asked. "I got stuck with the taxi fare. Aren't you ever going to tell me what's going on?"

I nodded and sat beside him. He lay the guitar down and turned to listen. After I described it all, he shook his head with rage.

"I wish I had been there," he said.

"You can't threaten them. It does no good. They're so arrogant, they know they'll always get out of whatever trouble they cause."

"I wouldn't just threaten them," Heyden said.

"I'm not going back there," I vowed. "I'm sick of pretending they are my family. They don't want me to be part of their family, and I don't want to be. Not anymore."

"You're better off," he said. Then he smiled. "So they made fun of the music we create together, huh? They're just jealous."

"I don't care what they think or say, Heyden. They can't ruin what we do, but I am worried for my uncle."

"That was surely just an idle threat. They would never go there. That sort of thing takes too much effort."

"I want to be sure he's all right, though. I'll go there tomorrow," I said.

"You look so tired. Shouldn't I call your stepfather and ask him to come to get you?"

"Not yet," I said. "Anyway, I'll call a cab and they'll

pay him when I get there. Maybe my mother will be asleep by then, and it will be easier."

"Whatever you say," Heyden told me.

I smiled and lay back. It felt good to sink my head into one of his pillows. He lay beside me, slipping his arm under and around my shoulders. I turned into him and closed my eyes. In moments I was asleep.

A clamor of voices and bright lights snapped open my eyes. I was alone in the bed and for a moment, I couldn't recall where I was or how I had gotten here. The confusion evaporated just before Heyden's door was opened. Miguel stood there, his shoulders hoisted, his mouth twisted in anger like I had never seen.

"What are you doing?" he shouted. I saw Heyden a few feet behind him.

"I—"

"Your mother is beside herself with worry. Thatcher called hours ago and told us you had run out of his house. We called the Palm Beach police and they've been scouring the highways and streets searching for you. Couldn't you have had the decency to call home, Hannah? How could you do such a thing to us? And now, with all that's happening? How could you do this!"

"I fell asleep. I didn't mean—"

"Just get up and get into the car, Hannah. *Now*!" Miguel screamed at me.

I hurried out of the bedroom, pausing by Heyden. He shook his head.

"I'm sorry," he said. "I didn't want to wake you. I knew you were exhausted and—"

"Hannah, get out," Miguel ordered. He turned to Heyden. "As for you, young man, I wouldn't advise you to call our home or encourage Hannah to come to your house, understand?"

"It's not his fault, Miguel!" I cried.

He burned his eyes into me and turned me around forcefully, his fingers like pincers in my shoulders.

"Out," he said, marching behind me, poking me to get me to move faster. His storm of rage was so fierce, I was afraid to defy him.

As we stepped out of the house, I tried to look back at Heyden, but Miguel shut the door behind us quickly.

"Get in the car!" he screamed. "Now!"

Moments later we were on our way back to Joya del Mar, Miguel's fury steaming the air between us. How could this night have turned so terrible? I never hated my twin half brothers more, but I never hated my life as much, either.

8

Leaving Home

For the rest of my life, no matter what I do, no matter how much or how hard I pursue any career or occupy my mind and my body with activities, I shall never forget nor diminish the memory of the events that followed when Miguel and I returned to Joya del Mar. Every little detail: where people were standing, what lights were on, what was said, and how each and every person there reacted to what was said, all of it is embedded in the blackest wall of my mind, each image rough and bright like some uncut but jagged diamond sparkling gleefully. Guilt would be forever an invisible necklace of thorns around my neck, tightening whenever the flood of these memories came rushing over me.

On the ride home from Heyden's house, Miguel calmed down enough to listen to my story. I told him the terrible things the twins had said and done.

"Why didn't you just call me then?" he asked. "I would have come to get you."

"I didn't want to add any more trouble and worry to what Mommy already had."

"So you ran off and then went to this boy's home without calling us?" He shook his head. "I just don't understand you, Hannah. I thought you were a great deal brighter than that. You've never disappointed us like this. I am afraid we have overestimated not only your intelligence, but your common sense. What were you thinking?"

"I thought I would rest up and come home and no one would be the less for it, Miguel. I didn't mean to fall asleep. I just didn't realize how exhausted I was mentally and physically. I didn't mean to cause all these problems," I moaned and began to cry again.

"All right, all right. There's no need to cry about it now, Hannah. I want to end this turmoil tonight as quickly as we can and let everyone get some very needed rest."

I ground the tears out of my eyes and took a deep breath.

"Why did they say such terrible things and do such terrible things? Daddy would never have said anything like that," I added.

Miguel was quiet.

"Well, would he?"

"You have to understand, Hannah, that when your mother and your father divorced, it was not a pleasant situation. I do not want to turn you against your father, and you cannot say I have ever said anything negative to you about him."

"I know. I know. They really don't like each other," I said. "Neither will let me forget it for a second."

"Well, it goes beyond just liking and disliking. Your father was not faithful. I don't think he will deny that, but the Eatons are a very proud family in Palm Beach. They just can't stand to be held accountable for any of their actions. They think they can buy their way through the Pearly Gates.

"Your Eaton grandparents, who have nothing to do with you, did not waste any time spreading stories about your mother so they could put on a good face in public and at their extravaganzas and big charity balls."

"Stories about her and Uncle Linden?"

"Well . . . yes," Miguel said. "Part of your uncle's mental difficulties concerned his relationship with your mother, and they took advantage of that."

"What do you mean?" I asked, my heart starting to thump. Could there be any truth to the rumors?

"In the beginning, when your mother did not reveal her true identity, Linden harbored some romantic feelings for her. He was a lost, lonely young man, often depressed and dejected. She burst onto his dismal scene like a bright and lovely new warm light and won his trust and affection.

"Later, when he learned who she was, he was deeply disappointed. Another sick joke pulled on him by Fate, he thought. He became even more bitter and was especially resentful of Thatcher and his attention to your mother and her growing affection for him. He grew up in Thatcher's shadow and was always somewhat envious of his success and popularity with women, I believe."

"Why didn't anyone ever tell me about all this?" I whined.

"It's not the sort of thing you sit your child down to discuss."

"I'm not a child anymore!" I exclaimed.

"No, you're not, and I suppose we should have had some frank discussions with you about it all. Your mother skirts around the issues whenever she talks to you about your uncle Linden. I know. I've heard her, but she was only trying to keep the sordid, ugly part of it from you."

"I'm old enough to hear anything, Miguel."

"It was done to protect you," he insisted.

"But I feel so stupid. My half brothers know more about all this."

"They don't know anything but what they have heard from their grandparents, I'm sure. Maybe they did over-hear Thatcher tell Danielle some of it. Maybe he was trying to belittle your mother in front of her or claim he loved Danielle more. I'm sure whatever the reason, it was a selfish one. He knows there's no truth to such a sordid lie.

"But," he continued after a moment's hesitation, "you should know that your uncle's final serious break-down occurred when he had the delusion you were his child. In his mental turmoil he fantasized a male female relationship with your mother. It's taken years of ther-apy, medication, and tender loving care to help him get over that delusion."

"Now I'm beginning to understand why he said some strange things the last time I visited with him," I admitted sadly.

"Like what?

"He was just confused, I guess. He told me my father had nothing to do with the baby, with little Claude."

Miguel was silent a moment, thinking. "Yes, I suppose he has his relapses, his trips down those old, strange highways, but for the most part, he's doing well," Miguel assured me.

"Yes, he is," I insisted.

I took another deep breath and settled back. Perhaps the worst was over, I thought. I just wouldn't go to my father's house anymore, and I would have nothing to do with the twins. I had lived without them in my life up until now. I saw no reason why I couldn't continue. I would apologize to Mommy profusely, I thought, and somehow, make it all up to her.

However, that opportunity was not to be. As we made the turn through the gated entrance of Joya del Mar, we could see red lights blinking.

"What the . . . what's that?" Miguel muttered.

"It's an ambulance!" I cried.

Miguel sped up and pulled alongside the ambulance. The doors were open, and we could see two paramedics bent over a gurney. Lila was in the open doorway of the house. She stood as still as a mannequin, her right hand up, the fingers bent and touching her temple, her left hand clutched in a fist at her side.

"What's happening here?" Miguel shouted at the paramedics.

One turned to him while the other continued doing what I would later learn was CPR. The gurney was high enough up to hide the tiny body of little Claude.

"We're tying to revive him," the paramedic told Miguel.

"What? Lila!" he screamed. "Where's Willow?"

"Oh, Mr. Fuentes, she's just lying in bed, staring up at the ceiling. I can't get her to say a word or get up or anything. I ran down here hoping to bring her good news."

"My son!" Miguel cried, more to himself than to me or the paramedics.

He then leaped into the ambulance and gazed down at the baby.

The paramedic who had spoken shook his head. He did it so slowly, it was truly like a slow-motion sequence in a movie. My ears began to ring. Some terribly loud noise was raging through my body. I looked up at Lila, who had crumbled against the doorjamb, her body shuddering like someone who had seized a live electric wire.

I realized what the terrible loud noise was.

It was coming from me. I was screaming as hard as I could, a single note, high-pitched, ricocheting off the front of Joya del Mar and shattering in the air around us.

The second paramedic took hold of Miguel as he began to collapse. He held him at the waist and kept him standing. I stopped screaming and hurried up to Lila, who turned and embraced me. We held on to each other with a desperation that froze my heart. Then I looked up the stairs. Mommy was coming down slowly, moving like a sleepwalker.

"Mommy!" I called. She didn't hear me. She continued toward us and emerged on the portico as Miguel came out of the ambulance.

He looked up at her. He was crying hard now, and I

remember how strange it looked for a grown man to bawl like a little boy. It made me cry harder, too.

Mommy started toward him, but not halfway there, she crumbled as if she had turned to liquid and poured down to her feet.

"MOMMY!" I screamed with all my strength and being.

"WILLOW!" Miguel cried and ran to her. The paramedics were at his side in seconds.

They gave her smelling salts and revived her, but she shook her head vigorously, wanting to deny reality certainly, and wanting only to return to her blissful state of unconsciousness. They kept her awake and, using another stretcher, lifted her and carried her back into the house at Miguel's direction, bringing her back to their bedroom.

Terrified and yet unable to stop myself from doing it, I went to the ambulance and gazed at little Claude. His little mouth was barely open. His eyes were shut. I touched his tiny fingers, realizing that I had not been with him very much at all when he was alive. How I wished my contact with him could somehow resurrect him. Wouldn't Mommy love me then? Of course, that was not to be.

"Goodbye, little Claude," I whispered and I stepped out. Lila put her arm around my shoulders, and we walked into the house.

"How did this happen?" I wondered aloud. Mommy had been practically still attached to my little brother through an invisible umbilical cord.

"She fell asleep. She tried not to, but she was exhausted, and when she woke, he was already in trouble," Lila explained through her sobs and tears. "I heard her screaming for Miguel, but he had already gone after you, so I went to the phone and called 911."

Her explanation felt like a ton of rocks falling on me and then turning to ice. Mommy had been shouting for Miguel, but he was gone to get me? I had been the one to pull him away at the most critical of moments?

I gazed up the stairway at the sound of the paramedics coming down, talking softly to themselves. I heard them say little Claude would have to be taken to the hospital for an autopsy.

Lila walked away, her head down.

"I'll make something, maybe coffee, maybe tea," she babbled to herself.

Slowly I headed upstairs, my legs feeling detached from the rest of me, carrying the rest of me like a true burden up the stairway. In the hallway outside of Mommy's room, I heard her wailing and pausing to continually ask Miguel if it was true, if Claude was really gone.

He repeated "I'm afraid so" each time until suddenly she began to shout at him.

"Where were you? Why weren't you here when I needed you, Miguel? Where were you?"

"I went to get Hannah, remember?"

"Hannah," she repeated. Never had my name sounded more like profanity to me.

"Yes. Remember I had located her at that boy's home."

Blood rushed into my face. Now she would know it was my fault. She would always think of it as my fault. I was responsible for Miguel being gone. If he had been here, he might have been able to do something or get the baby to medical help faster.

Suddenly all the jealousy I had felt, all the envy I had experienced turned dark and evil in my heart. It was as if a mask had been removed and behind it was the laughing devil himself taking pleasure in what he had done to me, what I had permitted him to do to me.

All of the nasty little innuendos I had said to Mommy were turned around and aimed back at me, striking me as painfully as sharp arrows. "You, you, you," each was saying. I could see Mommy pointing her finger toward me, accusing. She would press it into my heart.

I couldn't even imagine looking at her, and there was suddenly nothing I feared as much as her looking at me. No matter how much love she professed for me, no matter how many wonderful things she had said to me in the past, I would always see the accusation in her face; it would always linger and hover like some rotten slime behind the walls, seeping through at every opportunity. I would turn unexpectedly and see Mommy gazing at me with such fury and hatred, I would die a little more each and every time.

When she started to scream again, I backed away from her room. Miguel had his hands full trying to calm her and eventually gave up and called Dr. Jacobi, a close friend of theirs. He came over quickly to give Mommy a sedative. I wished he would give me one, too, I thought, maybe even give me too much.

While all this was going on, I sat on the floor at the foot of my bed and brought up my knees, squeezing myself into the tightest ball I could. I lowered my head to my folded arms and actually fell asleep for a while. Footsteps outside my door woke me occasionally, but when it was silent again, I fell in and out of sleep.

Later, Miguel found me there, and although I didn't recall it with much detail, he picked me up and lay me on my bed. I woke before dawn and listened for any sounds in the house. The silence worried me. I rose and walked softly and slowly to Mommy's bedroom, where I stood outside the door and listened for a long time. I could hear her moans and Miguel's soft, consoling voice and then quiet.

After I returned to my room, I tried to sleep a little longer, but I couldn't keep my eyes closed. Every creak, every tinkle caught my attention. It was as if my hearing had become as keen as a dog's or a cat's. Finally I gave up and rose, went to the bathroom, washed my face, and changed my clothes. By the time I was finished, I could hear Lila coming up the stairs with some breakfast for Mommy. I heard her shout that she didn't want anything, and I heard Miguel plead with her, warning her she would need her strength more than ever now.

Not once did I hear her ask for me. I was both grateful and disappointed simultaneously. I didn't have the courage to go to her, but I was also upset with the fact that she didn't want me at her side, that she didn't turn to me for any solace or support. I might as well have died with Claude, I thought. I really didn't know what to do.

Finally Miguel came to my room to see how I was.

"Good, you're up," he said. "Go see your mother."

"She doesn't want to see me," I moaned.

"Of course she does, Hannah. Don't pull any childish antics or moods now," he warned.

He looked at me so sternly, with eyes like cold steel. I had never seen him look at anyone this way, not even the drunken gardener who had called him terrible names in Spanish.

"You think it's my fault," I told him. "Don't you?"

"No. It's no one's fault, Hannah. It's God's will."

"Why would God want to take the life of a little baby just born? Why bother letting him be born?" I asked. I knew Miguel and his family had a deep faith, but right now that seemed so useless to me.

"We are not meant to know and understand God's will," he replied.

Convenient, I thought, but I wouldn't say it, although I wanted to say it very much. I wanted to turn my sense of guilt and responsibility toward Miguel's god, direct it like a spotlight on the churches, the Bibles, the choirs, and the prayers to expose the emptiness and exonerate myself.

"Just like an ant cannot hope to understand the mind of a man, we cannot hope to fully understand the mind of God. We are not gods," he insisted with a firmness that obviously gave him the strength to continue and be strong for Mommy.

Reluctantly I had to admire and even envy him for that. I nodded. With my head bowed, moving slowly, like someone heading toward her own funeral, I went to Mommy's room. She was lying there and looking up at the ceiling. She had a cold washcloth on her forehead.

"Mommy," I managed and she turned slowly, oh,

ever so slowly to me, and looked at me and shook her head.

"He's gone," she said.

"I know," I told her, my lips and my chin quivering. I was hoping she would lift her arms and urge me to run to her, but she turned away instead and gazed up at the ceiling again.

"He's gone," she chanted. "He was here for so short a time and now he's gone."

"I'm sorry, Mommy," I said. "I feel so sick and sad inside."

She closed her eyes.

I didn't know what else to say. Should I ask her if she was going to try to have another child? Would that sound too crass? Should I ask her if there was anything she wanted me to do? What could there possibly be to do? Dig a little grave? Lila would bring up anything she wanted to eat or drink. What was my purpose here now?

I looked back at Miguel, who was standing in the doorway. He lowered his eyes and then told me to go have some breakfast.

"It's going to be a very difficult time for all of us," he said. "We'll all need our strength to help each other get through it, Hannah."

I nodded and looked back at Mommy.

Suddenly, abruptly, she brought her hands to her swollen breasts and cried, "It's time to feed him!"

"Easy, Willow," Miguel said, coming in quickly.

"Oh," Mommy cried, "I ache so badly!"

"I'll call Dr. Jacobi, Willow."

"What good is that? What will he tell you? Bring my

baby back to me. Bring him back!" she demanded and began to pound her own body. Miguel had to hold her hands down. I winced with every blow as if the blows struck me. He held on to her firmly, and she stopped and settled down again, sinking back into herself like someone who wanted to disappear.

The funeral was so heavily attended that strangers thought a local dignitary had died. A sizable contingent came from the college. There were even some students of Miguel's. Of course, his family was large, relatives coming from Miami, as well as out of state. I never realized how many people Mommy knew and how many with whom she did business. I was surprised to see Daddy and half wondered if Mrs. Gouter hadn't been the one to remind him. Danielle was with him, too. I couldn't look at her. I was afraid she would have eyes full of accusations.

Mommy didn't seem to notice anyone. With glassy, empty eyes, she received their hugs and kisses and their words of sympathy, but I was sure she would remember none of it. She was on some sedation and barely able to walk and stand. Miguel was truly a tower of strength, not taking much time to serve his own grief until we were at the cemetery and the reality of little Claude's death was upon him. There, he cried softly.

When it was over, we returned to Joya del Mar, where Miguel and I greeted mourners. Daddy and Danielle did not come, but I was happy about that. Mommy didn't stay downstairs with Miguel and me. She just wanted to sleep. Food and drink and conversation lifted the shroud of gloom from our home for a little while, but after the last visitors expressed their final regrets and left, the pall rushed in with the power of the tides and once again deepened the shadows and the stillness in our house.

"Well," Miguel said, gazing at the empty room, "that's that. We've got to rebuild," he told me. I had no idea what that meant, but I nodded anyway. "I'll look in on your mother, Hannah," he said and went up to her.

Heyden had been afraid to come to the cemetery. I saw him at the church, but I barely acknowledged him. I was afraid to, but now I felt guilty about that. This was in no way his fault or had anything to do with him, yet somehow, he had been stained because I was at his home and had gone to him first after my fiasco at Daddy's house, rather than to Miguel and Mommy. If only I had . . . if only I had.

As far as I knew, Uncle Linden knew nothing of little Claude's death. I couldn't imagine Mommy wanting someone to tell him about it, and Miguel wouldn't have done so on his own. After all that had happened and had been said, I wasn't going to suggest he be told, either. That bothered me as much as what was directed at poor Heyden. Uncle Linden should have been given the opportunity to be with his family, to comfort and console Mommy and me.

I would wait, I thought, for the right time and then ask Miguel to bring it up with Mommy. If they wanted, I would take on the responsibility of informing Uncle Linden. I really believed he listened to me more than he listened to anyone else now anyway. I would be the best one to bring him the news and help him understand it.

For the remainder of the afternoon, I sat alone on the

rear loggia and looked out at the sea, watching the sinking sun change the shades of light and shadows. Eventually, Miguel came looking for me.

"How is she?" I asked when he stepped out on the loggia.

"As good as can be expected," he said.

I wanted to ask if she had asked for me, but I just looked out at the water.

"You should go up to her," he finally said.

"Okay."

How sad it was that my going up to see my mother to comfort her and give her love was so difficult for me now. I walked with very tentative steps, delaying the meeting as long as I could. She was sitting up in her bed, sipping some herbal tea when I stepped into the room.

"How are you, Mommy?" I asked.

"How can I be?" she replied. "It is truly as if a piece of me has been ripped away, a part of me has died. There's an emptiness in me that I don't think I'll ever fill, Hannah. My future has been taken away from me, and nothing will ever look beautiful, taste delicious, or feel good ever again. Pray to God every day that nothing like this happens to you," she said.

"It's happened to me, too," I protested. "He was my brother."

"No one but a mother could understand," she replied. "The relationship is too special, too close. No relationship compares to it. These are things I have always known, of course, but it's different when it's actually happening to you."

She sighed. "I'm the one who always advises people

to talk out their problems and feelings, and here I am hating every utterance, wishing I were mute. Perhaps I'll appreciate my clients more now," she said. "Just like them, I need time to mourn, to suffer."

"I don't want you to suffer, Mommy."

"Yes, well, it's too late for that, and it really doesn't matter what you want or I want, does it?" she said bitterly. "Miguel wants me to turn to faith. What did we do to have so deep and long a family curse put on us? How long do you pay for the sins of your fathers?" she asked. She wasn't asking me, of course. She was asking Fate itself.

She put her teacup down and lowered herself in the bed.

"Do me a favor, Hannah," she said, "and close the curtains. I want to sleep."

"But aren't you hungry or—"

"I just want to sleep," she said. "Close the door when you leave," she added and shut her eyes.

Maybe she was shutting them so she didn't have to look upon me, I thought, and did what she wanted.

Eventually Mommy emerged from her bedroom and from her state of mourning, but the gloom and the pall that had come into our home remained. She avoided lights and music. She ate only what she needed to survive and never with any gusto or appetite. Her work at the office was restricted to mostly office duties, reports, and some consultations for the time being.

Although I never heard her mention Miguel's having to fetch me that dreadful night, she avoided asking me anything about it as well. Nevertheless, I longed to tell

her what had happened at Daddy's home and what the
twins had said and done, but it was as if that day, those
hours were gone from her memory, and I was far too
frightened and nervous about bringing any of it up
myself.

Finally, one night at dinner, nearly ten days later, she
brought up Uncle Linden.

"I suppose he should know about little Claude," she
said.

"Do you want me to go over there?" Miguel asked
her.

"Half the time I wonder if he remembers who you
are, Miguel. No. I'll have to do it, I suppose."

"I can do it, Mommy," I offered.

She looked at me with a very strange, very foreign
expression. It gave me the eerie feeling she didn't
remember who I was. It was as if some stranger had
popped into the chair and dared to make such an offer
to do so personal a thing.

"No," she said. "He won't understand it if it comes
from you."

I didn't dare challenge her.

"I'll go with you at least, Willow," Miguel said.

"Fine. Let's do it this weekend," she said and continued to nibble at her food.

Later, without fully understanding why, I burst into
tears in my room. I kept my sobs subdued so no one
would hear me, and then I did my homework and went
to sleep.

At school Heyden had been avoiding me. I tried to
talk to him a few times, but he politely excused himself.
My girlfriends, even the most jealous ones, put aside

their jibes and sarcasm and were warmer to me out of sympathy. I accepted their consolation even though I had doubts about the sincerity. I needed someone to consider my feelings, offer me warm hugs and embraces and soft words.

The dreariness of Joya del Mar and the emptiness that had come into my own life reached a peak after Mommy and Miguel returned from visiting Uncle Linden late in the afternoon and telling him the tragic news. I waited anxiously at home, and when they came into the house, I immediately went to them and asked how he had taken it.

Miguel shook his head, meaning I should not pursue it, but Mommy did say, "He blamed it on me not listening to his advice. Can you believe that?"

My quizzical look brought a strange, eerie laugh out of her.

"He doesn't know what year this is, where he is, or what's happened. Maybe he's better off in limbo," she muttered.

"No," I made the mistake of saying too loud. She turned to me. "He's always been sensible with me, mostly," I said. "It was just with this, little Claude. . . ."

"Listen to her," Mommy said. "She doesn't need to go to college. She can hang her shingle out tomorrow. Your precious uncle is a disturbed man, Hannah. He will never, never, *never* leave that place. Get it in your head!" she screamed. "Why I went over there and subjected myself to his madness at a time like this, I'll never know.

"Yes," she quickly added, glaring at me. "I do know. It's your persistent concern for him and your making me feel guilty about him. Now see? What good has that done? He's no better off. He's worse, in fact. I forbid you to go there anymore. I absolutely forbid it!" she cried.

"Easy," Miguel told her.

She shook her head and marched upstairs.

"She's very upset. I'll see to her," Miguel said. "Let us know when dinner is ready. Maybe I can get her to eat something substantial tonight."

Let them know when dinner is ready, I thought. I'm just like another servant here now. But I didn't cry. My pool of tears was dry. I replaced sorrow with anger instead. How unfair it was to blame me for Uncle Linden. Would I be blamed for everything that happened to this family now?

My rage filled me with courage. Without anyone's permission, I charged out of the house and got into Mommy's car. In moments I was driving away and heading for Heyden's house. Whether he wanted to or not, he was going to listen to me. We would not be held accountable and punished for what happened. What we had together was good, and I was determined it would go on.

Fortunately, he was home when I arrived. When I stepped up to the front door, I could hear him practicing on his guitar. I knocked and waited, but he was singing as well, and he didn't hear me. The door was unlocked, so I entered.

"Heyden," I called. "Heyden."

He heard me and stopped playing.

"Hannah," he said, emerging from his room. "What are you doing here?"

"I came to see you. Don't you want me here?" I asked sharply.

"Sure, but . . . your stepfather said . . ."

"I don't care what he said or what anyone says, Heyden. There's nothing wrong with us seeing each other, and there is especially nothing wrong with us singing together."

He smiled.

"Never thought there was," he said with a shrug, "but who am I to take on the high and the mighty?"

"You're Heyden Reynolds and I'm Hannah Eaton, and we are the high and the mighty," I replied.

He laughed.

"C'mon, maybe I'll turn that into a song."

I laughed, too.

It was as if a damn had broken and all my joy and happiness, shut up and stifled, could come pouring out again. How I welcomed it.

As soon as I entered his bedroom, Heyden's eyes and mine met and told each other how much we had really missed each other. I was so hungry for affection and love, I couldn't wait for him to put his arms around me and bring his lips to mine. For me the kiss was like a long drink of water after traipsing through a desert. I wanted to remain in his arms forever.

This time my tears were tears of joy.

"Hey," he said, wiping them off my cheeks gently. "What's happening, Hannah?"

"Oh, Heyden, I am more than a stranger in my own house now. I feel so unwanted. And my mother has forbidden me to visit my Uncle Linden!"

"Why?"

"She blames me for everything, I know. If Miguel hadn't come for me, he might have been able to do something for little Claude. And now even my uncle's madness is somehow my fault."

"He didn't seem that mad to me," Heyden said.

"He isn't. My mother is just blind to everything but her own pain. I hate living there. I hate being there. I wish . . ."

"What?"

"I wish that somehow we could go away."

"Boy, don't I?" He shook his head. I sensed there was an added pain or weight on his shoulders.

"Something new?" I asked.

"You probably thought I was just afraid to talk to you at school and I was avoiding you because of your stepfather. Well, there was some of that, but the real reason was I didn't want you coming back to this place."

"Why not?" I thought a moment. Now that I realized it, it was unusually quiet. Where was Elisha? Why wasn't she playing her music too loudly? "Something to do with your sister? Something's happened to her?"

"She and two of her friends were caught with cocaine. Don't ask me how she and those friends of hers got a hold of as much as they did, but it was enough to have them all arrested. Because of her age, her name hasn't been in the papers. Of course, my mother is beside herself, and I didn't want to have anything to do with it.

"We called my father, but he can't get away from his gig without losing it. I'm supposed to keep him abreast of what happens next. She could go to some juvenile detention center, and if you ask me, she should."

"Where is she now?"

"Who knows. With her social worker maybe. That's a waste of time, too. In short," he said, "I couldn't be more ready or anxious to get away from it all, too."

We were both silent for a moment.

"Where would we go?" I finally asked.

He lay back on the bed and put his hands behind his head as he looked up at the ceiling.

"We could go on the road, try to get small jobs here and there as a duet. You're almost seventeen and certainly could pass for eighteen or nineteen."

"Are we good enough to get jobs?"

"Sure we are and we look good, too. At least, you do."

"I wonder if we really could do that," I said.

He sat up quickly. "Actually, I have had a wild idea for some time now, fantasizing about it ever since we started rehearsing."

"What?" I asked, my heart pounding with excitement.

"Everyone who runs away goes hitchhiking across country, sleeps in one slop house after another, or lives like a homeless person camped out in hallways and under bridges. The country is full of thousands of people our age and younger living like tramps, doing almost anything for a meal, a ride."

"How would we be different?"

He smiled. "We would rent a motor home," he said. "It's the cheapest way to travel. Most runaways eventually run out of money and end up on the streets. A motor home is economical housing, and we would be able to always be on the move, if we need be."

"That does sound like a good idea."

"Doesn't it?"

"But do you know anything about it, about getting one of those vehicles?"

He nodded. "I know where I can get one relatively cheap. I found it advertised on the Internet, but it's still a lot more money than I have," he added, his smile drifting off his face to be replaced by the face of reality.

"I don't have that much available, either. All my money is in a trust."

"I figured that."

"But what about my credit card?"

"I thought about that, too. The problem is once you use that, and every time you use it, you leave a trail, Hannah. I'm sure your mother and your father would come after us. You're still underage. I might even get into trouble taking you along," he said. "No," he continued, lying back again, "we're both trapped. "Without more money, some real money, it would be impossible," he said, quickly turning off the excitement in both our eyes.

"Maybe I could sell things," I suggested.

"It takes time to do that, and there's a good chance you would be discovered doing it. I've pawned things. I can tell you that you don't get anywhere near the value of what you have."

"I don't like feeling like this, feeling so helpless and trapped and unloved!" I cried and threw myself against him. He put his arm around me and stroked my hair.

"We are all in our own little cages, I guess, cages we didn't create for ourselves. Like your uncle in a way."

I buried my face in his chest to stifle my sobs and

tears. After a few moments I sat up and wiped my cheeks.

"I don't care what Mommy says. I'm going to visit Uncle Linden. He is surely terribly confused and alone after hearing the news. I can just imagine how he was left sitting in some corner of his room, wondering what was happening."

I got up.

"Now? You're going there now?"

"Yes," I said determinedly. "Would you come with me?"

He shrugged. "Sure," he said. "If we're going to get into trouble being together, we might as well do something worthwhile together."

I smiled. "You're the best friend I have now, Heyden."

"I want to be more than a friend, Hannah."

"You are," I said, and we kissed before starting out of the house.

It was dark now, but the sky was clear, and there was a quarter moon full of promise.

I got into the car.

"Wait," Heyden said and ran back to the house. When he emerged, he had his guitar with him.

"Might as well rehearse anyway. Maybe we'll hit the lottery or something. I'll leave my mother something, and we'll be on our way."

He strummed his guitar and played a few chords of *This Land is your land, this land is my land. . . .*

"Where is your mother?" I asked him.

"Just finishing work. She'll be home soon."

"Shouldn't you let her know where you are?" I asked

before starting the car. "I mean, with all that's happened to your sister?"

He shook his head. "I stopped doing that long ago, Hannah, and she stopped asking about the same time. The truth is," he said, "I've left home already. The only thing is I'm the only one who knows it."

I nodded with understanding.

"I think I have as well," I said, put the car in drive, and pulled away with Heyden strumming, trying to create something that sounded hopeful.

9

Leaving in a
Motor Home

Mrs. Robinson was very surprised to see us at the front door of the residency.

"Oh, dear," she said, "I was so sorry to hear the terrible news. You all must be so devastated."

"Yes, we are, Mrs. Robinson. Thank you. How is my uncle since my mother's visit?"

"He took it all very badly, I'm afraid, but two more visitors the same day will please him, I'm sure," she said, opening the screen door for us and stepping back.

"What do you mean, he took it all badly? What's happened to him?"

"Well, he didn't have any appetite at dinner tonight, but I think he will be fine," she said. "It's so muggy tonight; it's hard for anyone to be enthusiastic about anything, even if they didn't have a family tragedy. Naturally, he's a little depressed. However," she said, smiling, "I'm sure you'll cheer him up."

As usual Uncle Linden's door was closed. I knocked and waited. Mrs. Robinson had gone back to her living quarters and was not in the corridor. I knocked again and called to Uncle Linden. There was still no response. Worried now, I opened the door.

The room was in total darkness, but fortunately the silvery sliver of moon gave us enough illumination to see Uncle Linden sitting by the window, gazing out.

"Uncle Linden?" I said. "Why are you sitting in the dark?"

He did not turn. I glanced at Heyden, who looked concerned himself now, and then I crossed the room and touched Uncle Linden's left shoulder. He shuddered and slowly turned his head toward me.

"Willow? Have you come back?"

"No, Uncle Linden. It's Hannah."

"Oh," he said, his voice going flat.

"Why are you sitting in the dark, Uncle Linden?"

"Am I?" he asked. "I guess I didn't realize how long I've been sitting here."

Heyden found the light switch and snapped on the overhead fixture and the lamp in the corner. Uncle Linden blinked rapidly and smiled.

"Well," he said after a deep breath. "You're all right then?"

"Yes, I'm fine, Uncle Linden," I replied. "It's been very sad at home."

"Yes, I know," he said. He glanced out the window again. "I was just thinking of Joya del Mar. On nights like this I would go out on the beach and sit for hours listening to the ocean. I miss that."

"I know you do," I said. It was so cruel to continue keeping him here, locked in his private cage, as Heyden had said. "But it's not the same there," I added.

"Right, right. Who was it said you can't go home again?"

"Thomas Wolfe," Heyden replied quickly.

Uncle Linden looked at him.

"I remember you," he said. "You were here before. Heyden, isn't it?"

"Yes," Heyden replied smiling.

"And you write songs. Written anything new lately?"

"No, not lately, but I've got some new ideas," Heyden told him.

"So much for him not having his wits," I muttered.

Uncle Linden smiled.

"Good. As long as you're creative, you're still alive," he advised. He looked at me again, his brow creasing. "So things are not good at home. How could they be with such a tragedy?"

"No, Uncle Linden. Things are not good at either of our homes," I added, nodding at Heyden.

"Oh? Sorry about that, but sometimes there's not much you can do about it. No," he muttered more to himself than to us, "not much."

"You can leave," Heyden growled and flopped in the other chair.

Uncle Linden looked up. "What's that? Leave?" He shook his head. "I used to think about doing that, but I never had the self-confidence, and I couldn't leave my mother anyway, could I?" he asked, searching for confirmation.

"No, Uncle Linden, you couldn't," I said, patting his hand. I sat at the edge of his bed.

"It's very hard to leave a mother when you are all she has, very hard," he muttered.

"Mommy has changed so much since little Claude's death. I feel like a stranger in my own house," I told him. "I don't know if things will ever be like they were again."

He nodded. "I know what that's like," he said. "When we moved out of the main house, I felt like a stranger. And when we moved back, it was never the same. I tried to make it feel the same, put things back where they were, get rid of things the Eatons had left behind, but it was different. Everything changes. Sometimes, you just have to let go," he said.

"I'd like to," Heyden moaned.

"So, let go. What would you do?"

"We're going to continue developing our singing act together, Uncle Linden," I told him. "No matter who doesn't like it."

"Why would anyone not like it?" He thought a moment. "Is it one of those loud, heavy metal things?" he asked with a grimace and his hands over his ears.

"No," Heyden said, laughing. "Hardly."

"So?"

"There is just a great deal of sadness and blame raining down on us these days, Uncle Linden," I said, trying to explain. "We're caught in the middle."

"I've been in that sort of storm too often," he said, nodding. "And there isn't an umbrella strong enough."

Heyden shook his head. "Oh, yes, there is," he said. "Our music is our umbrella." He looked at me. "And it is strong enough."

"You don't say. Where would you two perform your music?" Uncle Linden asked. "On television?"

Heyden lit up and leaned forward.

"No, not right away. I'd love us to go on the road. There are hundreds of small places that would want an inexpensive but talented act like ours. We'd play for restaurants, nice bars, whatever. I know we can make a go of it and see a lot of this country at the same time. We would get all the experience we need. Mostly, we would get away for a while, a long while," he concluded.

"So you think you're that good, eh? People would listen to you and hire you on the spot?"

"Yes, I know we are that good," Heyden said with steely determination in his eyes as he looked at me. "My father's a musician. It's in my blood. I've been around it long enough and heard and seen singers and musicians who aren't half as good as we are."

"Now, there's a confident young man," Uncle Linden told me.

I smiled. "That he is, Uncle Linden."

"Well, you should go for it, then. Take a chance. I never did, and I sit here and regret it. All I can do now is stare out this window and wonder," Uncle Linden said. "Don't make my mistakes, Hannah. Seize the opportunity, if you have it."

"We don't have it, Uncle Linden. We have dreams."

"Well, that's a start." He thought a moment. "Why don't you have it?" he asked Heyden.

"It takes money, lots of money. I had this idea for us: We'd rent a motor home, you know, and we'd go on the road. That way we would always have a place to stay that wasn't some rat heap."

"Very interesting and very sensible," Uncle Linden said, nodding. "I've never really been in one of those, of course, but I imagine they can be comfortable enough."

"It's a small apartment on wheels!" Heyden said. "With a kitchen and room to sleep five. At least, the one I was looking at is," he concluded with a down note.

"And you say you would just get in it and go? If you could, you would do it immediately?"

"Absolutely. Wouldn't we, Hannah?"

I smiled. "I'm leaving on a motor home," I sang, parodying the famous song the folksingers Peter, Paul, and Mary sang.

Heyden laughed and added, "Don't know when I'll be back again."

We joined for, "Please, Uncle Linden, we've got to go."

He laughed and shook his head. "You guys are great. So how much is it you need really?"

"At least a few thousand," Heyden said. "We don't have enough to rent the motor home for a minimum of six months, which is what the owner requires, and stake ourselves for at least two weeks. We should get some work within that time."

"A few thousand, huh? I've got money. Lots of money and I don't have much use for it."

"We couldn't take your money, Uncle Linden," I said quickly. I didn't want Heyden to have any false hope.

"Oh, you won't be exactly taking it," he said.

He rose and walked over to the dresser drawer. Inside a sock he had hidden his bank account book. He held it up. "I have ten thousand dollars in here," he bragged.

"Ten thousand?"

"A little more." He opened the book and read, "Ten thousand, five hundred, and seventeen at the moment. Is that enough?"

"Sure is," Heyden said, brightening.

"We're not taking his money," I insisted.

"No, you're not taking it," Uncle Linden said. "I'm giving it to you as payment."

"Payment? Payment for what?" I asked quickly.

"For taking me, too," he said, smiling. "You're free to use it for whatever expenses are involved for the three of us."

Neither Heyden nor I spoke. We looked at each other and then at Uncle Linden.

"You want to leave Florida?" I asked.

"Oh, I know everyone thinks I'm comfortable and about as happy as I can be living here. I know exactly where I am and what it means. I stay because I don't want to be in anyone's way or make any more trouble than I have already made for my family. What little family I have, that is.

"But," he continued, crossing the room to look out his window again, "I'm really dying here. Sometimes, I feel like I'm in freeze frame, stuck and unable to move backward or forward. Don't misunderstand me—everyone here has always been good to me and pleasant. But I'm like a flower, wilting.

"My sunlight comes from what I can paint, and what I can paint here is limited to my memories, unfortunately. I'm sure there are many, many wonderful and beautiful things out there for me to see and paint.

"I wasn't completely honest with you before. Once I

did try to leave on my own. I started walking away from this place, but it was as if I hit an invisible glass wall. I had to stop, and I couldn't lift my foot to move forward. Finally, shaking and weak, I turned back and just dropped myself in the chair on the porch, feeling defeated."

"We can't take you away with us, Uncle Linden," I said softly.

"Why can't we?" Heyden asked.

"He's under a doctor's care here, Heyden."

"It doesn't sound like he needs a doctor to me, and besides, what's the doctor doing for him here? He's been here a long time. You told me that yourself."

"Heyden. . . ."

"I thought you always wanted to get him out of here."

"To bring him *home*, not to take him on the road!"

"Well, what's the difference? The motor home is a home, and you heard him. He wants to see new things, to stimulate his creativity. If you aren't creative, you're not alive," Heyden repeated.

I looked at Uncle Linden, who was smiling.

"Yes, yes," he said. "That's exactly it. The young man knows."

"Well, I *don't* know," I said, shaking my head.

But the whole idea suddenly looked possible, and my boasting and moaning began to frighten me.

"Well, I *do* know," Heyden fired back, all stirred up with hope. "Here's what we can do: I'll negotiate a price for the motor home and tell the owner we'll pay him cash. He'll want some sort of guarantee, so we can use your credit card for that, but he won't pass it through, so no one can use it to track us down.

"We can really do this," Heyden continued, his excitement building.

"Sure we can," Uncle Linden said, waving his bank book. "I've go what we need right here."

"We'll load up and head out. First, we'll take a scenic trip and give Uncle Linden a chance to see some of the beauty in this country, something else beside big, glitzy Palm Beach hotels, and then we'll head for New Orleans. My father will help us find work there, I'm sure."

Heyden was speaking so fast, I couldn't catch my breath following.

"I don't know, Heyden. I've got to think about this."

"Think about it," he said. "Meanwhile, I'll do all the research and planning necessary. Okay, Uncle Linden?"

"Count me in," he said. "You've just got to take me to the bank so I can transfer some money."

"We'll be back very soon and do just that."

"Heyden."

"What?"

"Nothing," I said, looking at Uncle Linden. His face had taken on such healthy color, and his eyes were the brightest I could recall. I stood up. "We've got to go, Uncle Linden. We'll be back soon."

"Very soon," Heyden promised him.

"Good. Good," Uncle Linden said. "What was that you sang? I'm leaving on a motor home?"

"Don't know when I'll be back again," Heyden followed.

"I do," Uncle Linden said. "Never."

Heyden laughed.

I opened the door quickly.

"C'mon, Heyden," I urged, practically pushing him out the door. "Good night, Uncle Linden."

"Good night, Hannah." He stepped up to me quickly and kissed me on the cheek. I couldn't recall him ever doing that before. It was always I who kissed him first.

"Thank you," he said. "Thank you for coming by and giving me something wonderful to think about."

"We're not just thinking about it, Uncle Linden. We're going to do it!" Heyden told him. Then he shook my uncle's hand, and we left. I walked quickly.

"Bye," Uncle Linden called from his doorway. "See you soon I hope."

"Everything all right?" Mrs. Robinson asked, stepping into the lobby of the home.

"Oh, yes, yes," I said. "He's fine."

"I thought as much. I know what good effect your visits have on him. Come back soon."

"We will," Heyden told her.

I hurried out the front door and down the steps to Mommy's car.

"Wait up," Heyden called. "You're practically running away from the place."

"Just get in, Heyden." I started the engine and he got in.

"What's the matter with you?"

"What's the matter with me?" I exclaimed. "How could you do that? How could you fill him with such a story, such an idea? Just imagine how disappointed he's going to be when we don't do it. He's had too many disappointments in his life already."

"Why won't we do it?"

"Please," I said, backing out of the driveway.

"Why won't we do it?" he demanded.

"We just won't. We were just talking, dreaming."

"I wasn't just talking. I told you. I've investigated this idea. I've been thinking and planning it for a while now. Maybe everything is just a childish fantasy to you, Hannah, but from where I sit, in the world I am living in, it's the only real hope I have. And from the way your uncle reacted and from the things he told us, it sounds like the only real hope he has, too."

"But how can we do that? How can we take someone like him on the road?"

"How were you going to take him home?"

"He would be near available medical attention all the time," I said.

"We wouldn't exactly be in the Outback, Hannah. We'd always be close to some sort of medical help. Besides, he doesn't sound like he needs any. It sounds like what he's getting is slowly killing him. You wanted to do something for him. This is it!" he emphasized.

I took a deep breath. I felt like I was falling, like I had impulsively started to row a canoe down a river and now I couldn't stop. The raging water had taken over, and it could drive me to the rocks!

"But take his money? I feel like we'd be taking advantage of him, Heyden."

"Why? We'd be giving him something he really wants and needs. Someday we'll pay him back. Besides," he said, sitting back, "it would be better to take him with us, and I don't mean just because of his money."

"What do you mean? How could it possibly be better?"

"It will help enormously to have an adult with us, especially him because he's your uncle. There's enough of a family resemblance to tell people he's your father."

"No," I said sharply. "That's the ugly rumor the twins were exploiting."

"So let's exploit it, too, only to help us and not hurt us. If people believe it, none will question why we are on the road and what we are trying to do. Don't you see how perfect this is?" he asked, the strain and frustration in his voice.

"I do. It's just . . ."

"Just what?"

"Just that I'm frightened, Heyden."

"To tell you the truth, Hannah, so am I, but what should I do? Remain here and let my mother and my sister drag me down, or go out there and seek a new and better life?

"And you, do you want to remain where you are, swimming in a pool of guilt and regret, coming home to unhappiness every day? I can tell you firsthand what that does to you. Before long, nothing will look good to you. You'll hate the morning because all it will be doing is starting another miserable day," he said and sat back again.

"Let me think about it," I relented.

"Right. Think about it," he said sharply.

My heart was pounding. When I dropped him off, I promised again that I would really think about it.

"You know what it's like to do that, Hannah? All this thinking and thinking? You ever stand on a diving board when you were younger?"

"Yes."

"Remember how the longer you looked down, the less courage you had? You had to concentrate on the technique, the process, and then just do it, otherwise, you would eventually retreat and you would never know what it could have been like. That's us. Think about it, but don't think about it too much, and whatever you do, don't look down," he advised, turned, and strode toward the front door of his dark house.

I drove home in such a daze, I didn't even remember the turns I had made.

"Where were you?" Mommy screamed down at me. She was at the top of the stairway, apparently alerted to my return the moment I opened the front door. She took a step down. "Well? Go on, tell me," she ordered.

"I had to go for a ride," I said.

"Where did you go, Hannah?"

"I went to see Heyden."

She took another step down. I looked behind her and down the hallway. Where was Miguel?

"And then where did you go?" she followed. It was obvious from the way she looked at me and the tone in her voice that she already knew the answer.

"I went to see Uncle Linden. I was worried about him after what you told me."

"Even though I forbade you to do it, you went ahead and did it, is that it?"

"I did what I thought was right, Mommy."

"You are not to use my car again. Ever!" she screamed. "Now go to your room and don't you dare to set foot off this property except to go to school, understand?"

"But—"

"I will not permit the madness to give life to the curse on this family. I will not permit it. I will fight it now, fight it tooth and nail," she vowed, lifting her right fist in the air.

She continued to look up at the ceiling.

"You took my baby, but you will regret it," she threatened.

Whom was she threatening? God? Fate? Me?

"Go to your room," she ordered, turned, and walked back upstairs.

I went looking for Miguel instead and found him in the library, sitting at the desk and sipping from a glass of bourbon, the bottle beside him. He was staring out the window, reminding me of Uncle Linden, actually.

"Miguel?"

He turned slowly. "Oh, Hannah. I came downstairs looking for you, wondering why you hadn't come up to tell me about dinner, and Lila said she heard you leave. You took Willow's car without her permission or mine?"

"I just felt I had to get away for a while."

"Your mother was very upset. She went to the phone, and she called Mrs. Robinson, who told her you and that boy had just left. Why did you do that, Hannah? Why? Are you deliberately adding fuel to the fire of her sorrow, my sorrow?"

"No, just the opposite."

"Just the opposite?" He shook his head. "You have a funny way of doing just the opposite. Selfish. That's all. Thinking only of yourself. Maybe you can't help it. Maybe you inherited it from your father," he said bitterly and took another sip of his straight bourbon.

"That's not fair, Miguel."

"I'm tired," he said. "Tired of protecting everyone, tired of fighting for happiness. Maybe there is something here we can't stop. Go on, Hannah. Go on to bed. You have to bear responsibility for your actions now. I'm not going to get in between you and your mother on this. I hope you'll come to your senses and make a change," he said and turned away. "I have my own pain to endure. I'm not taking on anyone else's for the moment," he muttered.

Stunned and deeply hurt, so much so I felt mortally wounded, I was speechless. This time my tears did burn my eyes. I let them roll down my cheeks and fly off with my quick stride out of the library, through the corridor, and up the stairs to my room where I slammed my door shut and sat on my bed, the fury in me feeling like a small hurricane building and building and threatening to burst and blow me apart. I wanted it to do just that.

What was it Miguel had said: He hoped I would make a change?

Yes, Miguel, that's exactly what I will do, I thought, and I went to my phone.

Heyden picked up after one ring.

"Hey," he said. "Sorry I was so hard on you. I understand what you're feeling, how scary this whole idea is for you, and I guess—"

"No, you don't," I said quickly. "Make the arrangements. We're taking Uncle Linden and we're leaving as soon as you can arrange it."

"Really?"

"Just do it!" I nearly screamed.

"Okay, okay. Hey," he said, "you're not going to regret this."

"What difference does it make what I regret and don't regret? I just want to do something good for someone and you're right: Taking Uncle Linden out of there is the best thing we can do for him. At least someone really wants me, needs me."

"Two someones," Heyden said. "Don't forget me."

"I won't," I said, smiling through my fury and drying my eyes.

"I'll get right on it," he promised.

"Oh, I can't use the car anymore, Heyden. How are we going to get back to Uncle Linden to tell him we're really going to do it and he should get his money transferred?"

"We'll use my moped. It will take us longer, but we can get over there. When we have to take him to the bank, we'll get a taxicab. These aren't big problems, Hannah. Trust me. I'll solve it all and take over from here."

"How can I do that? Mommy and Miguel are going to be sure I come right home from school. I've been forbidden to set foot off the property."

"So go right home. You can sneak out afterward, can't you?"

"Yes, I suppose I can."

All these little acts of disobedience were like little lies, tiny leaks that soon gushed and took over completely.

"Then there's no problem. We'll plan it all out in school tomorrow. Start packing," he said.

And that was just what I thought I would begin to do.

*   *   *

The following morning Heyden and I met like two conspirators in school, keeping ourselves far enough away from anyone else so no one could overhear any of our conversation. Half the time I found we were whispering. Oh, my friends were watching us and talking about us. I could see that, but none of them had any idea what we were plotting.

Heyden had downloaded a copy of the motor-home description with pictures on his computer and showed it to me.

"You can see we have lots of room for us and Uncle Linden," he said.

"What if he gets frightened, Heyden?"

"Of what?"

"He's never really been away. He's only been in hospitals and homes and Joya del Mar."

"He won't get frightened as long as we are confident," he insisted. "We have just got to keep our own fears and nervousness covered up well."

He looked down and then up and smiled.

"I made the deal."

"You did?"

"And once he heard it was for cash, it was even a better one than I originally thought. I have to bring the money to the owner as soon as possible. Right after you get home, you'll get out and we'll go to Uncle Linden and take him to the bank so he can make his withdrawal."

"But what if Mrs. Robinson gets wind of this? We can't just take him off in a cab. She lets me take him for walks, but she's never let me take him in a cab or in the car. I would need Mommy's permission first."

Heyden thought a moment.

"What we'll do is pretend we're just taking him for a walk, and about a block or so away we'll get the cab. Then we'll get the motor home and leave."

"Leave. You mean today?"

"Of course. I can't park the thing by my house. We've got to go. You told me last night to make the arrangements as soon as possible. I did exactly what you told me to do."

"But . . . what about my things?"

"You didn't pack a lot I hope?"

I looked down.

"You didn't pack at all, did you?" he asked, his voice dripping with disappointment.

I shook my head.

"Why not?"

"I don't know. I started to and then I was worried someone would see what I had done. I didn't think we were really going to go this soon."

"You called me. You led me to believe you had decided. You—"

"I know. I know. Don't keep telling me that."

I thought a moment.

He watched me, his face full of anticipation. He didn't even look as if he was breathing.

"All right," I said. "I know what I want to take. It won't take me fifteen minutes to put it all in a suitcase."

"Do you have something like a duffel bag, something soft so we can tie it to the moped?"

"No. At least, I don't think I do."

"Then fill up a pillowcase. That's what I did. And tie it and that'll do just fine."

"My dresses, shoes, blouses, and skirts, in a pillowcase?"

"Hannah, we don't need all that much to start. We'll get things as we go along. This isn't one of your ritzy vacations. We're going to be on the road, roughing it. We'll have to do the same for Uncle Linden: buy him what he needs as we go along. You're not thinking realistically. You're still not serious enough about this," Heyden said, shaking his head.

"Yes, I am," I insisted. "All right. I'll manage. I promise."

He thought a moment. "Go home from school now," he said suddenly.

"What?"

"Go on. Go complain about a stomachache or something and get picked up or delivered home. I can see you'll need a little more time to prepare, a lot more than I will."

"But . . ."

I was going to say I had to attend my next class. We were having an exam, but the ridiculousness of that struck me like a rock in my forehead. If I was really leaving, nothing I did here mattered anymore.

"What?" he asked, looking frantic.

"Nothing. Okay. I'm going to the nurse's office."

"Wait," he said as I started away.

"What, Heyden? I'm doing everything you want," I said, exasperated.

He smiled. "You don't know what time I'm coming by for you. We haven't decided on exactly where to meet outside your property. Some spy you'd make."

"Oh. Well, what time?"

He looked at his watch. "I'm cutting out of here at lunchtime. I'll pick you up at one-thirty. We need time to get Uncle Linden and get him to his bank."

"Okay," I said.

A part of me couldn't help wishing we would be discovered and stopped, and yet, there was a bigger part of me full of excitement and hope.

"Remember. Don't let anyone see you or know you're really leaving. Otherwise, they might find a way to stop us. Understand?"

"Yes," I said, my voice sounding so small I questioned for a moment that I had actually spoken.

"See you soon," he said and walked off.

The nurse called home, but Lila told her my mother was at her office, which was something that took me by surprise. The nurse called her there and told her I wasn't feeling well. She described my symptoms. I knew from the way the nurse spoke, listened, and nodded that my mother was diagnosing it as merely monthly cramps.

"You're probably right," the nurse said and hung up. She turned to me. "Your mother is calling someone named Ricardo to come for you," she said. "You can lie down until he arrives."

I wasn't surprised that Miguel couldn't come. He was in class, but even if it was only my monthlies, it did shock me that Mommy would send Ricardo and not come herself. I remember when I was little, Miguel used to gently criticize Mommy for doting too much on my every little complaint and every change in mood.

Once I even heard him say, "You must stop this paranoia, Willow. Hannah shows no signs of the manic depression your mother suffered and you think you suffer from time to time. It's only another ghost you must put to rest. Sometimes I think we should sell Joya del

Mar and go someplace else. Sometimes I think Linden is the only one with any sense among us."

How could she move so quickly from a mother who worried over my every frown and grimace to a mother who could send a gardener to pick up her ailing daughter? Was this to be my punishment for somehow contributing to little Claude's death? I couldn't wait to get home to fill that pillowcase, and that was just what I rushed to do as soon as Ricardo drove up to the front door. I practically leaped out of the car.

"I thought you were sick to your stomach," he called after me.

I charged up the stairs, into the house, and up the stairway to my room. For a moment I just stood in the middle and turned in circles. What would I take? What couldn't I stand to leave behind? Did it matter that much? Wasn't I ever coming back?

I started to choose toiletries and realized how foolish that was. Take only things you can't buy on the road, Hannah, I told myself and began to sift through my clothing. A pillowcase never looked as small to me as when I was trying to put in another skirt and another blouse. And shoes! I loved this pair and that. Didn't I need more than one pair of sneakers? What if we go into a much colder climate for a while? I should have a pair of boots, shouldn't I?

Pictures? No, none. I would just cry over them, I thought. What about dolls? There was that rag doll that Mommy gave me years ago, telling me my grandmother had made it for her and had modeled the doll's face after Mommy's from pictures she had. Was it wrong to take that doll out of this house? What if I somehow lost it?

No, I decided. I had to say goodbye to it for a while, perhaps a long, long while. No dolls, no remembrances of things past, no mementoes from parties and dances, even my own Sweet Sixteen party. It all belonged here, left in my past. Heyden and I were really starting a new life, and so was Uncle Linden.

With that sort of censorship in mind, it suddenly became easier to pack the pillowcase. I wouldn't even take my toothbrush. We would do as Heyden had said: buy what we needed as we went along.

When I was finished, I realized no one could look at this room and know I had left it. No one would suspect I was really gone, not for a while, but despite my anger and my new hope, I couldn't just walk out and close the door. That was too cruel.

I sat at my desk and debated with myself. Heyden had made it very clear that I tell no one I was leaving, not even give a hint. Yet I couldn't just walk out and let Mommy wait up for me, even though I had real doubts that she would. She would leave it up to Miguel, perhaps.

Maybe not. Maybe I was being too hard on her. No, I had to leave her something. I pulled my stationery out and stared at a blank page.

Dear Mommy and Miguel, I wrote. That was the easy part.

I know that in the beginning you will be very angry at me, maybe even angrier than you are at me now. In time I hope you will understand why I am doing this.

Whatever anyone says, I can't help but feel the clouds of blame and guilt hovering over my head every day here. I shall never forget that Miguel had to come for me when he was most needed here, and in my heart I fear you will never forget, either, Mommy. I know you don't hate me. I know you can't hate me, but for a while it will be as it has been, very hard for you to look at me and not think about it. I understand, but it's like living with a drill of fire pointing at me always.

You never saw so many faults in me as you do now, and you never had as much coldness in your voice when you spoke to me as you do now.

For the longest time I have been trying to get you and Miguel to understand I am not a child anymore. I need to be treated like an adult, to be trusted with the truth, whether it be ugly or not. Perhaps I am, as some of my friends think and most of my friends are, spoiled. Perhaps I have been protected too much.

I think the best way for me to mature is to go out on my own for a while, and I think the time we are apart will be good for all of us.

Just know that a day won't pass without my thinking of you and looking forward to the time when I can return and when we can be more than just mother and daughter, when we can be friends again as well.

Love,
Hannah

I put the letter in an envelope and left it on my pillow. Then I turned and walked to the door. I had to stand there for a while and look at each and every thing, no matter how small or how insignificant it might first appear. Everything had some sentimental significance and touched me in some way, even the view from my windows. I would never have a view like it or look out on what they looked out upon again.

Goodbye to all my childhood fears and my childhood fantasies, I thought, for all of it still lived somewhere within these walls, every cry, every sob, every laugh somewhere within them, resting, touched only by a dream or by a fleeting memory. This was a house with history, and mine was part of it. Years and years from now someone else surely would live here, and she might wonder about a chip in the wood, a scratch in the window, a piece of wrapping paper inside a closet. Perhaps my dreams would invade hers.

Forgive me, room, I thought. *You were never a disappointment, but what I seek now is outside and away.*

I turned and hurried out before anyone came home. In minutes I was walking quickly down the driveway, and moments later I was outside the gate. Heyden was there on his moped. He held up his hand, and I took a deep breath and hurried to him.

"I was getting worried," he said. "You're almost fifteen minutes late."

"Am I? Sorry."

"Good work," he said, holding my pillowcase. He tied it securely to the moped and patted the seat behind him. "Let's go. We have a lot to do."

I got on and placed my feet carefully. He started it, and we rolled forward.

I looked back once even though I had made a pact with myself not to look back. I just couldn't help it. Joya del Mar had its own powers. I could almost hear the flowers, the trees, the house itself calling to me, begging me not to go.

Or was that just the voice inside myself, tiny and frightened, soon to be drowned out by the roar of the wind passing my ears and the thunder of my own heartbeat?

10

On the Road

For a moment I thought Uncle Linden had forgotten every word we had spoken yesterday. He was sitting on the porch as usual, and he looked very relaxed and contented. The expression of surprise on his face when we pulled up on Heyden's moped convinced me he never really expected us to return, at least not as soon as this.

"Say," he said as we walked up to the porch, "shouldn't you guys be in school?" He checked his watch. "Today a holiday or something?"

"We've left school for good, Uncle Linden," I said. Just saying it made me tremble a little.

"Oh?"

"We're going ahead with the travel plans," Heyden said. "I've made all the arrangements. You remember everything we discussed last night, right?"

Uncle Linden smiled. "You mean, leaving on a motor home?"

"Yes, exactly."

Uncle Linden patted his jacket's breast pocket.

"My bank book is right here," he said. "I figured I'd keep it on me just in case."

"Great. Okay. Here's our plan. We're going for a walk. At the corner of the next block there's a drugstore. I'll have a cab meet us there. We'll go directly to the owner of the motor home and pick it up."

"That's good," Uncle Linden said. "That way no one here butts into my business."

"Hannah," Heyden said, turning to me. "Take Uncle Linden in and get only what is absolutely necessary from his room. Then tell Mrs. Robinson you're taking him for a walk."

"There's nothing in there that I want," Uncle Linden said suddenly and stood up. "Let's just go."

"But what about Mrs. Robinson?" I asked.

"No, he's right," Heyden said, lowering his voice. "If she knows he went off with us, she'll tell your parents, and they might get the police to stop us before we leave somehow. This will buy us that much more time undetected. C'mon. Let's make tracks while we can do it unnoticed."

He started away, and to my surprise, Uncle Linden, with a vigorous gait, followed. I looked back at the front door. No one had come upon us yet, but I was very nervous. I had never taken him away from the building without letting someone know. Then I thought, take him away from the building? What's that? You're taking him out of the whole state!

"Walk him to the drugstore," Heyden said, getting on the moped. "I don't want to leave this here. I'll meet you there."

He started up and drove off. I looked back at the residency again and then took Uncle Linden's hand, my heart thumping so hard I was sure he could feel the drumbeat in my fingers, and started across the street. We went nearly the whole block without speaking.

"Are you very sure you want to do this with us, Uncle Linden?" I asked.

"I'll let you in on a secret," he said, smiling. "I didn't sleep all night thinking about it."

"Really?"

"This is the nicest thing you could do for me, Hannah. Thank you," he said, and I walked faster.

By the time we arrived at the drugstore, Heyden had called for the taxicab.

"Where is your moped?" I asked, seeing our packed pillowcases beside him.

"Sold it," he said, "for twenty bucks." He showed me the bill.

"You sold it for only twenty dollars?"

"Had to get rid of it fast, and this young guy standing here waiting for a bus couldn't believe his luck."

"I'll bet," I said.

"I don't have any need for it now," Heyden declared, beaming.

Uncle Linden nodded. "He's right," he said. "It's like we're throwing all our excess weight overboard to keep the boat floating."

The taxicab arrived and we got in. Heyden gave him the bank's address, and in moments we were on our way. I had, in what was surely my mother's way of thinking, truly kidnapped my uncle.

Heyden asked the taxi driver to wait for us outside the bank and we entered. The suspicious way the tall, lean, bald-headed bank teller looked at us with his beady eyes made my heart skip beats, but Uncle Linden had identification in his wallet, and after the teller conferred with a female manager who was at a desk behind him, he returned to the window, smiled, and asked how Uncle Linden wanted the money. Uncle Linden turned to Heyden, who told him in what denominations to have it cashed. Less than twenty minutes later the three of us emerged, got back into the taxicab, and headed for the address for the motor home. The location was just outside of Jupiter Beach, which made it a very expensive taxi ride, but money didn't seem to matter very much anymore.

When we arrived, my heart sank. The motor home looked nothing like it had in the picture Heyden had showed me. I could see he was disappointed as well, but didn't want to reveal it. The compact mini motor home was built on a one-ton van cab. The door on the cab was banged in so badly, I wondered if it actually opened and closed. There were dents all over the coach's body. The window of the cabover had been hit with what looked like a BB pellet or a rock and although still intact, had a spidery web of cracks from one end to another. The front bumper was bashed on the right side and one of the tires was missing a wheel cover. Parts of the outside looked rusted, some places so badly they were peppered with holes.

"Heyden," I whispered. "Does it work?"

"Sure. The owner guarantees it's in good operating condition," he told me as we got out.

Uncle Linden was still smiling. It was as though he was looking through rose-colored glasses now and saw a brand-spanking-new vehicle instead of the wreck I saw before us.

"It doesn't matter what it looks like on the outside, Hannah," Heyden said as we started toward the A-frame old house with a small porch and anemic front lawn. It was scarred with patches of dirt and inundated with weeds. "It's what it will do for us that matters."

He turned to Uncle Linden. "Let me conclude our business arrangements, Uncle Linden."

"Sure, sure. Let's do it," he said, handing Heyden the envelope full of money.

Heyden went to the front door and knocked. No one came, so he knocked again, harder and louder.

"Didn't you tell the owner we were coming today?" I asked.

"Absolutely. I called him from the drugstore right after I called for the cab."

We waited, but still no one opened the door. Suddenly the door of the coach opened and a stout bald-headed man with just a patch of grayish brown hair behind each ear emerged. He was in a torn T-shirt and a pair of faded brown shorts that hung like an afterthought under his protruding belly. He was barefoot, one of his toenails so black, it looked dipped in ink.

"Yo there!" he called to us.

He had a can of beer in his left hand and took a gulp as he beckoned. Then he wiped his thick lips with the back of his right hand, crushed the emptied beer can in his left hand, and tossed it toward an opened garbage pail. The can hit the edge of the pail and bounced off to the right.

"Would you believe I was on the starting five of my high school basketball team?" he asked, laughing. He had a lower front tooth missing, and there were blotches of pale red over his cheeks and under his chin.

"Hi, I'm Heyden Reynolds. This is my uncle Linden Montgomery and his daughter Hannah."

"Pleased to meetcha," he said, offering Uncle Linden his thick-fingered hand, the fingertips of which were stained with nicotine.

Uncle Linden smiled and shook it.

"I know she don't look like much on the outside," the owner said, turning to the motor home, "but she runs like a thoroughbred, dependable. I take good care of it, and I'd expect you to do the same," he added, raising his untrimmed gray-brown eyebrows and lowering his head simultaneously. His jowls ballooned.

"Absolutely," Heyden said.

"She's all gassed up and ready to roll," the owner said. He looked at our pillowcases. "That all you taking?"

"No, we're picking other things up after we leave," Heyden said quickly.

"Good, good. You brought the money in cash?" he asked, directing himself to Uncle Linden now.

"Yes, yes, we did."

"And you have a credit card for me to use for some sort of guarantee?"

"Yes," I said when Heyden nodded to me. I produced the card and the owner took it, looked at it, looked at me, and then at Uncle Linden.

"I thought you said the name was Montgomery. This here card says Hannah Eaton?"

My heart sank.

Uncle Linden smiled. "This is my daughter," he said, "but my wife has remarried. This trip is a way for us to get to know each other again, if you get what I mean."

Heyden smiled. I had to admit to myself that Uncle Linden's quick thinking was impressive. I guess Heyden's right, I thought, Uncle Linden didn't need to be under any doctor's microscope.

"Oh. Oh, yeah, sure," the owner said, nodding, but he still looked suspicious. "Okay, let's do the paperwork. I've rented this baby out ten times without a single problem," he added, sounding more threatening now. "She has a rebuilt Ford engine under the hood. Should give you no trouble if you don't abuse her."

"We won't do that," Uncle Linden said with a calm sense of assurance that obviously impressed the owner.

He grunted. "I was just in there checking every appliance and everything else. Nothin's broken. You can go in there and confirm that while I go get the paperwork," he said and headed for the house.

"Thank you," Uncle Linden said.

He nodded and walked off.

Heyden looked at me and then at Uncle Linden.

"You're doing great, Uncle Linden. Thanks."

"Piece of cake," Uncle Linden said, still looking quite amused and excited. "Shall we?" he asked, gesturing toward the coach door.

"Right." Heyden opened it, and we all stepped up and in.

The first thing that struck me was the odor. It

smelled like stale beer and cheese. Of course, there was no linen of any sort, not that I would want to use it if there had been. Heyden and I checked the refrigerator, the stove, the microwave, and the sink. Everything did appear to be working despite appearances that would suggest otherwise.

"I hope the toilet works," I muttered to myself. All the faucets were rusty, stains in the sinks. The floor of the coach had a cheap linoleum broken in many places. The layout was simple with a bedroom in the rear. The sofa opened to produce another bed, the one Uncle Linden would have.

It suddenly occurred to me that Uncle Linden would know Heyden and I had slept together and would be sleeping together now. When I gazed at the one real bed, I felt myself flush with the realization. What would we do?

Heyden came up beside me, anticipating my thoughts.

"I'm sleeping in the cabover," Heyden whispered. "Don't worry about it."

I looked back at Uncle Linden, who was still smiling as he moved through the coach and then went to the driver's seat.

"It's been a long time since I drove!" he shouted back to us. "I'd better let you get it under way. Maybe later I'll take a turn at it."

"Right," Heyden said, smiling at me. "He's like a kid again."

We heard the door open and the owner stepped up.

"Well?" he said. "Everything's in order, right?"

"Yes," Heyden said quickly.

The owner handed my card back to me.

"I copied all the numbers down," he said and turned to Heyden. "You folks break anything, you folks fix it."

"We understand," Heyden said, trying desperately not to appear too anxious. He reminded me of a horse, chafing at the bit.

The owner held his gaze steady. "I hope so," he said.

Heyden handed him the cash, and he counted it out and then he gave Heyden the keys.

"I got the time marked down. The deal is six months to the day. You bring it back late, you pay for an extra day."

"Okay," Heyden said. "Thanks."

The owner looked at Uncle Linden, who was sitting in the driver's seat and gazing out as if he could already see the beautiful scenery.

"Yeah, well, mind everything I told you. The manuals are all here."

"Thanks again," Heyden said.

The owner looked at us one more time and then stepped out and closed the door.

Heyden turned to me.

"We've got it," he said, his eyes as bright and joyful as Christmas lights. "We're off, Uncle Linden," he said.

"What? Oh. Good, good," Uncle Linden said and got out of the driver's seat.

Heyden got into it, studied the dashboard a moment, and then started the engine. I thought it made a lot of noise, but he didn't seem to notice.

"Fasten your seatbelts!" he cried, then shifted and started out of the driveway. I had to admit he looked as if he had been driving motor homes for years. Seconds later we were moving down the street.

"I'm going to get us to the 95," he said. "We'll go for a while and then pull off and find a department store."

"Good plan," Uncle Linden said. He had taken the seat beside him.

I found I was holding my breath on and off. I actually felt a little numb.

We were doing it. We were actually leaving. Heyden started to hum what had become our theme song, *Leaving on a Motor Home*.

Surely this was a wonderful idea, I told myself. Look how happy Uncle Linden appears to be, looking out his window, watching the scenery pass, saying goodbye to the only world he has ever known, but a world that never wanted or welcomed him. He wasn't going off to start a new life the way we were exactly. He was escaping. And then I thought Heyden and I hadn't been living in a residency, but all three of us felt the same way.

We were all escaping.

It soon felt like a prolonged picnic, an outing that didn't end. About an hour and a half into the ride, Heyden decided it was time to pull off and get our shopping done. He took the first exit, and ten minutes later we pulled into the parking lot for a sprawling mall.

"What's first?" he asked.

"Let's get what we need for the house," I said.

"Yes, our house," Uncle Linden seconded.

Heyden drove toward the department store, and we got out of the motor home.

"She does drive well," he said, gesturing back at it as

we walked toward the entrance of the department store. "I guess he wasn't lying to us."

"I think you would have rented an old horse and buggy if you had to, Heyden."

"Probably," he admitted, laughing.

We went into the store and immediately began to behave like two people who had just arrived from a third-world country. Even Uncle Linden joined in on our childlike excitement, pouncing on the basic clothes and things he needed. After I filled our cart with what I considered the necessities—sheets, pillows, pillowcases and blankets, towels and washcloths—we bought decorative pictures in gilded frames, a clock, two area rugs, and, at Uncle Linden's insistence, a small television set and a DVD player.

"I've been asking for one of these back at the home, but Mrs. Robinson insisted it wasn't necessary. The other residents fall asleep watching television. What difference did it make how good the picture was?"

"Now you have it, Uncle Linden," Heyden told him.

"Yes. Now I have it."

I had to get another cart for our kitchen supplies, dishes, silverware, some pots and pans and paper goods. Our bill at the register was over three thousand dollars. Uncle Linden didn't hesitate to pay for it.

"We're cutting deeply into our bankroll," I warned Heyden.

"Don't worry about money. We're going to get work sooner than you can imagine," he assured me.

How I wished I had his confidence and optimism about everything. Was it because he came from so much darker a place than I did that he had so much sunlight in his eyes now? Where my steps and motions were tentative and cautious, his were quick and reckless. Buy this, do that, don't worry about tomorrow. How did he get such a warranty on the future? I wondered, and hoped that whatever left him with such sanguinity would infect me the same way soon.

Moving on to the supermarket, we truly behaved like people just let out of the loony bin. Uncle Linden lunged for cookies and cereals he hadn't had in ages. I tried to buy as sensibly as I could to keep our bill low, but between him and Heyden, both acting like children in a candy store, piling confections and ice cream into the cart, as well as cases of soda, I soon gave up. This bill reached over four hundred dollars.

We were so foolish, too, because our small refrigerator couldn't hold all the things that had to be kept frozen. We ended up having to eat a half dozen ice-cream pops. I chastised them both, but they only laughed and cried, "Pass me another before it melts!"

I went about organizing the bedrooms and the foods in our small cabinets. Three hours later we took exit 84 and pulled off the highway and parked in what was considered a scenic place. From where we were, we could see Canaveral and one of the space shuttle launch pads.

There I prepared our first dinner: a salad with macaroni and cheese.

"I don't want anyone to think I'm much of a cook," I warned. "I've never had to do much in the kitchen."

"Don't worry about it," Heyden said. "I have. I'll tackle the more complicated dinners, like steak and French fries."

Uncle Linden laughed and then declared my macaroni and cheese was ten times better than the slop Mrs. Robinson put out for her guests.

"She has no idea how to season anything. Now my mother, she was a good cook for someone who had been brought up like a princess. She liked to cook, to create different versions of different meals. 'You're an artist with paint, Linden,' she would tell me. 'I'll be one with food.' "

"Tell me more about her," I urged. It was always so difficult to get Mommy to talk about those days. Uncle Linden sat back, smiling at the pictures, events, and words he had begun to draw out of his well of memories.

"She had a peacefulness about her that would also manage to calm the storms raging inside me. I can't remember her raising her voice." He thought a moment. "She was the kind of person who makes you feel terrible for every and any passing moment of sadness or unhappiness you might have caused her." He shook his head. "Willow was like that, too."

It brought tears to my eyes to hear my mother's name mentioned. Had she found my note by now? Was she crying or raging with anger? Had they called the police? Did they know about Uncle Linden being with us or did everyone assume he had gone off on his own? Surely, Heyden's mother was contacted, too. What did she say? How sad and unhappy was she? Heyden hadn't mentioned her yet, nor had he mentioned his sister. If he had any regrets, they were so deeply buried, it would take days of intense psychotherapy to get him to reveal just the surfaces of them.

"Well," he said, breaking the heavy silence that had fallen among us. "It's time to get out the map and plan our trip."

He reached into his duffel bag and produced an automobile club map, spreading it on the table. Tracing with his finger, he pointed to a route that would take us through South Carolina. I saw the way that lit up Uncle Linden's eyes. We were indeed on a great adventure, and he was just as Heyden had suggested, a little boy again.

"I thought we would follow the so-called Savannah River Scenic Highway," he said. "There'll be plenty to see, plenty for Uncle Linden to appreciate as an artist."

"Oh, right," Uncle Linden said. "The next chance we get, I'll need to buy some supplies. I should have thought about that and gone back into the house for my easel and paints."

"We were in such a rush, we all forgot," I said. "Sorry."

"That's okay. I'll get new things. Time I did anyway," Uncle Linden said.

Like Heyden, he seemed incapable of being discouraged. Our trip was still far too filled with promise to entertain anything that might spoil it.

"After we go here, we'll bear southwest and head for New Orleans, where our opportunities to sing and make money will abound," Heyden declared. "We'll be there in a matter of a few days."

"New Orleans. I've always wanted to go there. There's an artist I like from New Orleans. He did all those swamp pictures with the Spanish moss hanging down like great cobwebs. Boy, this is great," Uncle

Linden said, clapping his hands together. "Let's keep going."

Heyden laughed.

"We can't ride all day and all night, Uncle Linden. Why don't we just settle in here for the night. It's a pretty enough spot," Heyden said.

"Okay. I'll watch one of those DVDs we bought."

"Sure. Let me set it up for you," Heyden told him and went right to it while I cleaned off the table and started to wash our dishes.

"I'll be right with you to help you with that, Hannah," Heyden said, leaning over the carton that held the DVD.

"I'm fine," I said. "I can dirty my little hands, too."

He laughed. "If all those snobby girls back in Palm Beach could see us now," he said.

"Yes."

I thought about them, about school, about what I had left behind. I couldn't think of anyone in my class who would trade living in Joya del Mar with its beautiful grounds and pool and beach for living in a battered motor home. Yet somehow, being on my own like this, with the whole world seemingly out there to be seen and explored, I didn't feel I had taken a giant step back-ward. The lives of my friends were truly predictable. It was all laid out before them, their maps, their scenic highways designed and chosen for them even before they were born perhaps. If they veered too far to the left or right, went too slowly or resisted going forward, they would be criticized and pressured to conform, not that many of them wanted to even approach anything nearly as rebellious as what I had done.

"There," Heyden said when he was able to start the movie for Uncle Linden, who sat in the living room chair looking as if he were sitting in the most expensive furniture set in the most luxurious room. "It's all set and ready for you, Uncle Linden."

"Thanks," he said, settling in the small, big-cushioned chair that looked so old and worn, I thought he would sink to the floor. He didn't seem to mind.

"Do you want something else, Uncle Linden? Coffee, tea, anything?"

"No, I'm fine. Thank you, Hannah."

Heyden winked at me and went to the coach door.

"How about a walk, Hannah?" he asked.

I looked at Uncle Linden.

"He'll be fine. Right, Uncle Linden?"

"What? Oh, yes, I'm fine. Don't worry about me."

I smiled and then I joined Heyden, and we stepped out of the coach.

"Let's not go too far, Heyden. Despite what he claims, he might get frightened."

"He's really all right, Hannah. I can see that he was shut up for no reason."

"I don't know. You don't know his history, how long it's taken for him to get to where he's at now. You do know that he gets terribly confused sometimes. Sometimes he goes into a depression that rivals a coma. You haven't seen that side of him yet."

"And I won't. That's not going to happen, not with us. Not now," Heyden insisted.

"Going off like this doesn't cure everything, Heyden. Let's not be unrealistic," I warned.

His smile faded and then came shooting back.

"No, it doesn't, but it's a start. Look, the first stars are out," he said. "You ever take time to look at the stars?"

"Yes. When I walk down to our beach."

"Yeah, I forgot," he said, disappointed. "You have always had your own private beach. Well, I'm in the middle of a city street, and with the lights all around me, it's hard to see stars or even care," he said bitterly. "At least, it was. Not anymore, never again," he vowed with such vehemence, I was actually frightened for a moment. He looked capable of doing anything to stay free of his past.

He saw the look in my face and smiled.

"Don't blame me for wanting this so much."

"I don't. I just want to keep our feet on the ground and be as realistic about it all as we can, Heyden."

"We will. I promise. This is our first free night, though, Hannah. Just tonight let's act like a couple of dreamers, okay?" he pleaded.

I smiled. "Okay."

He took my hand and we walked down to the beach where we could sit and look toward the space shuttle.

"I guess those guys really get away from it all up there," Heyden said. "I wonder if they feel like they're closer to God or something."

"I suppose when they see the world that way, they can have such a feeling."

Heyden looked at me. "When I'm with you, Hannah, I can, too. It's like being up there, I bet. Like floating in space, above everything, the noise, the static. It's all drowned out, and all I can see is you; all I can hear is you, and all I care to touch is you."

I smiled and looked down at the sand. "You're not even a bit afraid of what we're doing, Heyden?"

"Sure, I'm afraid. If I wasn't, I'd be worried about myself. Then I would know I'm completely bonkers, unrealistic. I know it's not going to be as easy as I make it sound, but I think it's possible, Hannah. I think we're possible. You've given me the hope, you and yes, Uncle Linden."

I looked up at him. With only the starlight, it was still easy to see his eyes burning with determination and what I surely thought was love. He leaned forward and kissed me softly. Then he lay back on the sand.

"I like the warmth in the sand afer the sun goes down, before night cools it. Don't you?"

"Yes," I said, lying back beside him.

"Pick two stars that are close to each other, and we'll claim them for ourselves," he said. "At least for the trip."

I read the night sky and then pointed to my right.

"I see them," Heyden said. "I'm the one on the right because the one on the left twinkles more."

"Oh, I'm twinkle toes now?"

He laughed. "To me you are," he said and kissed me again.

We embraced and I buried my head in the nook between his head and neck.

"Hold me, Heyden," I said. "Hold me as if I were going to fall off the edge of the world."

"Okay. I'll always hold you that way, Hannah."

So many promises coming so quickly, I thought. I was afraid they were like crepe paper and balloons, tinsel and lights to dress to keep us from seeing what was ordinary.

We were too young for so many promises, too poor to afford them yet. For us promises were still dreams and not plans. It was like floating on a magic carpet with the most dangerous thing being waking up. The air would be air again, and you could fall to the hard earth.

I said nothing, but Heyden felt my tension and fear. He kissed my forehead and cheek and brought his lips to mine, pressing hard as if he wanted to drive out any demons.

"It's going to be okay," he whispered.

I turned to lie back on his outstretched arm and gazed up at the still-emerging stars, each one another promise, too. But when the sun came up, when it was morning, they would be gone, I thought.

How would the world look to us the next day?

After a little while longer, we both decided it was time to go back to see how Uncle Linden was doing. It didn't surprise me to find him asleep in his chair, the movie still playing.

"That's funny. He was complaining about the other residents doing just that."

"He's exhausted. It was just as emotional for him to leave as it was for us," I said.

With Heyden's help, I pulled out the sofa bed and dressed it in the new linen and new pillows and pillow-cases. I fixed Uncle Linden's blanket for him, hoping he would soon wake up himself.

After that Heyden took his bedding and worked on the bed in the cabover. Then he turned off the movie, and Uncle Linden's eyes fluttered open. We both held our breaths. Would he finally realize where he was and what we had done? How would he take it?

"Oh," he said, scrubbing his cheeks and looking at where he was, "fell asleep, did I?"

"Your bed is all ready, Uncle Linden. I set out your new pajamas, too."

"I see that. Thanks, Hannah." He rose, gazed around, nodded, and smiled, then went into the bathroom.

Heyden and I let out simultaneous breaths of relief. Falling asleep had not left him confused. He was still quite aware of everything.

A few moments later Uncle Linden emerged and slipped into his bed.

"Comfortable?" I asked, completing a final cleanup and organization of our tiny kitchen.

"Absolutely. Sweet dreams everybody," he called.

Heyden was up and in his bed.

I started for mine.

"Hannah," Uncle Linden said.

I paused and turned to him. "Yes, Uncle Linden."

"It just occurred to me. This is the first time you and I have slept under the same roof. It's nice," he said, smiling. "Very nice."

I smiled through my teary eyes of happiness. "Yes, it is, Uncle Linden. Good night."

"Good night," he said, turning.

Heyden looked as if he was already asleep. I went into the bedroom and changed into the nightgown I had bought, and then I got into my bed, too. I had the window opened as wide as it could be to air out the coach, but that stale odor lingered. *Tomorrow, I'll do a better cleaning and disinfecting of the place,* I thought.

For a long time I just lay there with my eyes open,

not really thinking of anything in particular, just staring up at the stained yellow ceiling.

Was Mommy going to sleep?

Was she ranting and raving or was she crying in Miguel's arms?

Had I done a very terrible thing, something for which I would go straight to hell?

My two men were sleeping with far more content-ment than I could find. For me it was doomed to be a night of tossing and turning in a bed of regret and fear. When I finally did fall asleep, I dreamed about little Claude, and I woke up and felt tears on my cheeks. How wonderful it would have been to have had a little brother after all. Every note of jealousy I had sounded in myself was another pin of guilt sticking in my heart. I felt so miserable and so confused, I wished I could disappear.

Sleep did not return easily. It came on the back of total exhaustion, and what woke me was not the sun-light pouring through the small window, but the sounds of Heyden and Uncle Linden preparing the breakfast. Every part of me groaned a complaint when I rose and went to the door. The two of them were at the small table having coffee and talking. The map was spread before them again. They looked up with surprise.

"Morning, sleepyhead," Heyden called.

"Sorry I overslept."

"Hey, there are no schedules to follow here, no bells ringing and sending us from one room to another, except the bells in our own heads. The shower works," Heyden added. "Sorta."

"I slept well," Uncle Linden said. "I think it was the best night's sleep I've had in years."

He and Heyden returned their attention to the map and I worked at waking myself up. Heyden wasn't exaggerating when he used the word *sorta* for the tiny shower. It dripped out and it was not even warm.

"It's like being in the army," Heyden told me when I complained. "The famous two-minute shower."

"I didn't last one minute!"

"Well, soon we'll be able to afford a decent hotel," he promised. "Time to go on. We have many miles to cover."

Uncle Linden was already in the passenger's seat, anxiously waiting. Minutes later we were heading back toward the highway and north, creating more and more distance between home and ourselves. How appropriate it was for us to have parked near the space shuttle. It's how I felt this morning: jetting out into the great beyond, with all that once tied us to Mother Earth dropping away every passing moment.

When we crossed into Georgia, we stopped for lunch and found a place for Uncle Linden to get most of his art supplies. He had possessed art supplies most of his adult life, even when he was in a mental clinic because the work was considered therapeutic, but just because we were on our own, I think, with no one to supervise us, no rules to follow, no one to please or displease, he was like a little boy who had been given his first erector set or set of electric trains.

Both Heyden and I could see he was chafing at the bit in his anticipation of doing his first picture on the road, so we decided to have a picnic at the first opportunity to pull off the highway and enjoy the river itself. When we did that, Uncle Linden was too excited to eat. He set up his easel and began to frame out a picture.

"You two sit down there," he said, pointing to a clearing. "Spread your blanket out and just enjoy your lunch."

"But how about you, Uncle Linden?" I asked.

"I'll eat later. Go on. Don't worry about me," he commanded.

Heyden and I smiled at each other and took our food and blanket to where Uncle Linden wanted us. Heyden brought his guitar along, too. It was a magnificent day with just a few clouds that looked like egg whites pouring slowly over a blue skillet. As we sat and had our lunch, Uncle Linden worked away. We began to rehearse songs we thought we might do in any performance. After we sang each two or three times, Heyden decided whether or not we would keep it in our repertoire.

"We've got to get a good mix in here, Hannah," he instructed. "That way we can please more people."

We included love songs, soft rock, a few country songs, and what Heyden classified as classic standards. We worked so long and hard at it that neither of us realized how much time had passed until I noticed how low the sun had gotten. We had even forgotten about Uncle Linden, who never took a moment out to rest himself.

"We'd better get going. I was hoping to make more distance today," Heyden said. "Time to move on, Uncle Linden," he called.

"That's fine. I've done just about as much as I need to here," Uncle Linden said and began to gather his materials.

I folded the blanket. Heyden picked up our other things, and we headed back to the motor home, pausing to look at Uncle Linden's picture. He had left it on the easel while he took in his paints and brushes.

The scenery was done in a very interesting style, almost a Monet background, but the two people meant to be us were realistically depicted.

Heyden saw what I saw and leaned toward me to whisper as Uncle Linden was heading back.

"I look like him," he said.

All I could do was nod. I looked like my mother.

"Well?" Uncle Linden asked. "What do you think of my first work on the road?"

"It's amazing that you did so much so fast," Heyden said quickly.

"It's beautiful, Uncle Linden."

"I'll have to call it *View from a Motor Home* or something," he said, laughing.

Heyden took his easel, and he carried the picture back carefully. He put it safely next to the small sofa.

"I've got to make some time," Heyden said. "I'm going to push it a bit. Mount up."

We started out again, and once we were back on the highway, he did go faster than he had. I kept warning him not to violate the speed limit.

"We don't want to be pulled over by a traffic cop, Heyden. There might be too much explaining to do, or there might be one of what they call an all-points bulletin or something, right?"

"I know, I know, but it's getting dark fast. We should have paid more attention to the time," he said, angry at himself.

"I thought you told me there are no bells ringing to drive us," I chastised softly.

He raised his eyes at me. "We've still got to make distances, Hannah. I want to get us to the work as quickly as I can, you know."

"Then there are bells ringing for us, Heyden."

"All right," he relented. "I can see you'll always be reminding me of reality."

"And myself," I said. "And myself."

Just north of a city called Anderson in South Carolina, Heyden consulted the map and decided to take what looked like a shortcut.

"I'm sure we'll be able to find a good place to spend the night," he said.

I was nervous about leaving the well-traveled highway, but he was confident we would make better time and find a place to pull in for the night more easily this way. Uncle Linden was dozing on and off. He had taken something to drink, but he still hadn't eaten anything and I was worried. I wanted us to pull over so I could start dinner. We had been driving for hours and hours.

"Just let me go a few more miles," Heyden kept pleading.

I was standing over him practically the whole time. The road wasn't bad, but without lights and us not knowing where the next turn would be and how sharp it might be, he couldn't go too fast.

"We're fine," he kept muttering, and then suddenly we heard this terrible metallic groan that was followed by a terrific grinding noise. Following that, the motor home's engine lost all power.

"What the hell . . ."

"What is it?" I cried.

"I don't know. The engine just died on me, and the power steering has gone out."

He struggled to keep us straight and slow down the vehicle.

"Whaaa . . ." Uncle Linden said, stirring and looking out at the darkness before us.

"Engine trouble," Heyden muttered to him.

We came to a stop.

"Oh, no, Heyden."

"Don't panic," he said. "It might not be anything serious. Maybe a wire broke loose or something. Damn," he added when he scrounged about the glove compartment and the cabinets. "We don't have a flashlight, and we forgot to buy one."

"What are we going to do? How are you going to see? We can't light matches over a gas engine!" I cried.

"I know that. Don't you think I know that? Let me think."

"I told you not to leave the main highway, Heyden."

"I was just trying to make up for some lost time," he wailed.

"I'm hungry," Uncle Linden said suddenly. It seemed so unexpected and was so out of place for the situation, I couldn't help but laugh.

"He's right," Heyden said. "Let's just stay calm. We'll have dinner and wait until daylight."

"Right smack on the middle of this highway?"

"There's room for anyone to bypass us and see us."

"You hope."

"Well, what else do you want me to do? We'll leave some lights on."

"I wouldn't mind a good hamburger," Uncle Linden said.

Heyden looked at me. He knew what I was thinking: Uncle Linden wasn't just acting like a little boy from time to time, he was a little boy in so many ways. Almost all of his adult life, someone had taken care of him. *Responsibility* was always a word with a small *r*. What we had done was taken on that responsibility but with a capital *R*.

"Just take it easy. Relax. It'll all work out," Heyden assured me.

"Sure," I said and went to the refrigerator to get some of our meat out of the small freezer. When the light didn't go on, I felt a surge of new panic. "Heyden."

"What?"

"I think the electric went off, too."

"No." He jumped up and looked at the refrigerator. "Damn it," he said.

"All our food is going to spoil. We can't just stay here. Heyden," I said when he didn't reply.

"I know. I know. Don't you think I realize that? I'm not stupid."

I felt the tears come into my eyes. How terrible this was going to be: broken down on some country road, both of us runaways who took my uncle out of a residency. How could we be so naive and foolish to think we could do this? I had permitted so many emotions to block out my sense of reason. I had permitted my anger and my self-pity to possess me.

As if to bring an exclamation point to what I was thinking and what I had finally realized, we heard a loud clap of thunder. Somehow, neither I nor Heyden had noticed how quickly the sky had become overcast and how we had been driving right into the impending storm.

The first drops hit like a warning, and then they grew big and pelted the motor home, sounding like nails, slapping into the sides, the roof, and the front of the vehicle. It was a deafening sound.

I put my hands over my ears. "It's horrible!" I screamed.

"Easy," Uncle Linden suddenly said, as if he had just woken from a deep sleep. "Everything will be all right, Willow. I'm here."

Heyden looked at me with shock and fear scribbled madly over his face.

Willow?

The next clap of thunder came from my own heart.

11

Casa de la Luna

Even though we didn't have a flashlight, Heyden went out as soon as the rain let up to see if he could feel around the engine block and discover anything that he might be able to repair. I was too nervous to prepare any dinner, and Uncle Linden had gone back to sleep. I decided to go out and see if there was anything I could do to help. Just as I stepped out of the coach, a pair of headlights washed its light over us, and a pickup truck appeared, slowed, and came to a stop. It was so dark, it was hard to see who had driven up beside us. I joined Heyden and waited as the door opened and shut. A very big African-American man in a pair of coveralls came around the front of the truck. He looked to be at least six feet seven or eight. I wouldn't have called him fat, but I was willing to bet anyone he was well over two hundred and fifty pounds.

"Y'all have troubles?" he asked.

"Yes, sir, we do," Heyden said, "and we were foolish enough to leave home without a flashlight."

"I'm forgetting more and more myself these days," he said and reached into one of his deep coverall pockets to produce a flashlight. "I leave everything I can in these here coveralls so I don't forget stuff."

When he drew closer, I could see what hair he had was salt white. The stubble on his face was a mixture of salt and pepper. He had big features and the largest hands I had ever seen on a man.

"How's your battery?" he asked Heyden.

"It wasn't showing any problem."

"Well, go on and give her a turn or two and let me listen in," he said.

"Right." Heyden started away and then paused and looked at me. I could see he was concerned about leaving me alone with a stranger.

"I'm all right," I said. "Go try it."

He nodded and hurried back into the cab. A moment later we heard the engine grind.

"Whoa!" the man cried. Heyden stopped and then came out. "I know that sound. You deal with these things long enough, you learn what every tinkle means."

"What do you think it is?" Heyden asked.

"It sure sounds like you've blown a head gasket, I'm afraid."

"Is that a big thing?" I asked quickly.

"Big enough."

"Damn," Heyden said. "Expensive to fix, huh?"

"Somethin' like this, yeah, I imagine it ain't just one bail of cotton, as my daddy used to say."

"We're on sort of a budget," Heyden said shyly.

The big man glanced at the motor home and nodded. He probably thought, who else but someone on a budget would be driving something like this?

"I understand. Well," he said, dropping his flashlight back into his pants, "if I had the parts, I could fix it. This is an old engine in here. I recognize it. Done enough of them in my time."

"Could you really fix it?" Heyden asked.

"Sure. We got everything we need back at Casa de la Luna."

"Casa de la Luna?" I asked. "That means House of the Moon. What is it, a hotel?"

"Oh, it's just the old farm. Mrs. Lilliann Stanton named it that a while back and she gets awful mad if I don't call it that. It ain't but another half mile or so down the road. Y'all get in with me. We'll use the phone and see if a friend of mine back in Anderson can help. He's in the car cemetery business."

"Car cemetery?" I asked.

"Fancy name for junkyard, miss. C'mon," he beckoned and turned to the pickup truck.

"It's not just us," Heyden said.

"Pardon?"

"My father is in the motor home," I said.

"Oh." He looked back at the cab.

"He's been sick," I added quickly.

"Oh, that's too bad with this breakdown and all."

"I can ride in the back," Heyden said. "You go get Uncle Linden."

I turned away from the big man and made a face.

"We can't drag Uncle Linden someplace," I told him under my breath.

"You have any better ideas?" Heyden said. "Look where we are and what's happened."

"He's so confused as it is," I moaned. "Calling me Willow instead of Hannah."

"Confused is better than stranded," Heyden said.

"But what if he gets confused in front of strangers?"

"We'll have to take the chance, Hannah. We don't have much of a choice."

I looked back at the man.

"You need any help with him?" he asked, seeing my hesitation.

"No, sir. Thank you."

"Y'all don't have to call me sir. My name is Charles Anderson Dawson, but folks round here have always called me Chubs, except for Mrs. Stanton, that is. She won't call me anything but Charles. My own momma got so she called me Chubs. I was a big baby. My momma said I weigh close to eighteen pounds when I was born."

"Eighteen pounds!"

"I believe it," Heyden said.

"Course, that was more than eighty-one years ago now," Chubs added.

"Eighty-one?" Could he be telling the truth about anything? I wondered.

"Yes, ma'am. I can name all the Presidents during my lifetime, too."

"Go on, get Uncle Linden," Heyden said sharply. "It could start raining hard again any minute."

"Chances are it will. She ain't finished dumpin' her load yet," Chubs said, looking up and into the inky sky.

"Oh. I'm Heyden Reynolds, and this is my cousin Hannah. My uncle Linden is in the motor home."

Chubs nodded.

I went back in and nudged Uncle Linden. His eyes fluttered open. He looked up at me so strangely that for a moment I thought he was so confused, we were going to have new problems. Then he smiled.

"Time to eat?" he asked.

I released my trapped breath. At least he wasn't calling me Willow, and he'd remembered where we were.

"No, Uncle Linden. Someone came by and is willing to help us with the engine problems. We're going in his pickup truck back to his house to make some phone calls. We can't leave you here, and with our electric out, too, it makes no sense to stay here at the moment."

He just stared at me.

"You understand?"

"Oh. Sure. Let's go," he said, rising out of the seat.

"Wait," I said, turning before we stepped out, "I had to tell him you were my father, so I'll just call you Daddy in front of him and anyone else we meet, okay?"

"Of course you will," he said, smiling again.

It made me feel uneasy, but I just wanted to get all this over with as quickly as we could. He followed me out of the motor home.

"This is my father, Mr. Montgomery," I said, introducing him to Chubs.

"Pleased to meet you," Chubs said. His hand all but swallowed up Uncle Linden's. "Let's see if we can get you people back on your way."

"Yes, well, thank you," Uncle Linden said.

"You get into the truck with Hannah, Uncle Linden," Heyden instructed.

I led Uncle Linden to the truck, and he got in. Heyden leaped into the back. I got in and closed the door, and Chubs started up, shifted, and pulled away. I looked back at the crippled old motor home. To me it resembled a corpse that faded back into the darkness as we drove on. It probably belonged in Chub's friend's car cemetery.

"I've lived here all my life," Chubs began. "Worked for Mr. Stanton and his daddy from the day I could lift a hammer and hold a saw. We was once the biggest peach orchard round here. The farm then was a little more than 250 acres. We growed cling, semifree, and freestone peaches, harvesting cling all of May, semifree May and June, and freestone mid-June to the end of July. After Mr. Stanton Senior passed, we struggled along and eventually had to sell off about 170 acres to some land developers who wanted to build custom homes. Times got harder and harder for us, and without a son to take over, Mr. Stanton Junior just decided to let it all go. He sold off another fifty acres.

"Made me feel like the world was closing in on us from all sides. We had to let all the farm workers go until there was just me left to keep things up at the house and such. We raise all the vegetables we need, got some chickens, pigs and some cows, but it ain't nothin' like it once was."

"Casa de la Luna is an interesting name for a farm," I said.

"Is that what it's called?" Uncle Linden asked.

Chubs laughed. "During the good days, Mr. and Mrs. Stanton used to do a European trip every year. One year she come back from France throwing them parlez-vous's around and decided they just had to rename the farm Casa de le Luna cause of the way the moon spills itself over the place when it's full and such. Mr. Stanton, he just smiled at me and told me to go make a sign. He was always tryin' to please her until the day he died. He did what he could to make it seem as if they was still ridin' high.

"Where you folks from?" Chubs asked without pausing for a breath.

"We're from West Palm Beach," I said quickly. "This was supposed to be a little vacation for us."

"Well, it'll still be once we get you fixed and back on the road," he said optimistically. "What sort of work you in, Mr. Montgomery?"

"Work?"

"My father's an artist," I said quickly.

"An ar-tcest? No foolin'. You make pictures end up in museums and such?"

"No, not museums," Uncle Linden said, smiling. "Galleries."

"Oh, that right?" Chubs said, but I could tell from the hesitation in his voice that he didn't quite understand. "Well, long as you make a livin' at what you like to do, you're a lucky man in this world. Yes, sir."

"That's very, very true," Uncle Linden said. "Most of the people I knew who ended up where I am were depressed and upset about the way they had spent their lives."

"Don't say? Where is that?"

"What?"

"Where is you at?"

"Oh, my father means old friends he's known. People his age," I quickly explained.

"I don't have any old friends left, I'm afraid," Chubs said. "Left 'em behind, pushin' up daisies and such, as Mr. Stanton Senior used to say."

"Chubs is eighty-one, Daddy," I told Uncle Linden.

"Eighty-one? Remarkable. What's your secret?"

Chubs laughed. "Ain't got no secret, sir. I just get up every day and say, 'Hello, sunshine!' no matter what kind of day it is."

"That's your secret," Uncle Linden said. "You refuse to be unhappy and say no to gloom and doom. I haven't felt that way for a long, long time, but I feel that way now, now that we've left."

"That so? Well, I guess that's mighty good then, a mighty good thing. There she is ahead, Casa de le Luna!" Chubs cried, nodding.

I looked out at the two-story home. As we drew closer, I saw the barns, pigpen, and chicken coop, but the house looked as if it had been lifted out of a historic neighborhood in some city like Charleston and plopped right down in this farmland. It had a two-tiered entry porch with more slender Roman columns above. The home just looked too dainty and fancy for what was once a working farm home. It looked more like a home in which elegant parties were held for men in tuxedos and women in long gowns. I could almost hear the music and see the servants circulating with trays of hors d'oeuvres and champagne. No wonder Mrs. Stanton wanted to call it Casa de la Luna, I thought.

Closer yet, I could see more detail. There was a prominent center gable and side gable. The center gable was embellished with a semicircular window. The front windows were all aligned horizontally and vertically in symmetrical rows. A set of a half dozen steps led up to the short entry porch. The house was covered in a faded pink cream tinted stucco.

"Here we are," Chubs declared bringing the truck to a stop. "Mrs. Stanton, she is set in her ways and more forgetful than ever these days, but she's never been anything but the queen of Southern hospitality."

We all got out of the truck.

"Everything okay?" Heyden whispered.

"Yes."

Chubs led us up the steps to the front entrance.

"I made this here door myself," he said proudly and ran his hand over the embossed heavy dark oak.

"It's a work of art," Uncle Linden said.

"Well, thank you, sir. You bein' an ar-teest and all, that means somethin'."

He raised and lowered the ball-shaped knocker made of iron. We could hear the deep, hollow thump traveling through the inside of the house.

"I coulda put in one of them electric door buzzers, but Mrs. Lilliann, she wanted everything to be old-fashioned. Casa de la Luna," he added, smiling and shaking his head.

He had to strike the knocker again, and finally, a few seconds later, the door was opened by a small woman who looked barely five feet tall. She had a pretty face with hazel green eyes and dainty soft features highlighted by her full lips and graceful mouth. Her Confederate gray hair was thin but neatly swept up in a French twist. Two diamond stud earrings set in white gold twinkled in the light of an entryway teardrop chandelier. The earrings weren't ostentatious. They were just enough to accent. In fact, everything about her was elegant and stylish, especially her dark green sundress with bare shoulders and side panels that covered her elbows and lower arms. The color brought out the color of her eyes as well.

She wore a pair of matching green flats. I saw she had a beautiful diamond wedding band and an expensive-looking jeweled oval-shaped watch.

She smiled. "Oh, guests," she declared.

"Yes, ma'am. These nice people broke down in the motor home 'bout a mile down Peach Tree Road. I didn't want to leave them there while I find out if we can get a engine part they need."

"Of course you didn't, Charles. Please come in," she said, stepping back.

"Thank you," I said. "My name is Hannah. This is my father, Linden Montgomery, and my cousin, Heyden Reynolds."

"Why, I am pleased to meet y'all. Welcome to Casa de la Luna. Just go right into my sittin' room there, and I'll see that y'all get something cool to drink first. Charles, you do what you have to do to help these people, hear?"

"Yes, ma'am. That's what I intend to do. I'm gonna call Billy Donald."

"Don't tell me what you're going to do, Charles. Just do it," she said, whipping her consonants. Chubs smiled at us, seemingly enjoying the way this tiny woman ordered him about.

"Yes, ma'am," he said and walked down the hallway and off to the left.

"Please go in," she said, indicating the door on our right.

It was a large sitting room with only two small Tiffany lamps lit at the moment, each throwing a pattern of color over the almond-colored walls. When she turned on an overhead crystal chandelier, a wave of light brightened the room, and it was suddenly like an older woman who had been able to hide her age by using heavy makeup and staying mostly in shadows. The cold, cruel illumination revealed every wrinkle and imperfection. Like such a woman, the room was exposed for what it really was: a room full of very aged and tired furniture and worn area rugs.

However, looking about, I could see that it was truly once a very beautiful room. All of the cornices and moldings were elaborate. The grand fireplace was constructed of rich-looking fieldstone and had a dark cherry mantel upon which was set a miniature grandfather clock stuck on twelve, probably for years. Above it was a grand portrait of what had surely been the senior Mr. and Mrs. Stanton. I could tell from their early 1900s style of clothing and the fact that the woman didn't look at all like Lilliann Stanton. She had red hair and was much taller with coarser features.

Scattered about on tables and pedestals was a collection of small eclectic statuary that included cherubs, men in hunting outfits, Greek gods and goddesses, and one larger one that depicted a mother and daughter holding hands. Other pictures included landscapes in gilded frames.

The sofas and chairs were missing some of their elaborate tassels, the wooden frames worn in spots and the velvety cushions threadbare and pale. Everything looked a bit dusty and neglected, the room resembling some chamber forgotten a long time ago, left to come to a standstill just like the small grandfather clock. I wondered if Mrs. Stanton had entertained any guests for years. She didn't seem to notice any of the imperfections and made no attempt to apologize for the room's condition.

To our left on entering was the doorway to the dining room. It was dark, but I could see a very long table with upholstered high-back chairs and a chandelier above. There looked to be a long mirror on the right wall and a long china cabinet on the left with dinnerware visible behind closed glass doors.

"Please, just make yourselves comfortable. I'll see to some mint iced tea."

"Don't go out of your way, please," I said.

"Oh, it's not out of my way, darlin'. It's just across the hall," she said with a laughing voice that seemed to ring back to younger days.

Heyden smiled and shook his head. "I feel like we're on some strange movie set," he said. "Maybe they shot a scene from *Gone With the Wind* here or something."

"This is very lovely," Uncle Linden declared. As before when he first viewed the motor home, he seemed either unwilling or incapable of seeing imperfections and disappointments. He was certainly looking at the world through different eyes since we had left Florida, I thought, and wondered if that was something good or bad.

"I remember when Joya del Mar had glamorous rooms and exquisite furnishings like this. Once it, too, had style. That was before the Eatons came in and turned everything into glitz and opulence. Those people had no taste, no sense of elegance."

Maybe he was right, I thought, and looked again at the old artifacts, pictures, and statuary. As old and neglected as it all was, it at least had character.

"Well, I got good news and bad," Chubs said returning just after we sat. "Billy's got an engine that surely has what we need, but he had to leave to go to his son's house to celebrate a weddin' anniversary. We can't get what we need until tomorrow, I'm afraid."

"Oh," Heyden said, despondent.

"That's not such bad news," Lilliann Stanton declared as she walked in carrying a silver tray on which she had tumblers of iced tea. "Y'all will just stay over here at Casa de la Luna."

"Thank you," Heyden said, "but we can probably return to our motor home for the night."

"Don't forget what happened to the electricity," I whispered.

"We can make do," he said sharply.

"You got problems with the electric, too?" Chubs said, picking up on it.

"Refrigerator went out," Heyden said. "I haven't gone through the rest of the appliances yet."

"Well, all your food's gonna go bad."

"Charles, how could you leave that there?" Lilliann chastised.

"He didn't know about it, Mrs. Stanton."

"Well, you just drive right back to that vehicle and

get their things, hear? We'll put them away here and save what we can," she insisted.

"That's very kind of you," Uncle Linden said. "It's been a long time since anyone's been that kind to me."

Mrs. Stanton beamed. "Why, sir, I can't imagine why not. What's this world comin' to when people can't treat each other with some common decency?"

Uncle Linden nodded. "Exactly," he said sipping the iced tea. He held up the glass, twirling it in the light like some child mesmerized by the dancing colors and twinkling ice. "This is wonderful iced tea. I haven't had as good in years."

"Well, thank you, sir," she said. "It was my husband's favorite."

Then she looked at Chubs. "Are you still here, Charles?"

"I'm goin'. What we might want to do," he added, talking directly to Heyden now, "is tow that motor home back here tonight. Get it off the road. We're going to have to work on it here anyway. We'll take the tractor. I'll get everything together."

Heyden jumped up. "I'll do whatever I can to help you."

"That's a good idea, Heyden. If we're going to sleep here, we'll need some things from the motor home," I told him.

"Let me go along then and do what I can to help, too," Uncle Linden said.

"Oh, that ain't necessary, Mr. Montgomery. The young man and me can do what has to be done," Chubs said. "You just make yourself comfortable."

Just at that moment we heard footsteps on the stairway. Chubs looked at Mrs. Stanton and then at us. The worried expression on his face stirred my curiosity. Who was coming? Both Chubs and Mrs. Stanton had said Mr. Stanton was dead, and Chubs hadn't mentioned anyone else to us.

Whoever it was did not come to the sitting room doorway. Instead this person went directly into the dining room from the other side. I soon saw that it was a younger woman with long strawberry-blond hair that dropped limply down and over her shoulders. Even in the dimly lit room, I could see her bangs were too long. She practically had to part strands of hair to see. She was wearing a marine blue robe with a pair of what looked like men's soft leather slippers.

She turned so slowly toward us, it was like looking at someone in a dream. For a moment it did seem as if the world had come to a standstill. She was so frozen, and then she lifted her arms and cried, "Rosemary!"

Chubs didn't see her, but he immediately looked down at the floor. Mrs. Stanton hoisted her eyebrows and tucked her mouth in at the corners, releasing a small, but audible groan of despair.

The young woman started toward me. Heyden stepped up beside me protectively. The young woman stopped a few feet in front of me and shook her head. She was very pretty with an appropriate peach complexion to compliment her dazzlingly turquoise eyes. She had high cheekbones and a perfectly shaped mouth with full lips. There was a very slight cleft in her chin.

"When did you come home? Why didn't you come right upstairs to see me, Rosemary. Grandma," she said, turning to Mrs. Stanton, "why didn't you tell me Rosemary was home?"

To my surprise, Mrs. Stanton replied, "She just this moment arrived, Bess."

"Where's Nolan?" Bess asked, looking around. "Isn't he back, too?"

Mrs. Stanton shook her head slowly, her eyes blanketing with sadness. I looked at Heyden, whose eyes were wide with confusion. Chubs closed his and then turned slightly away. Uncle Linden looked pensive, concerned.

"Oh, well, at least Rosemary is back," Bess declared and threw her arms around me, pulling me close to her. She had the aroma of lavender about her, something that smelled like scented bath oils, I thought. Her embrace was strong, tight. I didn't struggle against it, but looked instead at Mrs. Stanton, who now seemed on the verge of tears.

Bess finally released me and then put her hands on my shoulders to hold me away stiff-armed while she looked into my face and scowled.

"You naughty, naughty girl, running off like that with your father and leaving us worried sick. I should be very, very angry with you, Rosemary, but I won't be," she said, dissolving the scowl into a soft, loving smile. "I'll be good and I'll make sure you're not unhappy anymore."

She dropped her right hand to seize my left and turned.

"Come along with me immediately," she said, "and see what improvements I've made in your room. Come on," she urged, tugging harder.

"But I'm not Rosemary," I protested.

Bess stopped, but clung tightly to my hand. She scowled again.

"Now, don't start that business again, Rosemary. You are who you are no matter what anyone tells you. Besides," she added, smiling, "why would you want to be anyone else?"

"But . . ."

"Tell her, Grandma."

I looked at Mrs. Stanton. She appeared to be breathing hard, her shoulders rising and falling with great effort. Whatever was happening was so terrible it was causing her to choke on her internal tears. Her face was losing color. She looked as if she might collapse.

"It's all right," I said quickly, indicating I could deal with this.

Bess didn't appear to be dangerous. She was someone who had obviously suffered some terrible emotional trauma. Years and years of nurturing Uncle Linden gave me the patience and compassion I needed for something like this, I thought, and besides, whether I wanted to admit to it or not, I was my mother's daughter.

"I'm fine. It's all right," I whispered with assurance.

Mrs. Stanton's face took on color immediately. The relief traveled up her neck and relaxed her shoulders. She looked at Bess, who was waiting anxiously for her response. She looked like she was holding her breath, in fact.

"You are Rosemary," Mrs. Stanton said to me and then recited, "You are your mother's daughter, my great-granddaughter, and you should be happy here. You never have run off with your Daddy."

"See?" Bess cried, releasing her breath. "Come along," she urged again and tugged my arm as she stepped toward the doorway. "Let's not waste another moment."

I followed her, glancing back once at Heyden, who looked frightened for me. I nodded my head to indicate I was fine and then continued to follow Bess, who rushed toward the stairway.

"All I have done since the day you left is plan and plan for your return," she said as she marched up ahead of me.

Heyden was at the bottom of the stairway, looking up. Chubs moved to his side.

"I'll be all right. Get the motor home," I said.

"We'll be back as soon as we can," Heyden promised.

I continued after Bess, who was now waiting at the top of the stairway.

"I can't forgive your father for telling you a story like that. Why, anyone who looked at the both of you for only a moment would see how strong the resemblance is. Of course Nolan is your father.

"He's ashamed of what he's done, I'm sure. That's why he's not back, too. I know. I shouldn't be able to forgive him for taking you away from me, but I will. We'll all forgive each other for everything and be a happy family again, won't we?"

I glanced back and saw Mrs. Stanton looking up at us with great concern.

"Yes," I said. "We will."

"This is so wonderful, so wonderful," she said and clapped her hands. "Come along. No, wait," she said, stopping me. "Close your eyes. I want this to be a really big surprise. Go on. Close your eyes."

I did so and she took my hand again. I opened my eyes enough to see that we were moving down the corridor toward a door on our right. She stopped before it and turned back to me, so I closed my eyes tightly.

"On the count of three, you can open your eyes, Rosemary. Ready?"

"Yes," I said.

"Good. One . . ."

I heard her open the door.

"Two. And three!" she screamed.

I opened my eyes and looked into the room.

To my surprise it was a beautiful room and a room obviously well kept. There was a four-poster canopied bed with a pink-and-white bedspread and large, fluffy pillows, at the center of which was the most beautiful stuffed black panther. It had absolutely luminous eyes and looked as if it was made with a rich velvet. On both sides of the bed were nightstands of the same eggshell white. One had a beautiful carousel on it, and the other had a *Wizard of Oz* clock with a replica of Dorothy with Toto at her feet.

Everything in the room was coordinated, from the white curtains with pink trim to the milk-white area rug with its apricot-tinted spirals. To the right was a long vanity table with an oval mirror framed in a pinkish white wood at the center. Everything on the table was neatly organized. Just to my left inside the door was a real old-fashioned school desk, the kind that had the desk attached to the seat. Books were stacked on it, the top one being a textbook for an American literature class. Next to the books was a notebook with a pen beside it. In the armoire on the right was a television set. On the walls to my left were shelves of books, dolls, framed art prints, and on the wall to my right was a poster from the *Wizard of Oz* film with Judy Garland.

Whereas the rest of the house I had seen looked stuck in time with its tired vintage furnishings, this room could be featured in a modern-day *House Beautiful* magazine, I thought. From the lamps to the fixtures, door handles and dresser drawer handles, it all glittered like new. The windows glistened, the colors were vibrant. It was like watching a black-and-white movie suddenly turn to Technicolor.

Bess moved quickly to the closet and opened it.

"Look!" she cried, standing back.

I walked in slowly and gazed in at the rows of what looked like brand-new clothing, some with tags still hanging from sleeves.

"Every time I go into Anderson, I find something you would like, Rosemary. I've even bought you new shoes to go with some of these outfits," she said, kneeling down to open a shoe box and show me its contents.

She stood up. "I knew you were coming back, my darlin', my sweet, darlin'. I knew it." She held my hands and smiled.

"The room is beautiful," I said.

"Yes. As it should be, as it should always be. Now come, sit with me," she said, pulling me to the bed with her. "And tell me everything you've been doing.

"No, wait," she added quickly, putting her finger to my lips. "Don't tell me anything. I don't want to know anything about all that. It doesn't matter. What matters is you are here now, and we'll be a family again."

She pouted. "You should never have believed him. How could you believe him? He was just angry at me for other things, and that was his way at getting back at me, Rosemary," she said and turned away to look down at the floor.

"Sometimes," she continued, "sometimes a woman needs to be left alone. She has other problems, woman's problems, and men just don't understand, Rosemary. They can't understand. They're selfish that way. They want to please themselves, satisfy their own needs.

"I thought you were too young for all this, but I was wrong. I was wrong, so wrong.

"But don't blame me for that. A mother doesn't want to admit that her little girl is grown up. Grown-up little girls don't want to be with Mommy all the time, now, do they? When you're a mother, you have to give up your baby, cut the umbilical cord, and let him or her go off, and no mother wants to do that, no real mother, no mother like me.

"Can you understand that? Can you?" she asked, pleading for the answer she wanted.

I stared at her. Yes, I could understand that, but it all made me think of Mommy and how little Claude's birth and death served to cut that umbilical cord abruptly. Part of us wants our mothers to let us go, and part of us resents it, I thought. Everything is so complicated. Yes, I could understand. I could even understand this woman's turmoil, although I knew nothing of the details.

"He poisoned you," she said suddenly.

"Poisoned me?" Is that what happened here? I wondered with terror.

"Poisoned you against me, turned me into some sort of ogre. He was angry at me, Rosemary, so angry at me. That's why he made up that story and filled you with all that poison just so you would follow him and leave me.

"But," she said, bouncing on the bed, "you realized all that was a lie, a great lie, didn't you? And that's why you came back to me.

"Look at yourself," she said, turning me so I could gaze into the vanity mirror. "Look at the way your eyes are shaped and your chin. How could you be anyone else but Nolan Simms's daughter?"

She scowled. "A father trying to turn his daughter against her own mother, trying to convince her that her mother slept in another man's bed after she was married and use that as a reason why he and she weren't doing what he wanted whenever he wanted. Disgusting, just disgusting.

"You're old enough to know that he wanted me to do animal things. He was a sick man, Rosemary, sick, sick, sick. Imagine, a grown man wanting to play doctor.

"Oh, but I shouldn't be telling you all these sordid, ugly things. It's gone. It's all gone and we're together and happy again.

"And just imagine how happy Grandma is going to be. She cried almost as much as I did when you left, Rosemary."

Her face changed again, filling with anger.

"She warned me about Nolan from the start, but a young woman doesn't want to listen to older people, doesn't want to have anyone make those kinds of decisions for her, does she? You won't, I know. It's just natural, but we feel so helpless, watching our youngsters make mistakes they could have avoided. That's why I was so hard on you, why I didn't want you wearing those clothes or piercing your ears, why I thought it was too soon for you to go out on dates and stay up so late, and why I tried to keep you from seeing those pornographic movies. I was just trying to protect you, honey. You know that now, don't you? Don't you?" she asked again, needing me to respond.

"Yes," I said.

"Oh, good, good. That's good. Your body changed so fast. You grew up too fast. It's like putting someone on a fast horse when she is just learning how to ride. It wasn't fair. Nature wasn't playing fair with you. I had to take charge. I had to lock you up sometimes and keep you safe. I had to keep those boys away from you, too, Rosemary. They were after only one thing. I told you and told you," she said, her face back to being hard and cold again. "That wasn't being crazy. Your father was just trying to turn you against me because I wasn't giving him what he wanted every time he wanted it. You understand that now, don't you? Sure you do. You wouldn't be back if you didn't, right? He finally admitted it, I bet."

She sighed and looked around. "This was my room when I was a little girl, you know. I had a canopy bed like that. My mother was so proud of it and so happy for me. Grandma used to chastise her for becoming so excited over things like this. 'You're spoilin' the child,' she would say, 'You're spoilin' the child.' "

She laughed and leaned toward me. "Meanwhile, she

was always giving me things on the side. Grandma. Grandma," she said, her voice drifting. "Oh, I'm suddenly so tired. Aren't you tired, Rosemary?"

"Yes," I said.

"Right. We should both get some sleep. In the morning . . . in the morning . . ." Her voice dropped as if she had forgotten what she was going to say.

She stood up. "I'm going to get some rest now. You wash up and get ready for bed and don't forget to brush your teeth well. Up and down, up and down," she chanted. Then she stared at me so hard and long I was sure she was going to say, "You're not Rosemary. Who are you?"

But instead, she turned and walked slowly to the door. When she reached it, she dipped her hand into her pocket and produced a key. She held it up.

"I have the key, but I won't lock your room. I won't lock it ever again, Rosemary. I promise."

She dropped the key into her pocket and then smiled and walked out.

I heard her go down the hallway to another door, open and close it, and then all was still.

I stood up, looked about the room for a moment. Something wasn't right; something was missing, I thought, and then realized there were no photographs. What about a picture of Rosemary? Weren't there any photographs of her and her parents?

I started out and down the stairs. Mrs. Stanton was in the sitting room with Uncle Linden. I could see they had been talking, and I wondered what sort of things he had told her. She looked very troubled. Her eyes lifted quickly to me when I appeared.

"How is she doing?" she asked quickly.

"She went to sleep."

"I'm so sorry I put you through all that, darlin', but it's a very heavy burden, very heavy."

"I'm all right," I assured her.

"Good." She looked at Uncle Linden and smiled. "I was just talking to your father, telling him about our tragedy. He's a very patient and compassionate man."

"We'll do whatever we can for you while we're here, Lilliann," he said. He said it with such confidence and assurance, I felt my eyebrows rise. Suddenly he was a tower of strength.

"What happened, Mrs. Stanton?" I asked. "And why are there no pictures of her? Nothing in her room, I noticed."

"I thought it best to put them away for now," she replied.

"I don't understand. Haven't you heard anything from them? Where did Rosemary and her father go?"

She looked at me, her lips quivering.

"I hope to heaven," she replied.

12

Daughters and Ghosts

As soon as I heard Heyden and Chubs returning, I rose and went out to see them towing the motor home up the driveway and parking it near the largest barn. Heyden had been standing behind Chubs on the tractor. I hurried to them.

"Are you all right?" he asked the moment he saw me.

"Yes. Oh, Heyden, it's all so sad."

"I know. Chubs told me the story on the way to the motor home."

Chubs glanced at us, nodded, and went to unhitch the motor home from the tractor.

"How horrible. First, her husband filled their daughter's head with all these stories and accusations, and then he talked her into running off with him."

"Chubs says they were killed that day in a head-on crash with a tractor trailer just two miles south of here on Peach Tree Road. He says the truck driver had no business taking that road. It's so narrow and full of curves. Mrs. Stanton refuses to go down that road ever since, and he has to drive an extra fifteen miles whenever there's a need to take her in that direction."

Chubs came up beside us, listening. "The crash was so bad," he said, "I'm sure there's still pieces of that car in the bushes. I gathered up most of it and got rid of it.

"Mrs. Bessie, she just won't accept the truth. It's all left her in a sort of driftin'," he explained, "like someone stuck in time, just waitin' on the clock to tick. She's been waitin' for that girl to come home ever since. You the first young woman stepped into the house since the accident, too. Hope and sorrow sure can change the way people sees things," he added. "Imagine lookin' at a stranger and thinkin' it's your only daughter. That's real desperation."

"But what does her grandmother say to her?" Heyden asked. "Why did she go along with Hannah being Rosemary?"

"Mrs. Lilliann, she doesn't disturb her with the truth. It's easier to just pretend the bad thing didn't happen. Otherwise, no tellin' what. She ain't the healthiest woman round here," he added.

"Mrs. Stanton?"

"No, Bessie."

"What's wrong with her?" I asked quickly.

Chubs looked very uncomfortable talking about it. His eyes went from us to the house. "You understand I don't poke my nose into anyone's affairs," he said.

"Sure," Heyden said.

"Heyden, let's not trouble Mr. Dawson anymore," I said, seeing how painful it was for Chubs to talk about it, too.

"Right."

Chubs looked from me to Heyden and back to me.

"When you're around the people you work for as much as I've been around the Stantons, you can't help but overhear stuff, but I don't go gossippin' about it."

Heyden nodded. "We understand, sure."

Chubs sighed. "Since they brought you into it, you should know somethin' about it, I guess."

He leaned back against the tractor wheel.

"Mrs. Bessie, she was born with heart problems. They took her to see lots of doctors. The truth is she wasn't even supposed to have a child. That's what I heard once."

He gazed at the house. I could see by the way his eyes grew smaller that he was remembering, reliving events, conversations and arguments.

"Everyone was afraid to raise his voice in that house. They walked on tiptoes, fussin' around Bessie, keepin' her from doin' too much. Poor girl, she wasn't allowed to do things other girls her age were doin'. She never been to a fun park, ride one of them roller coasters, and she was practically of marryin' age 'fore they'd let her go out on a date."

"How sad."

"That ain't the worst of it. First man she gets heavily involved with makes her pregnant. That was Mr. Simms. He was a no-account man, always blowin' off about himself, what great things he was goin' to do in business. He had all sorts of new ideas for this place. 'Caused Mr. Stanton to lose a pile of money, too, and after Mr. Stanton died, he considered himself the boss round here. Truth is, I almost quit a few times 'cause of him, but I kept thinkin' about Mrs. Lilliann."

"What about Bess's mother and father?" I asked.

"Mrs. Lilliann's daughter Jessica died when Bess was only ten. Bad cancer, like a wildfire in her body. Bess's daddy remarried 'bout two years afterward and moved on to California. He didn't have much to do with the family."

"He just left his daughter behind?" I asked.

Chubs shrugged. "He married a woman who wasn't interested in a ready-made family, especially one with a sickly daughter. He kept promisin' he'd send for her. In the beginnin' there were calls, and then they started growin' fewer and far between. Mrs. Lilliann took over the motherin'."

"How terrible for Bess," I said, looking toward the house too.

"Losin' her mother like that and then her father runnin' off with another woman left her shaky, to say the least," Chubs said, nodding. "She was always afraid somethin' terrible was waitin' around some corner like a wild cat ready to pounce on her. She had this way of lookin' at me when she saw me first thing in the mornin'."

"What way?" I asked.

"Well, it was like she was expectin' bad news all the time, anticipatin' it, holdin' her breath. I couldn't get my 'Good mornin' ' out fast enough, but when I did, I bellowed it and smiled and she relaxed. It made me feel good to see that."

He turned and looked down the driveway.

"But I guess she was right about the bad news. I remember that terrible night, the police cars with their lights turnin'. Soon as I saw that mournful parade comin' up the driveway, my heart sunk. I was workin' in the back here when Mr. Simms come out of the house with Rosemary, both carryin' suitcases and she carryin' that beautiful stuffed black cat under her arms. I knew if she was takin' that out of the house, somethin' was bad wrong. It had belonged to her grandma Jessica and was passed down.

"Anyway, Mr. Simms just looked at me like I was so much dirt or somethin' and drove off, squealin' his tires round the turn there.

"I went back to work and it was dark 'fore I quit. I just started to wash up, thinkin' about somethin' for dinner, when I seen the lights. I went out first, and this policeman, a local boy, Bobby Pine, steps out shakin' his head at me and sayin' 'It's bad, Chubs, real bad.'

"You know, Mrs. Bessie, she didn't even go to the funeral. She just lay up there in her room all week, and when anyone go to see her, she'd perk up and ask, 'Is Rosemary back? Did they come back yet?'

"She wouldn't hear nothin' 'bout anyone bein' dead and gone. No, sir. Those words drifted out of her head as fast as they drifted in. It was like . . . like she stepped out of the world each time and then stepped in and smiled and asked, 'Is she back yet? Is Rosemary back?'

"Got so I heard that in my sleep," he said.

"How sad. All of it is so sad," I said.

Heyden nodded.

"You did a kind thing lettin' her believe you was Rosemary," Chubs said. "Most people would just high-tail it outta here, for sure."

"Hannah's mother is a psychotherapist," Heyden told him. I thought he was about to reveal something about Uncle Linden, too, but he stopped.

Chubs raised his eyebrows. "That so? And your daddy and she couldn't get along anyway, huh?"

When someone is so forthcoming with you as Chubs had been with us, it made it doubly difficult to fabricate and deceive. I looked at Heyden and saw in his eyes that he didn't want to lie to this man anymore, either.

"My mother and father are divorced, Chubs, but the man who is with us is my uncle, not my father."

"That so?"

"We thought it would be easier if people thought he was my father. I'm sorry we didn't tell you the truth."

"Easier? Why easier?"

"Well, we're two young people in a motor home," I began.

Chubs looked from me to Heyden and then back to me.

"Y'all runnin' away or somethin'?"

"Just taking a vacation," Heyden replied with a wide smile.

Chubs nodded. "Like I said, I don't poke round other people's business. I just do what I got to do to help Mrs. Lilliann get by."

"Isn't there anyone else in the family who could have helped them?"

"There's some distant cousins, some on Mr. Stanton's side, some on hers, but they have little or nothin' to do with her. Mr. Stanton left her enough of a legacy to maintain what's here now, but not much more. We make do." He smiled. "We're both at the age when you don't complain for fear the Almighty will hear and decide to take you home. Neither of us is ready for that yet."

"You're a good man, Mr. Dawson," I said.

He shrugged. "I am what I am, for good or for worse. I'll be up early to get the parts we need to get you back on the road," he told Heyden.

"Whatever time, I'll go with you. You just let me know."

"Rooster will let us know," Chubs said. "It'll be before breakfast. I'll be in the truck," he said and stretched his big arms. "Time for bed. I have my own place behind the barn. Mr. Stanton Senior fixed it up for me long time ago. Got my own television and everythin' in there. See you in the mornin'," he added and walked off.

Heyden and I watched him.

"He's got a big heart to fit that big body of his," I said.

Heyden nodded and looked at the house. "What's Uncle Linden doing all this time?"

"I left him with Mrs. Stanton, talking. She seems to be enjoying his company, and he was very comfortable. He's doing a good job of reassuring her. You would be as surprised as I am at how strong he sounds. I guess when you see other people's troubles, you forget your own."

"I don't," Heyden said sharply. It sounded hard and selfish, but he did have so much more weight to carry than I had, I thought.

We walked back to the house and did find Mrs. Stanton and Uncle Linden still together, but in the dining room now, the chandelier lit.

"Your father told me you people didn't get to have any dinner tonight. I just told him how angry I am that no one said anything," Mrs. Stanton said, scowling. "No one's ever gone hungry in Lilliann Stanton's home. Just sit yourselves down here. I have some chicken and dumplings and green beans warming up."

"Let me help at least," I offered.

"Well, follow me into the kitchen, then. Go on, young man," she told Heyden. "Wash up if you like and then sit yourself at the table."

"You don't argue with Lilliann Stanton," Uncle Linden told us as if he had known her all his life. "She's fed pigs, milked cows, nurtured a garden, and harvested peaches from the day after her honeymoon until now."

I followed her into the kitchen.

"Your daddy's a very nice man," she said. "And an artist, too. I'd love to see one of his paintings."

"He started one. It's in the motor home. Maybe he'll show it to you," I said.

"That would be nice."

She stopped what she was doing and turned to me. "I want to thank you again for helping out back there. That took some sensitivity and consideration. You're a fine young lady."

"I'm sorry for all the trouble in your and Bess's life."

"Nothing you can do about stopping trouble when it

comes riding in on the back of a tornado. You make do and try to meet the test the Lord has set upon you. That's all," she said stoically and turned back to preparing the food.

I watched her move efficiently about her kitchen, this elderly lady who maintained her elegance and equilibrium even in the shadow of all her personal tragedy. What was it that gave some people spines of steel? Was it her faith, her pride, or just a heavy stream of determination, a refusal to permit Fate to defeat her that helped her maintain herself and carry so much weight on her small shoulders? How little it took for so many people years and years younger than she was to be reduced to whining and self-pity.

I suddenly thought more about myself and my running off like this. Did I take the easier route? Was I weak and selfish? Would Lilliann Stanton have ever run away from disappointment, conflict, and tension?

"After dinner," she said, "I'll get you what you need. You'll sleep in Rosemary's room, of course. Your father and your cousin can sleep in the downstairs guest rooms."

"Oh, I couldn't do that," I said. "That room is . . ." I wanted to say "kept like a shrine." It was almost sacrilegious to even consider it.

"Nonsense. It's a beautiful room. You'll be very comfortable in it, and why not use it? To tell you the truth," she said, turning back to me, "it would do my heart good to see it being used again."

"But—"

"Don't worry about Bess. She'll be asleep by the time you go up to bed," she assured me. "In the morning she might not even remember you. Charles will surely get you people on your way. He's a wonderful worker. My husband used to say he had a natural instinct for mechanical things. There wasn't anything on this farm he couldn't repair. The truth is I wouldn't know what to do without him. He's the closest friend I have," she added.

"Oh," she continued, swiping the air as if there was an annoying fly circling her, "we don't talk corn and mush to each other like that, but he knows how I feel and I know how he feels, how loyal and dedicated he is to us, has always been. I warned him not to die before me, or I would never forgive him," she said, and I smiled.

"Let's stop yapping like this and get those hungry men something to eat," she declared.

Uncle Linden never stopped raving about her dumplings. "I haven't had a meal like this since . . . I don't remember when," he said.

"Oh, go on with you, Mr. Montgomery. This is nothing much."

"Maybe not to you," he insisted, "but certainly to me."

"You live alone, do you?" she asked him, and Heyden and I paused and looked at each other and then Uncle Linden. He was very capable of forgetting our story. We were both afraid of how Mrs. Stanton would take the truth.

"I have for a long time," he replied and then looked at us, "but that's over. My mother was a very good cook," he continued, changing the subject, which let us relax. He went on to talk about Grandmother Grace and his growing up in Palm Beach. "Everyone else had personal cooks, but not us."

"I always enjoyed going to the ocean," Mrs. Stanton said. "We saw some wonderful sea resorts in Europe when we traveled. Since my husband died, I haven't been off this farm for more than a few hours to shop."

"Well, I'm sorry to hear that," Uncle Linden said. "Maybe when we get settled down, you'll come visit with us."

"Oh, my visiting days are long gone. This is enough of the world for me now," she said.

She insisted we have pieces of her peach cobbler, her speciality. It was delicious. Afterward, Heyden helped me and Mrs. Stanton clean up. Then she showed them to the guest rooms, settled them in, and returned to take me up to Rosemary's room. I was still full of trepidation about it, but she reassured me and repeated how pleased it would make her to have the room used by a nice young lady again. I wasn't about to be responsible for any more disappointment for her.

Inside the room, she paused beside me and closed her eyes for a moment.

"I know it sounds foolish, but sometimes I come in here and feel something so familiar, it's like Rosemary has just been in the room. You know how sometimes you can walk into a room and just know someone has been there moments before you. Maybe their bodies leave the air warmer or there's a whiff of someone's perfume or some man's cologne yet lingering. Maybe it's just the aroma of shampoo or scented soap, something, and you can't help but envision that person. He or she flashes before you like a shadow that lingered, an image in a mirror that didn't follow when she walked away, a reflection in the window, footsteps on the rug, a movement of air as he or she passes you by, something, and if you miss and have loved that person as much as I miss Rosemary and I loved Rosemary, you close your eyes and say, 'Yes,' to all the fantasies and images and wishes. You let yourself pretend.

"It's why I understand my granddaughter so well, why I don't disturb her illusions. There are things in this room," she continued, gazing about, "that haven't been touched by any other fingers than Rosemary's fingers. They are still exactly where she had left them.

"But don't be afraid to touch anything or move anything," she added quickly. "It's time we put it all to rest. Your coming is a blessed thing in more ways than you know. Maybe Someone higher up made it all happen."

"That beautiful stuffed black panther looks brand new," I said, nodding at it on the bed.

"It is brand new," she confessed. She shook her head guiltily. "God forgive me, but I went out and bought one just like the one Rosemary took with her that fateful night. I knew Bess wouldn't be able to look at this bed without seeing it there."

"It's never a bad thing to prevent someone from being unhappy," I said.

She smiled at me. "You're a lovely young lady, darlin'," she said. "Do you mind if I kiss you good night?"

"Oh, no," I replied quickly, realizing I was just staring at her.

She leaned toward me and kissed me softly on my cheek. "Good night, darlin'," she said, "Wake up healthy and strong."

I knew in my heart it was most probably the exact way she had said good night to Rosemary thousands of times.

"Thank you. Good night, Mrs. Stanton," I said.

She held her gentle smile and then turned and left, closing the door behind her so gently, it was as if the ghost or spirit she had sensed here had gone out.

I turned and looked at the room again.

Now that I knew what I did about Rosemary, I could imagine how lonely and frightened she must have been. I couldn't help visualizing her lying on that bed or sitting at the vanity table and wondering if the things her father had whispered in her ear were true. I knew how much she didn't want to turn against her mother. I knew that well.

Funnily enough, when I imagined her before me, I didn't see a stranger. I saw myself, vulnerable and alone. Young girls like she and myself have very thin skins covering our emotions. It takes so little to tear through and sting our trusting hearts. We want so much to believe and to trust our parents. Without that we are surely adrift in a nasty adult sea, the winds of deception tossing and spinning us around until we are too dizzy to face the day. We try to pass our time with our eyes closed, our ears covered, our footsteps so soft we attract little or no attention and make it back to our rooms, rooms like this one, sanctuaries full of dreams and memorabilia that had promised rainbows and candy cotton.

Don't look out the window, we warn ourselves. Don't look at the murky skies. Wait for the sunlight in the morning, the promise of a new day. Maybe all our disappointments will disappear like bad dreams. Maybe it isn't true; none of it is true. We are not alone after all. There is laughter and there is love waiting for us where they have always been waiting for us, and all the dark whispers and ugly faces are gone, popped like bubbles. Telling ourselves these things is the only way to lay our heads down on the pillows at night and trust the darkness enough to be unafraid of sleep.

It took a while for me to slip under the blanket on this beautiful bed. The bedding smelled fresh and clean, and I imagined that Bess took care of this room just the way she had taken care of it when Rosemary was alive and here. But lowering myself into this bed was truly like lowering myself into someone else's dreams.

A layer of clouds broke apart in the night sky, permitting a sliver of moonlight to cut through the darkness and pour through the curtains. Macabre shapes and shadows danced on the walls, imps and elves, nymphs and ogres, a variety of creatures silhouetted to perform on a nightmarish stage. I wanted to shut my eyes to them, but I couldn't. They were too powerful, too demanding.

Was this the way Rosemary went to sleep every night? Did she listen to the sounds in the house, hear muffled voices, soft crying, and realize she was hearing herself? Did she finally turn her back on the gleeful puppets dancing on the walls and close her eyes tightly, willing herself to remember laughter and song, birthdays and parties?

Like Rosemary, I have been told in so many different ways that I am not my father's daughter. He sired me, but I have been told I shouldn't want to be his daughter, that he is so different from me, from what is good in me. Like Rosemary, I have felt disappointment and betrayal, and like Rosemary, I am lying here feeling alone, confused, and lost. Where should I go? Whom should I trust?

I had the strange feeling that time was standing still, that the winds had stopped and all the clouds were pasted for the moment against the inky sky. Everyone in the world was holding his or her breath. Birds were frozen in the air. The earth itself had stopped turning on its axis. Only I could move, but it was as if I was moving through a set on a movie stage. I could touch things, touch people, but I felt nothing and they felt nothing. I couldn't scream or shout because it would all be stopped at my mouth and come back at me, echoing down through my very bones. I couldn't even tremble.

Almost in a panic, I battled to take a breath and then, as if my breath had done it, the door of the bedroom opened, the light behind it spilling in and followed by the silhouetted Bess dressed in her nightgown, tiptoing toward me, her arms folded under her breasts. She paused at the side of the bed.

"Rosemary," she whispered. "Are you still awake?"

Should I answer? I thought, but before I could decide, my mouth and tongue, controlled by something greater than myself or by something in me that made those decisions instinctively, replied.

"Yes."

"Oh, good. I was having a hard time falling asleep myself," she said and sat on the bed. She reached out and stroked my hair.

"It was such a shock for me when you told me you were having your first period. I don't know why our bodies are in such a rush. What's the point of having a twelve-year-old girl become capable of having a baby? She's still a baby herself, her mother's baby.

"It's a nasty trick that Nature pulls on us. I've barely had time to explain things to you, to warn you about boys. They live for only one thing, you know. Just like all the animals out there. They can't help it, I suppose, but that doesn't mean we have to be victims, now, does it? No, of course not.

"And just because you get married, don't think you're safe, Rosemary. Husbands don't care how difficult they can make it for their wives. They are truly God's most selfish creatures. Oh, I know they tell us that they can't help it. They have needs and those needs are in them from birth, but we all have needs and that doesn't mean we should be inconsiderate of others, does it?

"Of course it doesn't. If I'm too tired or not well, I shouldn't have to make him happy. He shouldn't blame me, and he shouldn't tell you that I'm the one who's selfish, now, should he?

"No, he shouldn't," she said. She sighed. "I wish we could all just get along. If everyone first thought about making someone else happy first, the world would be a happier place, wouldn't it?

"Of course it would." She stroked my hair again. "You just sleep and don't worry. Mommy will make sure it's all right. This getting your period isn't the end of the world. Well, maybe it's the end of one world, but it doesn't have to be a nasty thing. Just listen to me," she said and leaned closer.

"You have to think of what you have the way you would think of a safe. If you don't keep it locked, some selfish boy will take your treasure and leave you. Oh, he might promise he won't, but he will, because he won't be able to stop thinking of another treasure, and another. You're the poorer one for it, Rosemary. I know I was.

"Are you still having those cramps? Why do you think it's so unpleasant? I'll tell you why. It's because it's a warning. Every cramp is another alarm bell. Watch out. Beware. Keep the safe locked.

"There. I've told you some great secrets that only a mother and a daughter can share. Someday, when it's the right time for you, you will have a daughter and you will share the same secret, I hope."

She looked back at the door.

"He's waiting for me," she said. "He's been making all sorts of new promises. He has an endless well of promises, pulling up new ones constantly. Promises are contracts signed with dew. As soon as the sun comes up, they're gone.

"But you don't have to trouble yourself about any of this. Just think of sugarcane and bubbles, lollipops and magic, tinsel and crepe paper. Tomorrow, you and I will go for a walk to the lake, and just like always, we'll look for interesting flowers and toss little rocks in the water and listen to the birds gossip about us, okay?

"Nothing has changed, not really. You're still my little Rosemary."

She leaned over and kissed my forehead and then stood up.

"If he wants to go, he'll go. But you will never leave me, would you?"

"No," I said, seeing she was waiting for a reply.

"Good. Sleep tight, my sweetheart. Sleep well."

She turned and walked slowly out, moving in a dream again, and then she closed the door behind her. The clouds that had parted closed again, shutting away the sliver of moonlight. The room was completely dark. I hadn't moved a muscle.

As my eyes grew accustomed to the unlit room, I thought I saw a shadow thicken in the bathroom doorway until it took the shape of a young girl. My mind's just playing tricks on me, I told myself, but the shape lingered and was there even after I closed and opened my eyes.

Did I imagine it or did I hear a voice sharply whisper, "Stop it."

I couldn't swallow.

"Stop keeping me alive. She has to let me go. She has to mourn me, for even the dead need love. I'm waiting in these shadows, caught and trapped by her refusal to believe, to accept. You're not helping any. You have no right to be me, to put me on like a new dress and wear my feelings and my fears just to make yourself feel better.

"She hasn't even been to my grave." The voice began to drift back with "to my grave, to my grave, to my grave."

A moment later it was gone, and I released my breath and turned over in the bed, squeezing my eyes closed and willing myself to stop these imaginings. I tried to talk myself to sleep and finally did.

I began by fretting in and out of nightmares that mixed Bess and Mrs. Stanton in with Mommy and Miguel and even Daddy. The dreams woke me, and I found I was crying. My tears had wet the pillow.

Thinking about Bess, I couldn't help wondering if Mommy was wandering to and from my room tonight as well. My heart was so heavy, it took me most of the night to find another hour or so of sleep, and even that was restless and troubled. It was no wonder Heyden had to come up to see if I was all right. He had already been up and had gone with Chubs to the car cemetery to get the parts they needed to repair the motor home.

I heard the knock on my door, but not until he had struck it harder. For a moment I was very confused. I couldn't remember where I was. Then it came rushing back over me.

"Yes?" I called.

"It's me, Heyden. Can I come in?"

"Yes," I said, grinding as much of the sleep out of my eyes as I could, and sat up.

"Hey," he said, poking his head in first, "sleepyhead. I expected you to be downstairs with Mrs. Stanton and Uncle Linden having breakfast."

"What time is it?" I looked about the room for a clock and then reached for my watch where I had left it on the nightstand. "Ten!"

"Right," Heyden said, still laughing as he came into

the room. "Mrs. Stanton said she had been up to check on you, poked her head in and saw you were still sleeping, so she left you alone."

"What about Bess?" I asked quickly.

"Apparently she gets up even earlier than Chubs and goes for early morning walks when it's not raining."

"I'm surprised she didn't stop here first," I said, shaking my head.

"Mrs. Stanton isn't. She said she's not surprised Bess seems to have forgotten about us. It's part of her condition or something."

"She did tell me that might happen."

"She and your uncle are having a conversation about such things. Like any patient, he speaks like an expert about the things he's suffered and knows how they are treated, I guess. I don't think Mrs. Stanton has caught on yet, but I don't doubt she will soon. He's bound to say something that will reveal everything. I think the best thing for me to do is help Chubs and get us out of here as quickly as we can.

"Why did you sleep so long?" he asked. "Were you really that tired?"

"Oh, Heyden, I had such a terrible night. First, Bess came in here last night after I had gone to bed, and she talked to me as if I was Rosemary when Rosemary was only twelve years old. She said so many things that led me to understand how hard life might have been for Rosemary."

"I bet," Heyden said, "although this is a very nice room." He gazed about and looked at the television, the computer on the desk, and the clothes in the closet. "It all looks so new."

"Some of it is new. There are new garments in the closet with the tags still on them!"

"Well, it's not our problem. Get dressed, have some breakfast, and we'll get going as soon as we are able. It will take most of the day, I'm afraid."

I stared at him.

"Why are you looking so unhappy? We'll be okay. It didn't cost half as much as I feared it would, and Chubs is going to get it all done for us. We'll pay him, but it won't cost a quarter of what it would if we had to go to garage."

"I don't care about the money."

"So? What then?"

I looked down.

"What?"

"Last night," I said, slowly raising my head, "I saw Rosemary. She was here."

"What? The daughter? Are you saying she *is* alive?"

"No. It was like her spirit. She was angry, angry at me for encouraging Bess to fantasize and refuse to believe Rosemary is dead. She said she wanted to be mourned. She wanted to be loved in death, too, and she wanted to be free. She wanted to let go."

He smiled.

"I'm serious, Heyden."

"It was just all in your imagination. A place like this with kooky people like this can do that to you. That's why we want to get out of here as soon as possible."

"I don't think that was it."

"Oh, c'mon, Hannah. A ghost? A spirit? You feel guilty about what you did so you dream up something like that. That's all. I'm not even a student of psychology, and I can figure that out. Forget about it. Get dressed."

"I can't forget about it," I protested. "I want to do something to help."

"What could you do?" he practically screamed, raising his arms. "We have enough problems helping ourselves. Your uncle could do something strange any moment, Hannah. He's talking about setting up his easel out there and painting. You've got to come downstairs and occupy him until we're ready to leave. Now, that's what you can do," he said sharply.

"That's very selfish, Heyden. You just don't use people like this, take their hospitality, and rush off," I said.

"What are we supposed to do, leave a tip? Get real, Hannah Eaton," he snapped.

I felt the tears come into my eyes.

"I have all these problems to worry about, and now you're talking about a ghost complaining to you," he mumbled. "I'm going out to help Chubs. I hope you will do what I asked," he said and stormed out of the room, closing the door behind him.

It wasn't exactly the way I had hoped Heyden would react to all that I had told him. I was disappointed, but told myself he was probably very nervous and afraid that what he had done, what we had done, was a terrible mistake. He was anxious to make it all right and make it all happen.

I rose to dress and go down. He was right about Uncle Linden. I had to look after him, too.

Just before I left the room, I gazed out the window that faced the east field and saw him. He had done what Heyden said he wanted to do: He had set up his easel, but what startled me more was Bess. From where I was looking, it appeared he was organizing to do a picture of her, and she appeared to be a willing subject!

What would he paint?

Whom would he paint?

Maybe the ghosts were in us all, I thought. I caught my breath and hurried out, knowing full well that the revelations and surprises were far from over.

They waited for us, oh, too eagerly.

13

Rosemary's Portrait

"**H**e said it would be his way of repaying us for our hospitality," Mrs. Stanton said when I asked her about Uncle Linden and Bess. "It was his idea entirely. He looked out and saw her walking and turned to me and said, 'I think I'll do a picture of your granddaughter. She's a very beautiful young woman.

"Then he jumped up and went out to get his things, before I could say anything. I'm more surprised than you are, not that I don't think Bess is beautiful. She is, but what surprises me the most is that Bess is willing to do such a thing. She's always been a rather shy girl, and after the tragedy, you couldn't open her heart to anything that would bring her pleasure. I must say your father does have a very charming way about him. He's a very gentle, kind man."

"Yes, he is," I said, smiling. Why was it that

strangers could see Uncle Linden for what he really was quicker than people who knew him for years, especially Daddy?

"How about some eggs and grits?" she asked. "And I have some fresh homemade bread."

"I'm not that hungry, thank you. I'll just have some juice," I said, anxious to get out to Uncle Linden. Now, more than ever, despite his charm, I was as afraid as Heyden was that he might do or say something strange. Adding any more tension or disappointment to Mrs. Stanton's life, and especially to Bess's fragile world at this particular moment, would be horrible, I thought.

"Oh, that's no way for a girl your age to live. I know y'all are just rushing about, skipping this and that. You just sit yourself down there and let Grandma Stanton prepare one of her best breakfasts. Go on now or I'll order Chubs to *stop* working on your vehicle," she threatened playfully.

I had no choice, and besides, I could see the happiness my permitting her to dote over me brought to her. For too long her world had been overcast with dark gray clouds of sorrow. For one brief day or so, the clouds had parted, and there was enough sunshine to bring her back to happier times. If I was at least partly responsible for it, I was happy, too.

Mrs. Stanton rattled on and on about earlier days when her husband was alive and when her daughter was alive. Just talking about it flushed her face with so much pleasure that she looked as revived and buoyant as she probably was back then. I sat there vaguely aware of the smile that had settled comfortably in my own face. Her memories of happier times stirred my own. I could hear Mommy laughing again, see her and Miguel playfully teasing one another, recall our walks on the beach, our sailing trips and beach picnics, the parties and the music and the food Miguel's family took such pride in preparing and sharing with us.

Happiness like that was truly hard to hold on to. It was like a beautiful bird that perched for a while on a nearby branch, but the moment you got too close, would fly off and sail away, leaving you with only the memory. Cherish me as I am, it said, but never, never try to put me in a cage or tie me down. My picture can be pressed into scrapbooks, my voice can be recorded singing melodically. You can make a video of me and look at me repeatedly, but don't ask me to stay. I have other places to visit, other people to whom I must bring joy. I am happiness, a bird, fleeting and oh, so very precious.

How I knew that now, I thought.

"You haven't told me anything about your mother, dear," Mrs. Stanton said after she had served me my eggs and grits and slices of homemade bread. She sat with me at the kitchen table hovering like a mother hen making sure her chicks took in their nourishment.

"My mother is a psychotherapist," I began. "She is very successful, very well respected."

"In Palm Beach?"

"Her office is in West Palm Beach, but we live in Palm Beach."

"Isn't it very, very expensive to live there?"

"We inherited the property."

"I see. I'm sure it's hard for you not being able to be with both your parents. I feel so sorry for all those children from broken homes, sharing Thanksgiving and Christmas and even their own birthdays, I imagine. Is that what you do?"

"Sometimes, but you are right. It is hard, although my mother remarried and her new husband is a very nice man. He's a college teacher, and I get along very well with everyone in his family."

"I see. But so many personalities, so many people crowding into one small room and competing for your attention and love. It can't be easy."

"It isn't," I admitted. "Jealousy has its own room in my house," I said. "Sometimes, I feel like I have to dole out my feelings in teaspoons."

"My husband and I were married for fifty-one years. People were always asking how we did it, like it was something magical or supernatural."

"There has to be something special," I said. "You had to have some secret."

She laughed. "No secret, no magic. It was simply living up to the same vows everyone recites. Maybe more and more people recite them these days without thinking or understanding the words.

"I had a younger sister," she continued, tracing a line in the tablecloth with her thin right forefinger as she spoke, "who was always jealous of me. I knew it, but I pretended she wasn't. I did all I could to make her happy. She never married, and she died alone in her own bed. Once, when she went on and on about how lucky I had been to find a man so devoted to me, I looked her in the eyes and said, 'Mattie, you know as well as I do that you're just too self-centered to love someone else. Every man you meet realizes that, some sooner than others, and bids you a fond farewell.

" 'You know what love really is?' I lectured her. 'It's recognizing that the person you love isn't perfect and forgiving them for that. And then it's hoping that he or she will forgive you for not being perfect, too. It's tolerance and compromise and that takes a lot of selflessness, not selfishness. In the end we all have to realize that we are never going to be happy unless the person we love is happy, too. If that's not important to you, you are not in love, and it will come to some bad ending sooner than later.' "

"What did your sister say?" I asked. While she had spoken, I could think only of Mommy and myself and our need to forgive each other. The air around us was so still, too. I felt like an abrupt word, even a heavy breath, would shatter the special moment.

"Mattie?" She laughed and waved her hand at the memory of her sister. "She just looked at me like I belonged in some institution for the socially retarded and shook her head. 'That's all nonsense, romantic slop,' she said. 'If I want that, I'll watch my soap opera,' she added, and I thought, that's all you will ever do, Mattie, watch."

She pressed the tips of her fingers on the table a moment and looked deeply thoughtful.

"At best," she said, still looking down, "life is a balancing act between happiness and unhappiness." She sighed deeply and then she looked up at me and smiled.

"You like those grits? Made 'em with a secret ingredient my mother taught me."

"They're delicious," I said, scooping up the last spoonful. "Let me help with the dishes," I offered.

"Oh, no, darlin'. You go out and enjoy the beautiful day with your family. There's not much here to do, and it keeps my mind occupied."

I stood up and then paused just before turning to start away.

"My cousin told me you said Bess forgot about yesterday and last night," I said.

"Yes. Just as I suggested, she didn't do anything different from what she ordinarily does these days, so she might not think of you as Rosemary this morning. I really don't know if she even remembers you are here. Needless to say, there haven't been many opportunities for such a thing as what happened last night to happen. None of Rosemary's school friends ever come here. They rarely came when Rosemary was alive. You're the youngest visitor since the tragedy."

"Do you have her in some sort of therapy program or did you ever?"

She shook her head. "Time is the only therapy program she's in now. It's not easy to share your troubles with strangers."

She turned away, her shoulders slumping. How different this was from the world I knew, I thought. There, most parents wouldn't think twice about putting their children into some formal therapy. In fact, they don't think twice about putting themselves into it. Many of my friends at school talked about their parents being in some form of counseling or another. It was almost a sign of accomplishment, prestigious, and certainly never something about which someone would be ashamed.

"It's getting more and more difficult for people to

find a sense of themselves, have an identity with which they can be comfortable, settle in their own bodies," Mommy once told Miguel. "How many people out there look into a mirror and see a stranger or at least someone they would rather not see?"

"Don't knock it. It's your gold mine," he quipped.

"I don't know, Miguel. I don't know how long I can do this. I wonder more and more every day how my father was able to do it all of his adult life and enjoy it without it destroying him. He had a way of leaving it all outside his door when he came home from work. I'm not as strong as that."

"So, stop trying to be him. Be yourself," Miguel advised, and I remember wondering was that what Mommy was trying to do, and was that something I would try to do: be her? I was old enough to understand the implications. Would I be like the people she saw? Would I be struggling forever to find out who I am?

Wasn't that really what I was doing now with Heyden and Uncle Linden: running off to find another Hannah Eaton out there, a new one who could be happier and more contented with herself? Maybe that was just as big an illusion as the one Bess lived in, I thought.

I stepped out of the house and saw Chubs and Heyden working in front of the big barn. With their sleeves rolled up and the streaks of dirt on their cheeks and chins, they both looked like they were bathing in grease. But I could see they were chatting away happily, neither looking frustrated or disgusted with the work. Heyden waved when he saw me and then nodded toward the field on my right. There Uncle Linden stood before his easel. I saw Bess sitting on a large rock facing him. As I started toward them, my heart began to pound. Whom would she see when she saw me?

"Rosemary!" she called, answering my question when I was less than a dozen yards from them. Uncle Linden turned to me and smiled.

"Here she is," he declared. "Now I won't need this picture anymore."

He put a photograph aside.

"Hurry, Rosemary!" Bess cried. "Mr. Montgomery is working on putting you in the picture, too. He's been using the most recent picture of us, the one I always carry in my pocket."

So there *was* a picture of them that hadn't been hidden away, I thought. How could she look at it and look at me and still think I was her daughter, returning?

Bess was still wearing a robe and her hair was down, unbrushed, the breeze lifting and turning strands every which way. She looked wild, but yet very beautiful, natural and unspoiled.

"Come here," she said, patting the space beside her. "It's not hard to be a model, and you can move whenever you want, right, Linden?" she asked.

I raised my eyebrows. Linden? How did they get so close and familiar with each other so quickly?

Uncle Linden nodded. "Of course," he said. "All I have to do is take glimpses, little snapshots of my subject. They get locked in here," he said, pointing to his right temple. "I don't mean you should dance on the rock, but don't think you have to be as still as a statue."

"Hurry," Bess said. "We're getting our picture done by a very famous modern artist."

"Oh, not that famous, Bessie," he said. "I've sold a few pictures, that's all."

"You're the most famous artist who has ever stepped foot on *this* farm," she insisted, and they both laughed.

How well they are getting along, I thought. Some cynical person might say "It takes one to know one." They both have emotional and psychological problems. But perhaps it was just that they both instinctively understood how each craved some affection, some attention, and concern for their inner feelings. In that way they weren't so different from the rest of us after all.

I stepped up to the rock.

"Did Grandma make you a nice breakfast?"

"Yes," I said.

"She loves making you a nice breakfast. She loves doing everything for you, Rosemary. You are her favorite, even more so than I am, you know, but I'm not jealous. It's natural for a great-grandmother to love her great-grandchild more, especially when she is still a little girl. When I was a little girl, she loved me more than she loved my mother. 'You're spoiling her,' my mother would complain. 'I spoiled you, too,' she would say. 'It's her turn.' "

She laughed and looked around. "Isn't it a beautiful day, Rosemary?"

"Yes," I said.

It was. The sky was cobalt blue with just a patch of cloud here and there, all of them looking dabbed on one of Uncle Linden's canvases.

"We have had so many wonderful days like this together, haven't we, Rosemary? I was telling Mr.

Montgomery about our beautiful lake. He wants to see it. Maybe he should be painting it. After lunch we are all going for a nice walk to the lake, aren't we, Linden?"

"If you're up to it, Bessie, I would love to see it."

"Of course I'll be up to it. Why shouldn't I be? Isn't he the sweetest, most considerate man you have ever met, Rosemary? A perfect southern gentleman, too."

"Well, I'm from Palm Beach. Is that considered Southern?" he jokingly asked. "I have my doubts because most of the people I know there don't consider themselves Southerners. They are Sophisticates. They come from Sophistica, a separate country, even a separate world."

"Oh, that's so silly. Isn't he silly? Palm Beach isn't another country."

"Tell that to the citizens of Palm Beach," Uncle Linden muttered and peered over his easel at me. "They even speak a different language and say things like 'How ticky-tacky,' and 'shampoo' instead of 'champagne.'"

Bess laughed, her laugh light and airy and caught in the breeze that lifted her beautiful hair and made it dance over her forehead. How long has it been since she laughed like this? I wondered. How long since she had a small respite from her continuous grieving?

"Oh, what a delight you are. What a silly delight," she told Uncle Linden, who beamed with pleasure.

"I've been called a lot worse," he said. He shook his brush at Bess. "You can call me whatever you like, but don't call me late for dinner."

She laughed again and then, without much warning,

threw her arm around my shoulders and pulled me closer to her, kissing my forehead.

"Isn't she a beautiful child, Linden?"

"I wouldn't be painting her otherwise," he replied, "nor would I be painting you if you weren't a beautiful woman, Bessie. It's against my religion to paint anything ugly or unpleasant," he said. Her embarrassed laughter followed the blush that came quickly into her cheeks.

I couldn't help but be impressed with how charming Uncle Linden was being. Was he doing a good thing, or was it something that just prolonged the tragedy, and now, as I thought about what had happened last night and was still happening, made us a part of it?

"Just turn your head slightly to the right for me, Bessie," he told her, and she released me and did what he asked. "Yes," he said. "Perfect. You must have done this before."

"Me? I haven't."

"You've never worked as an artist's model? That's difficult to believe," he said and worked on.

Nothing I had seen him paint had given him as much pleasure, I thought, and then I remembered how nervous and troubled Mommy had been when he first had asked me to pose. This was different, though, I told myself. He wasn't painting me. He was painting Bess and Bess's Rosemary. I was just a stand-in for her. It was surely not the same thing.

Or was it? Was all of this the same thing: a fanning of the world of madness and illusion, strengthening the illness that had so gripped his mind most of his life, and was I now the one solely responsible for that?

We had taken too much on ourselves, Heyden, I thought, looking his way, far too much.

Nevertheless, Uncle Linden was more talkative and amusing than I had ever seen him. He rattled on and on, telling one funny Palm Beach story after another. Bess's laughter became our background music, and the more she laughed, the more he talked. He told her stories I had never heard, and he was very entertaining. How frustrated he must have been in the residency not having people to talk to who would stimulate his mind or encourage his creativity, I thought, comforting myself. Even if this wasn't forever, it was a wonderful interlude for him, too, wasn't it? It couldn't be all bad. Eventually Mommy would have to admit to that.

We paused to drink some fresh lemonade Mrs. Stanton brought out to us, and while we rested, Uncle Linden talked about his youth, living on a beach property, dreaming of sailing off to wonderful foreign lands.

"The truth is I never went more than a dozen or so miles from home, but sometimes, sometimes dreams are enough," he concluded.

"Yes," Bess said, nodding. "Sometimes they are."

I didn't say a word. I was more like an observer now. It was as if they had forgotten I was there, and I didn't want to spoil the magic for them.

We returned to modeling and creating the picture. Finally, literally hours after I had first joined them, we heard the tinkling of a bell.

"Oh, Grandma's calling us to lunch," Bess said.

"Wonderful. I'm absolutely famished. It's been a while since I've had so much fresh air. It stirs one's appetite," Uncle Linden said and then, looking at Bess, added, "All of one's appetites."

I almost fell off the rock with surprise at his flirtatious ways. Bess blushed and rose quickly. Uncle Linden covered his easel before either of us could have a look at what he had done, and then the three of us started for the house. Heyden and Chubs were still bent over the engine block, but when Chubs saw us walking back, he paused and said something to Heyden. He wiped his hands and then started toward us. I lingered in the rear, falling back. Bess, talking now with Uncle Linden, who was still telling one story after another, didn't seem to notice.

"I have a feeling your uncle isn't going to want to leave this place," Heyden said, smiling at him and Bess. "Mrs. Stanton still believes he's your father, right?"

"Yes, but I keep thinking that none of this is right, Heyden. We're all frauds."

He stopped, his hands on his hips. "No, we're not. We're helping the old lady get by, and what harm's any of it doing anyway, huh? Look at how happy that woman is," he said, nodding at Bess. "You want to go run up to her and tell her you're a fraud? Think that's the right thing to do? Think that will make you feel better?"

"No, but—"

"No, *buts*, then," he said. "Let's get something to eat. I'll go back to work. We're making headway. Maybe another few hours and then we can get on the road, and you won't have to feel like you're doing something terrible when you're not."

"I don't know if I want to get back on the road," I

said, avoiding his eyes. I gazed back at the rock and the easel out in the field instead.

"What? What are you saying, Hannah?"

"I haven't called my mother since we left."

"So? I haven't called mine, either, and what do you expect they will say when we do call them? Hope you're having a good time? Don't forget to send post-cards?"

Uncle Linden and Bess entered the house, their laughter echoing behind them.

"I'll tell you what they'll say," he continued. "They'll say we had better come home and come home right now or they'll send the police after us, and your mother will scream and yell at you for taking your uncle along."

"Maybe she won't," I said. "Maybe—"

"Maybe what?" he cried, his arms out.

"Maybe she's suffering like Bess," I blurted, my eyes so full of tears, I thought I had opened them under water.

He stared at me a moment.

"What are you saying, Hannah? You were the one who was suffering, remember? You were the one who was being treated like you were unwanted, remember? You were the one who said you felt guilty living in that house, right?"

"Yes," I said. "But—"

"But what? This isn't like going on a Sunday picnic or something. We took your uncle out of his home. We used his money. We took him to the bank and had him take it all out! We made a decision, choices, and we carried them out."

"Nothing was done that can't be corrected," I said.

"Corrected? *Corrected?* That suggests we did something wrong. We did nothing wrong."

I took a deep breath and looked at the house.

"Mrs. Stanton believes our coming here was something of a blessing. Well, maybe it was a blessing for all of us, especially for me. You think I imagined everything that happened last night in Rosemary's room. I know. Perhaps I did, but one way or another it happened, and it caused me to think about everything, Heyden.

"Bess lost her daughter tragically. Nothing can change that. My mother lost little Claude and nothing can change that, either. I saw what losing Rosemary has done to Bess. Losing little Claude was as traumatic for my mother, and now . . ."

"And now she's losing you. Is that it?" he asked.

"Yes. Except I can change that."

"Great. You lead me on. You get me to believe we can do this. You make a big deal over the music, and you give me hope and then you just stop and whine. I don't know. Maybe it's a mistake. We should go back."

"I feel terrible, Heyden. All of this sadness, tragedy, it makes me understand, and I feel terrible."

"Yeah, well, too bad for me, huh."

"Don't be so upset. You can still go on, can't you?"

He looked away, fuming. "Damn right, I can still go on. I'm not going back to an estate and fancy cars like you are."

He turned on me. "Maybe you *do* belong in the Palm Beach world, Hannah. Maybe deep down inside yourself you really *are* like all that."

"I'm not thinking of going back to that. I'm thinking of my mother," I moaned.

"Right. Fine. Thanks," he said and walked off.

"Heyden!"

He kept walking. I watched him a moment, sucked back my tears, and headed for the house.

By the time I walked in, they were all laughing around the table. Mrs. Stanton was serving a cold chicken salad with her mint iced tea and some of her bread. Uncle Linden was eating like he really was famished. Most of the time I saw him eat at the residency or anywhere, he pecked at his food, seemingly not enjoying a bite.

I saw how happy Mrs. Stanton was. She beamed over the two of them, growing happier and happier, every time Bess laughed or ate something.

"Hurry before these two devour it all," she called to me.

"I ate breakfast later than they did," I said. "I'm not as hungry."

"Well, sit and have something."

"It's harder work than you think being a model, Rosemary," Uncle Linden said, and I felt my blood freeze. He had avoided calling me that up until now, giving me the feeling he was only doing what I was doing: charitably humoring poor Bess, but the look on his face reminded me of times when he drifted off or said strange things to me at the residency, calling me Willow and speaking to me as though I were my mother.

He turned to Mrs. Stanton. "People don't realize that when they are nervous or intense, they are burning up calories, too. You don't have to plow a field or run a mile to build an appetite," he told her.

She listened attentively and nodded. "How very true."

"Of course, your food is so delicious, Mrs. Stanton, I would be hungry no matter what," he added, and she took on a smile that seemed to drop years from her face.

"Why, thank you, sir. That's very kind of you."

Mrs. Stanton looked at me, still standing and gaping at them all. "Where's Heyden?" she asked.

"Cleaning up and coming," I said, hoping that was exactly what he was doing.

"Well, don't you worry. Despite the way these two are consuming my salad, there is plenty more in the kitchen."

"Shouldn't have told us that," Uncle Linden warned. "We'll be asking for seconds, won't we, Bessie?"

"Yes," she said, laughing.

"Besides. We need our strength for the walk."

"What walk?" Mrs. Stanton asked.

I sat at the table and put some chicken salad on my plate.

"To your beautiful lake, right, Bess?" he said.

Mrs. Stanton's smile faded quickly. "You don't go to the lake anymore, Bess," she told her. "Remember?"

"Of course I go to the lake, Grandma. Rosemary and I were at the lake just yesterday, weren't we, Rosemary?" she asked me.

I stopped chewing and looked at Mrs. Stanton.

"Yes," I said.

"See?"

"I thought you promised me you wouldn't go

there, Bess. You wouldn't take Rosemary there. Remember?"

"It's all right. Mr. Montgomery will be with us, and he's thinking of painting it," she said, her lips quivering.

"But . . . there's a fence around the lake now, Bess. Remember? Charles built that fence for us." She looked at Uncle Linden. "With a fence around it, it wouldn't be pretty enough to paint," she said.

"I see. No, it might not."

"Yes, it will," Bess insisted.

"There are so many other beautiful places on the farm, Bess. Why don't you show Mr. Montgomery the remaining orchard, for example?"

"It's not the same," she said sharply. "I want to show him the lake."

Mrs. Stanton avoided Bess's eyes and smiled at me. "Some apple butter, darlin'?" she asked.

"Thank you," I said, taking the dish.

"Let me refresh the chicken salad," she said, rising and taking the bowl. She glanced back at me when she started for the kitchen.

"Let me help you, Grandma," I said and rose to follow.

When we stepped into the kitchen, she turned around quickly.

"She doesn't go there anymore," she said. "It's not actually a lake. It's a big pond, and I did have Charles build a fence around it."

"Why?"

"Sometimes Bess imagines different things happening to Rosemary. She wakes up after another nightmare and then acts on it. One morning she rose early and went to the pond because she had a dream that Rosemary was drowning. Luckily Charles saw her trampling down the high grass in her rush to get there, and he followed. He saw her gaze at the pond and then scream and run into the water. She was swimming frantically and crying for Rosemary. He realized she was soon actually struggling to stay afloat herself, and he got to her before she drowned.

"After that he and I decided to build a fence around it. It's a chain-link fence. She can't get to the water. If she goes there and looks at it, perhaps she doesn't see the fence. Her mind might play tricks on her, but at least she can't drown.

"Once she was gone for hours and we found her walking miles from here. She had dreamed that Rosemary had gotten lost, and she had gone out to find her.

"Now, whenever she goes out, no matter what he's doing, Charles follows and watches her. Sometimes she walks and talks aloud as if Rosemary is alongside her, he says. Sometimes she just walks in circles, mumbling to herself. When he thinks he has to, he calls to her and gets her to come home."

She dabbed her eyes with a napkin.

"I made up my mind that if something should happen to Charles or he left us for whatever reason, I would have to put her in some sort of place for her own protection, but until then, I do the best I can and pray nothing happens to her, that she doesn't do anything terrible to herself. Someday, maybe, she'll wake up and realize the truth and face it.

"We all have to wake up and face some unpleasant truth someday. All we can do is hope to be strong enough to carry it along with the other burdens life lays on us."

She took a deep breath and then looked at me.

"But you're too young to worry about these things, darlin'," she said, smiling and touching my face. "Soon your vehicle will be repaired, and you can leave all this behind you. Thank you for doing what you've done, and please thank your daddy, too."

It was on the tip of my tongue to blurt that he was *not* my daddy. He was my uncle and we were all running away. I wanted to tell her the truth. I wanted to be honest with her so much, but I was so afraid that she would see it as another form of betrayal and deceit in a normally dark world that for a few days at least had opened to some sunshine. How do you give someone such a gift and then take it away so quickly?

Uncle Linden's and Bess's laughter echoed from the dining room.

"Isn't that a wonderful sound?" she asked. "We haven't heard much of it for a long time."

"Yes," I said, practically in a whisper.

"I'd better get this replenished," Mrs. Stanton said, holding up the bowl. "Your cousin should be in there by now."

"What about Charles?"

"Oh, he won't eat much lunch. He likes to have a piece of fruit is all. All these years he's been with us, he still feels out of place eating in that formal dining room. I know and I don't force him to do it. He'll come in for birthdays and special occasions, but he's always been more comfortable where he's at. He knows I want him here whenever he wants to come. I guess we're all stuck in our ways. That's what being old does to you, darlin'. It hardens the grooves, tightens the doors, shuts the windows, and keeps you where life has taken you. Change is never easy, but when you reach our ages, it's nearly impossible. The only change left is the grave itself. And as you can see, I have more work to do before I retire.

"So," she said, "let me give you this little piece of wisdom: take your time making your big decisions, your turns and twists in life. Ponder those forks in the road because if you go too far, you never can go back, not really. No decision is too small. Live like everything you do will change the world, if not for you, for someone you love.

"That's it," she declared abruptly. "That's all the Grandma talk I'll be giving today. Enjoy. Tell your cousin I'm coming right out," she added.

"Thank you," I said and kissed her cheek. She beamed.

"Bless you, child," she said.

I hurried out to tell Heyden I had made a firm decision to go home, but when I stepped into the dining room, I saw he was still not there.

"Where's Heyden?" I asked Uncle Linden. He was in the middle of telling Bess a joke he recalled and held up his hand to ask me to wait.

"So the operator says, you're getting a busy signal because you're calling your own number, and the schizophrenic says, if you're so smart, lady, tell me, then why does someone else answer the phone?"

Bess roared with him.

"Heyden?" I asked.

Uncle Linden shook his head. "He didn't come in yet," he said and turned back to Bess and began to tell her another joke.

I hurried out of the house and stood on the front steps, looking toward the motor home. Neither Heyden nor Chubs was there, and Heyden was nowhere in sight. It was so quiet. Even the birds were hiding from the afternoon sun. My chest felt like a hive of ants were moving around inside it.

I walked quickly down to the motor home.

"Heyden!" I called. "Heyden!"

I listened but heard nothing. Then I walked around the side of the barn and called again. A door opened and Chubs emerged. He looked surprised.

"Somethin' wrong, miss?"

"I'm looking for Heyden. He didn't come in for lunch and I don't see him. Is he in there with you?"

"No, ma'am, he's not. I thought he was goin' in to lunch, too," Chubs said. "You look in the motor home?"

"No," I said, a surge of hope pushing out my panic. I rushed to it and opened the door. "Heyden?" I stepped into the coach, but he wasn't in there.

Chubs waited at the door.

"He's not here," I said.

"Hmm." Chubs stepped forward and gazed around the property. "Coulda taken a walk anywhere, I guess."

Something teased my brain and soon after became an image and a sound. I turned and rushed into the coach, looking everywhere. My fear found a solid place in my heart to set itself down firmly.

Heyden's guitar was gone!

Maybe he went somewhere to be alone and play it, I thought. He liked expressing his feelings through the music. I stepped out of the coach and listened again. Behind us in a patch of wildflowers, dozens of bees hummed, and from above us a jet plane dropped some thunder, but other than that, I heard nothing, nothing resembling music.

Chubs looked at his watch.

"He took his guitar," I moaned.

"We was going to start workin' again in about ten minutes. I'm sure he'll be back," Chubs said. "Meanwhile, I'll get to it."

He returned to thc engine. I sat in a shady place and watched the fields and the driveway, but Heyden didn't appear. After a while I heard a screen door open and close and saw Uncle Linden and Bess come out of the house. They walked toward the easel, and then, realizing I wasn't beside her, Bess stopped and looked around.

"Rosemary," she called. "Rosemary." Her voice filled with that familiar panic I had heard in my own when I had been calling for Heyden.

I stood up and waved. "I'm over here!" I shouted.

"Oh. Come back to the rock. Mr. Montgomery wants to finish what he's doing, and then wc'll take our walk."

"I'll be right there," I said.

They continued and I looked frantically in all directions.

Chubs raised himself from the engine and looked at me.

"He's not back," I said.

Chubs shook his head. Another thought occurred to me, and I hurried back into the motor home. I looked about and then my heart sank.

His guitar wasn't the only thing missing. Whatever he had taken along in the pillowcase was gone as well.

My worst fears were realized.

Heyden had left us.

14
Making the Right Decisions

I had never felt as lost and alone as I did at that moment. And disappointed in someone, too! How could Heyden do this? How could he be so angry and selfish?

Chubs stood there staring at me.

"What'cha goin' to do, miss?" he asked when I told him what I now believed.

"I don't know," I wailed, sucked back my tears, and looked down the long driveway. A part of me wanted to just run, run until I fell with exhaustion. A part of me wanted to sob and sob and sob. I bounced from fear to self-pity to anger, and then to a terrible sense of defeat that left me feeling weak and helpless. Chubs saw it all in my face, I think. He looked almost as upset as I did.

"Well, I'm almost finished here," he said. "In a little while, you can start out whenever you like."

"Start out?"

How? I thought. *Where to?* And who would drive this thing, me? Should I depend on Uncle Linden? It'd been years and years since he drove a car, much less something like this. We could get ourselves into even more trouble if we went back on the road.

"Rosemary!" Bess called again and waved harder, beckoning me.

Bring this all to an end, a voice inside was screaming at me. Stop it before it goes another step further.

Uncle Linden paused and turned my way, too. He raised his arms to ask what's going on?

I didn't know what to do. I started toward them, my mind reeling as it would had I just been spun around and around on a Ferris wheel.

"Oh, don't look so sad, Rosemary. We're not going to be sitting here much longer, are we, Linden?"

"Ten, fifteen minutes more is all I need. I have down what I want," he said.

I looked at him. I had to make him stop, make him understand.

"Heyden's gone," I said softly, hoping not only that Bess wouldn't hear, but more important, that she wouldn't hear the panic in my voice, which might set off her own.

"Gone?"

"He's run off, taken his things and run off."

Uncle Linden blinked his eyes rapidly. I could almost see reality seeping in under this wonderful day of illusion. He glanced at Bess and then turned back to me.

"Gone?" he asked, either failing to understand or refusing to understand.

"Yes," I said. "He took his guitar and his things and he left."

"But . . ." Uncle Linden looked at the motor home. "It's being repaired, isn't it?"

"It's almost done."

"Then . . . why did he leave?"

"I told him I wanted to return," I said. "I told him I thought we should go home."

"Oh."

He looked at Bess, who was sitting back now, bathing her face in the sunlight.

"I'm sorry, Uncle Linden," I said. "We haven't much choice now. We've got to get back."

He nodded. "Let's just finish here," he said and nodded at the rock. "Just a little longer."

Why? I wanted to ask, but seeing how he looked at Bess and how innocent and vulnerable she appeared, I understood. This was something he had to do; this was a gift he had to give.

I rejoined her at the rock, and he returned to his work. He looked more intense about it, more determined. Every once in a while I glanced at the driveway, hoping that Heyden had come to his senses, calmed down, and decided to come back, but there was no sight of him.

"Okay," Uncle Linden said, seeing how fidgety I was. "I have what I need. Thank you, ladies."

He stepped forward, took Bess's hand, and kissed it, following with a stage bow.

"I shall be eternally grateful," he said, and she laughed that thin laugh that reminded me of tinkling chandeliers.

We heard the motor home engine being started and a few moments later heard it run. Chubs stepped out and waved to us excitedly.

"Oh, my chariot has been repaired," Uncle Linden said. "Shall we inspect it, ladies?" he asked me and Bess.

She smiled, but suddenly looked more tentative and unsure of herself. She glanced at me and then turned and gazed at the field behind her as if something was drawing her to it. I looked as well and saw only little balls of insects circling madly in the afternoon sun.

"Would you escort me, Bess?" Uncle Linden pursued. "It will take only a few minutes," he added.

She glanced at me again, looking suddenly fearful, and then shook her head.

"No," she said. "I can't. I . . . I have to walk."

Uncle Linden smiled with confusion. "We will walk, Bess. Right after we talk to Mr. Dawson," he said.

She shook her head and looked at me, the fear blossoming in her eyes. I understood, I thought. She saw something threatening in the motor home. It would bring her back to reality because it would take me away. Rosemary would be gone again.

"I've got to walk," she insisted and started away.

"Bess!" Uncle Linden called.

"We've got to tell her the truth, Uncle Linden, the truth about everything."

"I know," he said, nodding. "Poor thing. She's so fragile. Every smile, every laugh is so thin and on the verge of shattering."

"We should pay Chubs for the work he has done for us," I said, looking his way. "I hope you didn't give Heyden all your money."

"No, no. He took only what we needed when we needed it. Yes, let's pay Chubs. Absolutely. Let's do that."

Bess hadn't gone far. About a hundred feet or so she began to walk in a circle as though the small flies had given her an idea. We started for the motor home. The front door of the house opened, and Mrs. Stanton came out and looked in Bess's direction. Even from this distance I could see the concern on her face.

What was I going to do? I hoped that perhaps Heyden was just hiding somewhere nearby and once he heard the engine started, he would come out, too, but I didn't see him anywhere. He was really gone.

As we approached, Chubs came forward, wiping his hands on a rag.

"She's about as good as she's gonna be," he said. "I've done all I can."

"Well, we appreciate what you've done. How much do we owe you?" Uncle Linden asked, taking out his remaining cash.

"You don't owe me anythin', sir. You and the young lady here have been kind to Mrs. Lilliann and Bess, and that's payment enough, thank you."

"Bess!" I heard Mrs. Stanton call, her voice full of apprehension.

I turned and looked at Bess. She was still walking in the circle, but walking faster and faster with her head down, mumbling.

"What is she doing?" I cried.

Bess stopped, turned, started in the opposite direction and then stopped and started another circle, moving faster yet and still talking to herself.

"Charles!" Mrs. Stanton screamed.

Chubs shot forward, Uncle Linden trailing behind him. I followed slowly.

"Now, now, Miss Bess, now, now," Chubs coaxed as he approached her.

She didn't stop until he reached out and took her arm. For a few moments she tottered, her legs still moving forward and then her body twisting. Suddenly she collapsed, folding up like a puppet whose strings were cut. Chubs didn't let her hit the ground. He caught her and in one easy, sweeping motion lifted her into his arms and started toward the house, carrying her as if she were only a child.

Uncle Linden stopped and watched as Chubs walked by. I came up beside him.

"She was doing so well," he said. "She was doing so well. She was happy. Wasn't she happy, Hannah?"

"Yes, Uncle Linden, but you knew it was only temporary."

"Poor thing," he said. He started after them and then stopped and turned to me, a look of confusion on his face. "What are we doing?" he asked, remembering what I had told him about Heyden.

"I don't know, Uncle Linden."

He shook his head. "I don't either," he said and shaking his head, continued toward the house.

I looked back at his easel and thought I might as well gather all his things together and put them in the motor home. One way or another, we weren't going to stay here much longer, I thought.

I closed up his paint case, putting the brushes back carefully, and then I went to take the canvas off the easel. The cloth covering it fell away, and I stood there gaping in shock. There were no definitive shapes, nothing that resembled Bess or me or even a young girl taken from a photograph. Everything was in the abstract, if it could even be called that. It was just a mix of lines, circles and colors. It could best be described as an artist's mad rambling perhaps, a nightmare of hues and shades, shadows and light. Did he actually look at this and see something? Did he believe anyone else could? Or was this all some sort of artistic note taking that he would later convert into a picture?

I gazed back at the house. They had all gone inside, including Uncle Linden. I couldn't imagine what Mrs. Stanton would think if she saw this. I quickly threw the cloth over the canvas and put it under my arm. I folded his easel and then grasped the handle of his paint case. Struggling, but somehow managing, I carried it all to the motor home and got it all inside.

Afterward, when I entered the house, I found Uncle Linden pacing in the foyer.

"What's going on?" I asked.

"They took her upstairs. She was still unconscious. What should we do?"

"What can we do, Uncle Linden?" I wanted to say we had our own problems now, but I didn't want to sound like Heyden. "She needs medical care."

"Yes," he said. "Perhaps."

Chubs appeared at the top of the stairway and started down.

"How is she?" I asked.

"She's breathin' all right. She's just . . . like she is, like she's been ever since. Often, she'll fall into these deep sleeps. Maybe she feels better that way," he said, shaking his head.

"Can we see her?" Uncle Linden asked quickly.

"I don't know. I don't know what good it'll do. Mrs. Lilliann is with her. You can go up and knock on the door, I suppose," he added. He rubbed his lower back. "Got word rain's comin'," he said. "It always does when I have an ache right here. More reliable than the weatherman."

We watched him leave the house, and then Uncle Linden turned to me and said, "We should at least see how she is before we decide to do anything."

"Okay," I said and followed him up the stairway.

We could hear Mrs. Stanton humming what sounded like a lullaby in Bess's bedroom. Uncle Linden paused at the open door and knocked on the jamb. We both looked in and saw Mrs. Stanton sitting on the bed and holding Bess's hand. Bess was under the blanket, her hair spread over the pillow, her face looking as pale as someone's who never set foot outside.

"How's she doing?" Uncle Linden asked.

"She's fine," Mrs. Stanton said, forcing a smile. "Just fine."

Bess turned slowly and looked at us.

"Who's that, Grandma?" She squinted at us. "They come about the peaches?"

"Yes," she said. "They've come about the peaches. I'll just take care of them, and then I'll be right back. You want some mint iced tea?"

"That would be nice. Thank you, Grandma."

Mrs. Stanton started to rise, but Bess seized her arm.

"Tell Rosemary to come in now, Grandma. Tell her

it's getting to be time for her bath. She's been outside long enough."

"I will, dear."

"Tell her I'll brush her hair afterward, just like always. Don't forget."

"I won't, darlin'. You just rest and everything will be all right."

"Yes. Everything will be all right," she parroted and turned away.

Mrs. Stanton fixed her blanket for her, brushed back her hair a little, kissed her on the forehead just as she would kiss a little girl, and then turned and walked out.

"It was all a bit too much for her, I'm afraid. I thought it might be. I'm sorry." She smiled at Uncle Linden. "You were very nice, though, a fresh drink of water, a cool breeze that came through the heat of all this sorrow. I'm grateful to the both of you.

"Charles says your vehicle is ready to roll, too. I guess you'll be on your way, then."

"No," I said quickly, too quickly. It raised her eyebrows.

"No? What do you mean, darlin'?"

"Heyden has run off," I told her. "He was the one who could drive that thing."

"Oh, dear, why would he run off?" she asked, pulling us farther way from Bess's bedroom door.

I glanced at Uncle Linden. He was looking back at the doorway, seemingly not hearing a word I was saying.

"I have to talk to you, Mrs. Stanton. We haven't told you the whole truth, I'm afraid," I said.

She held her smile, but her eyes darkened a bit.

"Oh, I see. We'll let's go downstairs. I do want to prepare some more iced tea and bring a glass of it up to Bess," she said and started away.

I reached out and gently grasped Uncle Linden's arm.

"Come on, Uncle Linden. We have to let her rest."

"Yes," he said. "She should rest."

He followed along and we descended the stairway. Mrs. Stanton was already down and turning to the kitchen. To me she looked as if she was running off, fleeing from me, fleeing from any more deception, any more lies. I got Uncle Linden to sit and wait in the living room. He promised he wouldn't go anywhere until I had returned. I thought he was beginning to look very tired and confused again himself, and that made my heart pound even faster and harder before I turned to go to speak to Mrs. Stanton.

She was at the stove in the kitchen heating water in which to steep her tea leaves. She glanced my way when I entered, but she turned back to the stove quickly as if she had to keep an eye on the pot.

"I'm sorry, Mrs. Stanton. I thought we would just leave right after the repair of the motor home, but with Heyden running off like this, I don't know what to do."

I thought she wasn't listening to me. She turned off the fire under the pot and began to pour the water into her teapot.

"Linden is not my father," I began.

She raised her shoulders as if to ward off an impending blow to the back of her neck. Then she turned slowly and looked at me, some anger seeping into her face.

"Not your father? I don't understand. Who is he, then?"

"He's my uncle. Heyden isn't my cousin. He is my boyfriend. We were all running away," I confessed quickly. I didn't think I could say it all if I didn't say it fast.

Curiosity replaced the small red patches of rage that had blossomed in her cheeks.

"Running away? Why? From whom?"

"We each had different reasons, different things we were fleeing. Heyden had come up with the idea of the motor home, and Uncle Linden had money he had earned from the sale of some of his pictures over the years. He was in what they call a residency, an interme-diate home between the mental clinic he had been in for years and living in what I guess is described as the out-side world. I hate to call it the normal world," I added.

She put her right palm against her chest and sank herself into the nearest chair.

"A mental clinic?" She looked toward the doorway as if she could see him. "What was wrong with him?"

"He was diagnosed as a severe manic depressive at the start. I've heard my mother say he also had charac-teristics of classic paranoia. I don't know all the techni-cal stuff. By the time I was old enough to visit with him on my own, he seemed fine to me. He was always lov-ing and gentle and always looked forward to my visits eagerly. We drew closer and closer until I was the one looking after him the most."

She shook her head. "You would never know any of that from talking to him."

I nodded. "Generally, he's fine and functions well.

He gets confused from time to time, but he has never been more charming than he has been here, and I think he really cares about Bess and is moved by her emotional pain.

"But it's like the blind leading the blind, Mrs. Stanton. I can't let it continue. I would feel responsible for any new problems. I *would be* responsible. I brought him here."

"I don't understand all this," she said, shaking her head again. "Why did you run away from your home? And why did that young man run away from his?"

"We were planing to become a singing act, but that's not why I ran off," I said.

I walked to the table and sat across from her. *Where do I begin?* I wondered. *How do I explain all this quickly so someone like Mrs. Stanton will understand and not think I'm simply a spoiled brat or as unbalanced as her granddaughter?*

"I have told you the truth about my family life," I started and continued in broad strokes until I got to Mommy's pregnancy and how our lives had changed, or at least, my life. When I finished with little Claude's death and how I felt I was being held accountable for it, she shook her head and muttered, "My, my, my, my."

"So when Heyden presented his plan to me and we saw how much my uncle Linden wanted to get out of that home, we just did it," I concluded. I had told her just enough about Heyden's home life to help her understand why he wanted to get away, too.

Mrs. Stanton rose without speaking and went to her teapot. She poured the tea through a strainer into a pitcher filled with ice, all the while not saying a word to me. Finally she paused and turned.

"My poor Rosemary can't come back to stop her mother's pain, but you can go back to your mama," she said. "And I'm sure she's in terrible pain, too."

"I know. That's what I intend to do. I'm sorry we didn't tell you the truth from the start, but Heyden didn't think we would be here that long, and I never anticipated doing what I did with Bess. Uncle Linden seemed to be doing so well with her, too, that I didn't want to spoil it and maybe cause you even more problems."

She nodded. "And so Heyden's run off because you wanted to go home and he thought you were betraying him?" she asked.

"Yes. I was hoping he would change his mind and come back here, but he hasn't. He was so angry with me."

"From the little you've told me, it doesn't appear that he has as much waiting for him if he does go home," she said.

"No, he doesn't, and he has been on his own for most of his life."

She shook her head. "I live here on this farm, in a real sense imprisoned by our family tragedy. Sometimes I feel sorry for myself. I don't suppose it can be helped. I think I'm missing so much out there. I don't have any social life anymore, haven't for years since my husband's death. Most of my friends are gone, and the ones who are still living are with their families and don't have the same independence they had.

"I watch the television, of course, but not a lot. Most

of the time, it puts me to sleep, but what I see on the news programs, the way it's all shown these days, makes me think it's all entertainment. How can people behave like that, do those things to each other, not that things like that didn't happen before, I'm sure. There just seems to be so much more of it, I think about it all, and I realize that maybe I'm not so bad off staying close to home, dealing with my own troubles."

"I'm sorry I brought our troubles here," I said.

She dropped her pensive look and smiled. "Oh, I don't believe you've done us any harm, darlin'. I still think you did us some good. At least poor Bess had a small respite from her pain. What are you going to do?"

"I thought I would call my father first and see if he could help us."

"Very wise," she said. She poured some mint iced tea into a tumbler and then into another. "I'll see that your uncle Linden gets some of this. He is fond of it," she said. "I do like him very much, and I hope he'll be all right."

"Me, too," I said, brushing some tears off my cheeks.

"You'll be fine, darlin'," she said. "Just go home. Go home to your mama. No matter what you think or feel, she's heartsick over you bein' gone. I'm sure of that. Pour yourself some iced tea if you like," she said and left with the tray.

I sat there trying to get my throat to open enough for me to talk on a phone. I did have some of her iced tea, and then I took a deep breath and went to the telephone. My fingers trembled as I punched in Daddy's office number. I thought it would be better to call him first. Despite the distance that had always been between us, I couldn't help thinking of my father as a man of action who seemed capable of moving mountains. He knew influential people, very, very wealthy people, and had even been invited to the White House. Surely, he would solve all my present problems with a snap of his fingers.

The familiar cold, official voice of Mrs. Gouter greeted me. If my father had told her anything about my running off, she didn't reveal it in her tone.

"He is at a meeting in Miami," she said. "I'll see if I can patch you through to his cellular."

I waited, finding it hard to take deep breaths. It felt as if a strap had been tightened around my back and chest, preventing it from expanding.

"Hannah?" I finally heard. "Where the hell are you?"

"I'm some place in South Carolina, Daddy, near a place called Anderson."

"South Carolina! How did you get there?"

"We rented a motor home. It broke down and—"

"A motor home? Was this your crazy uncle's idea?"

"No," I said.

"Well, you'd better just turn around, young lady, and get your rear end back home pronto. I'm very disappointed in you, especially after that bit you pulled with your brothers at the house. Danielle is still upset over it."

"That wasn't my fault, Daddy. I didn't get a chance to explain and—"

"Well, put an end to all this silly nonsense. Just get home," he said.

"I can't!" I screamed into the phone. "Daddy?" It

was silent. Had he hung up already? "Daddy?" There was no response. I clicked the receiver frantically and then realized he had hung up.

Panicked, I called his office again.

"Didn't you speak with him?" Mrs. Gouter sounded annoyed.

"We were cut off," I claimed. I could almost hear her lips click like a matchstick. Moments later she was back on the line.

"Your father cannot speak with you now. He has just gone into the courtroom."

"But I didn't get a chance to explain anything," I moaned.

"He said to tell you to get home immediately and not to call him again until you are home."

"I'm trying to get home, but I have no one to drive the motor home back and—"

"That's all he said. I have to pick up another call," she said sharply, and then she cut me off just as abruptly as Daddy had. The line went dead.

I stood there holding the receiver and feeling like an astronaut whose tether had snapped. I was floating in space, feeling lost and helpless. I had so hoped I wouldn't have to call Mommy and Miguel first. I wanted to spare them any more burdens, and I knew it wasn't going to be easy talking to them over the phone. Now I had no choice.

Lila answered the phone. I could hear how excited she was to hear that it was me calling. I had decided to ask first for Miguel, hoping he was there. He was.

"Hannah," he began, "*Agradezca a Dios*. Thank God. Where are you?"

Hearing his voice and his joy in hearing mine was so dramatic a contrast to what I had just gone through speaking with Daddy and his secretary that I just burst into tears.

"Miguel," I sobbed, my voice cracking so badly, I had actually pain in my throat trying to get the next few words out. "I need your help."

"What is it? Where are you? *Dios mio!*"

I sucked in enough breath to continue and explain all that had happened and where we were. The words flew out of my mouth so quickly, I was sure he didn't understand it all.

"A motor home?" he asked, astonished when I was finished.

"Yes."

"Dios mio. And Linden?" he asked.

"He's fine, Miguel. Really, he is." I took a deep breath and asked, "How's Mommy?"

"Whoever said, 'Physician, heal thyself,' couldn't imagine emotional and psychological illness," he replied as an answer.

"It's from the Bible," I said. "Luke. I used it in a term paper last year."

Miguel laughed. "We miss you so much, Hannah."

"I miss you, too," I said through my tears. "I'm so sorry, Miguel."

"Okay. Let's leave all that for later and concentrate on what we have to do to get you and Linden back home safely," he said. "You're sure Heyden has run off?"

"Yes. I'm afraid so."

"Let me have the telephone number there. I'll see what I can arrange and then get back to you."

I read it to him from the little label on the phone, and he said he would be calling back very soon. After I hung up, I had a sense of great relief. Miguel was a college professor. He didn't have the access to power and influence Daddy had, and yet he was the one who would come up with the solutions. The irony wasn't lost on me, but neither was the sadness and disappointment. I vowed I would never make a similar mistake in judgment again, and I hoped I wasn't optimistic in making it.

Mrs. Stanton returned to the kitchen, her face full of relief and joy.

"Your uncle wanted to see Bess very much. He was so insistent, I let him go up and he is sitting at her bedside and talking softly to her. When I left them, he was holding her hand, and she was smiling peacefully, looking just like she did when she was a little girl listening to a fairy tale. He has a way with him. Are you sure he wasn't one of the doctors at the clinic and not one of the patients?" she asked, smiling.

"I wish that were so," I said.

She nodded. "People who are in pain can help each other best sometimes," she said. "Were you able to reach your mother or your father on the phone?"

"I reached my stepfather," I told her. "He'll be calling soon with a plan to come get me, Uncle Linden, and the motor home."

"Good," she said. "In the meantime, I think I'll work on dinner for us all. I was thinking about making chicken with peaches. You can bet I have a good recipe for that. It's really my mother's."

"Oh, we cannot impose on your hospitality anymore, Mrs. Stanton."

"You're not imposin', darlin'. It's good to feel useful. Too often people my age are put out to pasture."

"You'll never be put out to pasture, Mrs. Stanton."

"Not if I can help it," she vowed.

We just looked at each other a moment, and then she hugged me.

"Everything will be fine, darlin'. You're making the right decisions now. You'll see."

How someone with all her burdens could even care amazed me and made me feel even sorrier than I did for all the trouble I had caused everyone. I held my tears back and thanked her. Then I went upstairs quietly and stood outside Bess's bedroom door, eavesdropping on Uncle Linden.

"My grandmother was the one who encouraged my art," I heard him say. "When I was a little boy, I would doodle on anything. Sometimes I did it on her tablecloths, and she would chastise me, but afterward, she would hand me a pad of plain paper and tell me to go off somewhere and draw her a picture.

"My mother bought me my first artist set when I was only nine. It was pretty sophisticated for a child. I had an easel and two dozen oil paints and acrylic brushes. It wasn't a toy. And then, when I was twelve, she located an art instructor who came around to give me lessons once a week.

"The Eatons were disdainful. I remember Thatcher would make fun of me or his friends would. They nicknamed me Van Gogh and told me to cut off an ear. Clowns. All of them, even now, despite their wealth. Every stupid thing they do is just on a bigger scale. That's all," he said with vehemence.

"Willow was different right from the beginning, though. She liked my work and let me paint her, just like you did, Bess. Later, as I told you, I sold a few pieces of my work to Palm Beach people who didn't care how much I wanted. I didn't want to sell my art to those kind of people. I really didn't think they liked the work. It was just another thing to them, know what I mean?"

He paused. I didn't hear her speak, so I looked through the door.

He was seated at the bedside, holding Bess's hand, but her eyes were closed, and it was apparent to me she had fallen asleep. I smiled because it didn't matter to Uncle Linden.

He continued to talk, to tell her about his love of art and some of the pictures he had done, and as he did so, he continued to hold on to her hand as well.

I heard the phone ringing, and a moment later Mrs. Stanton called to me.

"It's for you, darlin'," she said, and I hurried down to the phone. It was Miguel.

"All right. Here's the plan. I'm flying into an airport about thirty-six miles from Anderson. We'll be renting a car and coming to get you and Linden, Hannah."

"We? Is Mommy going to come on this trip?" I asked quickly, hopefully.

"No. There's no point in putting her through such a trip. I have Ricardo coming with me. He'll drive the motor home back. You, Linden, and I will return to the airport and make the last flight out. It will be a series of connecting flights that will bring us into West Palm Beach toward morning, but there is no better way to do it quickly, and quickly is what we want, Hannah," he said firmly.

"Okay."

"When I land and get the rental car, I'll call again. Have someone nearby who can give me clear directions to the Stanton farm, okay? We'll have to get things organized and turn right around. You understand?"

"Yes, Miguel."

"How is Linden doing now?"

"He's doing very well," I said.

"A journey like this could have been very traumatic for him."

"It wasn't," I said. "You don't have to worry about him. Really." I wanted to add he was doing better than I was, but I didn't.

"All right. I'm hoping to be there in three to four hours, Hannah."

"Okay," I said. "I'm sorry."

"So am I," he said. "So am I. Just hang on and take care of yourself."

I hung up. A moment later I heard Mrs. Stanton's hurried footsteps. When she stepped into the kitchen, she had to catch her breath.

"What's wrong?" I asked.

"You'd better go upstairs to your uncle," she said. "Quickly!"

15

A More-Happy Birthday

Uncle Linden was standing outside of Bess's bedroom, his ear against the door, which was now closed.

"What are you doing, Uncle Linden?" I asked.

He turned slowly, his eyes so distant they sent an electric surge of fear down my spine. He was more like a blind man, trying to understand from where my voice had come.

"Shhh," he said, bringing his finger to his lips. "Willow's sleeping. She's needs her rest."

"Oh, dear," Mrs. Stanton said, standing behind me on the stairway. "Why is he calling her Willow?"

"Did you close the door, Uncle Linden?"

"Of course. We've got to let her sleep. A pregnant woman needs her rest," he said.

"You see," Mrs. Stanton moaned. "He's not making any sense. I'll have to go get Charles."

"Wait," I pleaded. "Let me see what I can do first."

"But my Bess, she might be frightened."

"I think she's still asleep," I said. "She probably doesn't know the door is closed and he's out here."

I gently turned him from the door. "Uncle Linden, you have to come away from here now. We're going downstairs. We'll be going home soon."

"No, I have to stand guard. I have to stay here. Thatcher might return and annoy her."

"Thatcher can't return. He's gone for good, Uncle Linden. Don't worry. Come along. We want to rest before dinner. We have a long journey ahead of us. Please come with me," I pleaded, taking his hand.

He started to pull it away, but I held it tightly.

"Uncle Linden, think, think!" I urged, pumping his arm with every word, trying to shake him out of his trance. "You're here with me, Hannah. You're not in Joya del Mar. It's years and years later, Uncle Linden. I've already been born. You don't have to worry."

He turned back to the closed door. I tugged harder on his arm.

"Look at me!" I said sharply. "Look at me now, Uncle Linden," I demanded.

He turned and gazed into my face.

"You see it's Hannah. Hannah!"

"Hannah?"

"Come along, Uncle Linden. You're tired. You have to rest yourself. Remember how far we have come. Please," I said, still holding tightly to his hand.

Like someone whose blood had drained from his head and then started to slowly return, his face regained color, his eyes became less distant.

"Hannah?"

"Yes, it's Hannah," I said a little softer, calmer. "I'm here with you. Come along, Uncle Linden. You'll be fine. Everyone will be fine."

"Our Hannah?"

"Yes, Uncle Linden."

"Oh." He nodded, blinking fast, and then rubbing his forehead with his free hand. "I had such a bad dream." He looked around. "Where are we again?"

"We're at Mrs. Stanton's farmhouse in South Carolina. Remember? Our rented motor home broke down, and she was nice enough to take us in?"

"Oh, yes, right. I must have fallen asleep," he said. "I feel like I was walking in a dream."

"I think you were," I said, breathing with relief. I looked back at Mrs. Stanton and nodded. "He's all right now. Come on, Uncle Linden. Let's rest up downstairs."

I tugged him gently and he followed.

"Oh," he said when he saw Mrs. Stanton standing there on the stairs. "I hope I haven't caused any problems for you. I had a bad dream, I think."

"It's all right," she said. "You should rest. Go on down to the sitting room and relax, Mr. Montgomery. I'm preparing us a nice dinner."

"Thank you." He looked at me. "Let's get out of this nice lady's way, Hannah," he said as if I were the one holding us back from doing that.

I smiled. "Right, Uncle Linden."

I continued down the stairway with him while Mrs. Stanton went in to check on Bess. She joined us in the sitting room to say Bess was resting comfortably. She knew nothing of what had happened outside her door.

"Is he all right?" she asked.

"Fine," I said, looking at Uncle Linden, who had his head back on the big easy chair and his eyes closed.

"I'll see to dinner."

"I'm sorry about what happened."

"It just frightened me a little. I'm sure he's all right," she added.

I wasn't and I was now more anxious than ever that Miguel would arrive on time. It had been wrong to take Uncle Linden away. It was unfair to him, unfair to expect that Heyden and I could just drag him out to the world without all his support facilities and expect him to adjust and be successful. Mommy was right. She was always right.

I remained as close to Uncle Linden as I could right up until Mrs. Stanton began to set the table for dinner. He went in and out of dozing, and for a few moments every time he opened his eyes, he looked confused. When he saw me, he calmed down and closed his eyes again.

"You don't have to help me," she said. "Stay with him. I can see it makes you nervous, darlin'."

I saw she was setting the table for four, but it wasn't because she anticipated Bess coming down to dinner. She went out to find Chubs and ask him to join us. I knew it made her feel better to have him nearby, and I didn't blame her for that. I felt better, too.

Although my nerves made me feel there were a dozen grasshoppers in my stomach, I ate Mrs. Stanton's delicious dinner. Uncle Linden returned to his charming self, complimenting her on everything and making it seem as if I were the one who had experienced the dark dreams and not him. He and Chubs even had a conversation about growing peaches.

About an hour after we had finished dinner, Miguel called and I was able to put Chubs on the phone with him so he could give him very specific directions to the farm.

"He should be here within the hour," Chubs told me.

Uncle Linden had gone out to sit on the portico.

"Who are we waiting for again?" he asked when I went out to join him.

"Miguel, Mommy's husband."

"Oh, yes. I like him. He's a college teacher, right?"

"Yes, he is," I said. What was it that caused him to move in and out of memories, falling back into the past and then returning like someone who had gone under water and had fought his way back up to breathe again? There was still so much I didn't know about our family's past, but after being here nearly a day and seeing what pain and tragedy could cause, I wondered if I really wanted to know. Maybe like Uncle Linden, I was better off with some selective amnesia.

I was never so happy to see anyone as I was to see Miguel when he drove up to the Stanton farm with Ricardo. He had never hesitated to hold me and kiss me when I was a little girl, but as I grew older, I felt his restraint. Right now all I wanted to do was crash through it and have him embrace me. He did so willingly.

"Are you all right?" he asked.

"Yes."

"Hello, Linden," he said, extending his hand to him. "How are you doing?"

"I'm fine, Miguel." He squinted at the rented car. "I was hoping to see Willow with you."

"Oh, she's anxious to see you, too, but she wasn't up to this sort of trip. I'm sure you understand," he told him.

"Of course," Uncle Linden said.

Mrs. Stanton came out, and I introduced her to Miguel. Ricardo joined with Chubs and went to the motor home.

"Thank you for offering your hospitality and home to my daughter," Miguel said. Long ago he had dropped the word *step* from *daughter*, and I couldn't have been more happy about it than I was at the moment.

"She's a delightful young lady. I'm sure everything will be fine."

"I am, too," Miguel said. He turned to Uncle Linden. "Shall we start back, Linden?"

"What's that? Oh, yes, I suppose we should." He rose, but then hesitated and looked at the front door and Mrs. Stanton. "I'd like to say goodbye to Bess," he said.

Mrs. Stanton looked at me with surprise and concern. I wasn't expecting him to make that request, either.

"I'll come along," I said. She nodded and led him and me back into the house and up the stairs. She paused at the open bedroom door and stepped back to permit Uncle Linden to enter. He approached Bess slowly.

"I have to go now, Bess," he said.

She was staring ahead, but turned to look up at him. I remained back in the doorway, out of sight.

"I hope you'll be feeling better soon. I wanted to

thank you for being my model. I promise I'll finish the picture and get it to you soon."

She stared at him, her face unmoving.

"Maybe some day I'll return as well and we'll take that walk, okay?"

She nodded. I felt such a weight in my chest. They were looking at each other over chasms of emotional turmoil. Something desperate in them both was trying to touch, but there were so many obstacles in the way. *How sad and unfair,* I thought. Uncle Linden knelt down and kissed her quickly on the cheek. Then he turned from her and started for the doorway.

"Wait!" she cried.

He turned back.

"Don't forget," she said.

"No. I won't. That's a promise," he told her. "And I'm someone who keeps his promises," he added proudly.

He walked out and I started after him. Mrs. Stanton followed. At the front doorway she hugged me.

"God bless you, darlin'," she said. I held on to her for a long moment, and then I joined Uncle Linden in the rented car. Just as Miguel got behind the wheel, Uncle Linden cried, "Wait!"

"What is it, Linden?"

"My picture," he said. He started to get out.

"I brought it to the motor home already, Uncle Linden."

"Oh?"

"Ricardo will bring back all your things, Linden," Miguel promised. "He has the motor home's owner's address from the paperwork."

"Are you sure?"

"Absolutely," Miguel said. "I made sure to tell him."

"I hope so. I wouldn't want to lose that picture," Uncle Linden said.

Again I wondered what it was he saw in it, but I said nothing. Ricardo had already started away. I prayed he would remember.

As Miguel began to turn the car down the driveway, Chubs stepped out and held up his big hand to wave goodbye. I leaned out of the window and shouted, "Thank you, Mr. Dawson. Take care of them."

A smile spread across his face, and then in moments, he was left behind us in the darkness, along with the farmhouse and all that had happened.

It was as Miguel had described, a hard trip back. We nearly missed one connection, and we were delayed almost two hours on the final leg of the journey due to some scheduling problems. I dozed on and off on the planes and was actually asleep when we touched down in the West Palm Beach airport. Uncle Linden slept all the time, even when we were waiting in the airports.

Miguel thought it would be better if we took him to his residency first.

"Let him readjust, Hannah," he said. "Mrs. Robinson will help him, and then we'll bring him to the house in a day or so. I promise," he added with conviction when I raised my eyebrows with skepticism.

Surprisingly, when we arrived at the residency, Uncle Linden looked pleased. He got out quickly and, in his haste, almost forgot to say goodbye to me.

"And don't forget to come see me," he said. Mrs. Robinson greeted him at the door with a big welcome, as did one of the other residents. Seconds later we pulled away.

"We found the letter you left behind," Miguel said. "Willow has kept it beside her all this time. She has read it so often, the paper is beginning to shred." He shook his head. "You can't imagine how hard it was."

I swallowed down a throat lump.

"Does she hate me, Miguel?"

"Hardly," he replied. "Although she is about as fragile as that woman you described at the farm. You both have to be considerate of each other. That's all the advice I'm going to give," he concluded.

Despite all the dark corners of mystery and sadness that still lingered in Joya del Mar, I felt a surge of true joy when I saw it before me again, for to me, it had always been home. Never in more splendor with its vibrant flowers and beautiful grounds, its sparkling fountains and glistening stucco and glass, I felt as if it were smiling at me when we drove in and up to the main house.

I got out slowly, my body tired, my emotions tugged and stretched to their breaking point. Lila greeted me at the door, her face full of delight.

"I have a nice hot lunch waiting for you when you're ready," she told me.

I thanked her, but I went looking for Mommy. She wasn't in her bedroom, where I had expected she would be, and she wasn't anywhere in the house. Miguel had gone into his office. He had decided to step away and not even be an observer. Maybe wisely, I thought.

Finally I went out to the rear loggia. I looked down at the pool patio and saw her sitting with her back to the house, staring out at the water. She was wearing the shawl she had once given her mother. I started for her slowly, my heart pounding like the surf itself. The day had begun with an almost cloudless sky and now had some puffy globs of marshmallow being carried from east to west on the shoulders of the wind high above us. A sea breeze played impishly with the strands of Mommy's hair. She didn't seem to notice or care. She was so still, I thought perhaps she had fallen asleep.

When I reached her side, I stood there quietly, searching for a way to begin. Somehow, even though I had walked on air, she knew I was beside her.

"I remember the first time I met my mother as my mother, when my true identity was finally revealed," she began, not looking at me, her eyes fixed on the ocean. She could have been talking to herself. "I wanted to burst right out and ask, How could you leave me behind? How could you close the door and forget me? How could someone who was part of you, who had come from your blood and your every breath, be forgotten? I wanted to love her, but at the same time, I wanted to hate her.

"Her first reply came from her eyes. The pain was there in full brightness. Of course, after what she had been through here and at the clinic, she was afraid she wouldn't be able to care properly for a child, a baby. It had been the birth of Linden that had sent her reeling back into her darkness. And then there was concern for my father and for all the possible consequences of their forbidden love. She comforted herself with the knowledge that he would be my father, if not in name, at least in action, providing for me, watching over me.

She had no idea what hell my stepmother would create for me.

"What was clear to me was the realization that whatever were her faults and mistakes, she was my mother and I was her daughter, and in the end, in the final moments of this often difficult life, we would not escape that, nor would we want to deny it. We would never stop needing each other really. We could pretend we were beyond all that, perhaps, but as old-fashioned as it might sound, the tie that binds would not be unbroken. What we realized, she and I, was that forgiveness was everything, that love grew out of it and was nourished by it.

"We do so many painful things to each other, don't we?" Mommy asked and finally turned to me.

She didn't look sad. She hadn't been crying. She looked like she had most often looked to me, strong, wise, confident, my mother the doctor, my mother.

"Some of it we do deliberately. We can't fully contain our selfishness. We are, after all, only human with our envies and our pride. Some of it we do without fully realizing what we've done. We're careless, negligent. We blunder because we're too anxious or we move too quickly, and we regret that. Some of it we can't help because we've inherited things we still don't understand ourselves.

"But in the end, in the very end, when we have our quiet moments and we want to be honest, we know what we have done, and we desperately need to be forgiven.

"I did blame you for little Claude's death, Hannah. It was convenient to blame you and it helped me contend

with my own sorrow. Anger brought me a little ˌ
ironically. Of course, that was ridiculous, but I was
in a good state of mind, and I did not want to be.

"I did not want to understand or explain or justifˌ
anything. I wanted to hate God, hate Fate, hate anyone
or anything I could. I even hated myself, saw myself as
a victim of that curse again and blamed it on my own
heredity. Poor little Claude had to have been brought
into it.

"Of course, when my reason returned, I understood
how foolish and wrong all that was, but it was too late.
I had driven you from me."

"Mommy," I said, and she put up her hand.

"No, I did, Hannah. I am not going to deny it, and I
don't want you to fool yourself about that. What you
felt was real and was true. Your running away helped
me see it.

"Of course, I was angry again because you had taken
Linden with you, which at the time seemed an even
more defiant act."

"I shouldn't have," I admitted.

"Of course not, but not because of what I had told
you or forbidden you to do.

"You see, Hannah, I never wanted you to love your
uncle Linden and become as attached to him as much as
you have."

"Why not?"

She turned away.

"A long time ago, as you know, Linden developed an
unhealthy relationship to me in his own mind. The nervous breakdown that we have told you he suffered was
far more severe than we described. What Linden did in

d was try to cage me up in this very house. I could
died before giving birth to you. It was not a pleas-
thing. It was true madness, and it has taken all these
ears of therapy and care to bring him to the recupera-
tion he has enjoyed.

"But I never recuperated as I should have. I never
forgave him. I pretended I did. I hid behind all the medical and psychiatric activity and terminology I could,
but I have never held him lovingly, and I have never
permitted myself to care about him the way I should
have. I know that now, and in a way that is because of
you.

"I wonder myself if I haven't been afraid of Linden
all these years, afraid not just of him, but afraid of
something in me. Maybe some of what happened to
him was really my fault. I am constantly interrogating
myself, reviewing my past here, and wondering if I
hadn't encouraged him, perhaps out of a complicated
sense of sibling jealousy. My mother loved him beyond
life and I envied that.

"So you see, in a real sense I have to ask Linden to
forgive me, too. I don't know if he will ever be capable
of understanding why, but I am now and I need it."

"He couldn't hate you, ever," I assured her.

"Maybe not or maybe he never will understand why
he does. I know that sounds like a lot of psychiatric
mumbo jumbo, and perhaps in the end, that's all it is.
Perhaps things are simpler than we think they are, and
some day we'll all sit here together and share the wonder of our lives and laugh and be loving in an innocent
way.

"I suppose that's why we regret losing our child-

hood. It was a time when blue was simply blue, w
stars were simply stars, when smiles and laughter h.
no other purpose than to make us happy.

"That's all gone for you, too, now, Hannah, but there
are ways to replace it. Only it all depends on finding
someone who will help you love yourself again. Does
that make any sense to you?"

"Yes," I said.

"For me, you are that person, Hannah. You help me
care about myself. I need you to love me, Hannah. I
need you to forgive me."

"I love you, Mommy. I can't help it."

She smiled. "Nor can I help loving you. So," she
said, rising out of the patio chair, "let's begin by forgiving each other first."

She held out her arms and I rushed into her embrace.
For a very, very long moment we simply clung to each
other. It was as if the whole world had stepped back.

"Now," she said, taking my hand, "let's walk along
the beach, and you can begin to tell me all about this
crazy thing you did and all that happened along the
way."

We started walking and I did just that.

When I reached the end of my story, I told Mommy I
had called Daddy first to ask him to help me. I
explained what had happened, and she shook her head
and told me she wasn't surprised, but she thought I
should call him that night and tell him I was home anyway.

He wasn't home and thankfully, neither were my
twin brothers. The butler put Danielle on the phone.

said she would let my father know, but she sounded ry sad herself. I thought it was because she still believed I was to blame for what had happened at the house on the twins' birthday. I started to explain again, and she stopped me.

"You don't have to tell me anything, *cherie*. I know the truth. I know now just who my sons are," she said. I thought her voice cracked again, and I asked her if she was all right. She said she was and again assured me she would tell my father I was safely back home.

I expected to hear from him that night or at least the following day, but he didn't call. I called his office, and Mrs. Gouter told me he was out of town. She would give him the message when he called in for his messages. Again, the day passed and he didn't call. I decided to stop pursuing him.

As he had promised, Miguel brought Uncle Linden to Joya del Mar for lunch two days after we had returned. I could see Mommy was nervous about it, but Uncle Linden wasn't. He was very talkative and sat on the rear loggia making comments about this or that on the property, recalling things that had happened at the pool or on the beach front. I thought he had forgotten everything about our trip, until he paused at the end of his visit to tell me I should stop by when I had an opportunity because he wanted to show me the completed picture he had made of Bess and Rosemary. Mommy and I looked at each other with a little concern. She made arrangements to go to see him at the end of the week.

It had been a long time since she and I visited the residency together. Uncle Linden was very excited to see us, but not, as I thought at first, because Mommy was with me. No, he couldn't wait to bring us to his room so we could see his finished work of art. I had prepared Mommy for this, describing to her what I had discovered when I had gone to fetch his painting and put it in the motor home. We were both prepared to pretend we saw something that made sense.

Imagine the shock both of us experienced when we entered his room and saw the picture on his easel. It was a remarkable picture, Bess's likeness so exacting I could look at it and actually hear that thin and fragile laugh and see the vulnerability in her eyes. What interested me the most about the picture, however, was the rendering of Rosemary. The little girl beside her bore only the slightest resemblance to me and that was just in the color of her hair. She looked happy, too, so I imagined that the photograph Bess had given Uncle Linden was one taken before her husband had begun to poison Rosemary against her. I could see some of Bess in Rosemary and even something of Grandmother Stanton. Perhaps that had been Uncle Linden's contribution.

As in all of his recent pictures, the background was somewhat abstract, but the colors were vibrant and true, I thought.

"It's a wonderful picture, Linden," Mommy told him.

"I want you to help me get it to her," he said.

"We can do that right away. I'll have it packaged properly and sent express delivery," she promised.

"Good." He stepped back to admire his own work.

"And you did the little girl from a photograph?" Mommy asked, showing her admiration.

He turned and looked at her, shaking his head. "Oh, no, Willow," he said. "She was there. I saw her. Wasn't she, Hannah?"

I smiled. "Yes, Uncle Linden. She was there."

Afterward, we had some iced tea on the porch. Uncle Linden had gotten Mrs. Robinson to buy some mint tea. He made a point of telling us, however, that somehow, it didn't taste as good as Mrs. Stanton's.

"She has secret ingredients for everything, I bet. Next time I see her, I'll coax her into telling me," he said.

I thought it was nice that he expected there would be a next time. Mommy thought it was healthy for him to have a goal like that, to want to return to see someone else. He then revealed that he was writing letters, too.

"Well, when you're ready, then, Linden, you should take a trip like that," Mommy said.

"Yes. I should. When I'm ready," he agreed.

We took the picture with us when we left, and Mommy went directly to the packaging store to have it prepared and delivered. Afterward, we both agreed it was one of the nicest visits we had ever had with Uncle Linden.

"I am still amazed at how he did this picture, Mommy. What were all those lines and that mess I saw?"

"Maybe what you suspected; an artist's notes. Linden always had a visual mind, a real photographer's memory. He took his snapshots and kept them in his head along with the colors he saw and put down on that canvas. It is something amazing," she agreed. "Maybe he will come out of there one day," she concluded and

then looked at me and smiled, "but not to go o~
broken-down motor home."

I laughed with her. Time can make mistakes ~
trouble seem funny in retrospect, I thought, although
couldn't find it in myself to laugh or think lightly of
what Heyden had done.

One afternoon the following week, I called his house
just to see if there was any possibility he was home. He
hadn't returned to school and his absence was the
hottest topic of the week. Gradually it ended, and it was
almost as if he had never attended. My friends stopped
asking me about him, especially when they saw they
couldn't get any satisfactory responses. I really had
nothing to tell.

No one answered his telephone, so I tried it one
night and did get his mother. I asked for him and she
said she didn't know his whereabouts. She remembered
me, of course. I hesitated, but then I asked her about
Elisha.

"She's in one of those places for juvenile offenders,"
she said. I heard her start to sob and then stop and say,
"which is best for her."

I wished her good luck and hung up.

Occasionally, over the next week, I glanced at one or
another of the songs Heyden had written. I had my
copies. I even sang them, but after a while I put them
away. I wished I could put away the painful memories
as easily, but nothing lingered as vividly in my mind as
the vision of Heyden's angry face when he accused me
of betraying him.

Had I betrayed him?

Had I betrayed myself as well?

giveness, Mommy had said. It all begins with

Throughout this time I worked harder at my school assignments. I went sailing with Mommy and Miguel, and we went to his family restaurant more often. I met some new relatives on his side, and we had some wonderful family gatherings, one during which I was asked to sing a Cuban song I had learned at school, a song I knew was one of Miguel's favorites.

What I didn't know was they were planning a big party for my seventeenth birthday. It fell on the upcoming weekend, and what they had decided to do was close the restaurant and dedicate the night to me. Somehow, those friends of mine they had invited at school had managed to keep the secret. Mommy and Miguel had me believe we were just going out to dinner to celebrate my birthday, only when we arrived at the restaurant and entered, the party crowd of Miguel's family, my friends, all burst out with a "Surprise! Happy birthday!"

I was overwhelmed, but I did look for Daddy, Danielle, and the twins.

"I invited them," Mommy said when I asked her about them. "I made sure Mrs. Gouter knew to put it on your father's calendar, and as far as I knew, they were coming. Maybe, they'll still be coming," she said. "It's like your father to be late anyway. But let's not worry about it. Let's have a good time."

We did. There was music and wonderful food and a pile of presents that rivaled the one I saw my half brothers go through on their birthdays, except the gifts weren't as expensive, of course. I got up and sang with

Miguel's cousins. My friends at school who at
looked reluctant at being there and remained somew
clannish during the early part of the celebration grad
ally warmed to the food and music. Before the night
ended, they came to tell me how much they had enjoyed
themselves, and I even could see some envy. Ironically,
I, the daughter of a broken marriage, tossed about in a
sea of adult turmoil, was suddenly the one with family,
with people who loved and cared about me.

I remembered a line in Shakespeare's *Julius Caesar:
The eye sees not itself but by reflection.*

How true it was. We never see ourselves truly and
what we have unless and until we look into the faces of
others and see ourselves reflected.

How full my heart was, how much I loved Mommy
and Miguel. There was so much going on, I had actually forgotten Daddy and his family had not attended,
but the reason for that came at the end of the evening to
one of Mommy's friends, Morgan Williams, who had
been carrying her cellular.

I think it is true that you can feel and sense significant events, especially when they involve people close
to you. I heard Mrs. Williams call to Mommy as we
were saying good night to some of Miguel's relatives.
There was a drastic note in Mrs. Williams's voice.
Mommy's name came out like a cry for help. It was
enough to turn her with concern, her happy smile holding barely in a trembling of lips.

"Morgan?"

"Oh, my God, Willow," she said, walking toward us.

Miguel turned, too, and the three of us stood side by
side.

Courtney Lucas just called me. There was a ter-
ble boating accident early this evening involving
natcher's boys. Their speedboat hit another."

"And?" Mommy asked, her question hanging in the
air. Instinctively she had reached out for Miguel's hand,
and I had moved closer to her.

"One of the twins was killed," she said. "Cade."

Epilogue

Forgiveness

I suppose that there was some cruel and impish creature of Fate who had decided Cade would be killed on my birthday. The irony of that struck Mommy, too, but we didn't dwell on it, and she was quick to emphasize that I should in no way ever feel responsible.

"Too often," she said, "guilt is like some random infection people catch. There's no reason for it, but they suffer it until and unless we can help them see it doesn't belong with them."

I think I began by feeling the sorriest for Danielle, of course, but at the funeral and afterward, despite how he had treated me all my life, I ached for Adrian. He looked amputated, half of him gone. He did everything with an air of tentativeness and uncertainty, whether it be speaking or merely standing. I could see him checking for his brother at his side and saw how he realized

...as gone, forever and ever. It would be as if his sentences were only half completed, his laughter unfinished. Words spoken to a trusted second half would fall back into thoughts. Everywhere he went and every place he stood would seem deeper, wider, longer. Every sound he made would echo.

At the cemetery he looked years younger, a little boy clinging to Danielle, who was overcome with grief. It wasn't until then that Daddy appeared dazed. He was so calm and collected at church and afterward, greeting people with his professional, distinguished manner. Only when he looked at Mommy did I see his lips quiver. He and Mommy embraced for the longest time I had ever seen them hold each other, and I thought, how odd that is to see your mother and your father hold each other and think of it as remarkable. He smiled when I kissed him and then patted my hand as if I was the one who had experienced the deepest loss and not him or Danielle.

My nonfamily seemed impatient at church. I saw my younger cousins squirming uncomfortably. Asher Eaton, still a very distinguished-looking man, had the most sensitive and deeply saddened look of all on his face. Occasionally I caught him looking my way, and I thought he was even smiling at me. Bunny Eaton had her eyes closed as if she were sitting in a dentist's chair and waiting for it all to end. She did not come to the cemetery. I overheard someone in my nonfamily say she had never been in a cemetery, and when she is driving somewhere and a cemetery appears, she turns away quickly or closes her eyes.

Later we learned that their solution to all this grief

was to jet off to Paris for a shopping spree. Not once did
I hear anyone voice what was on most everyone's mind:
*The accident was the result of Bunny's spoiling those
boys.* They weren't mature enough to own and operate
such a powerful boat. They didn't have the self-
discipline.

And then, as if impish Fate were sprinkling salt on
wounds, the sordid story of Daddy's current infidelity
snaked its way into our home over the rumor highway.

"Your father's marriage is coming apart, Hannah,"
Mommy warned me soon afterward. "It wasn't strong
enough in the beginning and hardly strong enough to
weather such a tragedy and all these new complica-
tions."

In the end Adrian went off with Danielle to live in
France with her family. I never had a chance to say
goodbye to him. Just like all the news I learned about
that family, I heard about it from friends who were
more tuned into the Palm Beach social scene than I
was. I was sorry I had never had a chance to say goodbye to Danielle. I liked her. Perhaps I would see her
again and even see Adrian someplace, sometime. An
unpredictable future carried hope with it. That was its
best asset after all.

Despite my interest in a musical career or maybe
because of it, I followed Mommy's advice and decided
to pursue a liberal arts education first. I was starting my
senior year, and Mommy and I began to think about
colleges for me to consider. My life began to take some
shape, and I could feel myself moving forward like a
rocket that had dropped away its initial lift and was now
sailing with a definite sense of purpose.

Of course, I continued to visit Uncle Linden as often and for as long a visit as I could manage, and Mommy and Miguel had him visiting us at Joya del Mar more frequently. Mrs. Stanton had written to him to tell him how much Bess appreciated his picture. I called her and she told me Bess was doing better, and, because of our visit, she had gone ahead and made arrangements for Bess to get professional help. It was working. Bess had even gone to the cemetery.

In the fall Mommy made arrangements for Uncle Linden to visit the Stantons. It was her birthday present to him. She took care of all the transportation. He called a day after he had arrived there, especially to tell me that he had taken Bess on that walk and that he was inspired to do a picture of the lake despite the fence, which Chubs might soon take down anyway.

"I'm like Bess," Uncle Linden said. "I don't see the fence. I see the water and the ducks and the reflection of the foliage on the silvery surface."

"I can't wait to see your picture, Uncle Linden," I told him.

He promised that I would be the first, after Bess, of course.

One afternoon in October I returned from school and found a letter waiting for me on the entryway table. There was simply an HR and a New Orleans address on it. My heart immediately began to pound like a Caribbean steel drum. I didn't open it until I was out by the beach. There, I plopped myself down in the sand and with trembling fingers tore open the envelope. A clipping fell out first. It was from a music handout in New Orleans, and it featured Heyden with his guitar under the headline *Something Original in N'orlea...* talked about his songs being featured at a nightclub ... how he was part of his father's act now, handling t... intermissions and building his own reputation.

There was a letter included.

Dear Hannah,

It has taken me this long to write to you because I have not had the nerve to expect you would bother opening an envelope that I would send to you. I debated leaving my name and address off, but then I thought I would never know if you had received it, and besides, it was cowardly.

What I did to you in South Carolina was the most cowardly and selfish thing I have ever done, and I hope you believe me when I tell you not a day has gone by since when I don't stop and suffer regret about it.

I can't offer any decent defense of myself except to repeat what I had said that day. I had nothing to return to compared to you. I have another confession to make in that regard.

When you first came to me with your troubles, I knew in my heart that you were better off staying where you were and working them out because I knew in my heart that you had a loving mother and from what I saw of your stepfather, a very dedicated and loving man at home as well. I didn't discourage you when it came to running away because I wanted a means to run away myself.

However, believe me when I tell you I truly felt and still feel that we would have made a wonderful and successful act. It was just selfish of me to put that ahead of your own happiness.

As you can see, I'm beginning to get somewhere in this music business. It's not a great deal, but it's a start and I have grown closer to my father. We both feel bad about Elisha, and it's our hope that someday she can come to New Orleans. My mother seems content without all the problems. Perhaps she was just not meant to be a mother. I don't love her any less for it, but I don't think there is anything I can do, and I know she wouldn't want me to waste my life trying.

I've written a song about you. I'm refining it, but I expect to be singing it soon. Maybe someday someone will record it and you will hear it and you will think of me and the good times we had together and not the bad times. That's all I can expect and all I can ask.

As you know, your name means "grace," so I call the song "With the Grace of Her Smile."

*With the grace of her smile she lights up
    my day,*
*With the grace of her smile she drives the
    dark away,*
*With the grace of her smile she opens my
    heart*
*And in the glow of that smile, I can feel my
    life start. . . .*

That's how it begins. I won't put it all here. I want you to hear it. The music is so important to it, and I'd like you have some surprises. Good surprises from me for a change.

I wonder if you're smiling or if you're crumpling this up and tossing it in the garbage. I can't blame you if you do. I can only hope you don't, but not so long ago, although it seems so, you taught me how to hope.

Heyden

I didn't crumple it up and throw it away. I folded it and put it back into the envelope, and then I put the envelope in my dresser drawer and I didn't look at it again for some time. And then one day I went out to the dock and stood where Mommy had told me my grandmother had stood staring out at the sea at night, looking for the light of the boat that was to bring my grandfather back to her. I stood there with the wind snapping around me, and I watched the breakers and saw the clouds rushing across the blue sky, and I thought Mommy was right.

Forgiveness.

That's where it begins.

And I went upstairs and wrote a letter.